SO-BFB-251

Kit Smith

215

OLIVER TWIST

OLIVER TWIST

by

CHARLES DICKENS

A BANCROFT

CLASSIC

BANCROFT BOOKS

LONDON

BANCROFT BOOKS
49 – 53 Poland Street
London W . 1

First published in the "Bancroft Classics" 1966
This impression 1969

430 00079 0

CONTENTS

CONTENTS

CHAPTER 1

Treats of the place where Oliver Twist was born and of the circumstances attending his birth

AMONG other public buildings in a certain town, which for many reasons it will be prudent to refrain from mentioning, and to which I will assign no fictitious name, there is one anciently common to most towns, great or small–to wit, a workhouse; and in this workhouse was born, on a day and date which I need not trouble myself to repeat, inasmuch as it can be of no possible consequence to the reader, in this stage of the business at all events, the item of mortality whose name is prefixed to the head of this chapter.

For a long time after it was ushered into this world of sorrow and trouble, by the parish surgeon, it remained a matter of considerable doubt whether the child would survive to bear any name at all: in which case it is somewhat more than probable that these memoirs would never have appeared; or if they had, that being comprised within a couple of pages, they would have possessed the inestimable merit of being the most concise and faithful specimen of biography extant in the literature of any age or country.

Although I am not disposed to maintain that the being born in a workhouse is in itself the most fortunate and enviable circumstance that can possibly befall a human being, I do mean to say that in this particular instance it was the best thing for Oliver Twist that could by possibility have occurred. The fact is, that there was considerable difficulty in inducing Oliver to take upon himself the office of respiration–a troublesome practice, but one which custom has rendered necessary to our easy existence; and for some time he lay gasping on a little flock mattress, rather unequally poised between this world and the next: the balance being decidedly in favour of the latter. Now, if during this brief period Oliver had been surrounded by careful grand-mothers, anxious aunts, experienced nurses, and doctors of profound wisdom, he would most inevitably and indubitably have been killed in no time. There being nobody by, however, but a pauper old woman, who was rendered rather misty by an unwonted allowance of beer; and a parish surgeon, who did such matters by contract; Oliver and Nature fought out the point between them. The result was that, after a few struggles, Oliver breathed, sneezed, and proceeded to advertise to the inmates of the workhouse the fact of a new burden having been imposed upon the parish, by setting up as loud a cry as could reasonably have been expected from a male infant who had not been possessed of that very useful appendage, a voice, for a much longer space of time than three minutes and a quarter.

As Oliver gave this first proof of the free and proper action of his lungs, the patchwork coverlet, which was carelessly flung over the iron bedstead, rustled; the pale face of a young woman was raised feebly from the pillow; and a faint voice imperfectly articulated the words, "Let me see the child, and die."

The surgeon had been sitting with his face turned towards the fire, giving the palms of his hands a warm and a rub alternately. As the young woman spoke, he rose, and advancing to the bed's head, said, with more kindness than might have been expected of him,—

"Oh, you must not talk about dying yet."

"Lor bless her dear heart, no!" interposed the nurse, hastily depositing in her pocket a green glass bottle, the contents of which she had been tasting in a corner with evident satisfaction. "Lor bless her dear heart, when she has lived as long as I have, sir, and had thirteen children of her own, and all on 'em dead except two, and them in the wurkus with me, she'll know better than to take on in that way, bless her dear heart! Think what it is to be a mother, there's a dear young lamb, do."

Apparently this consolatory perspective of a mother's prospects failed in producing its due effect. The patient shook her head, and stretched out her hand towards the child.

The surgeon deposited it in her arms. She imprinted her cold white lips passionately on its forehead; passed her hands over her face; gazed wildly round; shuddered; fell back—and died. They chafed her breast, hands, and temples; but the blood had stopped for ever. They talked of hope and comfort. They had been strangers too long.

"It's all over, Mrs Thingummy!" said the surgeon at last.

"Ah, poor dear, so it is!" said the nurse, picking up the cork of the green bottle, which had fallen out on the pillow, as she stooped to take up the child. "Poor dear!"

"You needn't mind sending up to me, if the child cries, nurse," said the surgeon, putting on his gloves with great deliberation. "It's very likely it *will* be troublesome. Give it a little gruel if it is." He put on his hat, and pausing by the bedside on his way to the door, added, "She was a good-looking girl, too; where did she come from?"

"She was brought here last night," replied the old woman, "by the overseer's order. She was found lying in the street. She had walked some distance, for her shoes were worn to pieces; but where she came from, or where she was going to, nobody knows."

The surgeon leaned over the body, and raised the left hand. "The old story," he said, shaking his head; "no wedding-ring, I see. Ah! Good-night!"

The medical gentleman walked away to dinner; and the nurse, having once more applied herself to the green bottle, sat down on a low chair before the fire, and proceeded to dress the infant.

What an excellent example of the power of dress young Oliver Twist was! Wrapped in the blanket which had hitherto formed his only covering, he might have been the child of a nobleman or a beggar; it would have been hard for the haughtiest stranger to have assigned him his proper station in society. But now that he was enveloped in the old calico robes which had grown yellow in the same service, he was badged and ticketed, and fell into his place at once–a parish child–the orphan of a workhouse–the humble, half starved drudge–to be cuffed and buffeted through the world–despised by all and pitied by none. Oliver cried lustily. If he could have known that he was an orphan, left to the tender mercies of church-wardens and overseers, perhaps he would have cried the louder.

CHAPTER 2

Treats of Oliver Twist's growth, education, and board

FOR the next eight or ten months, Oliver was the victim of a systematic course of treachery and deception. He was brought up by the hand. The hungry and destitute situation of the infant orphan was duly reported by the workhouse authorities to the parish authorities. The parish authorities inquired with dignity of the workhouse authorities, whether there was no female then domiciled in "the house" who was in a situation to impart to Oliver Twist the consolation and nourishment of which he stood in need. The workhouse authorities replied with humility, that there was not. Upon this the parish authorities magnanimously and humanely resolved that Oliver should be "farmed" or, in other words, that he should be dispatched to a branch-workhouse some three miles off, where twenty or thirty other juvenile offenders against the poor-laws rolled about the floor all day, without the inconvenience of too much food or too much clothing, under the parental superintendence of an elderly female, who received the culprits at and for the consideration of sevenpence-halfpenny per small head per week. Sevenpence-halfpenny's worth per week is a good round diet for a child; a great deal may be got for sevenpence-halfpenny: quite enough to overload its stomach, and make it uncomfortable. The elderly female was a woman of wisdom and experience; she knew what was good for children: and she had a very accurate perception of what was good for herself. So, she appropriated the greater part of the weekly stipend to her own use, and consigned the rising parochial generation to even a shorter allowance than was originally provided for them: thereby finding in the lowest depth a deeper still; and proving herself a very great experimental philosopher.

It cannot be expected that this system of farming would produce any very extraordinary or luxuriant crop. Oliver Twist's ninth birthday found him a pale thin child, somewhat diminutive in stature, and decidedly small in circumference. But nature or inheritance had implanted a good sturdy spirit in Oliver's breast. It had had plenty of room to expand, thanks to the spare diet of the establishment; and perhaps to this circumstance may be attributed his having any ninth birthday at all. Be this as it may, however, it *was* his ninth birthday, and he was keeping it in the coal-cellar with a select party of two other young gentlemen, who, after participating with him in a sound thrashing, had been locked up therein for atrociously presuming to be hungry, when Mrs. Mann, the good lady of the house, was unexpectedly startled by the apparition of Mr. Bumble, the beadle, striving to undo the wicket of the garden-gate.

"Goodness gracious! is that you, Mr. Bumble, sir?" said Mrs. Mann, thrusting her head out of the window in well-affected ecstasies of joy. "(Susan, take Oliver and them two brats upstairs, and wash 'em directly.)– My heart alive! Mr. Bumble, how glad I am to see you, sure-ly!"

Now, Mr. Bumble was a fat man, and a choleric; so instead of responding to this open-hearted salutation in a kindred spirit, he gave the little wicket a tremendous shake, and then bestowed upon it a kick which could have emanated from no leg but a beadle's.

"Lor, only think," said Mrs. Mann, running out–for the three boys had been removed by this time,–"only think of that! That I should have forgotten that the gate was bolted on the inside, on account of them dear children. Walk in, sir, walk in, pray, Mr. Bumble, do, sir."

Although this invitation was accompanied with a curtsy that might have softened the heart of a churchwarden, it by no means mollified the beadle.

"Do you think this respectful or proper conduct, Mrs. Mann," inquired Mr. Bumble, grasping his cane, "to keep the parish officers a-waiting at your garden-gate, when they come here upon porochial business connected with the porochial orphans? Are you aweer, Mrs. Mann, that you are, as I may say, a porochial delegate, and a stipendiary?"

"I'm sure, Mr. Bumble, that I was only a-telling one or two of the dear children as is so fond of you, that it was you a-coming," replied Mrs. Mann, with great humility.

Mr. Bumble had a great idea of his oratorical powers and his importance. He had displayed the one, and vindicated the other. He relaxed.

"Well, well, Mrs. Mann," he replied, in a calmer tone, "it may be as you say it may be." Lead the way in, Mrs. Mann, for I come on business and have something to say."

Mrs. Mann ushered the beadle into a small parlour with a brick floor; placed a seat for him and officiously deposited his cocked hat and cane on the table before him. Mr. Bumble wiped from his forehead the perspiration which his walk had engendered; glanced complacently at the cocked hat; and smiled. Yes, he smiled. Beadles are but men; and Mr. Bumble smiled.

"Now don't you be offended at what I'm a-going to say," observed Mrs. Mann, with captivating sweetness. "You've had a long walk, you know, or I wouldn't mention it. Now, will you take a little drop of something, Mr. Bumble?"

"Not a drop. Not a drop," said Mr. Bumble, waving his right hand in a dignified, but placid manner.

"I think you will," said Mrs. Mann, who had noticed the tone of the refusal, and the gesture that had accompanied it. "Just a little drop, with a little cold water, and a lump of sugar."

Mr. Bumble coughed.

"Now, just a leetle drop," said Mrs. Mann, persuasively.

"What is it?" inquired the beadle.

"Why, it's what I'm obliged to keep a little of in the house, to put into the blessed infants' Daffy, when they ain't well, Mr. Bumble," replied Mrs. Mann, as she opened a corner cupboard, and took down a bottle and glass. "It's gin. I'll not deceive you, Mr. B. It's gin."

"Do you give the children Daffy, Mrs. Mann?" inquired Bumble, following with his eyes the interesting process of mixing.

"Ah, bless 'em, that I do, dear as it is," replied the nurse. "I couldn't see 'em suffer before my very eyes, you know, sir."

"No," said Mr. Bumble approvingly; "no, you could not. You are a humane woman, Mrs. Mann." (Here she set down the glass.) "I shall take a early opportunity of mentioning it to the board, Mrs.Mann." (He drew it towards him.) "You feel as a mother, Mrs. Mann." (He stirred the gin-and-water.) "I–I drink your health with cheerfulness, Mrs. Mann;" and he swallowed half of it.

"And now about business," said the beadle, taking out a leathern pocket-book. "The child that was half-baptized Oliver Twist is nine year old to-day."

"Bless him!" interposed Mrs. Mann, inflaming her left eye with the corner of her apron.

"And notwithstanding an offered reward of ten pound, which was afterwards increased to twenty pound–notwithstanding the most super-lative, and, I may say, supernat'ral exertions on the part of this parish," said Bumble, "we have never been able to discover who is his father, or what was his mother's settlement, name, or condition."

Mrs. Mann raised her hands in astonishment; but added, after a moment's reflection, "How comes he to have any name at all, then?"

The beadle drew himself up with great pride, and said, "I inwented it."

"You, Mr. Bumble!"

"I, Mrs. Mann. We name our fondlings in alphabetical order. The last was an S,–Swubble, I named him. This was a T,–Twist, I named *him*. The next one as comes will be Unwin, and the next Vilkins. I have got names ready made to the end of the alphabet, and all the way through it again, when we come to Z."

"Why, you're quite a literary character, sir!" said Mrs. Mann.

"Well, well," said the beadle, evidently gratified with the compliment; "perhaps I may be. Perhaps I may be, Mrs. Mann." He finished the gin-and-water, and added, "Oliver being now too old to remain here, the board have determined to have him back into the house. I have come out myself to take him there. So let me see him at once."

"I'll fetch him directly," said Mrs. Mann, leaving the room for that purpose. Oliver having had by this time as much of the outer coat of dirt, which encrusted his face and hands, removed as could be scrubbed off in one washing, was led into the room by his benevolent protectress.

"Make a bow to the gentleman, Oliver," said Mrs. Mann.

Oliver made a bow, which was divided between the beadle on the chair and the cocked hat on the table.

"Will you go along with me, Oliver?" said Mr. Bumble, in a majestic voice.

Oliver was about to say that he would go along with anybody with great readiness, when, glancing upwards, he caught sight of Mrs. Mann, who had got behind the beadle's chair, and was shaking her fist at him with a furious countenance. He took the hint at once, for the fist had been too often impressed upon his body not to be deeply impressed upon his recollection.

"Will *she* go with me?" inquired poor Oliver.

"No, she can't," replied Mr. Bumble. "But she'll come and see you sometimes."

This was no very great consolation to the child. Young as he was, however, he had sense enough to make a feint of feeling great regret at going away. It was no very difficult matter for the boy to call the tears into his eyes. Hunger and recent ill-usage are great assistants if you want to cry; and Oliver cried very naturally indeed. Mrs. Mann gave him a thousand embraces, and, what Oliver wanted a great deal more, a piece of bread and butter, lest he should seem too hungry when he got to the workhouse. With the slice of bread in his hand, and the little brown-cloth parish cap on his head, Oliver was then led away by Mr. Bumble from the wretched home where one kind word or look had never lighted the gloom of his infant years.

Oliver had not been within the walls of the workhouse a quarter of an hour, and had scarcely completed the demolition of a second slice of bread, when Mr. Bumble, who had handed him over to the care of an old woman, returned; and, telling him it was a board night, informed him that the board had said he was to appear before it forthwith.

Not having a very clearly defined notion of what a live board was, Oliver was rather astounded by this intelligence, and was not quite certain whether he ought to laugh or cry. He had no time to think about the matter, however; for Mr. Bumble gave him a tap on the head, with his cane, to wake him up, and another on the back to make him lively; and bidding him follow, conducted him into a large whitewashed room, where eight or ten fat gentlemen were sitting round a table. At the top of the table, seated in an armchair rather higher than the rest, was a particularly fat gentleman with a very round, red face.

"Bow to the board," said Bumble. Oliver brushed away two or three tears that were lingering in his eyes, and seeing no board but the table, fortunately bowed to that.

"What's your name, boy?" said the gentleman in the high chair.

Oliver was frightened at the sight of so many gentlemen, which made him tremble; and the beadle gave him another tap behind, which made him cry: and these two causes made him answer in a very low and hesitating voice; whereupon a gentleman in a white waistcoat said he was a fool. Which was a capital way of raising his spirits, and putting him quite at his ease.

"Boy," said the gentleman in the high chair, "listen to me. You know you're an orphan, I suppose?"

"What's that, sir?" inquired poor Oliver.

"The boy *is* a fool—I thought he was," said the gentleman in the white waistcoat.

"Hush!" said the gentleman who had spoken first. "You know you've got no father or mother, and that you were brought up by the parish, don't you?"

"Yes, sir," replied Oliver, weeping bitterly.

"What are you crying for?" inquired the gentleman in the white waistcoat. And to be sure it was very extraordinary. What *could* the boy be crying for?

"I hope you say your prayers every night," said another gentleman in a gruff voice; "and pray for the people who feed you, and take care of you—like a Christian."

"Yes, sir," stammered the boy. The gentleman who spoke last was unconsciously right. It would have been *very* like a Christian, and a marvellously good Christian, too, if Oliver had prayed for the people who fed and took care of *him*. But he hadn't, because nobody had taught him.

"Well! You have come here to be educated and taught a useful trade," said the red-faced gentleman in the high chair.

"So you'll begin to pick oakum to-morrow morning at six o'clock," added the surly one in the white waistcoat.

For the combination of both these blessings in the one simple process of picking oakum, Oliver bowed low by the direction of the beadle, and was then hurried away to a large ward, where, on a rough hard bed, he sobbed himself to sleep. What a noble illustration of the tender laws of England! They let the paupers go to sleep!

The room in which the boys were fed was a large stone hall, with a copper at one end; out of which the master, dressed in an apron for the purpose, and assisted by one or two women, ladled the gruel at meal-times. Of this festive composition each boy had one porringer, and no more—

except on occasions of great public rejoicing, when he had two ounces and a quarter of bread besides. The bowls never wanted washing. The boys polished them with their spoons till they shone again; and when they had performed this operation (which never took very long, the spoons being nearly as large as the bowls), they would sit staring at the copper, with such eager eyes, as if they could have devoured the very bricks of which it was composed; employing themselves, meanwhile, in sucking their fingers most assiduously, with the view of catching up any stray splashes of gruel that might have been cast thereon. Boys have generally excellent appetites. Oliver Twist and his companions suffered the tortures of slow starvation for three months. At last they got so voracious and wild with hunger, that one boy who was tall for his age, and hadn't been used to that sort of thing (for his father had kept a small cook's shop), hinted darkly to his companions, that unless he had another basin of gruel *per diem,* he was afraid he might some night happen to eat the boy who slept next him, who happened to be a weakly youth of tender age. He had a wild, hungry eye; and they implicitly believed him. A council was held; lots were cast who should walk up to the master after supper that evening and ask for more; and it fell to Oliver Twist.

The evening arrived, the boys took their places. The master, in his cook's uniform, stationed himself at the copper; his pauper assistants ranged themselves behind him; the gruel was served out; and a long grace was said over the short commons. The gruel disappeared; the boys whispered to each other, and winked at Oliver; while his next neighbours nudged him. Child as he was, he was desperate with hunger, and reckless with misery. He rose from the table; and advancing to the master, basin and spoon in hand, said, somewhat alarmed at his own temerity,–

"Please, sir, I want some more."

The master was a fat, healthy man; but he turned very pale. He gazed in stupefied astonishment on the small rebel for some seconds; and then clung for support to the copper. The assistants were paralyzed with wonder, the boys with fear.

"What!" said the master at length, in a faint voice.

"Please, sir," replied Oliver, "I want some more."

The master aimed a blow at Oliver's head with the ladle, pinioned him in his arms, and shrieked aloud for the beadle.

The board were sitting in solemn conclave, when Mr. Bumble rushed into the room in great excitement, and addressing the gentleman in the high chair, said,–

"Mr. Limbkins, I beg your pardon, sir! Oliver Twist has asked for more."

There was a general start. Horror was depicted on every countenance.

"For *more!*" said Mr. Limbkins. "Compose yourself, Bumble, and answer me distinctly. Do I understand that he asked for more, after he had eaten the supper allotted by the dietary?"

"He did, sir," replied Bumble.

"That boy will be hung," said the gentleman in the white waistcoat. "I know that boy will be hung."

Nobody controverted the prophetic gentleman's opinion. An animated discussion took place. Oliver was ordered into instant confinement; and a bill was next morning pasted on the outside of the gate, offering a reward of five pounds to anybody who would take Oliver Twist off the hands of the parish. In other words, five pounds and Oliver Twist were offered to any man or woman who wanted an apprentice to any trade, business, or calling.

"I never was more convinced of anything in my life," said the gentleman in the white waistcoat, as he knocked at the gate and read the bill next morning—"I never was more convinced of anything in my life, than I am that that boy will come to be hung."

Chapter 3

Oliver makes his first entry into public life

In great families, when an advantageous place cannot be obtained, either in possession, reversion, remainder, or expectancy, for the young man who is growing up, it is a very general custom to send him to sea. The board, in imitation of so wise and salutary an example, took counsel together on the expediency of shipping off Oliver Twist in some small trading vessel bound to a good unhealthy port; which suggested itself as the very best thing that could possibly be done with him; the probability being that the skipper would flog him to death, in a playful mood, some day after dinner, or would knock his brains out with an iron bar; both pastimes being, as is pretty generally known, very favourite and common recreations among gentlemen of that class.

Mr. Bumble had been dispatched to make various preliminary inquiries, with the view of finding out some captain or other who wanted a cabin-boy without any friends; and was returning to the workhouse to communicate the result of his mission, when he encountered, just at the gate, no less a person than Mr. Sowerberry, the parochial undertaker.

Mr. Sowerberry was a tall, gaunt, large-jointed man, attired in a suit of threadbare black, with darned cotton-stockings of the same colour, and shoes to answer. His features were not naturally intended to wear a smiling aspect, but he was in general rather given to professional jocosity. His step was elastic, and his face betokened inward pleasantry, as he advanced to Mr. Bumble and shook him cordially by the hand.

"I have taken the measure of the two women that died last night, Mr. Bumble," said the undertaker.

"You'll make your fortune, Mr. Sowerberry," said the beadle, as he thrust his thumb and forefinger into the proffered snuff-box of the undertaker; which was an ingenious little model of a patent coffin. "I say you'll make your fortune, Mr. Sowerberry," repeated Mr. Bumble, tapping the undertaker on the shoulder, in a friendly manner, with his cane.

"Think so?" said the undertaker in a tone which half admitted and half disputed the probability of the event. "The prices allowed by the board are very small, Mr. Bumble."

"So are the coffins," replied the beadle, with precisely as near an approach to a laugh as a great official ought to indulge in.

Mr. Sowerberry was much tickled at this—as of course he ought to be—and laughed a long time without cessation. "Well, well, Mr. Bumble," he said at length, "there's no denying that, since the new system of feeding has come in, the coffins are somewhat narrower and more shallow than they used to be; but we must have some profit, Mr. Bumble. Well-seasoned timber is an expensive article, sir; and all the iron handles come by canal from Birmingham."

"Well, well," said Mr. Bumble, "every trade has its drawbacks. A fair profit is, of course, allowable."

"Of course, of course," replied the undertaker; "and if I don't get a profit upon this or that particular article, why, I make it up in the long-run, you see—he! he! he!"

"Just so," said Mr. Bumble.

"Though I must say," continued the undertaker, resuming the current of observations which the beadle had interrupted—"though I must say, Mr. Bumble, that I have to contend against one very great disadvantage—which is, that all the stout people go off the quickest. The people who have been better off, and have paid rates for many years, are the first to sink when they come into the house. And let me tell you, Mr. Bumble, that three or four inches over one's calculation makes a great hole in one's profits; especially when one has a family to provide for, sir."

As Mr. Sowerberry said this with the becoming indignation of an ill-used man, and as Mr. Bumble felt that it rather tended to convey a reflection on the honour of the parish, the latter gentleman thought it advisable to change the subject. Oliver Twist being uppermost in his mind, he made him his theme.

"By-the-bye," said Mr. Bumble, "you don't know anybody who wants a boy, do you? A porochial 'prentice, who is at present a dead-weight—a millstone, as I may say, round the porochial throat? Liberal terms, Mr. Sowerberry, liberal terms!" As Mr. Bumble spoke, he raised his cane to the bill above him, and gave three distinct raps upon the words "five pounds;" which were printed thereon in Roman capitals of gigantic size.

"Gadso!" said the undertaker, taking Mr. Bumble by the gilt-edged lapelle of his official coat; "that's just the very thing I wanted to speak to you about. Why, you know, Mr. Bumble, I pay a good deal towards the poor's rates."

"Hem!" said Mr. Bumble, "Well?"

"Well," replied the undertaker, "I was thinking that if I pay so much towards 'em, I've a right to get as much out of 'em as I can, Mr. Bumble; and so–and so–I think I'll take the boy myself."

Mr. Bumble grasped the undertaker by the arm and led him into the building. Mr. Sowerberry was closeted with the board for five minutes; and it was arranged that Oliver should go to him that evening "upon liking,"–a phrase which means, in the case of a parish apprentice, that if the master finds, upon a short trial, that he can get enough work out of a boy without putting too much food into him, he shall have him for a term of years to do what he likes with.

When little Oliver was taken before "the gentlemen" that evening, and informed that he was to go, that night, as general house-lad to a coffin-maker's; and that if he complained of his situation, or ever came back to the parish again, he would be sent to sea, there to be drowned, or knocked on the head, as the case might be, he evinced so little emotion, that they, by common consent, pronounced him a hardened young rascal, and ordered Mr. Bumble to remove him forthwith.

Now, although it was very natural that the board, of all people in the world, should feel in a great state of virtuous astonishment and horror at the smallest tokens of want of feeling on the part of anybody, they were rather out in this particular instance. The simple fact was, that Oliver, instead of possessing too little feeling, possessed rather too much; and was in a fair way of being reduced, for life, to a state of brutal stupidity and sullenness by the ill-usage he had received. He heard the news of his destination in perfect silence; and, having had his luggage put into his hand–which was not very difficult to carry, inasmuch as it was all comprised within the limits of a brown paper parcel, about half a foot square by three inches deep–he pulled his cap over his eyes; and once more attaching himself to Mr. Bumble's coat cuff, was led away by that dignitary to a new scene of suffering.

For some time Mr. Bumble drew Oliver along without notice or remark; for the beadle carried his head very erect, as a beadle always should, and, it being a windy day, little Oliver was completely enshrouded by the skirts of Mr. Bumble's coat as they blew open, and disclosed to great advantage his flapped waistcoat and drab plush knee-breeches. As they drew near to their destination, however, Mr. Bumble thought it expedient to look down, and see that the boy was in good order for inspection by his new master, which he accordingly did, with a fit and becoming air of gracious patronage.

"Oliver!" said Mr. Bumble.

"Yes, sir," replied Oliver, in a low, tremulous voice.

"Pull that cap off your eyes, and hold up your head, sir."

Although Oliver did as he was desired at once, and passed the back of his unoccupied hand briskly across his eyes, he left a tear in them when he looked up at his conductor. As Mr. Bumble gazed sternly upon him, it rolled down his cheek. It was followed by another and another. The child made a strong effort, but it was an unsuccessful one. Withdrawing his other hand from Mr. Bumble's, he covered his face with both, and wept until the tears sprung out from between his thin and bony fingers.

"Well!" exclaimed Mr. Bumble, stopping short, and darting at his little charge a look of intense malignity—"well! Of *all* the ungreate-fullest, and worst-disposed boys as ever I see, Oliver, you are the—"

"No, no, sir," sobbed Oliver, clinging to the hand which held the well-known cane; "no, no, sir: I will be good indeed; indeed, indeed I will, sir! I am a very little boy, sir; and it is so–so—"

"So what?" inquired Mr. Bumble in amazement.

"So lonely, sir! So very lonely!" cried the child. "Everybody hates me. Oh! sir, don't, don't pray be cross to me!" The child beat his hand upon his heart; and looked in his companion's face with tears of real agony.

Mr. Bumble regarded Oliver's piteous and helpless look with some astonishment for a few seconds; hemmed three or four times in a husky manner; and after muttering something about "that trouble-some cough," bid Oliver dry his eyes and be a good boy. Then, once more taking his hand, he walked on with him in silence.

The undertaker, who had just put up the shutters of his shop, was making some entries in his day-book by the light of a most appropriately dismal candle, when Mr. Bumble entered.

"Aha!" said the undertaker, looking up from the book, and pausing in the middle of a word; "is that you, Bumble?"

"No one else, Mr. Sowerberry," replied the beadle. "Here, I've brought the boy." Oliver made a bow.

"Oh! that's the boy, is it?" said the undertaker, raising the candle above his head, to get a better view of Oliver. "Mrs. Sowerberry! will you have the goodness to come here a moment, my dear?"

Mrs. Sowerberry emerged from a little room behind the shop, and presented the form of a short, thin, squeezed-up woman, with a vixenish countenance.

"My dear," said Mr. Sowerberry, deferentially, "this is the boy from the workhouse that I told you of."

Oliver bowed again.

"Dear me!" said the undertaker's wife, "he's very small."

"Why, he *is* rather small," replied Mr. Bumble, looking at Oliver as if it were his fault that he was no bigger; "he *is* small. There's no denying it. But he'll grow, Mrs. Sowerberry–he'll grow."

"Ah! I dare say he will," replied the lady pettishly, "on our victuals and our drink. I see no saving in parish children, not I; for they always cost more to keep than they're worth. However, men always think they know best. There! Get downstairs, little bag o' bones." With this the undertaker's wife opened a side door, and pushed Oliver down a steep flight of stairs into a stone cell, damp and dark, forming the ante-room to the coal-cellar, and denominated "the kitchen;" wherein sat a slatternly girl, in shoes down at heel, and blue worsted stockings very much out of repair.

"Here, Charlotte," said Mrs. Sowerberry, who had followed Oliver down, "give this boy some of the cold bits that were put by for Trip. He hasn't come home since the morning so he may go without 'em. I daresay the boy isn't too dainty to eat 'em—are you, boy?"

Oliver, whose eyes had glistened at the mention of meat, and who was trembling with eagerness to devour it, replied in the negative; and a plateful of coarse broken victuals was set before him.

I wish some well-fed philosopher, whose meat and drink turn to gall within him, whose blood is ice, whose heart is iron, could have seen Oliver Twist clutching at the dainty viands that the dog had neglected. I wish he could have witnessed the horrible avidity with which Oliver tore the bits asunder with all the ferocity of famine. There is only one thing I should like better—and that would be to see the philosopher making the same sort of meal himself, with the same relish.

"Well," said the undertaker's wife, when Oliver had finished his supper—which she had regarded in silent horror, and with fearful auguries of his future appetite—"have you done?"

There being nothing eatable within his reach, Oliver replied in the affirmative.

"Then come with me," said Mrs. Sowerberry, taking up a dim and dirty lamp, and leading the way upstairs; "your bed's under the counter. You don't mind sleeping among the coffins, I suppose? But it doesn't much matter whether you do or don't, for you can't sleep anywhere else. Come—don't keep me here all night!"

Oliver lingered no longer, but meekly followed his new mistress.

CHAPTER 4

Oliver mingles with new associates. Going to a funeral for the first time, he forms an unfavourable notion of his master's business

OLIVER, being left to himself in the undertaker's shop, set the lamp down on a workman's bench, and gazed timidly about him with a feeling of awe and dread which many people a good deal older than he will be at no loss to understand. An unfinished coffin on black trestles, which stood in the middle of the shop, looked so gloomy and deathlike that a cold tremble came over him every time his eyes wandered in the direction of the dismal object—from which he almost expected to see some frightful form slowly rear its head to drive him mad with terror. Against the wall were arranged, in regular array, a long row of elm boards cut into the same shape; looking, in the dim light, like high-shouldered ghosts with their hands in their breeches-pockets. Coffin-plates, elm-chips, bright-headed nails, and shreds of black cloth, lay scattered on the floor; and the wall behind the counter was ornamented with a lively representation of two mutes in very stiff neck-cloths, on duty at a large private door, with a hearse drawn by four black steeds approaching in the distance. The shop was close and hot, and the atmosphere seemed tainted with the smell of coffins. The recess beneath the counter in which his flock mattress was thrust looked like a grave.

Oliver was awakened in the morning by a loud kicking at the outside of the shop-door; which, before he could huddle on his clothes, was repeated, in an angry and impetuous manner, about twenty-five times. When he began to undo the chain, the legs desisted, and a voice began.

"Open the door, will yer?" cried the voice which belonged to the legs which had kicked at the door.

"I will directly, sir," replied Oliver, undoing the chain, and turning the key.

"I suppose yer the new boy, a'n't yer?" said the voice through the keyhole.

"Yes, sir," replied Oliver.

"How old are yer?" inquired the voice.

"Ten, sir," replied Oliver.

"Then I'll whop yer when I get in," said the voice; "you just see if I don't, that's all, my work'us brat!" and having made this obliging promise, the voice began to whistle.

Oliver had been too often subjected to the process to which the very expressive monosyllable just recorded bears reference, to entertain the smallest doubt that the owner of the voice, whoever he might be, would redeem his pledge most honourably. He drew back the bolts with a trembling hand, and opened the door.

For a second or two, Oliver glanced up the street, and down the street, and over the way, impressed with the belief that the unknown, who had addressed him through the keyhole, had walked a few paces off, to warm himself; for nobody did he see but a big charity-boy, sitting on a post in front of the house, eating a slice of bread and butter, which he cut into wedges, the size of his mouth, with a clasp-knife, and then consumed with great dexterity.

"I beg your pardon, sir," said Oliver, at length, seeing that no other visitor made his appearance; "did you knock?"

"I kicked," replied the charity-boy.

"Did you want a coffin, sir?" inquired Oliver innocently.

At this the charity-boy looked monstrous fierce, and said that Oliver would want one before long if he cut jokes with his superiors in that way.

"Yer don't know who I am, I suppose, Work'us?" said the charity-boy, in continuation, descending from the top of the post, meanwhile, with edifying gravity.

"No, sir," rejoined Oliver.

"I'm Mister Noah Claypole," said the charity-boy, "and you're under me. Take down the shutters, yer idle young ruffian!"

With this, Mr. Claypole administered a kick to Oliver, and entered the shop with a dignified, air, which did him great credit. It is difficult for a large-headed, small-eyed youth, of lumbering make and heavy countenance to look dignified under any circumstances; but it is more especially so, when superadded to these personal attractions are a red nose and yellow smalls.

Oliver, having taken down the shutters, and broken a pane of glass in his efforts to stagger away beneath the weight of the first one to a small court at the side of the house in which they were kept during the day, was graciously assisted by Noah; who, having consoled him with the assurance that "he'd catch it," condescended to help him. Mr. Sowerberry came down soon after. Shortly afterwards, Mrs. Sowerberry appeared; and Oliver having "caught it," in fulfilment of Noah's prediction followed that young gentleman downstairs to breakfast.

"Come near the fire, Noah," said Charlotte. "I saved a nice little bit of bacon for you from master's breakfast. Oliver, shut that door at Mister Noah's back, and take them bits that I've put out on the cover of the bread-pan. There's your tea: take it away to that box, and drink it there, and make haste, for they'll want you to mind the shop. D'ye hear?"

"D'ye hear, Wor'kus?" said Noah Claypole.

"Lor, Noah!" said Charlotte, "what a rum creature you are! Why don't you let the boy alone?"

"Let him alone!" said Noah. "Why, everybody lets him alone enough, for the matter of that. Neither his father nor his mother will ever interfere with him. All his relations let him have his own way pretty well. Eh, Charlotte? He! he! he!"

"Oh, you queer soul!" said Charlotte, bursting into a hearty laugh, in which she was joined by Noah; after which, they both looked scornfully at poor Oliver Twist, as he sat shivering on the box in the coldest corner of the room, and ate the stale pieces which had been specially reserved for him.

Noah was a charity-boy, not a workhouse orphan. No chance-child was he, for he could trace his genealogy all the way back to his parents, who lived hard by; his mother being a washerwoman, and his father a drunken soldier, discharged with a wooden leg, and a diurnal pension of twopence-halfpenny and an unstatable fraction. The shop-boys in the neighbourhood had long been in the habit of branding Noah, in the public streets, with the ignominious epithets of "leathers," "charity," and the like; and Noah had borne them without reply. But now that fortune had cast in his way a nameless orphan, at whom even the meanest could point the finger of scorn, he retorted on him with interest.

Oliver had been sojourning at the undertaker's some three weeks or a month. Mr. and Mrs. Sowerberry–the shop, being shut up–were taking their supper in the little back-parlour, when Mr. Sowerberry, after several deferential glances at his wife, said,–

"My dear–" He was going to say more; but Mrs. Sowerberry looking up, with a peculiarly unpropitious aspect, he stopped short.

"Well," said Mrs. Sowerberry, sharply.

"Nothing, my dear, nothing," said Mr. Sowerberry.

"Ugh, you brute!" said Mrs. Sowerberry.

"Not at all, my dear," said Mr. Sowerberry, humbly. "I thought you didn't want to hear, my dear. I was only going to say—"

"Oh, don't tell me what you were going to say," interposed Mrs. Sowerberry. "I am nobody; don't consult me, pray. I don't want to intrude upon your secrets." As Mrs. Sowerberry said this, she gave a hysterical laugh, which threatened violent consequences.

"But, my dear," said Mr. Sowerberry, "I want to ask your advice."

"No, no, don't ask mine," replied Mrs. Sowerberry, in an affecting manner; "ask somebody else's." Here there was another hysterical laugh, which frightened Mr. Sowerberry very much. This is a very common and much-approved matrimonial course of treatment which is often very effective. It at once reduced Mr. Sowerberry to begging as a special favour to be allowed to say what Mrs. Sowerberry was most curious to hear. After a short altercation of less than three quarters of an hour's duration, the permission was most graciously conceded.

"It's only about young Twist, my dear," said Mr. Sowerberry. "A very good-looking boy, that, my dear."

"He need be, for he eats enough," observed the lady.

"There's an expression of melancholy in his face, my dear," resumed Mr. Sowerberry, "which is very interesting. He would make a delightful mute, my love."

Mrs. Sowerberry looked up with an expression of considerable wonderment. Mr. Sowerberry remarked it, and without allowing time for any observation on the good lady's part, proceeded:–

"I don't mean a regular mute to attend grown–up people, my dear, but only for children's practice. It would be very new to have a mute in proportion, my dear. You may depend upon it, it would have a most superb effect."

Mrs. Sowerberry, who had a good deal of taste in the undertaking way, was much struck by the novelty of this idea; but, as it would have been compromising her dignity to have said so under existing circumstances, she merely inquired, with much sharpness, why such an obvious suggestion had not presented itself to her husband's mind before? Mr. Sowerberry rightly construed this as an acquiescence in his proposition.

It was speedily determined, therefore, that Oliver should be at once initiated into the mysteries of the trade; and with this view, that he should accompany his master on the very next occasion of his services being required.

The occasion was not long in coming. Half an hour after breakfast next morning, Mr. Bumble entered the shop; and supporting his cane against the counter, drew forth his large leathern pocket-book, from which he selected a small scrap of paper, which he handed over to Sowerberry.

"Aha!" said the undertaker, glancing over it with a lively countenance; "an order for a coffin, eh?"

"For a coffin first. and a porochial funeral afterwards", replied Mr. Bumble, fastening the strap on the leathern pocket-book, which, like himself, was very corpulent.

"Bayton," said the undertaker, looking from the scrap of paper to Mr. Bumble. "I never heard the name before."

"We only heard of the family the night before last," said the beadle; "and we shouldn't have known anything about them then, only a woman who lodges in the same house made an application to the porochial committee for them to send the porochial surgeon to see a woman as was very bad. We had gone out to dinner; but his 'prentice (which is a very clever lad) sent 'em some medicine in a blacking-bottle, off-hand."

"Ah, there's promptness," said the undertaker.

"But, now she's dead, we've got to bury her; and that's the direction; and the sooner it's done the better."

Thus saying, Mr. Bumble put on his cocked hat wrong side first, in a fever of parochial excitement, and flounced out of the shop.

"Well," said Mr. Sowerberry, taking up his hat, "the sooner this job is done the better. Noah, look after the shop. Oliver, put on your cap, and come with me." Oliver obeyed, and followed his master on his professional mission.

There was neither knocker nor bell-handle at the open door where Oliver and his master stopped; so, groping his way cautiously through the dark passage, and bidding Oliver keep close to him and not be afraid, the undertaker mounted to the top of the first flight of stairs. Stumbling against a door on the landing, he rapped at it with his knuckles.

It was opened by a young girl of thirteen or fourteen. The undertaker at once saw enough of what the room contained to know it was the apartment to which he had been directed. He stepped in, and Oliver followed him.

There was no fire in the room; but a man was crouching, mechanically, over the empty stove. An old woman, too, had drawn a low stool to the cold hearth, and was sitting beside him. There were some ragged children in another corner; and in a small recess, opposite the door, there lay upon the ground something covered with an old blanket. Oliver shuddered as he cast his eyes towards the place, and crept involuntarily close to his master; for though it was covered up, the boy felt that it was a corpse.

The man's face was thin and very pale; his hair and beard were grizzly; and his eyes were bloodshot. The old woman's face was wrinkled; her two remaining teeth protruded over her under lip; and her eyes were bright and piercing. Oliver was afraid to look at either her or the man. They seemed so like the rats he had seen outside.

"She was my daughter," said the old woman, nodding her head in the direction of the corpse; and speaking with an idiotic leer, more ghastly than even the presence of death in such a place. "Lord, Lord! Well, it *is* strange that I who gave birth to her, and was a woman then, should be alive and merry now, and she lying there, so cold and stiff! Lord, Lord!–to think of it; it's as good as a play–as good as a play!"

As the wretched creature mumbled and chuckled in her hideous merriment, the undertaker turned to go away.

"Stop, stop!" said the old woman in a loud whisper. "Will she be buried to-morrow, or next day, or to-night? I laid her out; and I must walk, you know. Send me a large cloak–a good warm one, for it is bitter cold. We should have cake and wine, too, before we go! Never mind; send some bread–only a loaf of bread and a cup of water. Shall we have some bread, dear?" she said eagerly, catching at the undertaker's coat, as he once more moved towards the door.

"Yes, yes," said the undertaker, "of course, Anything, everything." He disengaged himself from the old woman's grasp, and, drawing Oliver after him, hurried away.

The next day (the family having been meanwhile relieved with a half-quartern loaf and a piece of cheese, left with them by Mr. Bumble himself) Oliver and his master returned to the miserable abode, where Mr. Bumble had already arrived, accompanied by four men from the workhouse, who were to act as bearers. An old black cloak had been thrown over the rags of the old woman and the man; and the bare coffin having been screwed down, was hoisted on the shoulders of the bearers and carried into the street.

"Now, you must put your best leg foremost, old lady!" whispered Sowerberry in the old woman's ear; "we are rather late, and it won't do to keep the clergyman waiting. Move on, my men– as quick as you like!"

Thus directed, the bearers trotted on under their light burden; and the two mourners kept as near them as they could. Mr. Bumble and Sowerberry walked at a good smart pace in front; and Oliver, whose legs were not so long as his master's, ran by the side.

There was not so great a necessity for hurrying as Mr. Sowerberry had anticipated, however; for when they had reached the obscure corner of the churchyard in which the nettles grew, and where the parish graves were made, the clergyman had not arrived; and the clerk, who was sitting by the vestry-room fire, seemed to think it by no means improbable that it might be an hour or so before he came. So they put the bier on the brink of the grave; and the two mourners waited patiently in the damp clay, with a cold rain drizzling down, while the ragged boys, whom the spectacle had attracted into the churchyard, played a noisy game at hide-and-seek among the tombstones, or varied their amusements by jumping backwards and forwards over the coffin. Mr. Sowerberry and Bumble, being personal friends of the clerk, sat by the fire with him, and read the paper.

At length, after the lapse of something more than an hour, Mr. Bumble, and Sowerberry, and the clerk, were seen running towards the grave. Immediately afterwards the clergyman appeared, putting on his surplice as he came along. Mr. Bumble then thrashed a boy or two, to keep up appearances; and the reverend gentleman, having read as much of the burial service as could be compressed into four minutes, gave his surplice to the clerk, and walked away again.

"Now, Bill!" said Sowerberry to the grave-digger, "fill up!"

It was no very difficult task, for the grave was so full that the uppermost coffin was within a few feet of the surface. The gave-digger shovelled in the earth; stamped it loosely down with his feet; shouldered his spade; and walked off, followed by the boys, who murmured very loud complaints at the fun being over so soon.

"Come, my good fellow!" said Bumble, tapping the man on the back. "They want to shut up the yard."

The man, who had never once moved since he had taken his station by the grave-side, started, raised his head, stared at the person who had addressed him, walked forward for a few paces, and fell down in a swoon. The crazy old woman was too much occupied in bewailing the loss of her cloak (which the undertaker had taken off) to pay him any attention, so they threw a can of cold water over him, and when he came to, saw him safely out of the churchyard, locked the gate, and departed on their different ways.

CHAPTER 5

Oliver being goaded by the taunts of Noah, rouses into action, and rather astonishes him

THE month's trial over, Oliver was formally apprenticed. It was a nice sickly season just at this time. In commercial phrases, coffins were looking up; and in the course of a few weeks, Oliver had acquired a great deal of experience. The success of Mr. Sowerberry's ingenious speculation exceeded even his most sanguine hopes. The oldest inhabitants recollected no period at which measles had been so prevalent, or so fatal to infant existence; and many were the mournful processions which little Oliver headed, in a hat-band reaching down to his knees, to the indescribable admiration and emotion of all the mothers in the town. As Oliver accompanied his master in most of his adult expeditions, too, in order that he might acquire that equanimity of demeanour and full command of nerve which are so essential to a finished undertaker, he had many opportunities of observing the beautiful resignation and fortitude with which some strong-minded people bear their trials and losses.

That Oliver Twist was moved to resignation by the example of these good people, I cannot, although I am his biographer, undertake to affirm with any degree of confidence; but I can most distinctly say, that for many months he continued meekly to submit to the domination and ill-treatment of Noah Claypole, who used him far worse than before, now that his jealousy was roused by seeing the new boy promoted to the black stick and hat-band, while he, the old one, remained stationary in the muffin-cap and leathers. Charlotte treated him badly, because Noah did; and Mrs. Sowerberry was his decided enemy because Mr. Sowerberry was disposed to be his friend; so, between these three on one side, and a glut of funerals on the other, Oliver was not altogether as comfortable as the hungry pig was, when he was shut up, by mistake, in the grain department of a brewery.

And now I come to a very important passage in Oliver's history; for I have to record an act, slight and unimportant perhaps in appearance, but which indirectly produced a most material change in all his future prospects and proceedings.

One day Oliver and Noah had descended into the kitchen at the usual dinner-hour, to banquet upon a small joint of mutton--a pound and a half of the worst end of the neck--when Charlotte being called out of the way, there ensued a brief interval of time, which Noah Claypole, being hungry and vicious, considered he could not possibly devote to a worthier purpose than aggravating and tantalizing young Oliver Twist.

Intent upon this innocent amusement, Noah put his feet on the table-cloth; and pulled Oliver's hair; and twitched his ears; and expressed his opinion that he was a "sneak;" and furthermore announced his intention of coming to see him hanged, whenever that desirable event should take place; and entered upon various other topics of petty annoyance, like a malicious and ill-conditioned charity-boy as he was. But, none of these taunts producing the desired effect of making Oliver cry, Noah attempted to be more facetious still; and in this attempt did what many small wits, with far greater reputations than Noah, sometimes do to this day, when they want to be funny--he got rather personal.

"Work'us," said Noah, "how's your mother?"

"She's dead," replied Oliver; "don't you say anything about her to me!"

Oliver's colour rose as he said this; he breathed quickly; and there was a curious working of the mouth and nostrils, which Mr. Claypole thought must be the immediate precursor of a violent fit of crying. Under this impression he returned to the charge.

"What did she die of, Work'us?" said Noah.

"Of a broken heart, some of our old nurses told me," replied Oliver, more as if he was talking to himself than answering Noah. "I think I know what it must be to die of that!"

"Tol de rol lol lol, right fol lairy, Work'us," said Noah, as a tear rolled down Oliver's cheek. "What's set you a snivelling now?"

"Not, *you*," replied Oliver, hastily brushing the tear away. "Don't think it."

"Oh, not me, eh?" sneered Noah.

"No, not you," replied Oliver, sharply. "There; that's enough. Don't say anything more to me about her; you'd better not!"

"Better not!" exclaimed Noah. "Well! Better not! Work'us don't be impudent. *Your* mother, too! She was a nice 'un, she was. Oh, Lor!" And here Noah nodded his head expressively, and curled up as much of his small red nose as muscular action could collect together for the occasion.

"Yer know, Work'us," continued Noah, emboldened by Oliver's silence, and speaking in a jeering tone of affected pity—of all tones the most annoying—"yer know, Work'us, it can't be helped now; and of course yer couldn't help it then; and I'm very sorry for it; and I'm sure we all are, and pity yer very much. But yer must know, Work'us, yer mother was a regular right-down bad 'un."

"What did you say?" inquired Oliver, looking up very quickly.

"A regular right-down bad 'un, Work'us," replied Noah, coolly. "And it's a great deal better, Work'us, that she died when she did, or else she'd have been hard labouring in Bridewell, or transported, or hung; which is more likely than either, isn't it?"

Crimson with fury, Oliver started up; overthrew the chair and table; seized Noah by the throat; shook him in the violence of his rage, till his teeth chattered in his head; and, collecting his whole force into one heavy blow, felled him to the ground.

A minute ago the boy had looked the quiet, mild, dejected creature that harsh treatment had made him. But his spirit was roused at last; the cruel insult to his dead mother had set his blood on fire. His breast heaved; his attitude was erect; his eye bright and vivid; his whole person changed, as he stood glaring over the cowardly tormentor who now lay crouching at his feet, and defied him with an energy he had never known before.

"He'll murder me!" blubbered Noah. "Charlotte! missis! Here's the new boy a-murdering of me! Help! help! Oliver's gone mad! Char—lotte!"

Noah's shouts were responded to by a loud scream from Charlotte, and a louder from Mrs. Sowerberry; the former of whom rushed into the kitchen by a side door, while the latter paused on the staircase till she was quite certain that it was consistent with the preservation of human life to come farther down.

"Oh, you little wretch!" screamed Charlotte, seizing Oliver with her utmost force, which was about equal to that of a moderately strong man in particularly good training. "Oh, you little un-grateful, mur-de-rous, hor-rid vil-lain!" And between every syllable, Charlotte gave Oliver a blow with all her might, accompanying it with a scream, for the benefit of society.

Charlotte's fist was by no means a light one; but, lest it should not be effectual in calming Oliver's wrath, Mrs. Sowerberry plunged into the kitchen, and assisted to hold him with one hand while she scratched his face with the other. In this favourable position of affairs Noah rose from the ground and pommelled him behind.

This was rather too violent exercise to last long. When they were all three wearied out, and could tear and beat no longer, they dragged Oliver, struggling and shouting but nothing daunted, into the dust-cellar, and there locked him up. This being done, Mrs. Sowerberry sank into a chair and burst into tears.

"Bless her, she's going off!" said Charlotte. "A glass of water, Noah, dear. Make haste!"

"Oh, Charlotte," said Mrs. Sowerberry, speaking as well as she could, through a deficiency of breath, and a sufficiency of cold water, which Noah had poured over her head and shoulders. "Oh! Charlotte, what a mercy we have not all been murdered in our beds!"

"Ah! mercy indeed, ma'am," was the reply. "I only hope this'll teach master not to have any more of these dreadful creatures, that are born to be murderers and robbers from their very cradle. Poor Noah! He was all but killed, ma'am, when I came in."

"Poor fellow!" said Mrs. Sowerberry, looking piteously on the charity-boy.

Noah, whose top waistcoat-button might have been somewhere on a level with the crown of Oliver's head, rubbed his eyes with the inside of his wrists while this commiseration was bestowed upon him, and performed some affecting tears and sniffs.

"What's to be done?" exclaimed Mrs. Sowerberry. "Your master's not at home; there's not a man in the house; and he'll kick that door down in ten minutes." Oliver's vigorous plunges against the bit of timber in question rendered this occurrence highly probable.

"Dear, dear! I don't know, ma'am," said Charlotte, "unless we send for the police-officers."

"Or the millingtary," suggested Mr. Claypole.

"No, no," said Mrs. Sowerberry, bethinking herself of Oliver's old friend. "Run to Mr. Bumble, Noah, and tell him to come here directly, and not to lose a minute; never mind your cap! Make haste! Make haste! You can hold a knife to that black eye as you run along, and it'll keep the swelling down."

Noah stopped to make no reply, but started off at his fullest speed; and very much it astonished the people who were out walking, to see the charity-boy tearing through the streets pell-mell, with no cap on his head, and a clasp-knife at his eye.

Chapter 6

Oliver continues refractory

Noah Claypole ran along the streets at his swiftest pace, and paused not once for breath, until he reached the workhouse gate. Having rested here for a minute or so, to collect a good burst of sobs and an imposing show of tears and terror, he knocked loudly at the wicket; and presented such a rueful face to the aged pauper who opened it, that even he, who saw nothing but rueful faces about him at the best of times, started back in astonishment.

"Why, what's the matter with the boy?" said the old pauper.

"Mr. Bumble! Mr. Bumble!" cried Noah, with well-affected dismay, and in tones so loud and agitated that they not only caught the ear of Mr. Bumble himself, who happened to be hardby, but alarmed him so much that he rushed into the yard without his cocked hat—which is a very curious and remarkable circumstance, as showing that even a beadle, acted upon by a sudden and powerful impulse, may be afflicted with a momentary visitation of loss of self-possession and forgetfulness of personal dignity.

"Oh, Mr. Bumble, sir!" said Noah. "Oliver, sir—Oliver has—"

"What? What?" interposed Mr. Bumble, with a gleam of pleasure in his metallic eyes. "Not run away; he hasn't run away, has he, Noah?"

"No, sir, no. Not run away, sir, but he's turned wicious," replied Noah. "He tried to murder me, sir; and then he tried to murder Charlotte; and then missis. Oh! what dreadful pain it is! Such agony, please, sir!" And here Noah writhed and twisted his body into an extensive variety of eel-like positions; thereby giving Mr. Bumble to understand that, from the violent and sanguinary onset of Oliver Twist, he had sustained severe internal injury and damage, from which he was, at that moment, suffering the acutest torture.

When Noah saw that the intelligence he communicated perfectly paralyzed Mr. Bumble, he imparted additional effect thereunto by bewailing his dreadful wounds ten times louder than before; and, when he observed a gentleman in a white waistcoat crossing the yard, he was more tragic in his lamentations than ever, rightly conceiving it highly expedient to attract the notice and rouse the indignation of the gentleman aforesaid.

The gentleman's notice was very soon attracted; for he had not walked three paces, when he turned angrily round, and inquired what that young cur was howling for, and why Mr. Bumble did not favour him with something which would render the series of vocular exclamations so designated, an involuntary process.

"It's a poor boy from the free-school, sir," replied Mr. Bumble, "who has been nearly murdered—all but murdered, sir—by young Twist."

"By Jove!" exclaimed the gentleman in the white waistcoat, stopping short. "I knew it! I felt a strange presentiment from the very first, that that audacious young savage would come to be hung!"

"He has likewise attempted, sir, to murder the female servant," said Mr. Bumble, with a face of ashy paleness.

"And his missis," interposed Mr. Claypole.

"And his master, too, I think you said, Noah?" added Mr. Bumble.

"No; he's out, or he would have murdered him," replied Noah. "He said he wanted to."

"Ah! Said he wanted to: did he, my boy?" inquired the gentleman in the white waistcoat.

"Yes, sir," replied Noah. "And please, sir, missis wants to know whether Mr. Bumble can spare time to step up there, directly, and flog him—'cause master's out."

"Certainly, my boy; certainly," said the gentleman in the white waistcoat, smiling benignly, and patting Noah's head, which was about three inches higher than his own. "You're a good boy—a very good boy. Here's a penny for you. Bumble, just step up to Sowerby's with your cane, and see what's best to be done. Don't spare him, Bumble."

"No, I will not, sir," replied the beadle, adjusting the wax-end which was twisted round the bottom of his cane for purposes of parochial flagellation.

"Tell Sowerberry not to spare him either. They'll never do anything with him without stripes and bruises," said the gentleman in the white waistcoat.

"I'll take care, sir," replied the beadle. And the cocked hat and cane having been by this time adjusted to their owner's satisfaction, Mr. Bumble and Noah Claypole betook themselves with all speed to the undertaker's shop.

Here the position of affairs had not at all improved, as Sowerberry had not yet returned, and Oliver continued to kick, with undiminished vigour, at the cellar-door. The accounts of his ferocity, as related by Mrs. Sowerberry and Charlotte, were of so startling a nature, that Mr. Bumble judged it prudent to parley before opening the door. With this view he gave a kick at the outside, by way of prelude; and then applying his mouth to the keyhole, said, in a deep and impressive tone,—

"Oliver!"

"Come; you let me out!" replied Oliver from the inside.

"Do you know this here voice, Oliver?" said Mr. Bumble.

"Yes," replied Oliver.

"Ain't you afraid of it, sir? Ain't you a—trembling while I speak, sir?" said Mr. Bumble.

"No!" replied Oliver, boldly.

An answer so different from the one he had expected to elicit, and was in the habit of receiving, staggered Mr. Bumble not a little. He stepped back from the keyhole; drew himself up to his full height; and looked from one to another of the three bystanders, in mute astonishment.

"Oh, you know, Mr. Bumble, he must be mad," said Mrs. Sowerberry. "No boy in half his senses could venture to speak so to you."

"Ah!" said Mr. Bumble, "the only thing that can be done now, that I know of, is to leave him in the cellar for a day or so till he's a little starved down; and then to take him out, and keep him on gruel all through his apprenticeship. He comes of a bad family. Excitable natures, Mrs. Sowerberry! Both the nurse and doctor said that that mother of his made her way here against difficulties and pain that would have killed any well-disposed woman weeks before."

At this point of Mr. Bumble's discourse, Oliver, just hearing enough to know that some further allusion was being made to his mother, recommenced kicking with a violence that rendered every other sound inaudible. Sowerberry returned at this junction; and Oliver's offence having been explained to him, with such exaggerations as the ladies thought best calculated to rouse his ire, he unlocked the cellar-door in a twinkling, and dragged his rebellious apprentice out by the collar.

Oliver's clothes had been torn in the beating he had received; his face was bruised and scratched; and his hair scattered over his forehead. The angry flush had not disappeared, however, and when he was pulled out of his prison, he scowled boldly on Noah, and looked quite undismayed.

"Now, you are a nice young fellow, ain't you?" said Sowerberry, giving Oliver a shake, and a box on the ear.

"He called my mother names," replied Oliver.

"Well, and what if he did, you little ungrateful wretch?" said Mrs. Sowerberry. "She deserved what he said, and worse."

"She didn't," said Oliver.

"She did," said Mrs. Sowerberry.

"It's lie!" said Oliver.

Mrs. Sowerberry burst into a flood of tears.

This flood of tears left Mr. Sowerberry no alternative. If he had hesitated for one instant to punish Oliver most severely, it must be quite clear to every experienced reader that he would have been, according to all precedents in disputes of matrimony established, a brute, an unnatural husband, an insulting creature, a base imitation of a man, and various other agreeable characters too numerous for recital within the limits of this chapter. To do him justice, he was, as far as his power went–it was not very extensive–kindly disposed towards the boy; perhaps because it was his interest to be so, perhaps because his wife disliked him. The flood of tears, however, left him no resource; so he at once gave him a drubbing, which satisfied even Mrs. Sowerberry herself, and rendered Mr. Bumble's subsequent application of the parochial cane rather unnecessary. For the rest of the day he was shut up in the back kitchen, in company with a pump and a slice of bread; and, at night, Mrs. Sowerberry, after making various remarks outside the door, by no means complimentary to the memory of his mother, looked into the room, and, amidst the jeers and pointings of Noah and Charlotte, ordered him upstairs to his dismal bed.

With the first ray of light that struggled through the crevices in the shutters, Oliver rose, and unbarred the door. One timid look around—one moment's pause of hesitation—he had closed it behind him, and was in the open street.

He looked to the right and to the left, uncertain whither to fly. He remembered to have seen the wagons, as they went out, toiling up the hill. He took the same route; and arriving at the footpath across the fields, which he knew, after some distance, led out again into the road, struck into it, and walked quickly on.

Along this same footpath Oliver well remembered he had trotted beside Mr. Bumble, when he first carried him to the workhouse from the farm. His way lay directly in front of the cottage. His heart beat quickly when he bethought himself of this, and he half resolved to turn back. He had come a long way though, and should lose a great deal of time by doing so. Besides, it was so early that there was very little fear of his being seen; so he walked on.

He reached the house. There was no appearance of its inmates stirring at that early hour. Oliver stopped, and peeped into the garden. A child was weeding one of the little beds; and as he stopped, he raised his pale face, and disclosed the features of one of his former companions. Oliver felt glad to see him before he went; for, though younger than himself, he had been his little friend and playmate. They had been beaten and starved, and shut up together, many and many a time.

"Hush, Dick!" said Oliver, as the boy ran to the gate and thrust his thin arm between the rails to greet him. "Is any one up?"

"Nobody but me," replied the child.

"You mustn't say you saw me, Dick," said Oliver. "I am running away. They beat and ill-use me, Dick; and I am going to seek my fortune some long way off. I don't know where. How pale you are!"

"I heard the doctor tell them I was dying," replied the child, with a faint smile. "I am very glad to see you, dear; but don't stop, don't stop!"

"Yes, yes, I will, to say good-bye to you," replied Oliver. "I shall see you again, Dick. I know I shall. You will be well and happy."

"I hope so," replied the child. "After I am dead, but not before. I know the doctor must be right, Oliver, because I dream so much of Heaven, and Angels, and kind faces that I never see when I am awake. Kiss me," said the child, climbing up the low gate, and flinging his little arms round Oliver's neck. "Good-bye, dear! God bless you!"

The blessing was from a young child's lips, but it was the first that Oliver had ever heard invoked upon his head; and through all the struggles and sufferings, and troubles and changes, of his after life, he never once forgot it.

CHAPTER 7

*Oliver walks to London. He encounters on the road a strange
sort of young gentleman*

OLIVER reached the stile at which the footpath terminated, and once more
gained the highroad. It was eight o'clock now. Though he was nearly five
miles away from the town, he ran and hid behind hedges, by turns, till
noon, fearing that he might be pursued and overtaken. Then he sat down
to rest by the side of a milestone, and began to think, for the first time,
where he had better go and try to live.

The stone by which he was seated bore, in large characters, an Intimation
that it was just seventy miles from that spot to London. The name awakened
a new train of ideas in the boy's mind. London!–that great large place!–
nobody, not even Mr. Bumble, could ever find him there. He had often
heard the old men in the workhouse, too, say that no lad of spirit need
want in London; and that there were ways of living in that vast city which
those who had been bred up in country parts had no idea of. It was the
very place for a homeless boy, who must die in the streets unless some one
helped him. As these things passed through his thoughts, he jumped upon
his feet, and again walked forward.

Oliver walked twenty miles that day, and all that time tasted nothing
but the crust of dry bread, and a few draughts of water which he begged
at the cottage-doors by the roadside. When the night came he turned into
a meadow, and, creeping close under a hayrick, determined to lie there till
morning.

He felt cold and stiff when he got up next morning, and so hungry that
he was obliged to exchange his only penny for a small loaf, in the very first
village through which he passed. He had walked no more than twelve miles
when night closed in again; for his feet were sore, and his legs so weak that
they trembled beneath him. Another night passed in the bleak damp air
made him worse, and when he set forward on his journey next morning
he could hardly crawl along.

In fact, if it had not been for a good-hearted turnpike-man, and a
benevolent old lady, Oliver's troubles would have been shortened by the
very same process which put an end to his mother's: in other words, he
would most assuredly have fallen dead upon the king's highway. But the
turnpike-man gave him a meal of bread and cheese; and the old lady,
who had a shipwrecked grandson wandering barefooted in some distant
part of the earth, took pity upon the poor orphan, and gave him what little
she could afford–and more–with such kind and gentle words, and such
tears of sympathy and compassion, that they sank deeper into Oliver's
soul than all the sufferings he had ever undergone.

Early on the seventh morning after he had left his native place, Oliver

limped slowly into the little town of Barnet. The window-shutters were
closed; the street was empty; not a soul had awakened to the business of
the day.

By degrees the shutters were opened; the window-blinds were drawn up;
and people began passing to and fro. Some few stopped to gaze at Oliver
for a moment or two, or turned round to stare at him as they hurried by;
but none relieved him, or troubled themselves to inquire how he came
there. He had no heart to beg. And there he sat.

He had been crouching on the step for some time, when he was roused
by observing that a boy, who had passed him carelessly some minutes
before, had returned, and was now surveying him most earnestly from the
opposite side of the way. He took little heed of this at first; but the boy
remained in the same attitude of close observation so long, that Oliver
raised his head, and returned his steady look. Upon this, the boy crossed
over, and, walking close up to Oliver, said,–

"Hallo! my covey, what's the row?"

The boy who addressed this inquiry to the young wayfarer was about
his own age, but one of the queerest-looking boys that Oliver had ever seen.
He was a snub-nosed, flat-browed, common-faced boy enough, and as dirty
a juvenile as one would wish to see; but he had about him all the airs and
manners of a man. He was short for his age, with rather bow-legs, and
little, sharp, ugly eyes. His hat was stuck on the top of his head so lightly,
that it threatened to fall off every moment–and would have done so very
often, if the wearer had not had a knack of every now and then giving his
head a sudden twitch, which brought it back to its old place again. He wore
a man's coat, which reached nearly to his heels. He had turned the cuffs
back, half way up his arm, to get his hands out of the sleeves, apparently
with the ultimate view of thrusting them into the pockets of his corduroy
trousers, for there he kept them.

"Hallo, my covey, what's the row?" said this strange young gentleman
to Oliver.

"I am very hungry and tired," replied Oliver, the tears standing in his
eyes as he spoke. "I have walked a long way. I have been walking these
seven days."

"Walking for sivin days!" said the young gentleman. "Oh, I see. Beak's
order, eh? But," he added, noticing Oliver's look of surprise, "I suppose
you don't know what a beak is, my flash com-pan-i-on."

Oliver mildly replied that he had always heard a bird's mouth described
by the term in question.

"My eyes, how green!" exclaimed the young gentleman. "Why, a beak's
a madgst'rate; and when you walk by a beak's order, it's not straight
forerd, but always a-going up, and nivir a-coming down agin. Was you
never on the mill?"

"What mill?" inquired Oliver.

"What mill!–why, *the* mill–the mill as takes up so little room that it'll work inside a Stone Jug; and always goes better when the wind's low with people than when it's high, acos then they can't get workmen. But come," said the young gentleman; "you want grub, and you shall have it. I'm at low-water-mark myself—only one bob and a magpie; but *as* far *as* it goes, I'll fork out and stump. Up with you on your pins. There! Now then! Morrice!"

Assisting Oliver to rise, the young gentleman took him to an adjacent chandler's shop, where he purchased a sufficiency of ready-dressed ham and a half-quartern loaf, or as he himself expressed it, "a fourpenny bran;" the ham being kept clean and preserved from dust by the ingenious expedient of making a hole in the loaf by pulling out a portion of the crumb, and stuffing it therein. Taking the bread under his arm, the young gentleman turned into a small public-house, and led the way to a tap-room in the rear of the premises. Here a pot of beer was brought in, by direction of the mysterious youth; and Oliver, falling to at his new friend's bidding, made a long and hearty meal, during the progress of which the strange boy eyed him from time to time with great attention.

"Going to London?" said the strange boy, when Oliver had at length concluded.

"Yes."

"Got any lodgings?"

"No."

"Money?"

"No."

The stranger boy whistled; and put his arms into his pockets, as far as the big coat sleeves would let them go.

"Do you live in London?" inquired Oliver.

"Yes. I do, when I'm at home," replied the boy. "I suppose you want some place to sleep in to-night, don't you?"

"I do indeed," answered Oliver. "I have not slept under a roof since I left the country."

"Don't fret your eyelids on that score," said the young gentleman "I've got to be in London to-night; and I knows a 'spectable old genelman as lives there, wot'll give you lodgings for nothink, and never ask for the change—that is, if any genelman he knows interduces you. And don't he know me? Oh, no! Not in the least! By no means. Certainly not!"

The young gentleman smiled, as if to intimate that the latter fragments of discourse were playfully ironical; and finished the beer as he did so.

This led to a more friendly and confidential dialogue; from which Oliver discovered that his friend's name was Jack Dawkins, and that among his intimate friends he was better known by the *sobriquet* of "The Artful Dodger."

As John Dawkins objected to their entering London before nightfall, it was nearly eleven o'clock when they reached the turnpike at Islington. They crossed from the Angel into St. John's Road, struck down the small street which terminates at Sadler's Wells Theatre; through Exmouth Street and Coppice Row; down the little court by the side of the workhouse; across the classic ground which once bore the name of Hockley-in-the-Hole; thence into Little Saffron Hill; and so into Saffron Hill the Great, along which the Dodger scudded at a rapid pace, directing Oliver to follow close at his heels.

Oliver was just considering whether he hadn't better run away when they reached the bottom of the hill. His conductor, catching him by the arm, pushed open the door of a house near Field Lane, and drawing him into the passage, closed it behind them.

"Now, then!" cried a voice from below, in reply to a whistle from the Dodger.

"Plummy and slam!" was the reply.

This seemed to be some watchword or signal that all was right; for the light of a feeble candle gleamed on the wall at the remote end of the passage, and a man's face peeped out from where a balustrade of the old kitchen staircase had been broken away.

"There's two on you," said the man, thrusting the candle farther out, and shading his eyes with his hand. "Who's the t'other one?"

"A new pal," replied Jack Dawkins, pulling Oliver forward.

"Where did he come from?"

"Greenland. Is Fagin upstairs?"

"Yes, he's a-sortin' the wipes. Up with you!" The candle was drawn back, and the face disappeared.

Oliver, groping his way with one hand, and having the other firmly grasped by his companion, ascended with much difficulty the dark and broken stairs, which his conductor mounted with an ease and expedition that showed he was well acquainted with them. He threw open the door of a back-room, and drew Oliver in after him.

The walls and ceiling of the room were perfectly black with age and dirt. There was a deal table before the fire; upon which were a candle, stuck in a ginger-beer bottle, two or three pewter pots, a loaf and butter, and a plate. In a frying-pan, which was on the fire, and which was secured to the mantelshelf by a string, some sausages were cooking; and standing over them, with a toasting-fork in his hand, was a very old shrivelled Jew, whose villainous-looking and repulsive face was obscured by a quantity of matted red hair. He was dressed in a greasy flannel gown, with his throat bare; and seemed to be dividing his attention between the frying-pan and a clothes-horse, over which a great number of silk handkerchiefs were hanging. Several rough beds, made of sacks, were huddled side by side on the floor; and seated round the table were four or five boys, none older than the Dodger, smoking long clay pipes, and drinking spirits with the air of middle-aged men. These all crowded about their associate as he whispered a few words to the Jew, and then turned round and grinned at Oliver; as did the Jew himself, toasting-fork in hand.

"This is him, Fagin," said Jack Dawkins; "my friend, Oliver Twist."

The Jew grinned, and, making a low obeisance to Oliver, took him by the hand, and hoped he should have the honour of his intimate acquaintance. Upon this the young gentlemen with the pipes came round him, and shook both his hands very hard, especially the one in which he held his little bundle. One young gentleman was very anxious to hang up his cap for him; and another was so obliging as to put his hands in his pockets, in order that, as he was very tired, he might not have the trouble of emptying them himself when he went to bed. These civilities would probably have been extended much further, but for a liberal exercise of the Jew's toasting-fork on the heads and shoulders of the affectionate youths who offered them.

"We are very glad to see you, Oliver–very," said the Jew. "Dodger, take off the sausages, and draw a tub near the fire for Oliver. Ah, you're a-staring at the pocket-handkerchiefs! eh, my dear? There are a good many of 'em, ain't there? We've just looked 'em out, ready for the wash; that's all, Oliver–that's all. Ha! ha! ha!"

The latter part of this speech was hailed by a boisterous shout from all the hopeful pupils of the merry old gentleman. In the midst of which they went to supper.

Oliver ate his share, and the Jew then mixed him a glass of hot gin and water; telling him he must drink it off directly, because another gentleman wanted the tumbler. Oliver did as he was desired. Immediately afterwards he felt himself gently lifted on to one of the sacks, and then he sank into a deep sleep.

CHAPTER 8

Containing further particulars concerning the pleasant old gentleman and his hopeful pupils

It was late next morning when Oliver awoke from a sound long sleep. There was no other person in the room but the old Jew, who was boiling some coffee in a saucepan for breakfast, and whistling softly to himself as he stirred it round and round with an iron spoon.

Although Oliver had roused himself from sleep, he was not thoroughly awake. He saw the Jew with his half-closed eyes, heard his low whistling, and recognized the sound of the spoon grating against the saucepan's sides; and yet the self-same senses were mentally engaged, at the same time, in busy action with almost everybody he had ever known.

When the coffee was done, the Jew drew the saucepan to the hob; and, standing in an irresolute attitude for a few minutes, as if he did not well know how to employ himself, turned round and looked at Oliver, and called him by his name. He did not answer, and was to all appearance asleep.

After satisfying himself upon this head, the Jew stepped gently to the door, which he fastened. He then drew forth, as it seemed to Oliver, from some trap in the floor, a small box, which he placed carefully on the table. His eyes glistened as he raised the lid and looked in. Dragging an old chair to the table, he sat down, and took from it a magnificent gold watch, sparkling with jewels.

"Aha!" said the Jew, shrugging up his shoulders, and distorting every feature with a hideous grin. "Clever dogs! clever dogs! Stanch to the last! Never told the old parson where they were. Never peached upon old Fagin! And why should they? It wouldn't have loosened the knot, or kept the drop up a minute longer. No, no, no! Fine fellows! Fine fellows!"

With these, and other muttered reflections of the like nature, the Jew once more deposited the watch in its place of safety. At least half a dozen more were severally drawn forth from the same box and surveyed with equal pleasure; besides rings, brooches, bracelets, and other articles of jewellery, of such magnificent materials and costly workmanship, that Oliver had no idea even of their names.

Having replaced these trinkets, the Jew took out another, so small that it lay in the palm of his hand. There seemed to be some very minute inscription on it; for the Jew laid it flat upon the table, and shading it with his hand, pored over it long and earnestly. At length he put it down, as if despairing of success; and leaning back in his chair, muttered,–

"What a fine thing capital punishment is! Dead men never repent; dead men never bring awkward stories to light. Ah, it's a fine thing for the trade! Five of 'em strung up in a row, and none left to play booty, or turn white-livered!"

As the Jew uttered these words, his bright dark eyes, which had been staring vacantly before him, fell on Oliver's face. The boy's eyes were fixed on his in mute curiosity; and, although the recognition was only for an instant–for the briefest space of time that can possibly be conceived–it was enough to show the old man that he had been observed. He closed the lid of the box with a loud crash; and, laying his hand on a bread-knife which was on the table, started furiously up. He trembled very much, though; for, even in his terror, Oliver could see that the knife quivered in the air.

"What's that?" said the Jew. "What do you watch me for? Why are you awake? What have you seen? Speak out, boy!–Quick–quick! for your life!"

"I wasn't able to sleep any longer, sir," replied Oliver, meekly. "I am very sorry if I have disturbed you, sir."

"You were not awake an hour ago?" said the Jew, scowling fiercely on the boy.

"No–no, indeed," replied Oliver.

"Are you sure?" cried the Jew, with a still fiercer look than before, and a threatening attitude.

"Upon my word I was not, sir," replied Oliver, earnestly. "I was not, indeed, sir."

"Tush, tush, my dear!" said the Jew, abruptly resuming his old manner, and playing with the knife a little, before he laid it down, as if to induce the belief that he had caught it up in mere sport. "Of course I know that, my dear. I only tried to frighten you. You're a brave boy. Ha! ha! you're a brave boy, Oliver!" The Jew rubbed his hands with a chuckle, but glanced uneasily at the box notwithstanding.

"Did you see any of these pretty things, my dear?" said the Jew, laying his hand upon it after a short pause.

"Yes, sir," replied Oliver.

"Ah!" said the Jew, turning rather pale. "They–they're mine, Oliver; my little property. All I have to live upon in my old age. The folks call me a miser, my dear–only a miser, that's all."

Oliver thought the old gentleman must be a decided miser to live in such a dirty place, with so many watches; but, thinking that perhaps his fondness for the Dodger and the other boys cost him a good deal of money, he only cast a deferential look at the Jew, and asked if he might get up.

"Certainly, my dear–certainly," replied the old gentleman. "Stay. There's a pitcher of water in the corner by the door. Bring it here; and I'll give you a basin to wash in, my dear."

Oliver got up, walked across the room, and stooped for one instant to raise the pitcher. When he turned his head the box was gone.

He had scarcely washed himself, and made everything tidy, by emptying the basin out of the window, agreeably to the Jew's directions, when the Dodger returned, accompanied by a very sprightly young friend, whom Oliver had seen smoking on the previous night, and who was now formally introduced to him as Charley Bates. The four sat down to breakfast on the coffee, and some hot rolls and ham, which the Dodger had brought home in the crown of his hat.

"Well," said the Jew, glancing slyly at Oliver, and addressing himself to the Dodger, "I hope you've been at work this morning, my dears?"

"Hard," replied the Dodger.

"As Nails," added Charley Bates.

"Good boys, good boys!" said the Jew. "What have *you* got, Dodger?"

"A couple of pocket-books," replied that young gentleman.

"Lined?" inquired the Jew, with eagerness.

"Pretty well," replied the Dodger, producing two pocket-books, one green and the other red.

"Not so heavy as they might be," said the Jew, after looking at the insides carefully; "but very neat and nicely made. Ingenious workman, ain't he, Oliver?"

"Very, indeed, sir," said Oliver.

"And what have you got, my dear?" said Fagin to Charley Bates.

"Wipes," replied Master Bates, at the same time producing four pocket-handkerchiefs.

"Well," said the Jew, inspecting them closely, "they're very good ones—very. You haven't marked them well, though, Charley; so the marks shall be picked out with a needle, and we'll teach Oliver how to do it. Shall us, Oliver, eh? Ha! ha! ha!"

"If you please, sir," said Oliver.

"You'd like to be able to make pocket-handkerchiefs as easy as Charley Bates, wouldn't you, my dear?" said the Jew.

"Very much indeed, if you'll teach me, sir," replied Oliver.

When the breakfast was cleared away, the merry old gentleman and the two boys played at a very curious and uncommon game, which was performed in this way. The merry old gentleman, placing a snuff-box in one pocket of his trousers, a note-case in the other, and a watch in his waistcoat pocket, with a guard chain round his neck, and sticking a mock diamond pin in his shirt, buttoned his coat tight round him, and putting his spectacle-case and handkerchief in his pockets, trotted up and down the room with a stick, in imitation of the manner in which old gentlemen walk about the streets any hour of the day. Sometimes he stopped at the fireplace, and sometimes at the door, making believe that he was staring with all his might into shop windows. At such times he would look constantly round him, for fear of thieves, and keep slapping all his pockets in turn, to see that he hadn't lost anything, in such a very funny and natural manner that Oliver laughed till the tears ran down his face. All this time the two boys followed him closely about; getting out of his sight so nimbly, every time he turned round, that it was impossible to follow their motions. At last the Dodger trod upon his toes, or ran upon his boot accidentally, while Charley Bates stumbled up against him behind; and in that one moment they took from him, with the most extraordinary rapidity, snuff-box, note-case, watch-guard, chain, shirt-pin, pocket-handkerchief—even the spectacle-case. If the old gentleman felt a hand in any one of his pockets, he cried out where it was; and then the game began all over again.

When this game had been played a great many times, a couple of young ladies called to see the young gentlemen; one of whom was named Bet, and the other Nancy. They wore a good deal of hair, not very neatly turned up behind, and were rather untidy about the shoes and stockings. They were not exactly pretty, perhaps; but they had a great deal of colour in their faces, and looked quite stout and hearty. Being remarkably free and agreeable in their manners, Oliver thought them very nice girls indeed. As there is no doubt they were.

These visitors stopped a long time. Spirits were produced, in consequence of one of the young ladies complaining of a coldness in her inside; and the conversation took a very convivial and improving turn. At length Charley Bates expressed his opinion that it was time to pad the hoof. This, it occurred to Oliver, must be French for going out; for directly afterwards, the Dodger, and Charley, and the two young ladies, went away together, having been kindly furnished by the amiable old Jew with money to spend.

"There, my dear," said Fagin, "that's a pleasant life, isn't it? They have gone out for the day."

"Have they done work, sir?" inquired Oliver.

"Yes," said the Jew; "that is, unless they should unexpectedly come across any when they are out; and they won't neglect it, if they do, my dear—depend upon it.

"Make 'em your models, my dear—make 'em your models," said the Jew, tapping the fire-shovel on the hearth to add force to his words; "do everything they bid you, and take their advice in all matters—especially the Dodger's, my dear. He'll be a great man himself, and will make you one too, if you take pattern by him.—Is my handkerchief hanging out of my pocket, my dear?" said the Jew, stopping short.

"Yes, sir," said Oliver.

"See if you can take it out without my feeling it, as you saw them do when we were at play this morning."

Oliver held up the bottom of the pocket with one hand, as he had seen the Dodger hold it, and drew the handkerchief lightly out of it with the other.

"Is it gone?" cried the Jew.

"Here it is, sir," said Oliver, showing it in his hand.

"You're a clever boy, my dear," said the playful old gentleman, patting Oliver on the head approvingly. "I never saw a sharper lad. Here's a shilling for you. If you go on in this way, you'll be the greatest man of the time. And now come here, and I'll show you how to take the marks out of the handkerchiefs."

Oliver wondered what picking the old gentleman's pocket in play had to do with his chances of being a great man. But, thinking that the Jew, being so much his senior, must know best, he followed him quietly to the table, and was soon deeply involved in his new study.

CHAPTER 9

Oliver becomes better acquainted with the characters of his new associates; and purchases experience at a high price. Being a short but very important chapter in this history

FOR many days Oliver remained in the Jew's room, picking the marks out of the pocket-handkerchiefs (of which a great number were brought home), and sometimes taking part in the game already described, which the two boys and the Jew played regularly every morning. At length he began to

languish for the fresh air, and took many occasions of earnestly entreating
the old gentleman to allow him to go out to work with his two companions.

Oliver was rendered the more anxious to be actively employed, by what
he had seen of the stern morality of the old gentleman's character. Whenever the Dodger or Charley Bates came home at night empty handed, he
would expatiate with great vehemence on the misery of idle and lazy
habits, and would enforce upon them the necessity of an active life by
sending them supperless to bed. On one occasion, indeed, he even went so
far as to knock them both down a flight of stairs; but this was carrying
out his virtuous precepts to an unusual extent.

At length one morning Oliver obtained the permission he had so eagerly
sought.

The three boys sallied out; the Dodger with his coat sleeves tucked up,
and his hat cocked, as usual; Master Bates sauntering along with his hands
in his pockets; and Oliver between them, wondering where they were
going, and what branch of manufacture he would be instructed in first.

They were just emerging from a narrow court not far from the open
square in Clerkenwell, which is yet called, by some strange perversion of
terms, "The Green", when the Dodger made a sudden stop, and, laying
his finger on his lip, drew his companions back again, with the greatest
caution and circumspection.

"What's the matter?" demanded Oliver.

"Hush!" replied the Dodger. "Do you see that old cove at the book-
stall?"

"The old gentleman over the way?" said Oliver. "Yes, I see him."

"He'll do," said the Dodger.

"A prime plant," observed Master Charley Bates.

Oliver looked from one to the other with the greatest surprise; but he
was not permitted to make any inquiries, for the two boys walked stealthily
across the road, and slunk close behind the old gentleman towards whom
his attention had been directed. Oliver walked a few paces after them, and,
not knowing whether to advance or retire, stood looking on in silent
amazement.

The old gentleman was a very respectable looking personage, with a
powdered head and gold spectacles. He had taken up a book from the
stall, and there he stood, reading away as hard as if he were in his elbow-
chair in his own study. What was Oliver's horror and alarm as he stood
a few paces off, looking on with his eyelids as wide open as they would
possibly go, to see the Dodger plunge his hand into the old gentleman's
pocket, and draw from thence a handkerchief; to see him hand the same
to Charley Bates; and finally to behold them both running away round the
corner at full speed!

In an instant the whole mystery of the handkerchiefs, and the watches,
and the jewels, and the Jew, rushed upon the boy's mind. He stood for a
moment, with the blood so tingling through all his veins from terror, that

he felt as if he were in a burning fire; then, confused and frightened, he took to his heels, and, not knowing what he did, made off as fast as he could lay his feet to the ground.

This was all done in a minute's space. In the very instant when Oliver began to run, the old gentleman, putting his hand to his pocket, and missing his handkerchief, turned sharp round. Seeing the boy scudding away at such a rapid pace, he very naturally concluded him to be the depredator; and, shouting "Stop thief!" with all his might, made off after him, book in hand.

But the old gentleman was not the only person who raised the hue-and-cry. The Dodger and Master Bates, unwilling to attract public attention by running down the open street, had merely retired into the very first doorway round the corner. They no sooner heard the cry, and saw Oliver running, than, guessing exactly how the matter stood, they issued forth with great promptitude, and shouting "Stop thief!" too, joined in the pursuit like good citizens.

Although Oliver had been brought up by philosophers, he was not theoretically acquainted with the beautiful axiom that self-preservation is the first law of nature. If he had been, perhaps he would have been prepared for this. Not being prepared, however, it alarmed him the more; so away he went like the wind, with the old gentleman and the two boys roaring and shouting behind him.

Stopped at last! A clever blow! He is down upon the pavement; and the crowd eagerly gather round him, each newcomer jostling and struggling with the others to catch a glimpse. "Stand aside!" "Give him a little air!" "Nonsense! he don't deserve it." "Where's the gentleman?" "Here he is, coming down the street." "Make room there for the gentleman!" "Is this the boy, sir?" "Yes."

Oliver lay, covered with mud and dust, and bleeding from the mouth, looking wildly round upon the heap of faces that surrounded him, when the old gentleman was officiously dragged and pushed into the circle by the foremost of the pursuers.

"Yes," said the gentleman, "I am afraid it is the boy."

"Afraid!" murmured the crowd. "That's a good 'un."

"Poor fellow!" said the gentleman. "He has hurt himself."

"*I* did that, sir," said a great, lubberly fellow, stepping forward; "and preciously I cut my knuckle agin' his mouth. *I* stopped him, sir."

The fellow touched his hat with a grin, expecting something for his pains; but the old gentleman, eyeing him with an expression of dislike, looked anxiously round, as if he contemplated running away himself, which it is very possible he might have attempted to do, and thus afforded another chase, had not a police officer (who is generally the last person to arrive in such cases) at that moment made his way through the crowd, and seized Oliver by the collar.

"Come, get up," said the man, roughly.

"It wasn't me, indeed, sir. Indeed, indeed, it was two other boys," said Oliver, clasping his hands passionately, and looking round.

"They are here somewhere."

"Oh, no, they ain't," said the officer. He meant this to be ironical, but it was true besides, for the Dodger and Charley Bates had filed off down the first convenient court they came to. "Come, get up!"

"Don't hurt him," said the old gentleman, compassionately.

"Oh, no, I won't hurt him," replied the officer, tearing his jacket half off his back in proof thereof. "Come, I know you; it won't do. Will you stand upon your legs, you young devil?"

Oliver, who could hardly stand, made a shift to raise himself on his feet, and was at once lugged along the streets by the jacket-collar at a rapid pace. The gentleman walked on with them by the officer's side; and as many of the crowd as could achieve the feat got a little ahead, and stared back at Oliver from time to time. The boys shouted in triumph; and on they went.

CHAPTER 10

Treats of Mr. Fang, the police magistrate; and furnishes a slight specimen of his mode of administering justice

THE offence had been committed within the district, and indeed in the immediate neighbourhood, of a very notorious metropolitan police officer. The crowd had only the satisfaction of accompanying Oliver through two or three streets, and down a place called Muttonhill, when he was led beneath a low archway, and up a dirty court, into this dispensary of summary justice, by the back way. It was a small paved yard into which they turned; and here they encountered a stout man with a bunch of whiskers on his face and a bunch of keys in his hand.

"What's the matter now?" said the man carelessly.

"A young fogle-hunter," replied the man who had Oliver in charge.

"Are you the party that's been robbed, sir?" inquired the man with the keys."

"Yes, I am," replied the old gentleman; "but I am not sure that this boy actually took the handkerchief. I–I would rather not press the case."

"Must go before the magistrate now, sir," replied the man. "His worship will be disengaged in half a minute. Now, young gallows."

This was an invitation for Oliver to enter through a door which he unlocked as he spoke, and which led into a stone cell. Here he was searched, and nothing being found upon him, locked up.

"There is something in that boy's face," said the old gentleman to himself as he walked slowly away, tapping his chin with the cover of the book in a thoughtful manner–"something that touches and interests me.

Can he be innocent? He looked like.–By-the-bye," exclaimed the old gentleman, halting very abruptly and staring up into the sky.–"Bless my soul!–where have I seen something like that look before?"

After musing for some minutes, the old gentleman walked, with the same meditative face, into a back anti-room opening from the yard; and there, retiring into a corner, called up before his mind's eye a vast amphitheatre of faces over which a dusky curtain had hung for many years. "No," said the old gentleman, shaking his head; "it must be imagination."

He was roused by a touch on the shoulder, and a request from the man with the keys to follow him into the office. He closed his book hastily, and was at once ushered into the imposing presence of the renowned Mr. Fang.

The office was a front parlour, with a panelled wall. Mr. Fang sat behind a bar, at the upper end; and on one side of the door was a sort of wooden pen, in which poor little Oliver was already deposited, trembling very much at the awfulness of the scene.

Mr. Fang was a lean, long-backed, stiff-necked, middle-sized man, with no great quantity of hair, and what he had growing on the back and sides of his head. His face was stern and much flushed.

The old gentleman bowed respectfully, and advancing to the magistrate's desk, said, suiting the action to the word, "That is my name and address, sir." He then withdrew a pace or two, and with another polite and gentlemanly inclination of the head waited to be questioned.

Now, it so happened that Mr. Fang was a that moment perusing a leading article in the newspaper of the morning, adverting to some recent decision of his, and commending him, for the three hundred and fiftieth time, to the special and particular notice of the Secretary of State for the Home Department. He was out of temper, and he looked up with an angry scowl.

"Who are you?" said Mr. Fang.

The old gentleman pointed with some surprise to his card.

"Officers!" said Mr. Fang, tossing the card contemptuously away with the newspaper, "who is this fellow?"

"My name, sir," said the old gentleman, speaking like a gentleman, "my name, sir, is Brownlow. Permit me to inquire the name of the magistrate who offers a gratuitous and unprovoked insult to a respectable person, under the protection of the bench." Saying this, Mr. Brownlow looked round the office as if in search of some person who would afford him the required information.

"Officer!" said Mr. Fang, throwing the paper on one side, "what's this fellow charged with?"

"He's not charged at all, your worship," replied the officer. "He appears against the boy, your worship."

His worship knew this perfectly well, but it was a good annoyance, and a safe one.

"Appears against the boy, does he?" said Fang, surveying Mr. Brownlow contemptuously from head to foot. "Swear him!"

"Before I am sworn, I must beg to say one word," said Mr. Brownlow, "and that is, that I really never, without actual experience, could have believed—"

"Hold your tongue, sir!" said Mr. Fang peremptorily.

"I will not, sir!" replied the old gentleman.

"Hold your tongue this instant, or I'll have you turned out of the office!" said Mr. Fang. "You're an insolent, impertinent fellow. How dare you bully a magistrate?"

"What!" exclaimed the old gentleman, reddening.

"Swear this person!" said Fang to the clerk. "I'll not hear another word. Swear him."

Mr. Brownlow's indignation was greatly roused, but, reflecting perhaps that he might only injure the boy by giving vent to it, he suppressed his feelings, and submitted to be sworn at once.

"Now," said Fang, "what's the charge against this boy? What have you got to say, sir?"

"I was standing at a book-stall—" Mr. Brownlow began.

"Hold your tongue, sir!" said Mr. Fang. "Policeman! Where's the policeman? Here, swear this policeman. Now, policeman, what is this?"

The policeman, with becoming humility, related how he had taken the charge; how he had searched Oliver, and found nothing on his person; and how that was all he knew about it.

"Are there any witnesses?" inquired Mr. Fang.

"None, your worship," replied the policeman.

Mr. Fang sat silent for some minutes, and then turning round to the prosecutor, said in a towering passion,—

"Do you mean to state what your complaint against this boy is, fellow, or do you not? You have been sworn. Now if you stand there refusing to give evidence, I'll punish you for disrespect to the bench; I will, by—"

By what, or by whom, nobody knows; for the clerk and jailer coughed very loud, just at the right moment, and the former dropped a heavy book upon the floor thus preventing the word from being heard—accidentally, of course.

With many interruptions, and repeated insults, Mr. Brownlow contrived to state his case; observing that, in the surprise of the moment, he had run after the boy because he saw him running away; and expressing his hope that, if the magistrate should believe him, although not actually the thief, to be connected with thieves, he would deal as leniently with him as justice would allow.

"He has been hurt already," said the old gentleman in conclusion. "And I fear," he added with great energy, looking towards the bar, "I really fear that he is very ill."

"Oh, yes; I dare say!" said Mr. Fang, with a sneer.–"Come, none of your tricks here, you young vagabond; they won't do. What's your name?"

Oliver tried to reply, but his tongue failed him. He was deadly pale, and the whole place seemed turning round and round.

"What's your name, you hardened scoundrel?" demanded Mr. Fang. "Officer, what's his name?"

This was addressed to a bluff old fellow, in a striped waistcoat, who was standing by the bar. He bent over Oliver, and repeated the inquiry; but finding him really incapable of understanding the question, and knowing that his not replying would only infuriate the magistrate the more, and add to the severity of his sentence, he hazarded a guess.

"He says his name's Tom White, your worship," said this kind-hearted thief-taker.

"Oh, he won't speak out, won't he?" said Fang. "Very well, very well. Where does he live?"

"Where he can, your worship," replied the officer, again pretending to receive Oliver's answer.

"Has he any parents?" inquired Mr. Fang.

"He says they died in his infancy, your worship," replied the officer, hazarding the usual reply.

At this point of the inquiry Oliver raised his head, and looking round with imploring eyes, murmured a feeble prayer for a draught of water.

"Stuff and nonsense!" said Mr. Fang; "don't try to make a fool of me."

"I think he really is ill, your worship," remonstrated the officer.

"I know better," said Mr. Fang.

"Take care of him, officer," said the old gentleman, raising his hands instinctively; "he'll fall down."

"Stand away, officer," cried Fang; "let him, if he likes."

Oliver availed himself of the kind permission, and fell heavily to the floor in a fainting fit. The men in the office looked at each other, but no one dared to stir.

"I knew he was shamming," said Fang, as if this were incontestable proof of the fact. "Let him lie there; he'll soon be tired of that."

"How do you propose to deal with the case, sir?" inquired the clerk in a low voice.

"Summarily," replied Mr. Fang. "He stands committed for three months –hard labour, of course. Clear the office."

The door was opened for this purpose, and a couple of men were preparing to carry the insensible boy to his cell, when an elderly man of decent but poor appearance, clad in an old suit of black, rushed hastily into the office and advanced towards the bench.

"Stop, stop! Don't take him away! For Heaven's sake, stop a moment!" cried the new-comer, breathless with haste.

Although the presiding Genii in such an office as this exercise a summary and arbitrary power over the liberties, the good name, the character, almost of the lives of Her Majesty's subjects, especially of the poorer class; and although, within such walls, enough fantastic tricks are daily played to make the angels blind with weeping; they are closed to the public, save through the medium of the daily press. Mr. Fang was consequently not a little indignant to see an unbidden guest enter in such irreverent disorder.

"What is this? Who is this? Turn this man out. Clear the office!" cried Mr. Fang.

"I will speak," cried the man; "I will not be turned out. I saw it all. I keep the book-stall. I demand to be sworn. I will not be put down. Mr. Fang, you must hear me. You must not refuse, sir."

The man was right. His manner was bold and determined; and the matter was growing rather too serious to be hushed up.

"Swear the fellow," growled Fang, with a very ill grace. "Now, man, what have you got to say?"

"This," said the man: "I saw three boys—two others and the prisoner here—loitering on the opposite side of the way, when this gentleman was reading. The robbery was committed by another boy. I saw it done; and I saw that this boy was perfectly amazed and stupefied by it." Having by this time recovered a little breath, the worthy book-stall keeper proceeded to relate, in a more coherent manner, the exact circumstances of the robbery.

"Why didn't you come here before?" said Fang, after a pause.

"I hadn't a soul to mind the shop," replied the man. "Everybody who could have helped me had joined in the pursuit. I could get nobody till five minutes ago; and I've run here all the way."

"The prosecutor was reading, was he?" inquired Fang, after another pause.

"Yes," replied the man. "The very book he has in his hand."

"Oh, that book, eh?" said Fang. "Is it paid for?"

"No, it is not," replied the man, with a smile.

"Dear me, I forgot all about it!" exclaimed the absent-minded old gentleman, innocently.

"A nice person to prefer a charge against a poor boy!" said Fang with a comical effort to look humane. "I consider, sir, that you have obtained possession of that book under very suspicious and disreputable circumstances; and you may think yourself very fortunate that the owner of the property declines to prosecute. Let this be a lesson to you, my man, or the law will overtake you yet. The boy is discharged. Clear the office."

"D—n me!" cried the old gentleman, bursting out with the rage he had kept down so long, "d—n me! I'll—"

"Clear the office!" said the magistrate. "Officers, do you hear! Clear the office!"

The mandate was obeyed, and the indignant Mr. Brownlow was conveyed out, with the book in one hand and the bamboo cane in the other, in a perfect frenzy of rage and defiance. He reached the yard, and his passion vanished for a moment. Little Oliver Twist lay on his back on the pavement, with his shirt unbuttoned, and his temples bathed with water; his face a deadly white, and a cold tremble convulsing his whole frame.

"Poor boy, poor boy!" said Mr. Brownlow, bending over him. "Call a coach, somebody, pray, directly."

A coach was obtained, and Oliver, having been carefully laid on one seat, the old gentleman got in and sat himself on the other.

"May I accompany you?" said the book-stall keeper, looking in.

"Bless me, yes, my dear friend," said Mr. Brownlow quickly. "I forgot you. Dear, dear! I have this unhappy book still! Jump in. Poor fellow! there's no time to lose."

The book-stall keeper got into the coach, and away they drove.

Chapter 11

In which Oliver is taken better care of than he ever was before.
And in which the narrative reverts to the merry old gentleman
and his youthful friends

The coach rattled away, down Mount Pleasant and up Exmouth Street, over nearly the same ground as that which Oliver had traversed when he first entered London in company with the Dodger; and, turning a different way when it reached the Angel at Islington, stopped at length before a neat house, in a quiet shady street near Pentonville. Here a bed was prepared without loss of time, in which Mr. Brownlow saw his young charge carefully and comfortable deposited; and here he was tended with a kindness and solicitude that knew no bounds.

But, for many days, Oliver remained insensible to all the goodness of his new friends. The sun rose and sank, and rose and sank again, and many times after that, and still the boy lay stretched on his uneasy bed, dwindling away beneath the dry and wasting heat of fever. The worm does not his work more surely on the dead body than does this slow creeping fire upon the living frame.

Weak, and thin, and pallid, he awoke at last from what seemed to have been a long and troubled dream. Feebly raising himself in the bed, with his head resting on his trembling arm, he looked anxiously round.

"What room is this? Where have I been brought to?" said Oliver. "This is not the place I went to sleep in."

He uttered these words in a feeble voice, being very faint and weak, but they were overheard at once; for the curtain at the bed's head was hastily drawn back, and a motherly old lady, very neatly and precisely dressed, rose as she withdrew, it, from an armchair close by, in which she had been sitting at needlework.

"Hush, my dear," said the old lady softly. "You must be very quiet, or you will be ill again; and you have been very bad—as bad as bad could be, pretty nigh. Lie down again; there's a dear!" With these words, the old lady very gently placed Oliver's head upon the pillow, and, smoothing back his hair from his forehead, looked so kindly and lovingly in his face, that he could not help placing his little withered hand in hers, and drawing it round his neck.

"Save us!" said the old lady, with tears in her eyes, "what a grateful little dear it is! Pretty creature! What would his mother feel if she had sat by him as I have, and could see him now?"

So Oliver kept very still; partly because he was anxious to obey the kind old lady in all things, and partly, to tell the truth, because he was completely exhausted with what he had already said.

Oliver dozed off again soon after this, and when he awoke it was nearly twelve o'clock. The old lady tenderly bade him good-night shortly afterwards, and left him in charge of a fat old woman, who had just come; bringing with her, in a little bundle, a small Prayer Book and a large night-cap. Putting the latter on her head and the former on the table, the old woman, after telling Oliver that she had come to sit up with him, drew her chair close to the fire and went off into a series of short naps, chequered at frequent intervals with sundry tumblings forward, and divers moans and chokings, which, however, had no worse effect than causing her to rub her nose very hard, and then fall asleep again.

And thus the night crept slowly on.

It had been bright day for hours when Oliver opened his eyes; and when he did so he felt cheerful and happy. The crisis of the disease was safely past. He belonged to the world again.

In three day's time he was able to sit in an easy-chair, well propped up with pillows; and, as he was still too weak to walk, Mrs. Bedwin had him carried downstairs into the little housekeeper's room which belonged to her, where, having sat him up by the fireside, the good old lady sat herself down too, and being in a state of considerable delight at seeing him so much better, forthwith began to cry most violently.

"Never mind me, my dear," said the old lady. "I'm only having a regular good cry. There; it's all over now, and I'm quite comfortable."

"You're very, very kind to me, ma'am," said Oliver.

"Well, never you mind that, my dear," said the old lady; "that's got nothing to do with your broth, and it's full time you had it. For the doctor says Mr. Brownlow may come in to see you this morning; and we must get up our best looks, because the better we look the more he'll be pleased." And with this, the old lady applied herself to warming up in a little saucepan a basinful of broth, strong enough to furnish an ample dinner, when reduced to the regulation strength, for three hundred and fifty paupers, at the very lowest computation.

"Are you fond of pictures, dear?" inquired the old lady, seeing that Oliver had fixed his eyes, most intently, on a portrait which hung against the wall, just opposite his chair.

"I don't quite know, ma'am," said Oliver, without taking his eyes from the canvas; "I have seen so few that I hardly know. What a beautiful mild face that lady's is!"

"Ah!" said the old lady, "painters always make ladies out prettier than they are, or they wouldn't get any custom, child. The man that invented the machine for taking likenesses might have known *that* would never succeed; it's a deal too honest. A deal," said the old lady, laughing very heartily at her own acuteness.

"Is—is that a likeness, ma'am?" said Oliver.

"Yes," said the old lady, looking up for a moment from the broth; "that's a portrait."

"Whose, ma'am?" asked Oliver eagerly.

"Why, really, my dear, I don't know," answered the old lady in a good-humoured manner. "It's not a likeness of anybody that you or I know, I expect, It seems to strike your fancy, dear."

"It is so very pretty," replied Oliver.

"Why, sure you're not afraid of it?" said the old lady, observing, in great surprise, the look of awe with which the child regarded the painting.

"Oh, no, no," returned Oliver quickly; "but the eyes look so sorrowful, and where I sit they seem fixed upon me. It makes my heart beat," added Oliver, in a low voice, "as if it was alive, and wanted to speak to me, but couldn't."

"Lord save us!" exclaimed the old lady, starting; "don't talk in that way, child. You're weak and nervous after your illness. Let me wheel your chair round to the other side, and then you won't see it. There!" said the old lady, suiting the action to the word; "you don't see it now, at all events."

Oliver *did* see it in his mind's eye as distinctly as if he had not altered his position; but he thought it better not to worry the kind old lady, so he smiled gently when she looked at him, and Mrs. Bedwin, satisfied that he felt more comfortable, salted and broke bits of toasted bread into the broth, with all the bustle befitting so solemn a preparation. Oliver got through it with extraordinary expedition, and had scarcely swallowed the last spoonful when there came a soft tap at the door. "Come in," said the old lady; and in walked Mr. Brownlow.

Now, the old gentleman came in as brisk as need be; but he had no sooner raised his spectacles on his forehead, and thrust his hands behind the skirts of his dressing-gown, to take a good long look at Oliver, than his countenance underwent a very great variety of odd contortions. Oliver looked very worn and shadowy from sickness, and made an ineffectual attempt to stand up, out of respect to his benefactor, which terminated in his sinking back into the chair again; and the fact is, if the truth must be told, that Mr. Brownlow's heart, being large enough for any six ordinary old gentlemen of humane disposition, forced a supply of tears into his eyes, by some hydraulic process which we are not sufficiently philosophical to be in a condition to explain.

"Poor boy, poor boy!" said Mr. Brownlow, clearing his throat. "How do you feel, my dear?"

"Very happy, sir," replied Oliver. "And very grateful indeed, sir, for your goodness to me."

"Good boy," said Mr. Brownlow, stoutly. "Have you given him any nourishment, Bedwin? Any slops, eh?"

"He has just had a basin of beautiful strong broth, sir," replied Mrs. Bedwin, drawing herself up slightly, and laying a strong emphasis on the last word, to intimate that between slops, and broth well compounded, there existed no affinity or connection whatsoever.

"Ugh!" said Mr. Brownlow, with a slight shudder; "a couple of glasses of port wine would have done him a great deal more good. Wouldn't they, Tom White, eh?"

"My name is Oliver, sir," replied the little invalid, with a look of great astonishment.

"Oliver!" said Mr. Brownlow–"Oliver what? Oliver White, eh?"

"No, sir; Twist–Oliver Twist."

"Queer name!" said the old gentleman. "What made you tell the magistrate your name was White?"

"I never told him so, sir," returned Oliver in amazement.

This sounded so like a falsehood that the old gentleman looked somewhat sternly in Oliver's face. It was impossible to doubt him; there was truth in every one of its thin and sharpened lineaments.

"Some mistake," said Mr. Brownlow. But, although his motive for looking steadily at Oliver no longer existed, the old idea of the resemblance between his features and some familiar face came upon him so strongly that he could not withdraw his gaze.

"I hope you are not angry with me, sir?" said Oliver, raising his eyes beseechingly.

"No, no," replied the old gentleman.–"Why! what's this? Bedwin, look here!"

As he spoke, he pointed hastily to the picture above Oliver's head, and then to the boy's face. There was its living copy. The eyes, the head, the mouth–every feature was the same. The expression was, for the instant, so precisely alike, that the minutest line seemed copied with a startling accuracy!

Oliver knew not the cause of this sudden exclamation, for, not being strong enough to bear the start it gave him, he fainted away. A weakness on his part which affords the narrative an opportunity of relieving the reader from suspense in behalf of the two young pupils of the Merry Old Gentleman, and of recording—

That when the Dodger and his accomplished friend Master Bates joined in the hue-and-cry which was raised at Oliver's heels in consequence of their executing an illegal conveyance of Mr. Brownlow's personal property, as has been already described, they were actuated by a very laudable and becoming regard for themselves.

It was not until the two boys had scoured, with great rapidity, through a most intricate maze of narrow streets and courts, that they ventured to halt, by one consent, beneath a low and dark archway. Having remained silent here just long enough to recover breath to speak, Master Bates uttered an exclamation of amusement and delight, and, bursting into an uncontrollable fit of laughter, flung himself upon a door-step, and rolled thereon in a transport of mirth.

"What's the matter?" inquired the Dodger.

"Ha! ha! ha!" roared Charley Bates.

"Hold your noise," remonstrated the Dodger, looking cautiously around. "Do you want to be grabbed, stupid?"

"I can't help it," said Charley—"I can't help it. To see him splitting away at that pace, and cutting round the corners, and knocking up against the posts, and starting on again as if he was made of iron as well as them, and me, with the wipe in my pocket, singing out arter him—oh, my eye!" The vivid imagination of Master Bates presented the scene before him in too strong colours. As he arrived at this apostrophe, he again rolled upon the door-step, and laughed louder than before.

"What'll Fagin say?" inquired the Dodger, taking advantage of the next interval of breathlessness on the part of his friend to propound the question.

"What?" repeated Charley Bates.

"Ah, what?" said the Dodger.

"Why, what should he say?" inquired Charley, stopping rather suddenly in his merriment; for the Dodger's manner was impressive. "What should he say?"

Mr. Dawkins whistled for a couple of minutes; then, taking off his hat, scratched his head, and nodded thrice.

"What do you mean?" said Charley.

"Toor rul lol loo, gammon and spinnage, the frog he wouldn't, and high cockolorum," said the Dodger, with a slight sneer on his intellectual countenance.

This was explanatory, but not satisfactory. Master Bates felt it so, and again said, "What do you mean?"

The Dodger made no reply; but putting his hat on again, and gathering the skirts of his long-tailed coat under his arm, thrust his tongue into his cheek, slapped the bridge of his nose some half-dozen times in a familiar but expressive manner, and turning on his heel, slunk down the court. Master Bates followed, with a thoughtful countenance.

The noise of footsteps on the creaking stairs, a few minutes after, roused the merry old gentleman as he sat over the fire with a saveloy and a small loaf in his left hand, a pocket-knife in his right, and a pewter pot on the trivet. There was a rascally smile on his white face as he turned round, and, looking sharply out from under his thick red eyebrows, bent his ear towards the door and listened intently.

"Why, how's this?" muttered the Jew, changing countenance; "only two of 'em? Where's the third? They can't have got into trouble. Hark!"

The footsteps approached nearer; they reached the landing. The door slowly opened, and the Dodger and Charley Bates entered, closing it behind them.

Chapter 12

Some new acquaintances are introduced to the intelligent reader; connected with whom various matters are related appertaining to this history

"What's become of the boy?" said the Jew, seizing the Dodger tightly by the collar, and threatening him with horrid imprecations. "Speak out, or I'll throttle you!"

"Why, the traps have got him, and that's all about it," said the Dodger, sullenly. "Come, let go o' me, will you!" And, swinging himself, at one jerk, clean out of the big coat, which he left in the Jew's hands, the Dodger snatched up the toasting-fork, and made a pass at the merry old gentleman's waistcoat, which, if it had taken effect, would have let a little more merriment out than could have been easily replaced in a month or two.

The Jew stepped back, in this emergency, with more agility than could have been anticipated in a man of his apparent decrepitude, and seizing up the pot, prepared to hurl it at his assailant's head. But Charley Bates, at this moment, calling his attention by a perfectly terrific howl, he suddenly altered its destination, and flung it full at that young gentleman.

"Why, what the blazes is in the wind now?" growled a deep voice. "Who pitched that 'ere at me? It's well it's the beer, and not the pot, as hit me, or I'd have settled somebody. I might have know'd as nobody but an infernal, rich, plundering, thundering old Jew could afford to throw away any drink but water—and not that, unless he done the River Company every quarter. Wot's it all about, Fagin? D— me, if my neckankercher ain't lined with beer! Come in, you sneaking warmint; wot are you stopping outside for, as if you was ashamed of your master? Come in!"

The man who growled out these words was a stoutly built fellow of about five-and-thirty, in a black velveteen coat, very soiled drab breeches, lace-up half-boots, and grey cotton stockings, which enclosed a very bulky pair of legs with large swelling calves–the kind of legs that, in such costume, always look in an unfinished and incomplete state without a set of fetters to garnish them. He had a brown hat on his head, and a dirty belcher handkerchief round his neck, with the long frayed ends of which he smeared the beer from his face as he spoke. He disclosed, when he had done so, a broad heavy countenance with a beard of three days' growth, and two scowling eyes, one of which displayed various parti-coloured symptoms of having been recently damaged by a blow.

"Come in–d'ye hear?" growled this engaging ruffian.

A white shaggy dog, with his face scratched and torn in twenty different places, skulked into the room.

"Why didn't you come in afore?" said the man. "You're getting too proud to own me afore company, are you? Lie down."

This command was accompanied with a kick which sent the animal to the other end of the room. He appeared well used to it, however; for he coiled himself up in a corner very quietly, without uttering a sound, and, winking his very ill-looking eyes about twenty times in a minute, appeared to occupy himself in taking a survey of the apartment.

"What are you up to?–ill-treating the boys, you covetous, avaricious, in-sa-ti-a-ble old fence?" said the man, seating himself deliberately. "I wonder they don't murder you! *I* would, if I was them. If I'd been your 'prentice, I'd have done it long ago; and–no, I couldn't have sold you afterwards, though, for you're fit for nothing but keeping as a curiosity of ugliness in a glass bottle, and I suppose they don't blow glass bottles large enough."

"Hush! hush! Mr. Sikes," said the Jew, trembling; "don't speak so loud."

"None of your mistering," replied the ruffian; "you always mean mischief when you come that. You know my name; out with it! I shan't disgrace it when the time comes."

"Well, well, then–Bill Sikes," said the Jew, with abject humility. "You seem out of humour, Bill."

"Perhaps I am," replied Sikes; "I should think *you* was rather out of sorts too, unless you mean as little harm when you throw pewter pots about as you do when you blab and—"

"Are you mad?" said the Jew, catching the man by the sleeve, and pointing towards the boys.

Mr. Sikes contented himself with tying an imaginary knot under his left ear, and jerking his head over on the right shoulder–a piece of dumb show which the Jew appeared to understand perfectly. He then, in cant terms, with which his whole conversation was plentifully besprinkled, but which would be quite unintelligible if they were recorded here, demanded a glass of liquor.

"And mind you don't poison it," said Mr. Sikes, laying his hat upon the table.

After swallowing two or three glasses of spirits, Mr. Sikes condescended to take some notice of the young gentlemen; which gracious act led to a conversation, in which the cause and manner of Oliver's capture were circumstantially detailed, with such alterations and improvements on the truth as to the Dodger appeared most advisable under the circumstances.

"I'm afraid," said the Jew, "that he may say something which will get us into trouble."

"That's very likely," returned Sikes, with a malicious grin. "You're blowed upon, Fagin."

"And I'm afraid, you see," added the Jew, speaking as if he had not noticed the interruption, and regarding the other closely as he did so— "I'm afraid that, if the game was up with us, it might be up with a good many more, and that it would come out rather worse for you than it would for me, my dear."

The man started, and turned fiercely round upon the Jew. But the old gentleman's shoulders were shrugged up to his ears, and his eyes were vacantly staring on the opposite wall.

"Somebody must find out wot's been done at the office," said Mr. Sikes in a much lower tone than he had taken since he came in.

The Jew nodded assent.

"If he hasn't peached, and is committed, there's no fear till he comes out again," said Mr. Sikes; "and then he must be taken care on. You must get hold of him somehow."

Again the Jew nodded.

How long they might have sat and looked at each other in a state of uncertainty not the most pleasant of its kind, it is difficult to say. It is not necessary to make any guesses on the subject, however; for the sudden entrance of the two young ladies whom Oliver had seen on a former occasion, caused the conversation to flow afresh.

"The very thing!" said the Jew. "Bet will go; won't you, my dear?"

"Where?" inquired the young lady.

"Only just up to the office, my dear," said the Jew coaxingly.

It is due to the young lady to say that she did not positively affirm that she would not, but that she merely expressed an emphatic and earnest desire to be "blessed" if she would; a polite and delicate evasion of the request, which shows the young lady to have been possessed of that natural good breeding which cannot bear to inflict upon a fellow-creature the pain of a direct and pointed refusal.

The Jew's countenance fell; and he turned from this young lady, who was gaily, not to say gorgeously, attired, in a red gown, green boots, and yellow curl-papers, to the other female.

"Nancy, my dear," said the Jew in a soothing manner, "what do *you* say?"

"That it won't do; so it's no use a-trying it on, Fagin," replied Nancy.

"What do you mean by that?" said Mr. Sikes, looking up in a surly manner.

"What I say, Bill," replied the lady collectedly.

"Why, you're just the very person for it," reasoned Mr. Sikes; "nobody about here knows anything of you."

"And as I don't want 'em to, neither," replied Nancy in the same composed manner, "it's rather more no than yes with me, Bill."

"She'll go, Fagin," said Sikes.

"No, she won't, Fagin, said Nancy.

"Yes, she will, Fagin," said Sikes.

And Mr. Sikes was right. By dint of alternate threats, promises, and bribes, the lady in question was ultimately prevailed upon to undertake the commission.

Accordingly, with a clean white apron tied over her gown, and her curl-papers tucked up under a straw bonnet–both articles of dress being provided from the Jew's inexhaustible stock–Miss Nancy prepared to issue forth on her errand.

"Stop a minute, my dear," said the Jew, producing a little covered basket. "Carry that in one hand; it looks more respectable, my dear."

"Give her a door-key to carry in her t'other one, Fagin," said Sikes; "it looks real and genivine like."

"Yes, yes, my dear, so it does," said the Jew, hanging a large street-door key on the forefinger of the young lady's right hand. "There; very good! very good indeed, my dear!" said the Jew, rubbing his hands.

"Oh, my brother! My poor, dear, sweet, innocent little brother!" exclaimed Nancy, bursting into tears, and wringing the little basket and the street-door key in an agony of distress. "What has become of him? Where have they taken him to? Oh, do have pity and tell me what's been done with the dear boy, gentlemen; do, gentlemen, if you please, gentlemen!"

Having uttered these words in a most lamentable and heartbroken tone, to the immeasurable delight of her hearers, Miss Nancy paused, winked to the company, nodded smilingly round, and disappeared.

Nancy made the best of her way to the police-office, whither, notwithstanding a little natural timidity consequent upon walking through the streets alone and unprotected, she arrived in perfect safety shortly afterwards.

Entering by the back way, she tapped softly with the key at one of the cell-doors, and listened. There was no sound within; so she coughed and listened again.

Still there was no reply; so she spoke.

"Nolly, dear?" murmured Nancy in a gentle voice: "Nolly?"

"Well!" cried a faint and feeble voice.

"Is there a little boy here?" inquired Nancy, with a preliminary sob.

"No," replied the voice; "God forbid!"

This was a vagrant of sixty-five, who was going to prison for *not* playing the flute–or in other words, for begging in the streets, and doing nothing for his livelihood. In the next cell was another man, who was going to the same prison for hawking tin saucepans without a licence; thereby doing something for his living, in defiance of the Stamp Office.

But, as neither of these criminals answered to the name of Oliver, or knew anything about him, Nancy made straight up to the bluff officer in the striped waistcoat, and with the most piteous wailings and lamentations, rendered more piteous by a prompt and efficient use of the street-door key and the little basket, demanded her own dear brother.

"I haven't got him, my dear," said the old man.

"Where is he?" screamed Nancy, in a distracted manner.

"Why, the gentleman's got him," replied the officer.

"What gentleman? Oh, gracious heavens! what gentleman?" exclaimed Nancy.

In reply to this incoherent questioning, the old man informed the deeply-affected sister that Oliver had been taken ill in the office, and discharged in consequence of a witness having proved the robbery to have been committed by another boy, not in custody; and that the prosecutor had carried him away in an insensible condition to his own residence, of and concerning which all the informant knew was, that it was somewhere at Pentonville, he having heard that word mentioned in the directions to the coachman.

In a dreadful state of doubt and uncertainty the agonized young woman staggered to the gate, and then, exchanging her faltering walk for a good, swift, steady run, returned by the most devious and complicated route she could think of to the domicile of the Jew.

Mr. Bill Sikes no sooner heard the account of the expedition delivered than he very hastily called up the white dog, and putting on his hat, expeditiously departed, without devoting any time to the formality of wishing the company good-morning.

"We must know where he is, my dears; he must be found," said the Jew, greatly excited. "Charley, do nothing but skulk about till you bring home some news of him. Nancy, my dear, I must have him found. I trust to you, my dear—to you and the Artful, for everything! Stay, stay," added the Jew, unlocking a drawer with a shaking hand; "there's money, my dears. I shall shut up this shop to-night. You'll know where to find me. Don't stop here a minute—not an instant, my dears!"

With these words he pushed them from the room; and carefully double-locking and barring the door behind them, drew from its place of concealment the box which he had unintentionally disclosed to Oliver. Then he hastily proceeded to dispose the watches and jewellery beneath his clothing.

A rap at the door startled him in this occupation. "Who's there?" he cried in a shrill tone.

"Me!" replied the voice of the Dodger through the keyhole.

"What now?" cried the Jew impatiently.

"Is he to be kidnapped to the other ken, Nancy says?" inquired the Dodger.

"Yes," replied the Jew, "wherever she lays hands on him. Find him, find him out, that's all! I shall know what to do next; never fear."

The boy murmured a reply of intelligence, and hurried downstairs after his companions.

"He has not peached so far," said the Jew as he pursued his occupation. "If he means to blab us among his new friends, we may stop his mouth yet."

CHAPTER 13

Comprising further particulars of Oliver's stay at
Mr. Brownlow's, with the remarkable prediction which one
Mr. Grimwig uttered concerning him when he went out on
an errand

OLIVER soon recovered from the fainting fit into which Mr. Brownlow's abrupt exclamation had thrown him; and the subject of the picture was carefully avoided, both by the old gentleman and Mrs. Bedwin, in the conversation that ensued, which indeed bore no reference to Oliver's history or prospects, but was confined to such topics as might amuse without exciting him. He was still too weak to get up to breakfast; but, when he came down into the housekeeper's room next day, his first act was to cast an eager glance at the wall, in the hope of again looking on the face of the beautiful lady. His expectations were disappointed, however, for the picture had been removed.

"Ah!" said the housekeeper, watching the direction of Oliver's eyes. "It is gone. you see."

"I see it is, ma'am," replied Oliver with a sigh. "Why have they taken it away?"

"It has been taken down, child, because Mr. Brownlow said that, as it seemed to worry you, perhaps it might prevent your getting well, you know," rejoined the old lady.

"Oh, no, indeed. It didn't worry me, ma'am," said Oliver. "I liked to see it. I quite loved it."

"Well, well!" said the old lady, good-humouredly; "you get well as fast as ever you can, dear, and it shall be hung up again. There! I promise you that. Now, let us talk about something else."

They were happy days those of Oliver's recovery. Everything was so quiet, and neat, and orderly, everybody so kind and gentle, that after the noise and turbulence in the midst of which he had always lived, it seemed like heaven itself. He was no sooner strong enough to put his clothes on properly, than Mr. Brownlow caused a complete new suit, and a new cap, and a new pair of shoes, to be provided for him.

One evening about a week later after the affair of the picture, as he was sitting talking to Mrs. Bedwin, there came a message down from Mr. Brownlow, that if Oliver Twist felt pretty well, he should like to see him in his study, and talk to him a little while.

"Bless us, and save us! Wash your hands, and let me part your hair nicely for you, child," said Mrs. Bedwin. "Dear heart alive! If we had known he would have asked for you, we would have put you a clean collar on, and made you as smart as sixpence!"

Thus encouraged, Oliver tapped at the study door. On Mr. Brownlow calling to him to come in, he found himself in a little back room quite full of books, with a window looking into some pleasant little gardens. There was a table drawn up before the window, at which Mr. Brownlow was seated reading. When he saw Oliver he pushed the book away from him, and told him to come near the table and sit down. Oliver complied, marvelling where the people could be found to read such a great number of books as seemed to be written to make the world wiser. Which is still a marvel to more experienced people than Oliver Twist, every day of their lives.

"There are a good many books, are there not, my boy?" said Mr. Brownlow, observing the curiosity with which Oliver surveyed the shelves that reached from the floor to the ceiling.

"A great number, sir," replied Oliver. "I never saw so many."

"You shall read them, if you behave well," said the old gentleman kindly; "and you will like that better than looking at the outsides–that is, in some cases, because there *are* books of which the backs and covers are by far the best parts."

"I suppose they are those heavy ones, sir," said Oliver, pointing to some large quartos, with a good deal of gilding about the binding.

"Not always those," said the old gentleman, patting Oliver on the head, and smiling as he did so; "there are other equally heavy ones, though of a much smaller size. How should you like to grow up a clever man, and write books, eh?"

"I think I would rather read them, sir," replied Oliver.

"What! wouldn't you like to be a bookwriter?" said the old gentleman.

Oliver considered a little while, and at last said he should think it would be a much better thing to be a bookseller; upon which the old gentleman laughed heartily, and declared he had said a very good thing. Which Oliver felt glad to have done, though he by no means knew what it was.

"Well, well," said the old gentleman, composing his features, "don't be afraid! We won't make an author of you while there's an honest trade to be learnt, or brickmaking to turn to."

"Thank you, sir," said Oliver. At the earnest manner of his reply, the old gentleman laughed again, and said something about a curious instinct, which Oliver, not understanding, paid no very great attention to.

"Now," said Mr. Brownlow, speaking if possible in a kinder, but at the same time in a much more serious manner than Oliver had ever known him assume yet, "I want you to pay great attention, my boy, to what I am going to say. I shall talk to you without any reserve, because I am sure you are as well able to understand me as many older persons would be."

"Oh, don't tell me you are going to send me away, sir, pray!" exclaimed Oliver, alarmed at the serious tone of the old gentleman's commencement. "Don't turn me out of doors to wander in the streets again. Let me stay here and be a servant. Don't send me back to the wretched place I came from. Have mercy upon a poor boy, sir!"

"My dear child," said the old gentleman, moved by the warmth of Oliver's sudden appeal, "you need not be afraid of my deserting you, unless you give me cause."

"I never, never will, sir," interposed Oliver.

"I hope not," rejoined the old gentleman. "I do not think you ever will. I have been deceived, before, in the objects whom I have endeavoured to benefit; but I feel strongly disposed to trust you, nevertheless; and I am more interested in your behalf than I can well account for, even to myself. The persons on whom I have bestowed my dearest love lie deep in their graves; but, although the happiness and delight of my life lie buried there too, I have not made a coffin of my heart, and sealed it up, for ever, on my best affections. Deep affliction has but strengthened and refined them."

As the old gentleman said this in a low voice, more to himself than to his companion, and as he remained silent for a short time afterwards, Oliver sat quite still.

"Well, well!" said the old gentleman at length, in a more cheerful tone, "I only say this because you have a young heart; and knowing that I have suffered great pain and sorrow, you will be more careful, perhaps, not to wound me again. You say you are an orphan, without a friend in the world; all the inquiries I have been able to make confirm the statement. Let me hear your story—where you came from, who brought you up, and how you got into the company in which I found you. Speak the truth, and you shall not be friendless while I live."

Oliver's sobs checked his utterance for some minutes. When he was on the point of beginning to relate how he had been brought up at the farm, and carried to the workhouse by Mr. Bumble, a peculiarly impatient little double-knock was heard at the street door, and the servant, running upstairs, announced Mr. Grimwig.

"Is he coming up?" inquired Mr. Brownlow.

"Yes, sir," replied the servant. "He asked if there were any muffins in the house; and when I told him yes, he said he had come to tea."

Mr. Brownlow smiled; and, turning to Oliver, said that Mr. Grimwig was an old friend of his, and he must not mind his being a little rough in his manners, for he was a worthy creature at bottom, as he had reason to know.

"Shall I go downstairs, sir?" inquired Oliver.

"No," replied Mr. Brownlow, "I would rather you remained here."

At this moment there walked into the room, supporting himself by a thick stick, a stout old gentleman, rather lame in one leg, who was dressed in a blue coat, striped waistcoat, nankeen breeches and gaiters, and a broad-brimmed white hat, with the sides turned up with green. A very small-plaited shirt-frill stuck out from his waistcoat; and a very long steel watch-chain, with nothing but a key at the end, dangled loosely below it. The ends of his white neckerchief were twisted into a ball about the size of an orange. The variety of shapes into which his countenance was twisted defy description. He had a manner of screwing his head on one side when he spoke, and of looking out of the corners of his eyes at the same time, which irresistibly reminded the beholder of a parrot. In this attitude he fixed himself the moment he made his appearance, and, holding out a small piece of orange peel at arm's length, exclaimed, in a growling, discontented voice,—

"Look here! do you see this? Isn't it a most wonderful and extraordinary thing that I can't call at a man's house but I find a piece of this poor surgeon's-friend on the staircase? I've been lamed with orange peel once, and I know orange peel will be my death at last. It will, sir; orange peel will be my death, or I'll be content to eat my own head, sir! Hallo! what's that?" looking at Oliver, and retreating a pace or two.

"This is young Oliver Twist, whom we were speaking about," said Mr. Brownlow.

Oliver bowed.

"You don't mean to say that's the boy who had the fever, I hope?" said Mr. Grimwig, recoiling a little more. "Wait a minute! Don't speak! Stop!" continued Mr. Grimwig, abruptly losing all dread of the fever in his triumph at the discovery; "that's the boy who had the orange! If that's not the boy, sir, who had the orange, and threw this bit of peel upon the staircase, I'll eat my head and his too."

"No, no, he has not had one," said Mr. Brownlow, laughing. "Come! put down your hat, and speak to my young friend."

"That's the boy, is it?" said Mr. Grimwig, at length.

"That is the boy," replied Mr. Brownlow.

"How are you, boy?" said Mr. Grimwig.

"A great deal better, thank you, sir," replied Oliver.

Mr. Brownlow, seeming to apprehend that his singular friend was about to say something disagreeable, asked Oliver to step downstairs and tell Mrs. Bedwin they were ready for tea; which, as he did not half like the visitor's manner, he was very happy to do.

As Mr. Grimwig, at tea, was graciously pleased to express his entire approval of the muffins, matters went on very smoothly; and Oliver, who made one of the party, began to feel more at his ease than he had yet done in the fierce old gentleman's presence.

"And when are you going to hear a full, true, and particular account of the life and adventures of Oliver Twist?" asked Grimwig of Mr. Brownlow, at the conclusion of the meal, looking sideways at Oliver, as he resumed the subject.

"To-morrow morning," replied Mr. Brownlow. "I would rather he was alone with me at the time. Come up to me to-morrow morning at ten o'clock, my dear."

"Yes, sir," replied Oliver. He answered with some hesitation, because he was confused by Mr. Grimwig's looking so hard at him.

"I'll tell you what," whispered that gentleman to Mr. Brownlow; "he won't come up to you to-morrow morning. I saw him hesitate. He is deceiving you, my good friend."

"I'll swear he is not," replied Mr. Brownlow warmly.

"If he is not," said Mr. Grimwig, "I'll—" and down went the stick.

"I'll answer for that boy's truth with my life!" said Mr. Brownlow, knocking the table.

"And I for his falsehood with my head!" rejoined Mr. Grimwig, knocking the table also.

"We shall see," said Mr. Brownlow, checking his rising anger.

"We will," replied Mr. Grimwig, with a provoking smile; "we will."

As fate would have it, Mrs. Bedwin chanced to bring in at this moment a small parcel of books which Mr. Brownlow had that morning purchased of the identical bookstall keeper who has already figured in this history. Having laid them on the table, she prepared to leave the room.

"Stop the boy, Mrs. Bedwin!" said Mr. Brownlow; "there is something to go back."

"He has gone, sir," replied Mrs. Bedwin.

"Call after him," said Mr. Brownlow; "it's particular. He is a poor man, and they are not paid for. There are some books to be taken back, too."

The street door was opened. Oliver ran one way, and the girl ran another, and Mrs. Bedwin stood on the step and screamed for the boy; but there was no boy in sight. Oliver and the girl returned, in a breathless state, to report that there were no tidings of him.

"Dear me, I am very sorry for that," exclaimed Mr. Brownlow; "I particularly wished those books to be returned to-night."

"Send Oliver with them," said Mr. Grimwig, with an ironical smile; "he will be sure to deliver them safely, you know."

"Yes, do let me take them, if you please, sir," said Oliver. "I'll run all the way, sir."

The old gentleman was just going to say that Oliver should not go out on any account, when a most malicious cough from Mr. Grimwig determined him that he should; and that by his prompt discharge of the commission, he should prove to him the injustice of his suspicions, on this head at least, at once.

"You *shall* go, my dear," said the old gentleman. "The books are on a chair by my table. Fetch them down."

Oliver, delighted to be of use, brought down the books under his arm in a great bustle, and waited, cap in hand, to hear what message he was to take.

"You are to say," said Mr. Brownlow, glancing steadily at Grimwig—"you are to say that you have brought those books back, and that you have come to pay the four pound ten I owe him. This is a five-pound note, so you will have to bring me back ten shillings change."

"I won't be ten minutes, sir," replied Oliver eagerly. Having buttoned up the bank-note in his jacket pocket, and placed the books carefully under his arm, he made a respectful bow, and left the room. Mrs. Bedwin followed him to the street-door, giving him many directions about the nearest way, and the name of the bookseller, and the name of the street, all of which Oliver said he clearly understood; and having superadded many injunctions to be sure and not take cold, the old lady at length permitted him to depart.

"Bless his sweet face!" said the old lady, looking after him. "I can't bear, somehow, to let him go out of my sight."

At this moment Oliver looked gaily round, and nodded before he turned the corner. The old lady smilingly returned his salutation, and, closing the door, went back to her own room.

"Let me see: he'll be back in twenty minutes at the longest," said Mr. Brownlow, pulling out his watch, and placing it on the table. "It will be dark by that time."

"Oh! you really expect him to come back, do you?" inquired Mr. Grimwig.

"Don t you?" asked Mr. Brownlow, smiling.

The spirit of contradiction was strong in Mr. Grimwig's breast at the moment, and it was rendered stronger by his friend's confident smile.

"No," he said, smiting the table with his fist, "I do not. The boy has a new suit of clothes on his back, a set of valuable books under his arm, and a five-pound note in his pocket. He'll join his old friends the thieves, and laugh at you. If ever that boy returns to this house, sir, I'll eat my head."

With these words he drew his chair closer to the table; and there the two friends sat, in silent expectation, with the watch between them.

It is worthy of remark, as illustrating the importance we attach to our own judgment, and the pride with which we put forth our most rash and hasty conclusions, that, although Mr. Grimwig was not by any means a bad-hearted man, and though he would have been unfeignedly sorry to see his respected friend duped and deceived, he really did, most earnestly and strongly, hope at that moment that Oliver Twist might not come back.

It grew so dark that the figures on the dial-plate were scarcely discernible; but there the two old gentlemen continued to sit, in silence, with the watch between them.

Chapter 14

Showing how very fond of Oliver Twist the merry old Jew and Miss Nancy were ·

In the obscure parlour of a low public-house, situated in the filthiest part of Little Saffron Hill–a dark and gloomy den, where a flaring gas-light burnt all day in the winter-time, and where no ray of sun ever shone in the summer–there sat brooding over a little pewter measure and a small glass, strongly impregnated with the smell of liquor, a man in a velveteen coat, drab shorts, half-boots and stockings, whom, even by that dim light, no experienced agent of police would have hesitated for one instant to recognize as Mr. William Sikes. At his feet sat a white-coated, red-eyed dog, who occupied himself, alternately, in winking at his master with both eyes at the same time, and in licking a large fresh cut on one side of his mouth which appeared to be the result of some recent conflict.

"Keep quiet, you warmint! keep quiet!" said Mr. Sikes, suddenly breaking silence. Whether his meditations were so intense as to be disturbed by the dog's winking, or whether his feelings were so wrought upon by his reflections that they required all the relief derivable from kicking an unoffending animal to allay them, is matter for argument and consideration. Whatever was the cause, the effect was a kick and a curse bestowed upon the dog simultaneously.

Dogs are not generally apt to revenge injuries inflicted upon them by their masters; but Mr. Sikes's dog, having faults of temper in common with his owner, and labouring, perhaps, at this moment, under a powerful sense of injury, made no more ado but at once fixed his teeth in one of the half-boots. Having given it a hearty shake, he retired, growling, under a form; thereby just escaping the pewter measure which Mr. Sikes levelled at his head.

"You would, would you?" said Sikes, seizing the poker in one hand, and deliberately opening with the other a large clasp-knife, which he drew from his pocket. "Come here, you born devil! Come here. D'ye hear?"

The dog no doubt heard, because Mr. Sikes spoke in the very harshest key of a very harsh voice; but appearing to entertain some unaccountable objection to having his throat cut, he remained where he was, and growled more fiercely than before, at the same time grasping the end of the poker between his teeth, and biting at it like a wild beast.

This resistance only infuriated Mr. Sikes the more, who, dropping on his knees, began to assail the animal most furiously. The dog jumped from

right to left, and from left to right, snapping, growling, and barking; the
man thrust and swore, and struck and blasphemed; and the struggle was
reaching a most critical point for one or other, when, the door suddenly
opening, the dog darted out, leaving Bill Sikes with the poker and the
clasp-knife in his hands.

There must always be two parties to a quarrel, says the old adage.
Mr. Sikes being disappointed of the dog's participation, at once transferred
his share in the quarrel to the new-comer.

"What the devil do you come in between me and my dog for?" said
Sikes, with a fierce gesture.

"I didn't know, my dear, I didn't know," replied Fagin, humbly--for
the Jew was the new-comer.

"Didn't know, you white-livered thief!" growled Sikes. "Couldn't you
hear the noise?"

"Not a sound of it, as I'm a living man, Bill," replied the Jew.

"Oh, no! You hear nothing, you don't," retorted Sikes with a fierce
sneer. "Sneaking in and out, so as nobody hears how you come or go! I
wish you had been the dog, Fagin, half a minute ago."

"Why?" inquired the Jew with a forced smile.

" 'Cause the Government, as cares for the lives of such men as you, as
haven't half the pluck of curs, lets a man kill a dog how he likes," replied
Sikes, shutting up the knife with a very expressive look; "that's why."

The Jew rubbed his hands, and, sitting down at the table, affected to
laugh at the pleasantry of his friend. He was obviously very ill at ease,
however.

"Grin away," said Sikes, replacing the poker, and surveying him with
savage contempt--"grin away. You'll never have the laugh at me, though,
unless it's behind a night-cap. I've got the upper hand over you, Fagin;
and d-- me, I'll keep it. There! if I go, you go; so take care of me."

"Well, well, my dear," said the Jew, "I know all that; we--we--have a
mutual interest, Bill--a mutual interest."

"Humph," said Sikes, as if he thought the interest lay rather more on the
Jew's side than on his. "Well, what have you got to say to me?"

"It's all passed safe through the melting-pot," replied Fagin; "and this
is your share. It's rather more than it ought to be, my dear; but as I know
you'll do me a good turn another time, and--"

"Stow that gammon," interposed the robber, impatiently. "Where is it?
Hand over!"

"Yes, yes, Bill; give me time, give me time," replied the Jew, soothingly.
"Here it is! All safe!" As he spoke he drew forth an old cotton handkerchief
from his breast, and, untying a large knot in one corner, produced a small
brown-paper packet. Sikes, snatching it from him, hastily opened it, and
proceeded to count the sovereigns it contained.

"Is this all?" inquired Sikes.

"All," replied the Jew.

"You haven't opened the parcel and swallowed one or two as you come along, have you?" inquired Sikes suspiciously. "Don't put on an injured look at the question; you've done it many a time. Jerk the tinkler."

These words, in plain English, conveyed an injunction to ring the bell. It was answered by another Jew–younger than Fagin, but nearly as vile and repulsive in appearance.

Bill Sikes merely pointed to the empty measure. The Jew, perfectly understanding the hint, retired to fill it–previously exchanging a remarkable look with Fagin, who raised his eyes for an instant as if in expectation of it, and shook his head in reply so slightly that the action would have been almost imperceptible to an observant third person. It was lost upon Sikes, who was stooping at the moment to tie the boot-lace which the dog had torn. Possibly, if he had observed the brief interchange of signals, he might have thought that it boded no good to him.

"Is anybody here, Barney?" inquired Fagin, speaking, now that Sikes was looking on, without raising his eyes from the ground.

"Dot a shoul," replied Barney, whose words, whether they came from the heart or not, made their way through the nose.

"Nobody?" inquired Fagin, in a tone of surprise, which perhaps might mean that Barney was at liberty to tell the truth.

"Dobody but Biss Dadsy," replied Barney.

"Nancy!" exclaimed Sikes. "Where? Strike me blind, if I don't honour that 'ere girl for her native talents."

"She's bid havid a plate of boiled beef id the bar," replied Barney.

"Send her here," said Sikes, pouring out a glass of liquor. "Send her here."

Barney looked timidly at Fagin, as if for permission. The Jew remaining silent, and not lifting his eyes from the ground, he retired, and presently returned, ushering in Nancy, who was decorated with bonnet, apron, basket, and street-door key complete.

"You are on the scent, are you, Nancy?" inquired Sikes, proffering the glass.

"Yes, I am, Bill," replied the young lady, disposing of its contents; "and tired enough of it I am, too. The young brat's been ill, and confined to the crib; and—"

"Ah, Nancy, dear!" said Fagin, looking up.

Now, whether a peculiar contraction of the Jew's red eyebrows, and a half-closing of his deeply-set eyes, warned Miss Nancy that she was disposed to be too communicative, is not a matter of much importance. The fact is all we need care for here; and the fact is, that she suddenly checked herself, and, with several gracious smiles upon Mr. Sikes, turned the conversation to other matters. In about ten minutes' time Mr. Fagin was seized with a fit of coughing; upon which Nancy pulled her shawl over her shoulders and declared it was time to go. Mr. Sikes, finding that he was walking a short part of her way himself, expressed his intention of accompanying her; and they went away together, followed, at a little distance, by the dog, who slunk out of a backyard as soon as his master was out of sight.

Meanwhile, Oliver Twist, little dreaming that he was within so very short a distance of the merry old gentleman, was on his way to the book-stall. When he got into Clerkenwell, he accidentally turned down a by-street which was not exactly in his way; but not discovering his mistake until he had got half-way down it, and knowing it must lead in the right direction, he did not think it worth while to turn back, and so marched on, as quickly as he could, with the books under his arm.

He was walking along, thinking how happy and contented he ought to feel, and how much he would give for only one look at poor little Dick—who, starved and beaten, might be weeping bitterly at that very moment—when he was startled by a young woman screaming out very loud, "Oh, my dear brother!" and he had hardly looked up to see what the matter was, when he was stopped by having a pair of arms thrown tight round his neck.

"Don't," cried Oliver, struggling. "Let go of me. Who is it? What are you stopping me for?"

The only reply to this was a great number of loud lamentations from the young woman who had embraced him, and who had a little basket and a street-door key in her hand.

"Oh my gracious!" said the young woman, "I've found him! Oh Oliver! Oliver! Oh, you naughty boy, to make me suffer such distress on your account! Come home, dear—come. Oh, I've found him! Thank gracious goodness heavens, I've found him!" With these incoherent exclamations the young woman burst into another fit of crying, and got so dreadfully hysterical that a couple of women who came up at the moment asked a butcher's boy with a shiny head of hair, anointed with suet, who was also looking on, whether he didn't think he had better run for the doctor. To which the butcher's boy who appeared of a lounging, not to say indolent disposition, replied that he thought not.

"Oh, no, no; never mind," said the young woman, grasping Oliver's hand—"I'm better now. Come home directly, you cruel boy! Come!"

"Why, it's Nancy!" exclaimed Oliver, who now saw her face for the first time, and started back in irrepressible astonishment.

"You see he knows me!" cried Nancy, appealing to the bystanders. "He can't help himself. Make him come home, there's good people, or he'll kill his dear mother and father, and break my heart!"

"What the devil's this?" said a man, bursting out of a beer-shop, with a white dog at his heels; "young Oliver! Come home to your poor mother, you young dog. Come home directly."

"I don't belong to them. I don't know them. Help! help!" cried Oliver, struggling in the man's powerful grasp.

"Help!" repeated the man. "Yes; I'll help you, you young rasca! What

books are these? You've been a-stealing 'em, have you? Give 'em here."
With these words the man tore the volumes from his grasp, and struck
him on the head.

"That's right!" cried a looker-on, from a garret window. "That's the
only way of bringing him to his senses!"

"To be sure!" cried a sleepy-faced carpenter, casting an approving look
at the garret window.

"It'll do him good!" said the two women.

"And he shall have it, too!" rejoined the man, administering another
blow, and seizing Oliver by the collar. "Come on, you young villain! Here,
Bull's-eye! mind him, boy! Mind him!"

Weak with recent illness, stupefied by the blows and the suddenness of
the attack, terrified by the fierce growling of the dog and the brutality of
the man, and overpowered by the conviction of the bystanders that he
really was the hardened little wretch he was described to be—what could
one poor child do? Darkness had set in; it was a low neighbourhood; no
help was near; resistance was useless. In another moment he was dragged
into a labyrinth of dark narrow courts, and forced along them at a pace
which rendered the few cries he dared to give utterance to wholly unintelligible.

The gas-lamps were lighted; Mrs. Bedwin was waiting anxiously at the
open door; the servant had run up the street twenty times, to see if there
were any traces of Oliver; and still the two old gentlemen sat perseveringly
in the dark parlour, with the watch between them.

CHAPTER 15

*Relates what became of Oliver Twist, after he had been
claimed by Nancy*

THE narrow streets and courts at length terminated in a large open space,
scattered about which were pens for beasts, and other indications of a
cattle-market. Sikes slackened his pace when they reached this spot, the
girl being quite unable to support any longer the rapid rate at which they
had hitherto walked. Turning to Oliver, he roughly commanded him to
take hold of Nancy's hand.

"Do you hear?" growled Sikes, as Oliver hesitated and looked round.

They were in a dark corner, quite out of the track of passengers. Oliver
saw, but too plainly, that resistance would be of no avail. He held out his
hand, which Nancy clasped tight in hers.

"Give me the other," said Sikes, seizing Oliver's unoccupied hand.
"Here, Bull's-eye!"

The dog looked up and growled.

"See here, boy!" said Sikes, putting his other hand to Oliver's throat; "if he speaks ever so soft a word, hold him! D'ye mind?"

The dog growled again, and licking his lips, eyed Oliver as if he were anxious to attach himself to his windpipe without delay.

"He's as willing as a Christian, strike me blind if he isn't!" said Sikes, regarding the animal with a kind of grim and ferocious approval. "Now you know what you've got to expect, master, so call away as quick as you like; the dog will soon stop that game. Get on, young 'un!"

Bull's-eye wagged his tail in acknowledgment of this unusually endearing form of speech, and giving vent to another admonitory growl for the benefit of Oliver, led the way onward.

It was Smithfield that they were crossing, although it might have been Grosvenor Square for anything Oliver knew to the contrary. The night was dark and foggy. The lights in the shops could scarcely struggle through the heavy mist, which thickened every moment and shrouded the streets and houses in gloom, rendering the strange place still stranger in Oliver's eyes, and making his uncertainty the more dismal and depressing.

They had hurried on a few paces, when a deep church-bell struck the hour. With its first stroke, his two conductors stopped, and turned their heads in the direction whence the sound proceeded.

"Eight o'clock, Bill," said Nancy, when the bell ceased.

"What's the good of telling me that? I can hear it, can't I?" replied Sikes.

"I wonder whether *they* can hear it," said Nancy.

"Of course they can," replied Sikes. "It was Bartlemy time when I was shopped; and there warn't a penny trumpet in the fair as I couldn't hear the squeaking on. Arter I was locked up for the night, the row and din outside made the thundering old jail so silent, that I could almost have beat my head out against the iron plates of the door."

"Poor fellows!" said Nancy, who still had her face turned towards the quarter in which the bell had sounded. "Oh, Bill, such fine young chaps as them!"

"Yes; that's all you women think of," answered Sikes. "Fine young chaps! Well, they're as good as dead, so it don't much matter."

With this consolation, Mr. Sikes appeared to repress a rising tendency to jealousy; and clasping Oliver's wrist more firmly, told him to step out again.

"Wait a minute!" said the girl. "I wouldn't hurry by, if it was you that was coming out to be hung the next time eight o'clock struck, Bill. I'd walk round and round the place till I dropped, if the snow was on the ground, and I hadn't a shawl to cover me."

"And what good would that do?" inquired the unsentimental Mr. Sikes. "Unless you could pitch over a file and twenty yards of good stout rope, you might as well be walking fifty mile off, or not walking at all, for all the good it would do me. Come on, will you, and don't stand preaching there."

The girl burst into a laugh, drew her shawl more closely round her, and they walked away. But Oliver felt her hand tremble, and looking up in her face as they passed a gas-lamp, saw that it had turned a deadly white.

They walked on, by little-frequented and dirty ways, for a full half-hour—meeting very few people, and those appearing, from their looks, to hold much the same position in society as Mr. Sikes himself. At length they turned into a very filthy narrow street nearly full of old-clothes shops. The dog running forward, as if conscious that there was no further occasion for his keeping on guard, stopped before the door of a shop that was closed and apparently untenanted. The house was in a ruinous condition; and on the door was nailed a board intimating that it was to let, which looked as if it had hung there for many years.

"All right," cried Sikes, glancing cautiously about.

Nancy stopped below the shutters, and Oliver heard the sound of a bell. They crossed to the opposite side of the street, and stood for a few moments under a lamp. A noise, as if a sash window were gently raised, was heard, and soon afterwards the door softly opened. Mr. Sikes then seized the terrified boy by the collar with very little ceremony, and all three were quickly inside the house.

The passage was perfectly dark. They waited while the person who had let them in chained and barred the door.

"Anybody here?" inquired Sikes.

"No," replied a voice, which Oliver thought he had heard before.

"Is the old 'un here?" asked the robber.

"Yes," replied the voice; "and precious down in the mouth he has been. Won't he be glad to see you? Oh, no!"

The style of this reply, as well as the voice which delivered it, seemed familiar to Oliver's ears; but it was impossible to distinguish even the form of the speaker in the darkness.

"Let's have a glim," said Sikes, "or we shall go breaking our necks, or treading on the dog. Look after your legs if you do! That's all."

"Stand still a moment, and I'll get you one," replied the voice. The receding footsteps of the speaker were heard; and in another minute the form of Mr. John Dawkins, otherwise the Artful Dodger, appeared. He bore in his right hand a tallow candle stuck in the end of a cleft stick.

The young gentleman did not stop to bestow any other mark of recognition upon Oliver than a humorous grin, but, turning away, beckoned the visitors to follow him down a flight of stairs. They crossed an empty kitchen; and, opening the door of a low earthy-smelling room, which seemed to have been built in a small backyard, were received with a shout of laughter.

"Oh, my wig, my wig!" cried Master Charles Bates, from whose lungs the laughter had proceeded; "here he is! oh, cry, here he is! Oh, Fagin,

look at him; Fagin, do look at him! I can't bear it; it is such a jolly game,
I can't bear it. Hold me, somebody, while I laugh it out."

With this irrepressible ebullition of mirth, Master Bates laid himself
flat on the floor, and kicked convulsively for five minutes in an ecstasy
of facetious joy. Then jumping to his feet, he snatched the cleft stick from
the Dodger, and, advancing to Oliver, viewed him round and round; while
the Jew, taking off his nightcap, made a great number of low bows to the
bewildered boy. The Artful, meantime, who was of a rather saturnine
disposition, and seldom gave way to merriment when it interfered with
business, rifled Oliver's pockets with steady assiduity.

"Look at his togs, Fagin!" said Charley, putting the light so close to his
new jacket as nearly to set him on fire. "Look at his togs—superfine cloth,
and the heavy-swell cut! Oh, my eye, what a game! And his books, too;
nothing but a gentleman, Fagin!"

"Delighted to see you looking so well, my dear," said the Jew, bowing
with mock humility. "The Artful shall give you another suit, my dear, for
fear you should spoil that Sunday one. Why didn't you write, my dear,
and say you were coming? We'd have got something warm for supper."

At this Master Bates roared again—so loud that Fagin himself relaxed,
and even the Dodger smiled; but as the Artful drew forth the five-pound
note at that instant, it is doubtful whether the sally or the discovery
awakened his merriment.

"Hallo! what's that?" inquired Sikes, stepping forward as the Jew seized
the note. "That's mine, Fagin."

"No, no, my dear," said the Jew. "Mine, Bill, mine. You shall have the
books."

"If that ain't mine," said Bill Sikes, putting on his hat with a determined
air—"mine and Nancy's, that is, I'll take the boy back again."

The Jew started. Oliver started too, though from a very different cause,
for he hoped that the dispute might really end in his being taken back.

"Come! Hand over, will you?" said Sikes.

"This is hardly fair, Bill—hardly fair, is it, Nancy?" inquired the Jew.

"Fair, or not fair," retorted Sikes, "hand over, I tell you! Do you think
Nancy and me has got nothing else to do with our precious time but to
spend it in scouting arter, and kidnapping, every young boy as gets
grabbed through you? Give it here, you avaricious old skeleton; give it
here!"

With this gentle remonstrance Mr. Sikes plucked the note from between
the Jew's finger and thumb; and looking the old man coolly in the face,
folded it up small, and tied it in his neckerchief.

"That's for our share of the trouble," said Sikes; "and not half enough
neither. You may keep the books, if you're fond of reading. If you ain't,
sell 'em."

"They're very pretty," said Charley Bates, who, with sundry grimaces,
had been affecting to read one of the volumes in question; "beautiful

writing, isn't it, Oliver?" At sight of the dismayed look with which Oliver regarded his tormentors, Master Bates, who was blessed with a lively sense of the ludicrous, fell into another ecstasy, more boisterous than the first.

"They belong to the old gentleman," said Oliver, wringing his hands, "to the good, kind, old gentleman who took me into his house, and had me nursed, when I was near dying of the fever. Oh, pray send them back—send him back the books and money! Keep me here all my life long; but pray, send them back. He'll think I stole them, the old lady, all of them were so kind to me, will think I stole them; Oh, do have mercy upon me, and send them back!"

With these words, which were uttered with all the energy of passionate grief, Oliver fell upon his knees at the Jew's feet, and beat his hands together in perfect desperation.

"The boy's right," remarked Fagin, looking covertly round, and knitting his shaggy eyebrows into a hard knot. "You're right, Oliver, you're right; they *will* think you have stolen 'em. Ha! ha!" chuckled the Jew, rubbing his hands; "it couldn't have happened better if we had chosen our time!"

"Of course it couldn't," replied Sikes; "I know'd that directly I see him coming through Clerkenwell, with the books under his arm. It's all right enough. They're soft-hearted psalm-singers, or they wouldn't have taken him in at all; and they'll ask no questions after him fear they should be obliged to prosecute, and so get him lagged. He's safe enough."

Oliver had looked from one to the other while these words were being spoken, as if he were bewildered and could scarcely understand what passed; but when Bill Sikes concluded, he jumped suddenly to his feet, and tore wildly from the room, uttering shrieks for help, which made the bare old house echo to the roof.

"Keep back the dog, Bill!" cried Nancy, springing before the door, and closing it, as the Jew and his two pupils darted out in pursuit—"keep back the dog; he'll tear the boy to pieces."

"Serve him right!" cried Sikes, struggling to disengage himself from the girl's grasp. "Stand off from me, or I'll split your head against the wall."

"I don't care for that, Bill; I don't care for that," screamed the girl, struggling violently with the man; "the child shan't be torn down by the dog, unless you kill me first."

"Shan't he!" said Sikes, setting his teeth fiercely. "I'll soon do that, if you don't keep off."

The housebreaker flung the girl from him to the farther end of the room, just as the Jew and the two boys returned, dragging Oliver among them.

"What's the matter here?" said Fagin, looking round.

"The girl's gone mad, I think," replied Sikes savagely.

"No, she hasn't," said Nancy, pale and breathless from the scuffle—"no, she hasn't, Fagin; don't think it."

"Then keep quiet, will you?" said the Jew, with a threatening look.

"No, I won't do that neither," replied Nancy, speaking very loud. "Come! what do you think of that?"

Mr. Fagin was sufficiently well acquainted with the manners and customs of that particular species of humanity to which Nancy belonged to feel tolerably certain that it would be rather unsafe to prolong any conversation with her at present. With the view of diverting the attention of the company, he turned to Oliver.

"So you wanted to get away, my dear, did you?" said the Jew, taking up a jagged and knotted club which lay in a corner of the fireplace; "eh?"

Oliver made no reply. But he watched the Jew's motions, and breathed quickly.

"Wanted to get assistance; called for the police, did you?" sneered the Jew, catching the boy by the arm. "We'll cure you of that, my young master."

The Jew inflicted a smart blow on Oliver's shoulders with the club, and was raising it for a second when the girl, rushing forward, wrested it from his hand. She flung it into the fire with a force that brought some of the glowing coals whirling out into the room.

"I won't stand by and see it done, Fagin!" cried the girl. "You've got the boy, and what more would you have? Let him be—let him be, or I shall put that mark on some of you that will bring me to the gallows before my time."

The girl stamped her foot violently on the floor as she vented this threat; and with her lips compressed, and her hands clenched, looked alternately at the Jew and the other robber, her face quite colourless from the passion of rage into which she had gradually worked herself.

"Why, Nancy!" said the Jew, in a soothing tone, after a pause, during which he and Mr. Sikes had stared at one another in a disconcerted manner, "you—you're more clever than ever to-night. Ha! ha! my dear, you are acting beautifully."

"Am I?" said the girl. "Take care I don't overdo it. You will be the worse for it, Fagin, if I do; and so I tell you in good time to keep clear of me."

There is something about a roused woman, especially if she add to all her other strong passions the fierce impulses of recklessness and despair, which few men like to provoke. The Jew saw that it would be hopeless to affect any further mistake regarding the reality of Miss Nancy's rage; and shrinking involuntarily back a few paces, cast a glance, half-imploring and half-cowardly, at Sikes, as if to hint that he was the fittest person to pursue the dialogue.

Mr. Sikes, thus mutely appealed to, and possibly feeling his personal pride and influence interested in the immediate reduction of Miss Nancy to reason, gave utterance to about a couple of score of curses and threats, the rapid production of which reflected great credit on the fertility of his invention. As they produced no visible effect on the object against whom they were discharged, however, he resorted to more tangible arguments.

"What do you mean by this?" said Sikes, backing the inquiry with a very common imprecation concerning the most beautiful of human features, which, if it were heard above only once out of every fifty thousand times that it is uttered below, would render blindness as common a disorder as measles—"what do you mean by it? Burn my body? Do you know who you are, and what you are?"

"Oh, yes, I know all about it," replied the girl, laughing hysterically, and shaking her head from side to side, with a poor assumption of indifference.

"Well, then, keep quiet," rejoined Sikes, with a growl like that he was accustomed to use when addressing his dog, "or I'll quiet you for a good long time to come."

The girl laughed again, even less composedly than before; and, darting a hasty look at Sikes, turned her face aside, and bit her lip till the blood came.

"You're a nice one," added Sikes, as he surveyed her with a contemptuous air, "to take up the humane and genteel side! A pretty subject for the child, as you call him, to make a friend of!"

"God Almighty help me, I am!" cried the girl passionately; "and I wish I had been struck dead in the street, or had changed places with them we passed so near to-night, before I had lent a hand in bringing him here. He's a thief, a liar, a devil! all that's bad, from this night forth. Isn't that enough for the old wretch without blows?"

"Come, come, Sikes," said the Jew, appealing to him in a remonstratory tone, and motioning towards the boys, who were eagerly attentive to all that passed; "we must have civil words—civil words, Bill."

"Civil words!" cried the girl, whose passion was frightful to see. "Civil words, you villain! Yes; you deserve 'em from me. I thieved for you when I was a child not half as old as this!" pointing to Oliver. "I have been in the same trade and in the same service for twelve years since. Don't you know it? Speak out! don't you know it?"

"Well, well," replied the Jew, with an attempt at pacification; "and if you have, it's your living!"

"Ay, it is!" returned the girl, not speaking but pouring out the words in one continuous and vehement stream. "It is my living; and the cold, wet, dirty streets are my home; and you are the wretch that drove me to them long ago, and that'll keep me there, day and night, day and night, till I die!"

"I shall do you a mischief," interposed the Jew, goaded by these reproaches—"a mischief worse than that, if you say much more!"

The girl said nothing more; but tearing her hair and dress in a transport of frenzy, made such a rush at the Jew as would probably have left signal marks of her revenge upon him, had not her wrists been seized by Sikes at the right moment, upon which she made a few ineffectual struggles, and fainted.

"She's all right now," said Sikes, laying her down in a corner. "She's uncommon strong in the arms when she's up in this way."

The Jew wiped his forehead, and smiled, as if it were a relief to have the disturbance over; but neither he, nor Sikes, nor the dog, nor the boys, seemed to consider it in any other light than a common occurrence incidental to business.

"It's the worst of having to do with women," said the Jew, replacing his club; "but they're clever, and we can't get on, in our line, without 'em Charley, show Oliver to bed."

"I suppose he'd better not wear his best clothes to-morrow, Fagin, had he?" inquired Charley Bates.

"Certainly not," replied the Jew, reciprocating the grin with which Charley put the question.

Master Bates, apparently much delighted with his commission, took the cleft stick, and led Oliver into an adjacent kitchen where there were two or three of the beds on which he had slept before; and here, with many uncontrollable bursts of laughter, he produced the identical old suit of clothes which Oliver had so much congratulated himself upon leaving off at Mr. Brownlow's, and the accidental display of which, to Fagin, by the Jew who purchased them, had been the very first clue received of his whereabouts.

"Pull off the smart ones," said Charley, "and I'll give 'em to Fagin to take care of. What fun it is!"

Poor Oliver unwillingly complied. Master Bates, rolling up the new clothes under his arm, departed from the room, leaving Oliver in the dark, and locking the door behind him.

The noise of Charley's laughter, and the voice of Miss Betsy, who opportunely arrived to throw water over her friend, and perform other feminine offices for the promotion of her recovery, might have kept many people awake under more happy circumstances than those in which Oliver was placed. But he was sick and weary, and he soon fell sound asleep.

Chapter 16

Oliver's destiny continuing unpropitious, brings a great man to London to injure his reputation

Mr. Bumble emerged at early morning from the workhouse gate, and walked, with portly carriage and commanding steps, up the High Street. He was in the full bloom and pride of beadlehood, his cocked hat and coat were dazzling in the morning sun, and he clutched his cane with the vigorous tenacity of health and power. Mr. Bumble always carried his head high; but this morning it was higher than usual. There was an abstraction in his eye, an elevation in his air, which might have warned an observant stranger that thoughts were passing in the beadle's mind too great for utterance.

Mr. Bumble stopped not to converse with the small shopkeepers and others who spoke to him, deferentially, as he passed along. He merely returned their salutations with a wave of his hand, and relaxed not in his dignified pace until he reached the farm where Mrs. Mann tended the infant paupers with parochial care.

"Drat that beadle!" said Mrs. Mann, hearing the well-known shaking at the garden gate, "if it isn't him at this time in the morning!—Lauk, Mr. Bumble, only think of its being you! Well, dear me, it is a pleasure, that is! Come into the parlour, sir, please."

The first sentence was addressed to Susan; and the exclamations of delight were uttered to Mr. Bumble, as the good lady unlocked the garden gate, and showed him, with great attention and respect, into the house.

"Mrs. Mann," said Mr. Bumble, not sitting upon, or dropping himself into a seat, as any common jackanapes would, but letting himself gradually, and slowly down into a chair; "Mrs. Mann, ma'am, good-morning."

"Well, and good-morning to you, sir," replied Mrs. Mann, with many smiles; "and hoping you find yourself well, sir!"

"So-so, Mrs. Mann," replied the beadle. "A porochial life is not a bed of roses, Mrs. Mann."

"Ah, that it isn't, indeed, Mr. Bumble," rejoined the lady. And all the infant paupers might have chorused the rejoinder with great propriety, if they had heard it.

A porochial life, ma'am," continued Mr. Bumble, striking the table with his cane, "is a life of worrit, and vexation, and hardihood; but all public characters, as I may say, must suffer prosecution."

Mrs. Mann, not very well knowing what the beadle meant, raised her hands with a look of sympathy, and sighed.

"Ah! you may well sigh, Mrs. Mann!" said the beadle.

Finding she had done right, Mrs. Mann sighed again; evidently to the satisfaction of the public character, who, repressing a complacent smile by looking sternly at his cocked hat, said,

"Mrs. Mann, I am a-going to London."

"Lauk, Mr. Bumble!" cried Mrs. Mann, starting back.

"To London, ma'am," resumed the inflexible beadle, "by coach—I and two paupers, Mrs. Mann. A legal action is a-coming on, about a settlement, and the board has appointed me—me, Mrs. Mann—to depose to the matter before the quarter-sessions at Clerkinwell. And I very much question," added Mr. Bumble, drawing himself up, "whether the Clerkinwell Sessions will not find themselves in the wrong box before they have done with me."

"Oh! you mustn't be too hard upon them, sir," said Mrs. Mann, coaxingly.

"We are forgetting business, ma'am," said the beadle! "here is your porochial stipend for the month."

Mr. Bumble produced some silver money, rolled up in paper, from his pocket-book; and requested a receipt, which Mrs. Mann wrote.

"It's very much blotted, sir," said the farmer of infants; "but it's formal enough, I dare say. Thank you, Mr. Bumble, sir; I am very much obliged to you, I'm sure."

Mr. Bumble nodded blandly, in acknowledgment of Mrs. Mann's curtsy, and inquired how the children were.

"Bless their dear little hearts!" said Mrs. Mann, with emotion, "they're as well as can be, the dears! Of course, except the two that died last week. And little Dick."

"Isn't that boy no better?" inquired Mr. Bumble.

Mrs. Mann shook her head.

"He's a ill-conditioned, wicious, bad-disposed porochial child that," said Mr. Bumble, angrily. "Where is he?"

"I'll bring him to you in one minute, sir," replied Mrs. Mann. "Here, you, Dick!"

After some calling, Dick was discovered. Having had his face put under the pump, and dried upon Mrs. Mann's gown, he was led into the awful presence of Mr. Bumble the beadle.

The child was pale and thin, his cheeks were sunken, and his eyes large and bright. The scanty parish dress—the livery of his misery—hung loosely on his feeble body; and his young limbs had wasted away, like those of an old man.

Such was the little being who stood trembling beneath Mr. Bumble's glance, not daring to lift his eyes from the floor, and dreading even to hear the beadle's voice.

"Can't you look at the gentleman, you obstinate boy?" said Mrs. Mann.

The child meekly raised his eyes, and encountered those of Mr. Bumble.

"What's the matter with you, porochial Dick?" inquired Mr. Bumble with well-timed jocularity.

"Nothing, sir," replied the child faintly.

"I should think not," said Mrs. Mann, who had of course laughed very much at Mr. Bumble's humour. "You want for nothing, I'm sure."

"I should like—" faltered the child.

"Hey-day!" interposed Mrs. Mann, "I suppose you're going to say that you *do* want for something, now? Why, you little wretch—"

"Stop, Mrs. Mann, stop!" said the beadle, raising his hand with a show of authority. "Like what, sir—eh?"

"I should like," faltered the child, "if somebody that can write would put a few words down for me on a piece of paper; and fold it up and seal it; and keep it for me, after I am laid in the ground."

"Why, what does the boy mean?" exclaimed Mr. Bumble, on whom the earnest manner and wan aspect of the child had made some impression, accustomed as he was to such things. "What do you mean, sir?"

"I should like," said the child, "to leave my dear love to poor Oliver Twist; and to let him know how often I have sat by myself and cried to think of his wandering about in the dark nights with nobody to help him. And I should like to tell him," said the child, pressing his small hands together, and speaking with great fervour, "that I was glad to die when I was very young; for, perhaps, if I had lived to be a man, and had grown old, my little sister, who is in heaven, might forget me, or be unlike me; and it would be so much happier if we were both children there together."

Mr. Bumble surveyed the little speaker from head to foot with indescribable astonishment, and, turning to his companion, said, "They're all in one story, Mrs. Mann. That out-dacious Oliver has demogalized them all!"

"I couldn't have believed it, sir!" said Mrs. Mann, holding up her hands, and looking malignantly at Dick. "I never see such a hardened little wretch!"

"Take him away, ma'am!" said Mr. Bumble imperiously. "This must be stated to the board, Mrs. Mann."

"I hope the gentlemen will understand that it isn't my fault, sir?" said Mrs. Mann, whimpering pathetically.

"They shall understand that, ma'am; they shall be acquainted with the true state of the case," said Mr. Bumble. "There, take him away. I can't bear the sight on him."

Dick was immediately taken away, and locked up in the coal-cellar. Mr. Bumble shortly afterwards took himself off, to prepare for his journey.

At six o'clock next morning, Mr. Bumble, having exchanged his cocked hat for a round one, and encased his person in a blue greatcoat with a cape to it, took his place on the outside of the coach, accompanied by the criminals whose settlement was disputed; with whom, in due course of time, he arrived in London. He experienced no other crosses on the way than those which originated in the perverse behaviour of the two paupers, who persisted in shivering, and complaining of the cold, in a manner which Mr. Bumble declared caused his teeth to chatter in his head, and made him feel quite uncomfortable, although he had a greatcoat on.

Having disposed of these evil-minded persons for the night, Mr. Bumble sat himself down in the house at which the coach stopped, and took a temperate dinner of steaks, oyster sauce, and porter. Putting a glass of hot gin-and-water on the chimney-piece, he drew his chair to the fire; and, with sundry moral reflections on the too-prevalent sin of discontent and complaining, composed himself to read the paper.

The very first paragraph upon which Mr. Bumble's eyes rested was the following advertisement:–

"FIVE GUINEAS REWARD

"WHEREAS a young boy, named Oliver Twist, absconded, or was enticed, on Thursday evening last, from his home, at Pentonville; and has not since been heard of. The above reward will be paid to any person who will give such information as will lead to the discovery of the said Oliver Twist, or tend to throw any light upon his previous history, in which the advertiser is, for many reasons, warmly interested."

And then followed a full description of Oliver's dress, person, appearance, and disappearance, with the name and address of Mr. Brownlow at full length.

Mr. Bumble opened his eyes; read the advertisement, slowly and carefully, three several times; and in something more than five minutes was on his way to Pentonville, having actually, in his excitement, left the glass of hot gin-and-water untasted.

"Is Mr. Brownlow at home?" inquired Mr. Bumble of the girl who opened the door.

To this inquiry the girl returned the not uncommon but rather evasive reply of "I don't know. Where do you come from?"

Mr. Bumble no sooner uttered Oliver's name in explanation of his errand, than Mrs. Bedwin, who had been listening at the parlour door, hastened into the passage in a breathless state.

"Come in—come in," said the old lady; "I knew we should hear of him. Poor dear! I knew we should! I was certain of it. Bless his heart! I said so all along."

Having said this, the worthy old lady hurried back into the parlour again, and, seating herself on a sofa, burst into tears. The girl, who was not quite so susceptible, had run upstairs meanwhile, and now returned with a request that Mr. Bumble would follow her immediately, which he did.

He was shown into the little back study, where sat Mr. Brownlow and his friend Mr. Grimwig, with decanters and glasses before them. The latter gentleman at once burst into the exclamation,—

"A beadle! A parish beadle, or I'll eat my head."

"Pray don't interrupt just now," said Mr. Brownlow. "Take a seat, will you?"

Mr. Bumble sat himself down, quite confounded by the oddity of Mr. Grimwig's manner. Mr. Brownlow moved the lamp, so as to obtain an uninterrupted view of the beadle's countenance, and said, with a little impatience,—

"Now, sir, you come in consequence of having seen the advertisement?"

"Yes, sir," said Mr. Bumble.

"And you *are* a beadle, are you not?" inquired Mr. Grimwig.

"I am a porochial beadle, gentlemen," rejoined Mr. Bumble proudly.

"Of course," observed Mr. Grimwig aside to his friend, "I knew he was. A beadle all over!"

Mr. Brownlow gently shook his head to impose silence on his friend, and resumed,–

"Do you know where this poor boy is now?"

"No more than nobody," replied Mr. Bumble.

"Well, what *do* you know of him?" inquired the old gentleman. "Speak out, my friend, if you have anything to say. What *do* you know of him?"

"You don't happen to know any good of him, do you?" said Mr. Grimwig caustically, after an attentive perusal of Mr. Bumble's features.

Mr. Bumble, catching at the inquiry very quickly, shook his head with portentous solemnity.

"You see?" said Mr. Grimwig, looking triumphantly at Mr. Brownlow.

Mr. Brownlow looked apprehensively at Mr. Bumble's pursed-up countenance, and requested him to communicate what he knew regarding Oliver in as few words as possible.

Mr. Bumble put down his hat, unbuttoned his coat, folded his arms, inclined his head in a retrospective manner, and, after a few moments' reflection, commenced his story.

It would be tedious if given in the beadle's words, occupying, as it did, some twenty minutes in the telling; but the sum and substance of it was, that Oliver was a foundling, born of low and vicious parents; that he had, from his birth, displayed no better qualities than treachery, ingratitude, and malice; that he had terminated his brief career in the place of his birth by making a sanguinary and cowardly attack on an unoffending lad, and running away in the night-time from his master's house. In proof of his really being the person he represented himself, Mr. Bumble laid upon the table the papers he had brought to town; and folding his arms again, awaited Mr. Brownlow's observations.

I fear it is all too true," said the old gentleman sorrowfully, after looking over the papers. "This is not much for your intelligence; but I would gladly have given you treble the money if it had been favourable to the boy."

It is not at all improbable that if Mr. Bumble had been possessed of this information at an earlier period of the interview, he might have imparted a very different colouring to his little history. It was too late to do it now, however; so he shook his head gravely, and, pocketing the five guineas, withdrew.

Mr. Brownlow paced the room to and fro for some minutes, evidently so much disturbed by the beadle's tale that even Mr. Grimwig forbore to vex him further.

At length he stopped and rang the bell violently.

"Mrs. Bedwin," said Mr. Brownlow, when the housekeeper appeared, "that boy Oliver is an impostor."

"It can't be, sir. It cannot be," said the old lady energetically.

6 Oliver

"I tell you he is," retorted the old gentleman. "What do you mean he can't be? We have just heard a full account of him from his birth, and he has been a thorough-paced little villain all his life."

"I never will believe it, sir," replied the old lady firmly. "Never!"

"You old women never believe anything but quack-doctors and lying story-books," growled Mr. Grimwig. "I knew it all along. Why didn't you take my advice in the beginning? You would, if he hadn't had a fever, I suppose, eh? He was interesting, wasn't he? Interesting! bah!" And Mr. Grimwig poked the fire with a flourish.

"He was a dear, grateful, gentle child, sir," retorted Mrs. Bedwin, indignantly. "I know what children are, sir, and have done these forty years; and people who can't say the same, shouldn't say anything about them. That's my opinion!"

This was a hard hit at Mr. Grimwig, who was a bachelor. As it extorted nothing from that gentleman but a smile, the old lady tossed her head, and smoothed down her apron preparatory to another speech, when she was stopped by Mr. Brownlow.

"Silence!" said the old gentleman, feigning an anger he was far from feeling. "Never let me hear the boy's name again. I rang to tell you that. Never—never, on any pretence, mind! You may leave the room, Mrs. Bedwin. Remember I am in earnest."

There were sad hearts at Mr. Brownlow's that night.

Oliver's heart sank within him when he thought of his good kind friends; it was well for him that he could not know what they had heard, or it might have broken outright.

CHAPTER 17

In which a notable plan is discussed and determined on

IT was a chill, damp, windy night, when the Jew, buttoning his greatcoat tight round his shrivelled body, and pulling the collar up over his ears so as completely to obscure the lower part of his face, emerged from his den. He paused on the step as the door was locked and chained behind him; and having listened while the boys made all secure, and until their retreating footsteps were no longer audible, slunk down the street as quickly as he could.

The house to which Oliver had been conveyed was in the neighbourhood of Whitechapel. The Jew stopped for an instant at the corner of the street, and, glancing suspiciously round, crossed the road and struck off in the direction of Spitalfields.

He kept on his course, through many winding and narrow ways until he reached Bethnal Green; then, turning suddenly off to the left, he soon became involved in the maze of the mean and dirty streets which abound in that close and densely populated quarter.

The Jew was evidently too familiar with the ground he traversed, however, to be at all bewildered, either by the darkness of the night or by the intricacies of the way. He hurried through several alleys and streets; and at length turned into one, lighted only by a single lamp at the farther end. At the door of a house in this street he knocked; and having exchanged a few muttered words with the person who opened it, walked upstairs.

A dog growled as he touched the handle of a room-door, and a man's voice demanded who was there.

"Only me, Bill; only me, my dear," said the Jew, looking in.

"Bring in your body then," said Sikes. "Lie down, you stupid brute! Don't you know the devil when he's got a greatcoat on?"

Apparently the dog had been somewhat deceived by Mr. Fagin's outer garment; for as the Jew unbuttoned it, and threw it over the back of a chair, he retired to the corner from which he had risen, wagging his tail as he went, to show that he was as well satisfied as it was in his nature to be.

"Well!" said Sikes.

"Well, my dear," replied the Jew. "Ah! Nancy."

The latter recognition was uttered with just enough of embarrassment to imply a doubt of its reception; for Mr. Fagin and his young friend had not met since she had interfered in behalf of Oliver. All doubts upon the subject, if he had any, were speedily removed by the young lady's behaviour. She took her feet off the fender, pushed back her chair, and made Fagin draw up his, without saying more about it; for it was a cold night, and no mistake.

"It *is* cold, Nancy dear," said the Jew, as he warmed his skinny hands over the fire. "It seems to go right through one," added the old man, touching his side.

"It must be a piercer if it finds its way through *your* heart," said Mr. Sikes. "Give him something to drink, Nancy. Burn my body, make haste! It's enough to turn a man ill to see his lean old carcass shivering in that way, like a ugly ghost just rose from the grave."

Nancy quickly brought a bottle from a cupboard, in which there were many, which, to judge from the diversity of their appearance, were filled with several kinds of liquids. Sikes, pouring out a glass of brandy, bade the Jew drink it off.

"Quite enough, quite, thankye, Bill," replied the Jew, putting down the glass, after just setting his lips to it.

"What! you're afraid of our getting the better of you, are you?" inquired Sikes, fixing his eyes on the Jew. "Ugh!"

With a hoarse grunt of contempt, Mr. Sikes seized the glass, and threw the remainder of is contents into the ashes—as a preparatory ceremony to filling it again for himself, which he did at once.

The Jew glanced round the room, as his companion tossed down the second glassful; not in curiosity, for he had seen it often before, but in a restless and suspicious manner which was habitual to him. It was a meanly-furnished apartment, with nothing but the contents of the closet to induce the belief that its occupier was anything but a working man; and with no more suspicious articles displayed to view than two or three heavy bludgeons which stood in a corner, and a "life-preserver" that hung over the chimney-piece.

"There," said Sikes, smacking his lips, "now I'm ready."

"For business?" inquired the Jew.

"For business," replied Sikes; "so say what you've got to say."

"About the crib at Chertsey, Bill?" said the Jew, drawing his chair forward, and speaking in a very low voice.

"Yes. Wot about it?" inquired Sikes.

"Ah! you know what I mean, my dear," said the Jew. "He knows what I mean, Nancy; don't he?"

"No, he don't," sneered Mr. Sikes. "Or he won't; and that's the same thing. Speak out and call things by their right names; don't sit there, winking, and blinking and talking to me in hints, as if you warn't the very first that thought about the robbery. What d'ye mean?"

"Hush, Bill, hush!" said the Jew, who had in vain attempted to stop this burst of indignation; "somebody will hear us, my dear—somebody will hear us."

"Let 'em hear," said Sikes; "I don't care." But as Mr. Sikes *did* care, upon reflection, he dropped his voice as he said the words, and grew calmer.

"There, there," said the Jew, coaxingly. "It was only my caution—nothing more. Now, my dear, about that crib at Chertsey; when is it to be done, Bill, eh?—when is it to be done? Such plate, my dear, such plate!" said the Jew, rubbing his hands, and elevating his eyebrows in a rapture of anticipation.

"Not at all," replied Sikes, coldly.

"Not to be done at all!" echoed the Jew, leaning back in his chair.

"Not, not at all," rejoined Sikes. "At least it can't be a put-up job, as we expected."

"Then it hasn't been properly gone about," said the Jew, turning pale with anger. "Don't tell me."

"But I will tell you," retorted Sikes. "Who are you that's not to be told? I tell you that Toby Crackit has been hanging about the place for a fortnight, and he can't get one of the servants into a line."

"Do you mean to tell me, Bill," said the Jew, softening as the other grew heated, "that neither of the two men in the house can be got over?"

"Yes, I do mean to tell you so," replied Sikes. "The old lady has had 'em these twenty years, and if you were to give 'em five hundred pounds, they wouldn't be in it."

"And yet," said the old man, dropping his hands on his knees, "it's a sad thing, my dear, to lose so much when we had set our hearts upon it."

"So it is," said Mr. Sikes. "Worse luck!"

A long silence ensued, during which the Jew was plunged in deep thought, with his face wrinkled into an expression of villainy perfectly demoniacal. Sikes eyed him furtively from time to time. Nancy, apparently fearful of irritating the housebreaker, sat with her eyes fixed upon the fire, as if she had been deaf to all that passed.

"Fagin," said Sikes, abruptly breaking the stillness that prevailed, "is it worth fifty shiners extra, if it's safely done from the outside?"

"Yes," said the Jew, as suddenly rousing himself.

"Is it a bargain?" inquired Sikes.

"Yes, my dear, yes," rejoined the Jew, his eyes glistening, and every muscle in his face working, with the excitement that the inquiry had awakened.

"Then," said Sikes, thrusting aside the Jew's hand with some disdain, "let it come off as soon as you like. Toby and I were over the garden-wall the night afore last, sounding the panels of the door and shutters. The crib's barred up at night like a jail; but there's one part we can crack, safe and softly."

"Which is that, Bill?" asked the Jew eagerly.

"Why," whispered Sikes, "as you cross the lawn—"

"Yes, yes," said the Jew, bending his head forward, with his eyes almost starting out of it.

"Umph!" cried Sikes, stopping short, as the girl, scarcely moving her head, looked suddenly round, and pointed for an instant to the Jew's face. "Never mind which part it is. You can't do it without me, I know; but it's best to be on the safe side when one deals with you."

"As you like, my dear, as you like," replied the Jew. "Is there no help wanted but yours and Toby's?"

"None," said Sikes. "'Cept a centre–bit and a boy. The first we've both got, the second you must find us."

"A boy," exclaimed the Jew. "Oh! then it's panel, eh?"

"Never mind wot it is!" replied Sikes. "I want a boy; and he mustn't be a big 'un."

"Now, Fagin," said Nancy with a laugh, "tell Bill at once about Oliver!"

"Ha! you're a clever one, my dear; the sharpest girl I ever saw!" said the Jew, patting her on the neck. "It *was* about Oliver, I was going to speak, sure enough. Ha! ha! ha!"

"What about him?" demanded Sikes.

"He's the boy for you, my dear," replied the Jew in a hoarse whisper, laying his finger on the side of his nose, and grinning frightfully.

"He!" exclaimed Sikes.

"Have him, Bill!" said Nancy. "I would, if I was in your place. He mayn't be so much as any of the others; but that's not what you want, if he's only to open a door for you. Depend upon it he's safe one, Bill."

"I know he is," rejoined Fagin. "He's been in good training these last few weeks; and it's time he began to work for his bread. Besides, the others are all too big."

"Well, he is just the size I want," said Mr. Sikes, ruminating.

"And will do everything you want, Bill, my dear," interposed the Jew; "he can't help himself—that is, if you frighten him enough."

"Frighten him?" echoed Sikes. "It'll be no sham frightening, mind you. If there's anything queer about him when we once get into the work, in for a penny, in for a pound. You won't see him alive again, Fagin. Think of that before you send him. Mark my words!" said the robber, poising a crowbar which he had drawn from under the bedstead.

"Ah, to be sure," said the Jew. "When is it to be done, Bill?"

"I planned, with Toby, the night arter to-morrow," rejoined Sikes in a surly voice, "if he heerd nothing from me to the contrary."

"Good," said the Jew; "there's no moon."

"No," rejoined Sikes.

"It's all arranged about bringing off the swag,[1] is it?" asked the Jew.

Sikes nodded.

"And about—"

"Oh, ah, it's all planned," rejoined Sikes, interrupting him. "Never mind particulars. You'd better bring the boy here to-morrow night; I shall get off the stones an hour arter daybreak. Then you hold your tongue, and keep the melting-pot ready; and that's all you'll have to do."

After some discussion, in which all three took an active part, it was decided that Nancy should repair to the Jew's next evening when the night had set in, and bring Oliver away with her.

These preliminaries adjusted, Mr. Sikes proceeded to drink brandy at a furious rate, and to flourish the crowbar in an alarming manner; yelling forth, at the same time, most unmusical snatches of song, mingled with wild execrations. At length, in a fit of professional enthusiasm, he insisted upon producing his box of housebreaking tools; which he had no sooner stumbled in with, and opened for the purpose of explaining the nature and properties of the various implements it contained, and the peculiar beauties of their construction, than he fell over it upon the floor, and went to sleep where he fell.

"Good-night, Nancy," said the Jew, muffling himself up as before.

"Good-night."

Their eyes met, and the Jew scrutinized her narrowly. There was no flinching about the girl. She was as true and earnest in the matter as Toby Crackit himself could be.

The Jew again bade her good-night; and bestowing a sly kick upon the prostrate form of Mr. Sikes, while her back was turned, groped downstairs.

[1] Booty.

Chapter 18

Wherein Oliver is delivered over to Mr. William Sikes

WHEN Oliver awoke in the morning, he was a good deal surprised to find that a new pair of shoes, with strong thick soles, had been placed at his bedside, and that his old ones had been removed. At first he was pleased with the discovery, hoping that it might be the forerunner of his release; but such thoughts were quickly dispelled on his sitting down to breakfast along with the Jew, who told him, in a tone and manner which increased his alarm, that he was to be taken to the residence of Bill Sikes that night.

"To-to-stop there, sir?" asked Oliver anxiously.

"No, no, my dear; not to stop there," replied the Jew. "We shouldn't like to lose you. Don't be afraid, Oliver, you shall come back to us again. Ha! ha! ha! We won't be so cruel as to send you away, my dear. Oh, no, no!"

The old man, who was stooping over the fire toasting a piece of bread, looked round as he bantered Oliver thus, and chuckled, as if to show that he knew he would still be very glad to get away if he could.

"I suppose," said the Jew, fixing his eyes on Oliver, "you want to know what you're going to Bill's for-eh, my dear?"

Oliver coloured, involuntarily, to find that the old thief had been reading his thoughts; but boldly said, Yes, he did want to know.

"Why, do you think?" inquired Fagin, parrying the question.

"Indeed I don't know, sir," replied Oliver.

"Bah!" said the Jew, turning away with a disappointed countenance from a close perusal of the boy's face. "Wait till Bill tells you, then."

The Jew seemed much vexed by Oliver's not expressing any greater curiosity on the subject; but the truth is, that although he felt very anxious, he was too much confused by the earnest cunning of Fagin's looks, and his own speculations, to make any further inquiries just then. He had no other opportunity; for the Jew remained very surly and silent till night, when he prepared to go abroad.

"You may burn a candle," said the Jew, putting one upon the table. "And here's a book for you to read, till they come to fetch you. Take heed, Oliver, take heed!" said the old man, shaking his right hand before him in a warning manner. "He's a rough man, and thinks nothing of blood when his own is up. Whatever falls out, say nothing; and do what he bids you. Mind!" Placing a strong emphasis on the last word, he suffered his features gradually to resolve themselves into a ghastly grin, and, nodding his head, left the room.

Oliver leaned his head upon his hand when the old man disappeared, and pondered, with a trembling heart, on the words he had just heard. He remained lost in thought for some minutes, when a rustling noise aroused him.

"What's that?" he cried, starting up, and catching sight of a figure standing by the door. "Who's there?"

"Me—only me," replied a tremulous voice.

Oliver raised the candle above his head, and looked towards the door. It was Nancy.

"Put down the light," said the girl, turning away her head. "It burts my eyes."

Oliver saw that she was very pale, and gently inquired if she were ill. The girl threw herself into a chair, with her back towards him, and wrung her hands, but made no reply.

"God forgive me!" she cried after a while; "I never thought of this."

"Has anything happened?" asked Oliver. "Can I help you? I will if I can. I will, indeed."

She rocked herself to and fro, caught her throat, and, uttering a gurgling sound, struggled and gasped for breath.

"Nancy!" cried Oliver, "what is it?"

The girl beat her hands upon her knees, and her feet upon the ground, and, suddenly stopping, drew her shawl close around her, and shivered with cold.

Oliver stirred the fire. Drawing her chair close to it, she sat there, for a little time, without speaking; but at length she raised her head, and looked round.

"I don't know what comes over me sometimes," said she, affecting to busy herself in arranging her dress; "it's this damp, dirty room, I think. Now, Nolly, dear, are you ready?"

"Am I to go with you?" asked Oliver.

"Yes; I have come from Bill," replied the girl. "You are to go with me."

"What for?" said Oliver, recoiling.

"What for?" echoed the girl, raising her eyes, and averting them again the moment they encountered the boy's face. "Oh, for no harm."

He stepped forward and said that he was ready.

"Hush!" said the girl, stooping over him, and pointing to the door as she looked cautiously round. "You can't help yourself. I have tried hard for you, but all to no purpose. You are hedged round and round; and if ever you are to get loose from here, this is not the time."

Struck by the energy of her manner, Oliver looked up in her face with great surprise. She seemed to speak the truth; her countenance was white and agitated, and she trembled with very earnestness.

She pointed, hastily, to some livid bruises on her neck and arms, and continued with great rapidity:—

"Remember this! and don't let me suffer more for you just now. If I could help you, I would; but I have not the power. They don't mean to harm you; and whatever they make you do is no fault of yours. Hush! every word from you is a blow for me. Give me your hand. Make haste! Your hand!"

She caught the hand which Oliver instinctively placed in hers, and, blowing out the light, drew him after her up the stairs. The door was opened quickly by some one shrouded in the darkness, and was as quickly closed when they had passed out. A hackney cabriolet was in waiting. With the same vehemence which she had exhibited in addressing Oliver, the girl pulled him in with her, and drew the curtains close. The driver wanted no directions, but lashed his horse into full speed without the delay of an instant.

The girl still held Oliver fast by the hand, and continued to pour into his ear the warnings and assurances she had already imparted. All was so quick and hurried that he had scarcely time to recollect where he was, or how he came there, when the carriage stopped at the house to which the Jew's steps had been directed on the previous evening.

For one brief moment Oliver cast a hurried glance along the empty street, and a cry for help hung upon his lips. But the girl's voice was in his ear, beseeching him in such tones of agony to remember her, that he had not the heart to utter it. While he hesitated, the opportunity was gone, for he was already in the house, and the door was shut.

"This way," said the girl, releasing her hold for the first time. "Bill!"

"Hallo!" replied Sikes, appearing at the head of the stairs with a candle. "Oh! that's the time of day. Come on!"

This was a very strong expression of approbation, an uncommonly hearty welcome, from a person of Mr. Sikes's temperament. Nancy, appearing much gratified thereby, saluted him cordially.

"Bull's-eye's gone home with Tom," observed Sikes, as he lighted them up. "He'd have been in the way."

"That's right," rejoined Nancy.

"So you've got the kid," said Sikes, when they had all reached the room, closing the door as he spoke.

"Yes; here he is," replied Nancy.

"Did he come quiet?" inquired Sikes.

"Like a lamb," rejoined Nancy.

"I'm glad to hear it," said Sikes, looking grimly at Oliver; "for the sake of his young carcass, as would otherways have suffered for it. Come here, young 'un; and let me read you a lectur', which is as well got over at once."

Thus addressing his new pupil, Mr. Sikes pulled off Oliver's cap and threw it into a corner; and then, taking him by the shoulder, sat himself down by the table, and stood the boy in front of him.

"Now, first; do you know wot this is?" inquired Sikes, taking up a pocket-pistol which lay on the table.

Oliver replied in the affirmative.

"Now it's loaded," said Mr. Sikes.

"Yes, I see it is, sir," replied Oliver.

"Well," said the robber, grasping Oliver's wrist tightly, and putting the barrel so close to his temple that they touched; at which moment the boy could not repress a start–"if you speak a word when you're out o' doors with me, except when I speak to you, that loading will be in your head without notice. So, if you *do* make up your mind to speak without leave, say your prayers first."

Having bestowed a scowl upon the object of this warning, to increase its effect, Mr. Sikes continued:–

"As near as I know, there isn't anybody as would be asking very partickler arter you, if you *was* disposed of; so I needn't take this devil-and-all of trouble to explain matters to you, if it warn't for your own good. D'ye hear me?"

"The short and the long of what you mean," said Nancy, speaking very emphatically, and slightly frowning at Oliver, as if to bespeak his serious attention to her words, "is, that if you're crossed by him in this job you have on hand, you'll prevent his ever telling tales afterwards by shooting him through the head; and will take your chance of swinging for it, as you do for a great many other things in the way of business, every month of your life."

"That's it!" observed Mr. Sikes, approvingly; "women can always put things in fewest words. Except when it's a-blowing up; and then they lengthens it out. And now that he's thoroughly up to it, let's have some supper, and get a snooze before starting."

In pursuance of this request, Nancy quickly laid the cloth, and, disappearing for a few minutes, presently returned with a pot of porter and a dish of sheep's heads; which gave occasion to several pleasant witticisms on the part of Mr. Sikes, founded upon the singular coincidence of "jemmies" being a cant name common to them, and also to an ingenious implement much used in his profession.

Supper being ended–it may be easily conceived that Oliver had no great appetite for it–Mr. Sikes disposed of a couple of glasses of spirits and water, and threw himself upon the bed, ordering Nancy, with many imprecations in case of failure, to call him at five precisely. Oliver stretched himself in his clothes by command of the same authority on a mattress upon the floor; and the girl, mending the fire, sat before it, in readiness to rouse them at the appointed time.

For a long time Oliver lay awake, thinking it not impossible that Nancy might seek that opportunity of whispering some further advice; but the girl sat brooding over the fire, without moving, save now and then to trim the light. Weary with watching and anxiety, he at length fell asleep.

When he awoke the table was covered with tea things, and Sikes was thrusting various articles into the pockets of his greatcoat, which hung over the back of a chair; while Nancy was busily engaged in preparing breakfast. It was not yet daylight, for the candle was still burning, and it was quite dark outside. A sharp rain, too, was beating against the window panes, and the sky looked black and cloudy.

"Now then!" growled Sikes, as Oliver started up; "half-past five! Look sharp, or you'll get no breakfast, for it's late as it is."

Oliver was not long in making his toilet; and, having taken some breakfast, replied to a surly inquiry from Sikes, by saying that he was quite ready.

Nancy, scarcely looking at the boy, threw him a handkerchief to tie round his throat; and Sikes gave him a large rough cape to button over his shoulders. Thus attired, he gave his hand to the robber, who, merely pausing to show him, with a menacing gesture, that he had the pistol in a side-pocket of his greatcoat, clasped it firmly in his and, exchanging a farewell with Nancy, led him away.

Oliver turned, for an instant, when they reached the door, in the hope of meeting a look from the girl. But she had resumed her old seat in front of the fire, and sat perfectly motionless before it.

CHAPTER 19

The expedition

IT was a cheerless morning when they got into the street-blowing and raining hard, and the clouds looking dull and stormy.

By the time they had turned into the Bethnal Green Road the day had fairly begun to break. Many of the lamps were already extinguished; a few country wagons were slowly toiling on towards London; and now and then a stage-coach, covered with mud, rattled briskly by, the driver bestowing, as he passed, an admonitory lash upon the heavy wagoner, who, by keeping on the wrong side of the road, had endangered his arriving at the office a quarter of a minute after his time. As they approached the City, the noise and traffic gradually increased; and when they threaded the streets between Shoreditch and Smithfield it had swelled into a roar of sound and bustle.

Turning down Sun Street and Crown Street, and crossing Finsbury Square, Mr. Sikes struck, by way of Chiswell Street, into Barbican; thence into Long Lane; and so into Smithfield, from which latter place arose a tumult of discordant sounds that filled Oliver Twist with surprise and amazement.

They held their course at this rate until they had passed Hyde Park Corner, and were on their way to Kensington, when Sikes relaxed his pace, until an empty cart, which was at some little distance behind, came up. Seeing "Hounslow" written on it, he asked the driver, with as much civility as he could assume, if he would give them a lift as far as Isleworth.

"Jump up," said the man. "Is that your boy?"

"Yes; he's my boy," replied Sikes, looking hard at Oliver, and putting his hand abstractedly into the pocket where the pistol was.

"Your father walks rather too quick for you, don't he, my man?" inquired the driver, seeing that Oliver was out of breath.

"Not a bit of it," replied Sikes, interposing. "He's used to it. Here, take hold of my hand, Ned. In with you!"

Thus addressing Oliver, he helped him into the cart; and the driver pointing to a heap of sacks, told him to lie down there and rest himself.

At length they came to a public-house called the Coach and Horses, a little way beyond which another road appeared to turn off. And here the cart stopped.

Sikes dismounted with great precipitation, holding Oliver by the hand all the while; and lifting him down directly, bestowed a furious look upon him, and tapped the side-pocket with his fist in a very significant manner.

"Good-bye, boy," said the man.

"He's sulky," replied Sikes, giving him a shake–"he's sulky. A young dog! Don't mind him."

"Not I!" rejoined the other, getting into his cart. "It's a fine day, after all." And he drove away.

Sikes waited until he had fairly gone, and then, telling Oliver he might look about him if he wanted, once again led him forward on his journey.

They turned round to the left, a short way past the public-house; and then, taking a right-hand road, walked on for a long time, passing many large gardens and gentlemen's houses on both sides of the way, and stopping for nothing but a little beer, until they reached a town. Here, against the wall of a house, Oliver saw written up in pretty large letters, "Hampton." They lingered about in the fields for some hours. At length they came back into the town, and turning into an old public-house with a defaced sign-board, ordered some dinner by the kitchen fire.

The kitchen was an old, low-roofed room, with a great beam across the middle of the ceiling; and benches, with high backs to them, by the fire, on which were seated several rough men in smock-frocks, drinking and smoking. They took no notice of Oliver, and very little of Sikes; and as Sikes took very little notice of them, he and his young comrade sat in a corner by themselves without being much troubled by their company.

They had some cold meat for dinner; and sat here so long after it, while Mr. Sikes indulged himself with three or four pipes, that Oliver began to feel quite certain they were not going any farther. Being much tired with the walk, and getting up so early, he dozed a little at first; and then, quite overpowered by fatigue and the fumes of the tobacco, fell asleep.

It was quite dark when he was awakened by a push from Sikes. Rousing himself sufficiently to sit up and look about him, he found that worthy in close fellowship and communication with a labouring man, over a pint of ale.

"So, you're going on to Lower Halliford, are you?" inquired Sikes.

"Yes, I am," replied the man, who seemed a little the worse–or better, as the case might be–for drinking; "and not slow about it neither. My horse hasn't got a load behind him going back, as he had coming up in the mornin'; and he won't be long a-doing of it. Here's luck to him! Ecod! he's a good 'un!"

"Could you give my boy and me a lift as far as there?" demanded Sikes, pushing the ale towards his new friend.

"If you're going directly, I can," replied the man, looking out of the pot. "Are you going to Halliford?"

"Going on to Shepperton," replied Sikes.

"I'm your man as far as I go," replied the other.

After the exchange of a few compliments they bade the company good-night, and went out. The horse was standing outside, ready harnessed to the cart. Oliver and Sikes got in without any further ceremony; and the man to whom he belonged, having lingered for a minute or two "to bear him up," and to defy the hostler and the world to produce his equal, mounted also. Then they started off at great speed, and rattled out of the town right gallantly.

Sunbury was passed through, and they came again into the lonely road. Two or three miles more, and the cart stopped. Sikes alighted; and taking Oliver by the hand, they once again walked on.

They turned into no house at Shepperton, as the weary boy had expected; but still kept walking on, in mud and darkness, through gloomy lanes and over cold open wastes, until they came within sight of the lights of a town at no great distance. On looking intently forward Oliver saw that the water was just below them, and that they were coming to the foot of a bridge.

Sikes kept straight on until they were close upon the bridge, and then turned suddenly down a bank upon the left.

"The water!" thought Oliver, turning sick with fear. "He has brought me to this lonely place to murder me!"

He was about to throw himself on the ground and make one struggle for his young life, when he saw that they stood before a solitary house, all ruinous and decayed. There was a window on each side of the dilapidated entrance, and one story above; but no light was visible. It was dark, dismantled, and, to all appearance, uninhabited.

Sikes, with Oliver's hand still in his, softly approached the low porch, and raised the latch. The door yielded to the pressure, and they passed in together.

CHAPTER 20

The burglary

"HALLO!" cried a loud, hoarse voice, directly they had set foot in the passage.

"Don't make such a row," said Sikes, bolting the door. "Show a glim, Toby."

"Aha, my pal," cried the same voice–"a glim, Barney, a glim! Show the gentleman in, Barney; and wake up first, if convenient."

A pair of slipshod feet shuffled, hastily, across the bare floor of the room and there issued, from the door on the right hand, first, a feeble candle, and next the form of the same individual who has been heretofore described as labouring under the infirmity of speaking through his nose, and officiating as waiter at the public-house on Saffron Hill.

"Bister Sikes!" exclaimed Barney, with real or counterfeit joy; "cub id, sir; cub id."

Muttering a curse upon his tardiness, Sikes pushed Oliver before him, and they entered a low dark room with a smoky fire, two or three broken chairs, a table, and a very old couch; on which, with his legs much higher than his head, a man was reposing at full length, smoking a long clay pipe. He was dressed in a smartly-cut snuff-coloured coat, with large brass buttons, an orange neckerchief, a coarse, staring, shawl-pattern waistcoat, and drab breeches. Mr. Crackit (for he it was) had no very great quantity of hair, either upon his head or face, but what he had was of a reddish dye, and tortured into long corkscrew curls, through which he occasionally thrust some very dirty fingers ornamented with large common rings.

"Bill, my boy!" said this figure, turning his head towards the door, "I'm glad to see you. I was almost afraid you'd given it up, in which case I should have made a personal wentur."

"Now," said Sikes, "if you'll give us something to eat and drink while we're waiting, you'll put some heart in us, or in me, at all events. Sit down by the fire, younker, and rest yourself; for you'll have to go out with us again to-night, though not very far off."

Sikes having satisfied his appetite (Oliver could eat nothing but a small crust of bread which they made him swallow), the two men laid themselves down on chairs for a short nap. Oliver retained his stool by the fire, and Barney, wrapped in a blanket, stretched himself on the floor, close outside the fender.

They slept, or appeared to sleep, for some time; nobody stirring but Barney, who rose once or twice to throw coals upon the fire. Oliver fell into a heavy doze-imagining himself straying along through the gloomy lanes, or wandering about the dark churchyard, or retracing some one or other of the scenes of the past day, when he was roused by Toby Crackit jumping up and declaring it was half-past one.

In an instant the other two were on their legs, and all were actively engaged in busy preparation. Sikes and his companion enveloped their necks and chins in large dark shawls, and drew on their greatcoats; while Barney, opening a cupboard, brought forth several articles, which he hastily crammed into the pockets.

"Barkers for me, Barney," said Toby Crackit.

"Here they are," replied Barney, producing a pair of pistols. "You loaded them yourself."

"All right!" replied Toby, stowing them away. "The persuaders?"

"I've got 'em," replied Sikes.

"Crape, keys, centre-bits, darkies—nothing forgotten?" inquired Toby, fastening a small crowbar to a loop inside the skirt of his coat.

"All right," rejoined his companion. "Bring them bits of timber, Barney. That's the time of day."

With these words, he took a thick stick from Barney's hands, who, having delivered another to Toby, busied himself in fastening on Oliver's cape.

"Now, then!" said Sikes, holding out his hand. "Look out, Barney."

The man went to the door, and returned to announce that all was quiet. The two robbers issued forth with Oliver between them. Barney having made all fast, rolled himself up as before, and was soon asleep again.

It was now intensely dark. The fog was much heavier than it had been in the early part of the night, and the atmosphere was so damp that, although no rain fell, Oliver's hair and eyebrows, within a few minutes after leaving the house, had become stiff with the half-frozen moisture that was floating about. They crossed the bridge, and kept on towards the lights which he had seen before. They were at no great distance off; and, as they walked pretty briskly, they soon arrived at Chertsey.

"Slap through the town," whispered Sikes; "there'll be nobody in the way to-night to see us."

Toby acquiesced; and they hurried through the main street of the little town, which at that late hour was wholly deserted. A dim light shone at intervals from some bedroom window, and the hoarse barking of dogs occasionally broke the silence of the night. But there was nobody abroad, and they had cleared the town as the church-bell struck two.

Quickening their pace, they turned up a road upon the left hand. After walking about a quarter of a mile, they stopped before a detached house surrounded by a wall, to the top of which Toby Crackit, scarcely pausing to take breath, climbed in a twinkling.

"The boy next," said Toby. "Hoist him up; I'll catch hold of him."

Before Oliver had time to look round, Sikes had caught him under the arms, and in three or four seconds he and Toby were lying on the grass on the other side. Sikes followed directly. And they stole cautiously towards the house.

And now, for the first time, Oliver, well-nigh mad with grief and terror, saw that housebreaking and robbery, if not murder, were the objects of the expedition. He clasped his hands together and involuntarily uttered a subdued exclamation of horror. A mist came before his eyes, the cold sweat stood upon his ashy face, his limbs failed him, and he sank upon his knees.

"Get up!" murmured Sikes, trembling with rage, and drawing the pistol from his pocket; "get up, or I'll strew your brains upon the grass."

"Oh! for God's sake, let me go!" cried Oliver; "let me run away and die in the fields. I will never come near London—never, never! Oh! pray have mercy on me, and do not make me steal. For the love of all the bright Angels that rest in heaven, have mercy upon me!"

The man to whom this appeal was made swore a dreadful oath, and had cocked the pistol, when Toby, striking it from his grasp, placed his hand upon the boy's mouth and dragged him to the house.

"Hush!" cried the man, "it won't answer here. Say another word, and I'll do your business myself with a crack on the head. That makes no noise; and is quite as certain, and more genteel. Here, Bill, wrench the shutter open. He's game enough now, I'll engage. I've seen older hands of his age took the same way, for a minute or two, on a cold night."

Sikes, invoking terrific imprecations upon Fagin's head for sending Oliver on such an errand, plied the crowbar vigorously, but with little noise. After some delay, and some assistance from Toby, the shutter to which he had referred swung open on its hinges.

It was a little lattice-window, about five feet and a half above the ground, at the back of the house, which belonged to a scullery, or small brewing-place, at the end of the passage. The aperture was so small that the inmates had probably not thought it worth while to defend it more securely; but it was large enough to admit a boy of Oliver's size, nevertheless. A very brief exercise of Mr. Sikes's art sufficed to overcome the fastening of the lattice, and it soon stood wide open also.

"Now listen, you young limb," whispered Sikes, drawing a dark lantern from his pocket, and throwing the glare full on Oliver's face; "I'm a-going to put you through there. Take this light; go softly up the steps straight afore you, and along the little hall to the street door; unfasten it, and let us in."

"There's a bolt at the top you won't be able to reach," interposed Toby. "Stand upon one of the hall chairs. There are three there, Bill, with a jolly large blue unicorn and a gold pitchfork on 'em, which is the old lady's arms."

"Keep quiet, can't you?" replied Sikes, with a threatening look. "The room door is open, is it?"

"Wide," replied Toby, after peeping in to satisfy himself. "The game of that is, that they always leave it open with a catch, so that the dog, who's got a bed in here, may walk up and down the passage when he feels wakeful. Ha! ha! Barney 'ticed him away to-night. So neat!"

Although Mr. Crackit spoke in a scarcely audible whisper, and laughed without noise, Sikes imperiously commanded him to be silent, and to get to work. Toby complied, by first producing his lantern, and placing it on the ground; and then by planting himself firmly with his head against the wall beneath the window, and his hands upon his knees, so as to make a step of his back. This was no sooner done than Sikes, mounting upon him, put Oliver gently through the window with his feet first, and, without leaving hold of his collar, planted him safely on the floor inside.

"Take this lantern," said Sikes, looking into the room. "You see the stairs afore you?"

Oliver, more dead than alive, gasped out, "Yes." Sikes, pointing to the street-door with the pistol-barrel, briefly advised him to take notice that he was within shot all the way, and that if he faltered, he would fall dead that instant.

"It's done in a minute," said Sikes, in the same low whisper. "Directly I leave go of you, do your work. Hark!"

"What's that?" whispered the other man.

They listened intently.

"Nothing," said Sikes, releasing his hold of Oliver. "Now!"

In the short time he had had to collect his senses the boy had firmly resolved that, whether he died in the attempt or not, he would make one effort to dart upstairs from the hall and alarm the family. Filled with this idea, he advanced at once, but stealthily.

"Come back!" suddenly cried Sikes aloud. "Back! back!"

Scared by the sudden breaking of the dead stillness of the place, and by a loud cry which followed it, Oliver let his lantern fall, and knew not whether to advance or fly.

The cry was repeated–a light appeared–a vision of two terrified, half-dressed men at the top of the stairs swam before his eyes–a flash–a loud noise–a smoke–a crash somewhere, but where, he knew not–and he staggered back.

Sikes had disappeared for an instant; but he was up again, and had him by the collar before the smoke had cleared away. He fired his own pistol after the men, who were already retreating, and dragged the boy up.

"Clasp your arm tighter," said Sikes, as he drew him through the window. "Give me a shawl here. They've hit him. Quick! Damnation, how the boy bleeds!"

Then came the loud ringing of a bell, mingled with the noise of fire-arms, and the shouts of men, and the sensation of being carried over uneven ground at a rapid pace. And then the noises grew confused in the distance, and a cold deadly feeling crept over the boy's heart; and he saw or heard no more.

CHAPTER 21

Which contains the substance of a pleasant conversation between Mr. Bumble and a lady; and shows that even a beadle may be susceptible on some points

THE night was bitter cold. The snow lay on the ground, frozen into a hard thick crust, so that only the heaps that had drifted into by-ways and corners were affected by the sharp wind that howled abroad; which, as if expending increased fury on such prey as it found, caught it savagely up in clouds, and, whirling it into a thousand misty eddies, scattered it in air.

Such was the aspect, when Mrs. Corney, the matron of the workhouse to which our readers have been already introduced as the birthplace of Oliver Twist, sat herself down before a cheerful fire in her own little room, and glanced with no small degree of complacency at a small round table, on which stood a tray of corresponding size, furnished with all necessary materials for the most grateful meal that matrons enjoy. In fact, Mrs. Corney was about to solace herself with a cup of tea.

She had just tasted her first cup when she was disturbed by a soft tap at the room door.

"Oh, come in with you!" said Mrs. Corney, sharply. "Some of the old women dying, I suppose. They always die when I'm at meals. Don't stand there letting the cold air in, don't. What's amiss now, eh?"

"Nothing, ma'am, nothing," replied a man's voice.

"Dear me!" exclaimed the matron, in a much sweeter tone, "is that Mr. Bumble?"

"At your service, ma'am," said Mr. Bumble, who had been stopping outside to rub his shoes clean and to shake the snow off his coat, and who now made his appearance, bearing the cocked hat in one hand and a bundle in the other. "Shall I shut the door, ma'am?"

The lady modestly hesitated to reply, lest there should be any impropriety in holding an interview with Mr. Bumble with closed doors. Mr. Bumble taking advantage of the hesitation, and being very cold himself, shut it without further permission.

"Hard weather, Mr. Bumble," said the matron.

"Hard, indeed, ma'am," replied the beadle. "Anti-porochial weather this, ma'am. We have given away, Mrs. Corney, we have given away a matter of twenty quartern loaves, and a cheese and a half, this very blessed afternoon; and yet them paupers are not contented. This is the port wine, ma'am, that the board ordered for the infirmary–real, fresh, genuine port wine; only out of the cask this forenoon, clear as a bell, and no sediment!"

Having held the first bottle up to the light, and shaken it well to test its excellence, Mr. Bumble placed them both on the top of a chest of drawers; folded the handkerchief in which they had been wrapped; put it carefully in his pocket, and took up his hat as if to go.

"You'll have a very cold walk, Mr. Bumble," said the matron.

"It blows, ma'am," replied Mr. Bumble, turning up his coat-collar, "enough to cut one's ears off."

The matron looked from the little kettle to the beadle, who was moving towards the door; and as the beadle coughed preparatory to bidding her good-night, bashfully inquired whether–whether he wouldn't take a cup of tea?

Mr. Bumble instantly turned back his collar again, laid his hat and stick upon a chair, and drew another chair up to the table. As he slowly seated himself he looked at the lady. She fixed her eyes upon the little teapot. Mr. Bumble coughed again, and slightly smiled.

Mrs. Corney rose to get another cup and saucer from the closet. As she sat down, her eyes once again encountered those of the gallant beadle; she coloured, and applied herself to the task of making his tea. Again Mr. Bumble coughed—louder this time than he had coughed yet.

"Sweet? Mr. Bumble," inquired the matron, taking up the sugar-basin.

"Very sweet, indeed, ma'am," replied Mr. Bumble. He fixed his eyes on Mrs. Corney as he said this; and if ever a beadle looked tender, Mr. Bumble was that beadle at that moment.

The tea was made, and handed in silence. Mr. Bumble, having spread a handkerchief over his knees to prevent the crumbs from sullying the splendour of his shorts, began to eat and drink; varying these amusements, occasionally, by fetching a deep sigh, which, however, had no injurious effect upon his appetite, but, on the contrary, rather seemed to facilitate his operations in the tea and toast department.

The beadle drank his tea to the last drop, finished a piece of toast, whisked the crumbs off his knees, wiped his lips, and deliberately kissed the matron.

"Mr. Bumble," cried that discreet lady in a whisper; for the fright was so great that she had quite lost her voice—"Mr. Bumble, I shall scream!" Mr. Bumble made no reply, but in a slow and dignified manner put his arm round the matron's waist.

As the lady had stated her intention of screaming, of course she would have screamed at this additional boldness, but that the exertion was rendered unnecessary by a hasty knocking at the door; which was no sooner heard than Mr. Bumble darted, with much agility, to the wine-bottles, and began dusting them with great violence, while the matron sharply demanded who was there. It is worthy of remark, as a curious physical instance of the efficacy of a sudden surprise in counteracting the effects of extreme fear, that her voice had quite recovered all its official asperity.

"If you please, mistress," said a withered old female pauper, hideously ugly, putting her head in at the door, "Old Sally is a-going fast."

"Well, what's that to me?" angrily demanded the matron. "I can't keep her alive, can I?"

"No, no, mistress," replied the old woman, "nobody can; she's far beyond the reach of help. I've seen a many people die—little babes and great strong men—and I know when death's a-coming, well enough. But she's troubled in her mind; and when the fits are not on her—and that's not often, for she is dying very hard—she says she has got something to tell, which you must hear. She'll never die quiet till you come, mistress."

At this intelligence the worthy Mrs. Corney muttered a variety of invectives against old women who couldn't even die without purposely annoying their betters; and muffling herself in a thick shawl which she hastily caught up, briefly requested Mr. Bumble to stay till she came back, lest anything particular should occur, and bidding the messenger walk fast, and not be all night hobbling up the stairs, followed her from the room with a very ill grace, scolding all the way.

CHAPTER 22

Treats of a very poor subject. But is a short one; and may be found of some importance in this history

IT was no unfit messenger of death that had disturbed the quiet of the matron's room. Her body was bent by age, her limbs trembled with palsy, and her face, distorted into a mumbling leer, resembled more the grotesque shaping of some wild pencil than the work of Nature's hand.

The old crone tottered along the passages, and up the stairs, muttering some indistinct answers to the chidings of her companion; and being at length compelled to pause for breath, gave the light into her hand, and remained behind to follow as she might, while the more nimble superior made her way to the room where the sick woman lay.

It was a bare garret-room, with a dim light burning at the farther end. There was another old woman watching by the bed; and the parish apothecary's apprentice was standing by the fire, making a toothpick out of a quill.

"Cold night, Mrs. Corney," said this young gentleman, as the matron entered.

"Very cold indeed, sir," replied the mistress in her most civil tones, and dropping a curtsy as she spoke.

"You should get better coals out of your contractors," said the apothecary's deputy, breaking a lump on the top of the fire with the rusty poker; "these are not at all the sort of thing for a cold night."

"They're the board's choosing, sir," returned the matron. "The least they could do would be to keep us pretty warm, for our places are hard enough."

The conversation was here interrupted by a moan from the sick woman.

"Oh!" said the young man, turning his face towards the bed, as if he had previously quite forgotten the patient, "it's all U.P. there, Mrs. Corney."

"It is, is it, sir?" asked the matron.

"If she lasts a couple of hours, I shall be surprised," said the apothecary's apprentice, intent upon the toothpick's point. "It's a break-up of the system altogether. Is she dozing, old lady?"

The attendant stooped over the bed to ascertain, and nodded in the affirmative.

"Then perhaps she'll go off in that way, if you don't make a row," said the young man. "Put the light on the floor—she won't see it there."

The attendant did as she was told, shaking her head meanwhile, to intimate that the woman would not die so easily. Having done so, she resumed her seat by the side of the other nurse, who had by this time returned. The mistress, with an expression of impatience, wrapped herself in her shawl, and sat at the foot of the bed.

The apothecary's apprentice, having completed the manufacture of the toothpick, planted himself in front of the fire, and made good use of it for ten minutes or so, when, apparently growing rather dull, he wished Mrs. Corney joy of her job, and took himself off on tip-toe.

When they had sat in silence for some time, the two old women rose from the bed, and crouching over the fire, held out their withered hands to catch the heat. The flame threw a ghastly light on their shrivelled faces, and made their ugliness appear perfectly terrible, as, in this position, they began to converse in a low voice.

While they were thus employed, the matron, who had been impatiently watching until the dying woman should awaken from her stupor, joined them by the fire, and sharply asked how long she was to wait.

"Not long, mistress," replied the second woman, looking up into her face. "We have none of us long to wait for Death. Patience, patience! He'll be here soon enough for us all."

"Hold your tongue, you doting idiot!" said the matron sternly. "You, Martha, tell me–has she been in this way before?"

"Often," answered the first woman.

"But will never be again," added the second one; "that is, she'll never wake again but once–and mind, mistress, that won't be for long."

"Long or short," said the matron snappishly, "she won't find me here when she does wake. And take care, both of you, how you worry me again for nothing. It's no part of my duty to see all the old women in the house die; and I won't–that's more. Mind that, you impudent old harridans. If you make a fool of me again, I'll soon cure you, I warrant you!"

She was bouncing away, when a cry from the two women, who had turned towards the bed, caused her to look round. The patient had raised herself upright, and was stretching her arms towards them.

"Who's that?" she cried in a hollow voice.

"Hush, hush!" said one of the women, stooping over her. "Lie down, lie down!"

"I'll never lie down again alive!" said the woman, struggling. "I *will* tell her! Come here! Nearer! Let me whisper in your ear."

She clutched the matron by the arm, and forcing her into a chair by the bedside, was about to speak, when, looking round, she caught sight of the two old women bending forward in the attitude of eager listeners.

"Turn them away," said the woman drowsily. "Make haste! make haste!"

The two old crones, chiming in together, began pouring out many piteous lamentations that the poor dear was too far gone to know her best friends, and were uttering sundry protestations that they would never leave her, when the superior pushed them from the room, closed the door, and returned to the bedside. On being excluded, the old ladies changed their tones, and cried through the keyhole that old Sally was drunk–which, indeed, was not unlikely, since, in addition to a moderate dose of opium prescribed by the apothecary, she was labouring under the effects of a final taste of gin-and-water which had been privately administered, in the openness of their hearts, by the worthy old ladies themselves.

"Now listen to me," said the dying woman aloud, as if making a great effort to revive one latent spark of energy. "In this very room–in this very bed–I once nursed a pretty young creatur' that was brought into the house with her feet cut and bruised with walking, and all soiled with dust and blood. She gave birth to a boy, and died. Let me think–what was the year again?"

"Never mind the year," said the impatient auditor; "what about her?"

"Ay," murmured the sick woman, relapsing into her former drowsy state, "what about her–what about–I know!" she cried, jumping fiercely up, her face flushed, and her eyes starting from her head–"I robbed her, so I did! She wasn't cold–I tell you she wasn't cold when I stole it!"

"Stole what, for God's sake?" cried the matron, with a gesture as if she would call for help.

"*It!*" replied the woman, laying her hand over the other's mouth–"the only thing she had. She wanted clothes to keep her warm, and food to eat; but she had kept it safe, and had it in her bosom. It was gold, I tell you!– rich gold, that might have saved her life!"

"Gold!" echoed the matron, bending eagerly over the woman as she fell back. "Go on, go on–yes–what of it? Who was the mother? When was it?"

"She charged me to keep it safe," replied the woman, with a groan, "and trusted me as the only woman about her. I stole it in my heart when she first showed it me hanging round her neck; and the child's death, perhaps, is on me besides! They would have treated him better if they had known it all!"

"Known what?" asked the other. "Speak!"

"The boy grew so like his mother," said the woman, rambling on, and not heeding the question, "that I could never forget it when I saw his face. Poor girl! poor girl! She was so young, too! such a gentle lamb! Wait; there's more to tell. I have not told you all, have I?"

"No, no," replied the matron, inclining her head to catch the words as they came more faintly from the dying woman. "Be quick, or it may be too late!"

"The mother," said the woman, making a more violent effort than before –"the mother, when the pains of death first came upon her, whispered in my ear that if her baby was born alive, and thrived, the day might come when it would not feel so much disgraced to hear its poor young mother named. 'And oh, kind Heaven!' she said, folding her thin hands together, whether it be boy or girl, raise up some friends for it in this troubled world, and take pity upon a lonely, desolate child, abandoned to its mercy!' "

"The boy's name?" demanded the matron.

"They *called* him Oliver," replied the woman feebly. "The gold I stole was—"

"Yes, yes—what?"

She was bending eagerly over the woman to hear her reply; but drew back instinctively as she once again rose, slowly and stiffly, into a sitting posture, then clutching the coverlet with both hands, muttered some indistinct sound in her throat, and fell lifeless on the bed.

"Stone dead!" said one of the old women, hurrying in as soon as the door was opened.

"And nothing to tell, after all," rejoined the matron, walking carelessly away.

The two crones, to all appearance too busily occupied in the preparations for their dreadful duties to make any reply, were left alone, hovering about the body.

CHAPTER 23

Wherein Mrs. Corney relates her harrowing experience to Mr. Bumble

MRS. CORNEY, hurrying into the room, threw herself, in a breathless state, on a chair by the fireside, and covering her eyes with one hand, placed the other over her heart, and gasped for breath.

"Mrs. Corney," said Mr. Bumble, stooping over the matron, "what is this, ma'am? has anything happened, ma'am? Pray answer me; I'm on—on—" Mr. Bumble, in his alarm, could not immediately think of the word "tenter-hooks," so he said, "broken bottles."

"Oh, Mr. Bumble," cried the lady, "I've been so dreadfully put out!"

"Put out, ma'am!" exclaimed Mr. Bumble; "who has dared to—? I know!" said Mr. Bumble, cheeking himself with native majesty, "this is them wicious paupers!"

"It's dreadful to think of," said the lady, shuddering.

"Then *don't* think of it, ma'am," rejoined Mr. Bumble.

"I can't help it," whimpered the lady.

"Then take something, ma'am," said Mr. Bumble, soothingly. "A little of the wine?"

"Not for the world!" replied Mrs. Corney. "I couldn't—oh! The top shelf in the right-hand corner—oh!" Uttering these words, the good lady pointed distractedly to the cupboard, and underwent a convulsion from internal spasms. Mr. Bumble rushed to the closet, and snatching a pint green-glass bottle from the shelf thus incoherently indicated, filled a teacup with its contents, and held it to the lady's lips.

"I'm better now," said Mrs. Corney, falling back after drinking half of it.

Mr. Bumble raised his eyes piously to the ceiling in thankfulness, and bringing them down again to the brim of the cup, lifted it to his nose.

"Peppermint," exclaimed Mrs. Corney, in a faint voice, smiling gently on the beadle as she spoke. "Try it! There's a little—a little something else in it."

Mr. Bumble tasted the medicine with a doubtful look, smacked his lips, took another taste, and put the cup down empty.

"It's very comforting," said Mrs. Corney.

"Very much so indeed, ma'am," said the beadle. As he spoke, he drew a chair beside the matron, and tenderly inquired what had happened to distress her.

"Nothing," replied Mrs. Corney. "I am a foolish, excitable, weak creetur."

"Not weak, ma'am," retorted Mr. Bumble, drawing his chair a little closer. "Are you a weak creetur, Mrs. Corney?"

"We are all weak creeturs," said Mrs. Corney, laying down a general principle.

"So we are," said the beadle.

Nothing was said on either side for a minute or two afterwards. By the expiration of that time Mr. Bumble had illustrated the position by removing his left arm from the back of Mrs. Corney's chair, where it had previously rested, to Mrs. Corney's apron-string, round which it gradually became entwined.

"We are all weak creeturs," said Mr. Bumble.

Mrs. Corney sighed.

"Don't sigh, Mrs. Corney," said Mr. Bumble.

"I can't help it," said Mrs. Corney. And she sighed again.

"This is a very comfortable room, ma'am," said Mr. Bumble, looking round. "Another room and this, ma'am, would be a complete thing."

"It would be too much for one," murmured the lady.

"But not for two, ma'am," rejoined Mr. Bumble, in soft accents. "Eh, Mrs. Corney?"

Mrs. Corney dropped her head, when the beadle said this. The beadle dropped his, to get a view of Mrs. Corney's face. Mrs. Corney, with great propriety, turned her head away, and released her hand to get at her pocket-handkerchief; but insensibly replaced it in that of Mr. Bumble.

"The board allow you coals, don't they, Mrs. Corney?" inquired the beadle, affectionately pressing her hand.

"And candles," replied Mrs. Corney, slightly returning the pressure.

"Coals, candles, and house-rent firee," said Mr. Bumble. "Oh, Mrs. Corney, what a Angel you are!"

The lady was not proof against this burst of feeling. She sank into Mr.

Bumble's arms; and that gentleman, in his agitation, imprinted a passionate kiss upon her chaste nose.

"Such porochial perfection!" exclaimed Mr. Bumble rapturously. "You know that Mr. Slout is worse to-night, my fascinator?"

"Yes," replied Mrs. Corney bashfully.

"He can't live a week, the doctor says," pursued Mr. Bumble. "He is the master of this establishment; his death will cause a wacancy; that wacancy must be filled up. Oh, Mrs. Corney, what a prospect this opens! What a opportunity for a joining of hearts and housekeepings!"

Mrs. Corney sobbed.

"The little word?" said Mr. Bumble, bending over the bashful beauty. "The one little, little, little word, my blessed Corney?"

"Ye–ye–yes!" sighed out the matron.

"One more," pursued the beadle; "compose your darling feelings for only one more. When is it to come off?"

Mrs. Corney twice essayed to speak, and twice failed. At length, summoning up courage, she threw her arms round Mr. Bumble's neck, and said it might be as soon as ever he pleased, and that he was "a irresistible duck."

Matters being thus amicably and satisfactorily arranged, the contract was solemnly ratified in another teacupful of the peppermint mixture, which was rendered the more necessary by the flutter and agitation of the lady's spirits. While it was being disposed of, she acquainted Mr. Bumble with the old woman's decease.

"Very good," said the gentleman, sipping his peppermint. "I'll call at Sowerberry's as I go home, and tell him to send to-morrow morning. Was it that as frightened you, love?"

"It wasn't anything particular, dear," said the lady evasively.

"It must have been something, love," urged Mr. Bumble. "Won't you tell your own B.?"

"Not now," rejoined the lady; "one of these days. After we're married, dear."

"After we're married!" exclaimed Mr. Bumble. "It wasn't any impudence from any of them male paupers as—"

"No, no, love!" interposed the lady hastily.

"If I thought it was," continued Mr. Bumble–"if I thought as any one of 'em had dared to lift his vulgar eyes to that lovely countenance—"

"They wouldn't have dared to do it, love," responded the lady.

"They had better not!" said Mr. Bumble, clenching his fist. "Let me see any man, porochial or extra-porochial, as would presume to do it, and I can tell him that he wouldn't do it a second time!"

Unembellished by any violence of gesticulation, this might have seemed no very high compliment to the lady's charms; but as Mr. Bumble accompanied the threat with many warlike gestures, she was much touched with this proof of his devotion, and protested, with great admiration, that he was indeed a dove.

The dove then turned up his coat-collar, and put on his cocked hat; and, having exchanged a long and affectionate embrace with his future partner, once again braved the cold wind of the night, merely pausing for a few minutes. in the male paupers' ward, to abuse them a little with a view of satisfying himself that he could fill the office of workhouse-master with needful acerbity. Assured of his qualifications, Mr. Bumble left the building with a light heart, and bright visions of his future promotion, which served to occupy his mind until he reached the shop of the undertaker.

Now, Mr. and Mrs. Sowerberry having gone out to tea and supper, and Noah Claypole not being at any time disposed to take upon himself a greater amount of physical exertion than is necessary to a convenient performance of the two functions of eating and drinking, the shop was not closed, although it was past the usual hour of shutting up. Mr. Bumble tapped with his cane on the counter several times; but, attracting no attention, and beholding a light shining through the glass window of the little parlour at the back of the shop, he made bold to peep in and see what was going forward; and when he saw what *was* going forward, he was not a little surprised.

The cloth was laid for supper, and the table was covered with bread and butter, plates and glasses, a porter-pot, and a wine-bottle. At the upper end of the table Mr. Noah Claypole lolled negligently in an easy-chair, with his legs thrown over one of the arms, an open claspknife in one hand, and a mass of buttered bread in the other. Close beside him stood Charlotte, opening oysters from a barrel, which Mr. Claypole condescended to swallow with remarkable avidity. A more than ordinary redness in the region of the young gentleman's nose, and a kind of fixed wink in his right eye, denoted that he was in a slight degree intoxicated; and these symptoms were confirmed by the intense relish with which he took his oysters, for which nothing but a strong appreciation of their cooling properties, in cases of internal fever, could have sufficiently accounted.

"Here's a delicious fat one, Noah, dear!" said Charlotte! "try him, only this one."

"What a delicious thing is a oyster!" remarked Mr. Claypole, after he had swallowed it. "What a pity it is a number of 'em should ever make you feel uncomfortable; isn't it, Charlotte?"

"It's quite a cruelty," said Charlotte.

"So it is," acquiesced Mr. Claypole. "An't yer fond of oysters?"

"Not overmuch," replied Charlotte. "I like to see you eat 'em, Noah, dear, better than eating 'em myself."

"Lor!" said Noah reflectively; "how queer!"

"Have another," said Charlotte. "Here's one with such a beautiful delicate beard!"

"I can't manage any more", said Noah; "I'm very sorry. Come here, Charlotte, and I'll kiss yer."

"What!" said Bumble, bursting into the room. "Say that again, sir."

Charlotte uttered a scream, and hid her face in her apron. Mr. Claypole, without making any further change in his position than suffering his legs to reach the ground, gazed at the beadle in drunken terror.

"Say it again, you wile, owdacious fellow!" said Mr. Bumble. "How dare you mention such a thing, sir? And how dare you encourage him, you insolent minx? Kiss her!" exclaimed Mr. Bumble, in strong indignation. "Faugh!"

"I didn't mean to do it!" said Noah, blubbering. "She's always a-kissing of me, whether I like it or not."

"Oh, Noah," cried Charlotte reproachfully.

"Yer are; yer know ye are!" retorted Noah. "She's always a-doing of it, Mr. Bumble, sir; she chucks me under the chin, please, sir, and makes all manner of love!"

"Silence!" cried Mr. Bumble sternly. "Take yourself downstairs, ma'am. Noah, you shut up the shop; say another word till your master comes home at your peril; and when he does come home, tell him that Mr. Bumble said he was to send an old woman's shell after breakfast to-morrow morning. Do you hear, sir? Kissing!" cried Mr. Bumble, holding up his hands. "The sin and wickedness of the lower orders in this porochial district is frightful. If parliament don't take their abominable courses under consideration, this country's ruined, and the character of the peasantry gone for ever!" With these words, the beadle strode, with a lofty and gloomy, air, from the undertaker's premises.

CHAPTER 24

Looks after Oliver, and proceeds with his adventures

"WOLVES tear your throats!" muttered Sikes, grinding his teeth. "I wish I was among some of you; you'd howl the hoarser for it."

As Sikes growled forth this imprecation, with the most desperate ferocity that his desperate nature was capable of, he rested the body of the wounded boy across his bended knee, and turned his head for an instant to look back at his pursuers.

"Stop, you white-livered hound!" cried the robber, shouting after Toby Crackit, who, making the best use of his long legs, was already ahead. "Stop!"

The repetition of the word brought Toby to a dead standstill. For he was not quite satisfied that he was beyond the range of pistol-shot, and Sikes was in no mood to be played with.

"Bear a hand with the boy!" roared Sikes, beckoning furiously to his confederate. "Come back!"

Toby made a show of returning; but ventured, in a low voice, broken for want of breath, to intimate considerable reluctance as he came slowly along.

"Quicker!" cried Sikes, laying the boy in a dry ditch at his feet, and drawing a pistol from his pocket. "Don't play booty with me."

"It's all up, Bill!" cried Toby; "drop the kid, and show 'em your heels." With this parting advice, Mr. Crackit, preferring the chance of being shot by his friend to the certainty of being taken by his enemies, fairly turned tail, and darted off at full speed. Sikes clenched his teeth; took one look round; threw over the prostrate form of Oliver the cape in which he had been hurriedly, muffled; ran along the front of the hedge, as if to distract the attention of those behind from the spot where the boy lay; paused, for a second, before another hedge which met it at right angles; and whirling his pistol high into the air, cleared it at a bound, and was gone.

"Ho, ho, there!" cried a tremulous voice in the rear. "Pincher! Neptune! Come here, come here!"

The dogs, who, in common with their masters, seemed to have no particular relish for the sport in which they were engaged, readily answered to the command; and three men, who had by this time advanced some distance into the field, stopped to take counsel together.

"My advice, or, leastways, I should say, my *orders* is," said the fattest man of the party, "that we 'mediately go home again."

"I am agreeable to anything which is agreeable to Mr. Giles," said a shorter man, who was by no means of a slim figure, and who was very pale in the face, and very polite, as frightened men frequently are.

"I shouldn't wish to appear ill-mannered, gentlemen," said the third, who had called the dogs back; "Mr. Giles ought to know."

"Certainly," replied the shorter man; "and whatever Mr. Giles says, it isn't our place to contradict him. No, no, I know my sitiwation! Thank my stars, I know my sitiwation." To tell the truth, the little man *did* seem to know his situation, and to know perfectly well that it was by no means a desirable one, for his teeth chattered in his head as he spoke.

This dialogue was held between the two men who had surprised the burglars, and a travelling tinker, who had been sleeping in an outhouse, and who had been roused, together with his two mongrel curs, to join in the pursuit. Mr. Giles acted in the double capacity of butler and steward to the old lady of the mansion; and Brittles was a lad-of-all-work, who, having entered her service a mere child, was treated as a promising young boy still, though he was something past thirty.

Encouraging each other with such converse as this, but keeping very close together, notwithstanding, and looking apprehensively round whenever a fresh gust rattled through the boughs, the three men hurried back to a tree, behind which they had left their lantern, lest its light should inform the thieves in what direction to fire. Catching up the light, they made the best of their way home at a good round trot; and long after their dusky forms had ceased to be discernible, it might have been seen twinkling and dancing in the distance, like some exhalation of the damp and gloomy atmosphere through which it was swiftly borne.

Morning drew on apace. The air became more sharp and piercing as its first dull hue–the death of night rather than the bird of day–glimmered faintly in the sky. The objects which had looked dim and terrible in the darkness grew more and more defined, and gradually resolved into their familiar shapes. The rain came down thick and fast, and pattered, noisily, among the leafless bushes. But Oliver felt it not as it beat against him; for he still lay stretched, helpless and unconscious, on his bed of clay.

At length a low cry of pain broke the stillness that prevailed; and uttering it, the boy awoke. His left arm, rudely bandaged in a shawl, hung heavy and useless at this side; and the bandage was saturated with blood. He was so weak that he could scarcely raise himself into a sitting posture; and when he had done so, he looked feebly round for help, and groaned with pain. Trembling in every joint, from cold and exhaustion, he made an effort to stand upright; but, shuddering from head to foot, fell prostrate on the ground.

After a short return of the stupor in which he had been so long plunged, Oliver, urged by a creeping sickness at his heart which seemed to warn him that if he lay there he must surely die, got upon his feet and essayed to walk. His head was dizzy, and he staggered to and fro like a drunken man. But he kept up, nevertheless, and, with his head drooping languidly on his breast, went stumbling onward, he knew not whither.

Thus he staggered on, creeping, almost mechanically, between the bars of gates, or through hedge-gaps, as they came in his way, until he reached a road. Here the rain began to fall so heavily that it roused him.

He looked about, and saw that at no great distance there was a house, which perhaps he could reach. He summoned up all his strength for one last trial, and bent his faltering steps towards it.

As he drew nearer to this house, a feeling came over him that he had seen it before. He remembered nothing of its details, but the shape and aspect of the building seemed familiar to him.

That garden wall! On the grass inside he had fallen on his knees last night and prayed the two men's mercy. It was the very same house they had attempted to rob.

Oliver felt such fear come over him when he recognized the place that, for the instant, he forgot the agony of his wound, and thought only of flight. Flight! he could scarcely stand; and if he were in full possession of all the best powers of his slight and youthful frame, whither could he fly? He pushed against the garden-gate; it was unlocked, and swung open on its hinges. He tottered across the lawn, climbed the steps, knocked faintly at the door, and, his whole strength failing him, sunk down against one of the pillars of the little portico.

It happened that about this time Mr. Giles, Brittles, and the tinker, were recruiting themselves, after the fatigues and terrors of the night, with tea and sundries, in the kitchen. Not that it was Mr. Giles's habit to admit to too great familiarity the humbler servants, towards whom it was rather his wont to deport himself with a lofty affability, which, while it gratified, could not fail to remind them of his superior position in society. But death, fires, and burglary make all men equals; so Mr. Giles sat with his legs stretched out before the kitchen fender, leaning his left arm on the table, while with his right he illustrated a circumstantial and minute account of the robbery, to which his hearers (but especially the cook and housemaid, who were of the party) listened with breathless interest.

"It was about half-past two," said Mr. Giles, "or I wouldn't swear that it mightn't have been a little nearer three, when I woke up, and, turning round in my bed, as it might be so (here Mr. Giles turned round in his chair, and pulled the corner of the table-cloth over him to imitate bed-clothes), I fancied I heerd a noise."

At this point of the narrative the cook turned pale, and asked the housemaid to shut the door, who asked Brittles, who asked the tinker, who pretended not to hear.

"I heerd it now, quite apparent," resumed Mr. Giles. " 'Somebody,' I says, 'is forcing off a door, or window; what's to be done? I'll call up that poor lad, Brittles, and save him from being murdered in his bed, or his throat,' I says, 'may be cut from his right ear to his left without his ever knowing it.' "

Here all eyes were turned upon Brittles, who fixed his upon the speaker, and stared at him with his mouth wide open, and his face expressive of the most unmitigated horror.

"I tossed off the clothes," said Giles, throwing away the table-cloth, and looking very hard at the cook and housemaid, "got softly out of bed, seized the loaded pistol that always goes upstairs with the plate-basket, and walked on tip-toes to his room. 'Brittles,' I says, when I had woke him, 'don't be frightened!' "

Mr. Giles had risen from his seat, and taken two steps with his eyes shut, to accompany his description with appropriate action, when he started violently, in common with the rest of the company, and hurried back to his chair. The cook and housemaid screamed.

"It was a knock," said Mr. Giles, assuming perfect serenity. "Open the door, somebody."

Mr. Giles, as he spoke, looked at Brittles; but that young man, being naturally modest, probably considered himself nobody, and so held that the inquiry could not have any application to him; at all events, he tendered no reply. Mr. Giles directed an appealing glance at the tinker; but he had suddenly fallen asleep. The women were out of the question.

"If Brittles would rather open the door in presence of witnesses," said Mr. Giles, after a short silence, "I am ready to make one."

"So am I," said the tinker, waking up as suddenly as he had fallen asleep.

Brittles capitulated on these terms. Mr. Giles held on fast by the tinker's arm (to prevent his running away, as he pleasantly said), and gave the word of command to open the door. Brittles obeyed; and the group, peering timorously over each other's shoulders, beheld no more formidable object than poor little Oliver Twist, speechless and exhausted, who raised his heavy eyes, and mutely solicited their compassion.

"A boy," exclaimed Mr. Giles, valiantly pushing the tinker into the background. "What's the matter with the–eh?–why–Brittles–look here–don't you know?"

Brittles, who had got behind the door to open it, no sooner saw Oliver than he uttered a loud cry. Mr. Giles, seizing the boy by one leg and one arm (fortunately not the broken limb) lugged him straight into the hall, and deposited him at full length on the floor thereof.

In the midst of all this noise and commotion there was heard a sweet female voice, which quelled it in an instant.

"Giles!" whispered the voice from the stair-head.

"I'm here, miss," replied Mr. Giles. "Don't be frightened, miss; I ain't much injured. He didn't make a very desperate resistance, miss, I was soon too many for him."

"Hush!" replied the young lady: "you frighten my aunt as much as the thieves did. Is the poor creature much hurt?"

"Wounded desperate, miss," replied Giles, with indescribable complacency.

"He looks as if he was a-going, miss," bawled Brittles, in the same manner as before. "Wouldn't you like to come and look at him, miss, in case he should?"

"Hush, pray; there's a good man!" rejoined the young lady. "Wait quietly one instant, while I speak to aunt."

With a footstep as soft and gentle as the voice the speaker tripped away; and soon returned, with the direction that the wounded person was to be carried, carefully, upstairs to Mr. Giles's room; and that Brittles was to saddle the pony and betake himself instantly to Chertsey, from which place he was to dispatch, with all speed, a constable and a doctor.

"But won't you take one look at him first, miss?" asked Mr. Giles, with as much pride as if Oliver were some bird of rare plumage that he had skilfully brought down. "Not one little peep, miss?"

"Not now for the world," replied the young lady. "Poor fellow! Oh! treat him kindly, Giles, for my sake!"

The old servant looked up at the speaker, as she turned away, with a glance as proud and admiring as if she had been his own child. Then, bending over Oliver, he helped to carry him upstairs, with the care and solicitude of a woman.

Chapter 25

Has an introductory account of the inmates of the house to which Oliver resorted

In a handsome room—though its furniture had rather the air of old-fashioned comfort than of modern elegance—there sat two ladies at a well-spread breakfast-table. Mr. Giles, dressed with scrupulous care in a full suit of black, was in attendance upon them.

Of the two ladies, one was well advanced in years; but the highbacked oaken chair in which she sat was not more upright than she. Dressed with the utmost nicety and precision, in a quaint mixture of bygone costume, with some slight concessions to the prevailing taste, which rather served to point the old style pleasantly than to impair its effect, she sat, in a stately manner, with her hands folded on the table before her. Her eyes (and age had dimmed but little of their brightness) were attentively fixed upon her young companion.

The younger lady was in the lovely bloom and spring-time of womanhood. She was not past seventeen. Cast in so slight and exquisite a mould, so mild and gentle, so pure and beautiful, that earth seemed not her element, nor its rough creatures her fit companions. The very intelligence that shone in her deep blue eye, and was stamped upon her noble head, seemed scarcely of her age or of the world; and yet the changing expression of sweetness and good-humour, the thousand lights that played about the face and left no shadow there, above all, the smile, the cheerful, happy smile, were made for Home, for fireside peace and happiness.

She was busily engaged in the little offices of the table.

"And Brittles has been gone upwards of an hour, has he?" asked the old lady, after a pause.

An hour and twelve minutes, ma'am," replied Mr. Giles, referring to a silver watch, which he drew forth by a black ribbon.

"He is always slow," remarked the old lady.

Mr. Giles was apparently considering the propriety of indulging in a respectful smile himself, when a gig drove up to the garden-gate, out of which there jumped a fat gentleman, who ran straight up to the door, and who, getting quickly into the house, by some mysterious process, burst into the room, and nearly overturned Mr. Giles and the breakfast-table together.

"I never heard of such a thing!" exclaimed the fat gentleman. "My dear Mrs. Maylie—bless my soul—in the silence of night, too—I *never* heard of such a thing!"

With these expressions of condolence, the fat gentleman shook hands with both ladies, and drawing up a chair, inquired how they found themselves.

"You ought to be dead, positively dead with the fright," said the fat gentleman. "Why didn't you send? Bless me, my man should have come in a minute; and so would I; and my assistant would have been delighted; or anybody, I'm sure, under such circumstances. Dear, dear! So unexpected! In the silence of night, too!"

The doctor seemed especially troubled by the fact of the robbery having been unexpected, and attempted in the night time, as if it were the established custom of gentlemen in the housebreaking way to transact business at noon, and to make an appointment, by the two-penny post, a day or two previous.

"And you, Miss Rose," said the doctor, turning to the young lady, "I—"

"Oh! very much so, indeed," said Rose, interrupting him; "but there is a poor creature upstairs whom aunt wishes you to see."

"Ah! to be sure," replied the doctor, "so there is. That was your handiwork, Giles, I understand."

Mr. Giles, who had been feverishly putting the tea-cups to rights, blushed very red, and said that he had had that honour.

"Honour, eh?" said the doctor. "Well, I don't know; perhaps it's as honourable to hit a thief in a back kitchen as to hit your man at twelve paces. Fancy that he fired in the air, and you've fought a duel, Giles."

Mr. Giles, who thought this light treatment of the matter an unjust attempt at diminishing his glory, answered respectfully that it was not for the like of him to judge about that; but he rather thought it was no joke to the opposite party.

"Gad, that's true!" said the doctor. "Where is he? Show me the way. I'll look in again, as I come down, Mrs. Maylie. That's the little window that he got in at, eh? Well, I couldn't have believed it!"

Talking all the way, he followed Mr. Giles upstairs, and while he is going upstairs the reader may be informed that Mr. Losberne, a surgeon in the neighbourhood, known through a circuit of ten miles round as "the doctor," had grown fat, more from good-humour than from good living, and was as kind and hearty, and withal as eccentric, an old bachelor, as will be found in five times that space by any explorer alive.

The doctor was absent much longer than either he or the ladies had anticipated. A large flat box was fetched out of the gig; and a bedroom bell was rung very often; and the servants ran up and down stairs perpetually: from which tokens it was justly concluded that something important was going on above. At length he returned, and in reply to an anxious inquiry after his patient, looked very mysterious, and closed the door carefully.

"This is a very extraordinary thing, Mrs. Maylie," said the doctor, standing with his back to the door, as if to keep it shut.

"He is not in danger, I hope?" said the old lady.

"Why, that would *not* be an extraordinary thing, under the circumstances," replied the doctor; "though I don't think he is. Have you seen this thief?"

"No," rejoined the old lady.

"Nor heard anything about him?"

"No."

"I beg your pardon, ma'am," interposed Mr. Giles, "but I was going to tell you about him when Doctor Losberne came in."

"Rose wished to see the man," said Mrs. Maylie, "but I wouldn't hear of it."

"Humph!" rejoined the doctor; "there is nothing very alarming in his appearance. Have you any objection to see him in my presence?"

"If it be necessary," replied the old lady, "certainly not."

Chapter 26

Of the happy life Oliver began to lead with his kind friends

OLIVER'S ailings were neither slight nor few. In addition to the pain and delay attendant on a broken limb, his exposure to the wet and cold had brought on fever and ague; which hung about him for many weeks, and reduced him sadly. But at length he began, by slow degrees, to get better, and to be able to say sometimes, in a few tearful words, how deeply he felt the goodness of the two sweet ladies, and how ardently he hoped that, when he grew strong and well again, he could do something to show his gratitude—only something which would let them see the love and duty with which his breast was full—something, however slight, which would prove to them that their gentle kindness had not been cast away, but that the poor boy whom their charity had rescued from misery, or death, was eager to serve them with his whole heart and soul.

"Poor fellow!" said Rose, when Oliver had been one day feebly endeavouring to utter the words of thankfulness that rose to his pale lips, "you shall have many opportunities of serving us, if you will. We are going into the country, and my aunt intends that you shall accompany us. The quiet place, the pure air, and all the pleasures and beauties of spring, will restore you in a few days; and we will employ you in a hundred ways when you can bear the trouble."

"The trouble!" cried Oliver. "Oh! dear lady, if I could but work for you; if I could only give you pleasure by watering your flowers, or watching your birds, or running up and down, the whole day long to make you happy; what would I give to do it!"

"You shall give nothing at all," said Miss Maylie, smiling; "for, as I told you before, we shall employ you in a hundred ways; and if you only take half the trouble to please us that you promise now, you will make me very happy indeed."

"Happy, ma'am!" cried Oliver; "how kind of you to say so!"

"You will make me happier than I can tell you," replied the young lady. "To think that my dear good aunt should have been the means of rescuing any one from such sad misery as you have described to us would be an unspeakable pleasure to me; but to know that the object of her goodness and compassion was sincerely grateful and attached, in consequence, would delight me more than you can well imagine. Do you understand me?" she inquired, watching Oliver's thoughtful face.

"Oh, yes, ma'am, yes!" replied Oliver, eagerly; "but I was thinking that I am ungrateful now."

"To whom?" inquired the young lady.

"To the kind gentleman, and the dear old nurse, who took so much care of me before," rejoined Oliver. "If they knew how happy I am, they would be pleased, I am sure."

"I am sure they would," rejoined Oliver's benefactress; "and Mr. Losberne has already been kind enough to promise that, when you are well enough to bear the journey, he will carry you to see them."

"Has he, ma'am?" cried Oliver, his face brightening with pleasure. "I don't know what I shall do for joy when I see their kind faces once again!"

In a short time Oliver was sufficiently recovered to undergo the fatigue of this expedition, and one morning he and Mr. Losberne set out accordingly, in a little carriage which belonged to Mrs. Maylie. When they came to Chertsey Bridge, Oliver turned very pale, and uttered a loud exclamation.

"What's the matter with the boy?" cried the doctor, as usual, all in a bustle. "Do you see anything–hear anything–feel anything–eh?"

"That, sir," cried Oliver, pointing out of the carriage window. "That house!"

"Yes; well, what of it?–Stop, coachman. Pull up here," cried the doctor.– "What of the house, my man; eh?"

"The thieves; the house they took me to," whispered Oliver.

"The devil it is!" cried the doctor. "Hallo, there! let me out!"

But before the coachman could dismount from his box, he had tumbled out of the coach by some means or other, and running down to the deserted tenement, began kicking at the door like a madman.

"Hallo!" said a little, ugly, hump-backed man, opening the door so suddenly that the doctor, from the very impetus of his last kick, nearly fell forward into the passage. "What's the matter here?"

"Matter!" exclaimed the other, collaring him without a moment's reflection. "A good deal. Robbery is the matter."

"There'll be murder the matter, too," replied the hump-backed man, coolly, "if you don't take your hands off. Do you hear me?"

"I hear you," said the doctor, giving his captive a hearty shake. "Where's–confound the fellow, what's his rascally name–Sikes; that's it. Where's Sikes, you thief?"

The hump-backed man stared, as if in excess of amazement and indignation; and twisting himself, dexterously, from the doctor's grasp, growled forth a volley of horrid oaths, and retired into the house. Before he could shut the door, however, the doctor had passed into the parlour, without a word of parley. He looked anxiously round: not an article of furniture, not a vestige of anything animate or inanimate, not even the position of the cupboards, answered Oliver's description!

"Now!" said the hump-backed man, who had watched him keenly, "what do you mean by coming into my house in this violent way? Do you want to rob me, or to murder me? Which is it?"

"Did you ever know a man come out to do either in a chariot and pair,. you ridiculous old vampire?" said the irritable doctor.

"What do you want, then?" demanded the hunchback. "Will you take yourself off, before I do you a mischief? Curse you!"

"As soon as I think proper," said Mr. Losberne, looking into the other parlour, which, like the first, bore no resemblance whatever to Oliver's account of it. "I shall find you out, some day, my friend."

"Will you?" sneered the ill-favoured cripple. "If you ever want me, I'm here. I haven't lived here mad, and all alone, for five-and-twenty years, to be scared by you. You shall pay for this; you shall pay for this." And so saying, the misshapen little demon set up a hideous yell, and danced upon the ground, as if frantic with rage.

"Stupid enough, this," muttered the doctor to himself; "the boy must have made a mistake. Here! Put that in your pocket, and shut yourself up again." With these words he flung the hunchback a piece of money, and returned to the carriage.

"I am an ass!" said the doctor, after a long silence. "Did you know that before, Oliver?"

"No, sir."

"Then don't forget it another time."

"An ass," said the doctor again, after a further silence of some minutes. "Even if it had been the right place, and the right fellows had been there, what could I have done single-handed? And if I had had assistance, I see no good that I should have done, except leading to my own exposure, and an unavoidable statement of the manner in which I have hushed up this business. That would have served me right, though. I am always involving myself in some scrape or other by acting on impulse; and it might have done me good."

As Oliver knew the name of the street in which Mr. Brownlow resided, they were enabled to drive straight thither. When the coach turned into it, his heart beat so violently that he could scarcely draw his breath.

"Now, my boy, which house is it?" inquired Mr. Losberne.

"That! that!" replied Oliver, pointing eagerly out of the window. "The white house. Oh! make haste! Pray, make haste! I feel as if I should die; it makes me tremble so."

"Come, come!" said the good doctor, patting him on the shoulder. "You will see them directly, and they will be overjoyed to find you safe and well."

"Oh! I hope so!" cried Oliver. "They were so good to me–so very, very good to me."

The coach rolled on. It stopped. No; that was the wrong house–the next door. It went on a few paces, and stopped again. Oliver looked up at the windows, with tears of happy expectation coursing down his face.

Alas! the white house was empty, and there was a bill in the window, "To let."

"Knock at the next door," cried Mr. Losberne, taking Oliver's arm in his.–"What has become of Mr. Brownlow, who used to live in the adjoining house, do you know?"

The servant did not know, but would go and inquire. She presently returned, and said that Mr. Brownlow had sold off his goods, and gone to the West Indies, six weeks before. Oliver clasped his hands, and sank feebly backwards.

"Has his housekeeper gone, too?" inquired Mr. Losberne, after a moment's pause.

"Yes, sir," replied the servant. "The old gentleman, the housekeeper, and a gentleman who was a friend of Mr. Brownlow's all went together."

"Then turn towards home again," said Mr. Losberne to the driver; "and don't stop to bait the horses till you get out of this confounded London."

"The book-stall keeper, sir!" said Oliver. "I know the way there. See him, pray, sir! Do see him!"

"My poor boy, this is disappointment enough for one day," said the doctor. "Quite enough for both of us. If we go to the book-stall keeper's, we shall certainly find that he is dead, or has set his house on fire, or run away. No; home again straight!" And, in obedience to the doctor's impulse, home they went.

This bitter disappointment caused Oliver much sorrow and grief, even in the midst of his happiness; for he had pleased himself, many times during his illness, with thinking of all that Mr. Brownlow and Mrs. Bedwin would say to him, and what delight it would be to tell them how many long days and nights he had passed in reflecting on what they had done for him, and in bewailing his cruel separation from them. The hope of eventually clearing himself with them, too, and explaining how he had been forced away, had buoyed him up and sustained him under many of his recent trials; and now the idea that they should have gone so far, and carried with them the belief that he was an impostor and a robber–a belief which might remain uncontradicted to his dying day–was almost more than he could bear.

The circumstance occasioned no alteration, however, in the behaviour of his benefactors. After another fortnight, when the fine warm weather had fairly begun, and every tree and flower was putting forth its young leaves and rich blossoms, they made preparations for quitting the house at Chertsey for some months. Sending the plate, which had so excited the Jew's cupidity, to the bankers, and leaving Giles and another servant in care of the house, they departed to a cottage at some distance in the country, and took Oliver with them.

It was a happy time. The days were peaceful and serene; the nights brought with them neither fear nor care--no languishing in a wretched prison, or associating with wretched men--nothing but pleasant and happy thoughts. Every morning he went to a white-headed old gentleman who lived near the little church, who taught him to read better, and to write; and spoke so kindly, and took such pains, that Oliver could never try enough to please him. Then he would walk with Mrs. Maylie and Rose, and hear them talk of books; or perhaps sit near them in some shady place, and listen whilst the young lady read, which he could have done until it grew too dark to see the letters. Then he had his own lessons for the next day to prepare, and at this he would work hard, in a little room which looked into the garden, till evening came slowly on, when the ladies would walk out again, and he with them; listening with such pleasure to all they said, and so happy if they wanted a flower that he could climb to reach, or had forgotten anything he could run to fetch, that he could never be quick enough about it. When it became quite dark, and they returned home, the young lady would sit down to the piano, and play some pleasant air, or sing, in a low and gentle voice, some old song which it pleased her aunt to hear. There would be no candles lighted at such times as these; and Oliver would sit by one of the windows, listening to the sweet music, in a perfect rapture.

So three months glided away; three months which, in the life of the most blessed and favoured of mortals, might have been unmingled happiness, and which, in Oliver's were true felicity indeed. With the purest and most amiable generosity on one side, and the truest, warmest, soul-felt gratitude on the other, it is no wonder that, by the end of that short time, Oliver Twist had become completely domesticated with the old lady and her niece, and that the fervent attachment of his young and sensitive heart was repaid by their pride in, and attachment to, himself.

CHAPTER 27

*Wherein the happiness of Oliver and his friends experiences
a sudden check*

SPRING flew swiftly by, and summer came; and if the village had been beautiful at first, it was now in the full glow and luxuriance of its richness. Still the same quiet life went on at the little cottage, and the same

cheerful serenity prevailed among its inmates. Oliver had long since grown
stout and healthy; but health or sickness made no difference in his warm
feelings to those about him, though they do in the feelings of a great many
people. He was still the same gentle, attached, affectionate creature that
he had been when pain and suffering had wasted his strength, and when
he was dependent for every slight attention and comfort on those who
tended him.

One beautiful night they had taken a longer walk than was customary
with them; for the day had been unusually warm, and there was a brilliant
moon, and a light wind had sprung up which was unusually refreshing.
Rose had been in high spirits, too, and they had walked on in merry
conversation, until they had far exceeded their ordinary bounds. Mrs. Maylie
being fatigued, they returned more slowly home. The young lady, merely
throwing off her simple bonnet, sat down to the piano as usual. After
running abstractedly over the keys for a few minutes, she fell into a low
and very solemn air; and, as she played it, they heard her sob, as if she
were weeping.

"Rose, my dear!" said the elder lady.

Rose made no reply, but played a little quicker, as though the words had
roused her from some painful thoughts.

"Rose, my love!" cried Mrs. Maylie, rising hastily, and bending over
her. "What is this? In tears? My dear child, what distresses you?"

"Nothing, aunt; nothing," replied the young lady. "I don't know what
it is–I can't describe it–but I feel—"

"Not ill, my love?" interposed Mrs. Maylie.

"No, no! Oh, not ill," replied Rose, shuddering, as though some deadly
chillness were passing over her while she spoke; "I shall be better presently.
Close the window, pray!"

Oliver hastened to comply with her request. The young lady, making
an effort to recover her cheerfulness, strove to play some livelier tune; but
her fingers dropped powerless on the keys, and covering her face with her
hands, she sank upon a sofa, and gave vent to the tears which she was now
unable to repress.

"My child!" said the elderly lady, folding her arms about her, "I never
saw you thus before."

"I would not alarm you if I could avoid it," rejoined Rose; "but indeed
I have tried very hard, and cannot help this. I fear I *am* ill, aunt."

She was, indeed, for when candles were brought they saw that, in the
very short time which had elapsed since their return home, the hue of her
countenance had changed to a marble whiteness.

Oliver, who watched the old lady anxiously, observed that she was
alarmed by these appearances; and so, in truth, was he, but, seeing that she
affected to make light of them, he endeavoured to do the same, and they
so far succeeded that when Rose was persuaded by her aunt to retire for
the night, she was in better spirits, and appeared even in better health,

assuring them that she felt certain she should rise in the morning quite well.

"I hope," said Oliver, when Mrs. Maylie returned, "that nothing is the matter. She don't look well tonight, but—"

The old lady motioned to him not to speak, and, sitting herself down in a dark corner of the room, remained silent for some time. At length she said, in a trembling voice,-

"I hope not, Oliver. I have been very happy with her for some years–too happy, perhaps. It may be time that I should meet with some misfortune; but I hope it is not this."

"What?" inquired Oliver.

"The heavy blow," said the old lady, "of losing the dear girl who has so long been my comfort and happiness."

"Oh! God forbid!" exclaimed Oliver, hastily.

"Amen to that, my child!" said the old lady, wringing her hands.

An anxious night ensued. When morning came, Rose was in the first stage of a high and dangerous fever.

"We must be active, Oliver, and not give way to useless grief," said Mrs. Maylie, laying her finger on her lip, as she looked steadily into his face; "this letter must be sent, with all possible expedition, to Mr. Losberne. It must be carried to the market-town–which is not more than four miles off, by the footpath across the fields–and thence dispatched, by an express on horseback, straight to Chertsey. The people at the inn will undertake to do this; and I can trust to you to see it done, I know."

Oliver could make no reply, but looked his anxiety to be gone at once.

"Here is another letter," said Mrs. Maylie, pausing to reflect; "but whether to send it now, or wait until I see how Rose goes on, I scarcely know. I would not forward it unless I feared the worst."

"Is it for Chertsey, too, ma'am?" inquired Oliver, impatient to execute his commission, and holding out his trembling hand for the letter.

"No," replied the old lady, giving it to him mechanically. Oliver glanced at it, and saw that it was directed to Harry Maylie, Esquire, at some great lord's house in the country; where, he could not make out.

"Shall it go, ma'am?" asked Oliver, looking up, impatiently.

"I think not," replied Mrs. Maylie, taking it back. "I will wait until to-morrow."

With these words she gave Oliver her purse, and he started off, without more delay, at the greatest speed he could muster. . . .

It was something to feel certain that assistance was sent for, and that no time had been lost. Oliver hurried up the inn-yard with a somewhat lighter heart, and was turning out of the gateway when he accidentally stumbled against a tall man wrapped in a cloak, who was at that moment coming out of the inn door.

"Ha!" cried the man, fixing his eyes on Oliver, and suddenly recoiling. "What the devil's this?"

"I beg your pardon, sir," said Oliver; "I was in a great hurry to get home, and didn't see you were coming."

"Death!" muttered the man to himself, glaring at the boy with his large dark eyes. "Who would have thought it? Grind him to ashes! He'd start up from a marble coffin to come in my way!"

The man shook his fist and gnashed his teeth as he uttered these words incoherently. He advanced towards Oliver, as if with the intention of aiming a blow at him, but fell violently on the ground, writhing and foaming in a fit.

Oliver gazed for a moment at the struggles of the madman (for such he supposed him to be), and then darted into the house for help. Having seen him safely carried into the hotel, he turned his face homewards, running as fast as he could to make up for lost time, and recalling, with a great deal of astonishment and some fear the extraordinary behaviour of the person from who he had just parted.

The circumstance did not dwell long in his recollection, however; for when he reached the cottage there was enough to occupy his mind, and to drive all considerations of self completely from his memory.

Rose Maylie had rapidly grown worse, and before midnight was delirious. A medical practitioner, who resided on the spot, was in constant attendance upon her; and after first seeing the patient, he had taken Mrs. Maylie aside, and pronounced her disorder to be one of a most alarming nature. "In fact," he said, "it would be little short of a miracle if she recovered."

How often did Oliver start from his bed that night, and stealing out, with noiseless footstep, to the staircase, listen for the slightest sound from the sick chamber! How often did a tremble shake his frame, and cold drops of terror start upon his brow, when a sudden trampling of feet caused him to fear that something too dreadful to think of had even then occurred! And what had been the fervency of all the prayers he had ever uttered, compared with those he poured forth now, in the agony and passion of his supplication for the health and life of the gentle creature who was tottering on the deep grave's verge.

Morning came, and the little cottage was lonely and still. People spoke in whispers; anxious faces appeared at the gate, from time to time; and women and children went away in tears. All the livelong day, and for hours after it had grown dark, Oliver paced softly up and down the garden, raising his eyes every instant to the sick chamber, and shuddering to see the darkened window, looking as if death lay stretched inside. Mr. Losberne arrived. "It is hard," said the good doctor, turning away as he spoke; "so young, so much beloved, but there is very little hope."

CHAPTER 28

*Contains some introductory particulars relative to a young
gentleman who now arrives upon the scene; and a new
adventure which happened to Oliver*

THE night was fast closing in when Oliver returned homewards, laden with
flowers which he had culled, with peculiar care, for the adornment of the
sick chamber. As he walked briskly along the road, he heard behind him
the noise of some vehicle approaching at a furious pace. Looking round,
he saw that it was a post-chaise, driven at great speed; and as the horses
were galloping, and the road was narrow, he stood leaning against a gate
until it should have passed him.

As he dashed on, Oliver caught a glimpse of a man in a white nightcap,
whose face seemed familiar to him, although his view was so brief that he
could not identify the person. In another second or two the nightcap was
thrust out of the chaise-window, and a stentorian voice bellowed to the
driver to stop, which he did, as soon as he could pull up his horses. Then
the nightcap once again appeared, and the same voice called Oliver by his
name.

"Here!" cried the voice. "Master Oliver, what's the news? Miss Rose!
Master O-li-ver!"

"Is it you, Giles?" cried Oliver, running up to the chaise-door.

Giles popped out his nightcap again, preparatory to making some reply,
when he was suddenly pulled back by a young gentleman who occupied
the other corner of the chaise, and who eagerly demanded what was the
news.

"In a word!" cried the gentleman, "better or worse?"

"Better, much better!" replied Oliver, hastily.

"Thank Heaven!" exclaimed the gentleman.

The gentleman said not another word, but opening the chaise-door,
leaped out, and taking Oliver hurriedly by the arm, led him aside.

"You are quite certain? There is no possibility of any mistake on your
part, my boy, is there?" demanded the gentleman in a tremulous voice.
"Pray do not deceive me by awakening any hopes that are not to be
fulfilled."

"I would not for the world, sir," replied Oliver. "Indeed, you may
believe me. Mr. Losberne's words were that she would live to bless us all
for many years to come. I heard him say so."

All this time Mr. Giles, with the white nightcap on, had been sitting
upon the steps of the chaise, supporting an elbow on each knee, and wiping
his eyes with a blue cotton pocket-handkerchief dotted with white spots.

"I think you had better go on to my mother's in the chaise, Giles," said
the young gentleman. "I would rather walk slowly on, so as to gain a little
time before I see her. You can say I am coming."

"I beg your pardon, Mr. Harry," said Giles, giving a final polish to his ruffled countenance with the handkerchief, "but if you would leave the postboy to say that, I should be very much obliged to you. It wouldn't be proper for the maids to see me in this state, sir; I should never have any more authority with them if they did."

"Well," rejoined Harry Maylie, smiling, "you can do as you like. Let him go on with the luggage, if you wish it, and do you follow with us. Only first exchange that nightcap for some more appropriate covering, or we shall be taken for madmen."

Mr. Giles, reminded of his unbecoming costume, snatched off and pocketed his nightcap, and substituted a hat of grave and sober shape, which he took out of the chaise. This done, the postboy drove off, and Giles, Mr. Maylie, and Oliver, followed at their leisure.

As they walked along, Oliver glanced from time to time with much interest and curiosity at the newcomer. He seemed about five-and-twenty years of age, and was of the middle height; his countenance was frank and handsome; and his demeanour singularly easy and prepossessing. Notwithstanding the difference between youth and age, he bore so strong a likeness to the old lady, that Oliver would have had no great difficulty in imagining their relationship, even if he had not already spoken of her as his mother.

Mrs. Maylie was anxiously waiting to receive her son when he reached the cottage, and the meeting did not take place without great emotion on both sides.

"Mother!" whispered the young man, "why did you not write before?"

"I did," replied Mrs. Maylie; "but on reflection, I determined to keep back the letter until I had heard Mr. Losberne's opinion."

"But why," said the young man, "why run the chance of that occurring which so nearly happened? If Rose had—I cannot utter that word now—if this illness had terminated differently, how could you ever have forgiven yourself? How could I ever had known happiness again?"

"If that *had* been the case, Harry," said Mrs. Maylie, "I fear your happiness would have been effectually blighted; and that your arrival here, a day sooner or a day later, would have been of very, very little import."

"And who can wonder if it be so, mother?" rejoined the young man; "or why should I say, *if?* It is—it is—you know it, mother—you must know it!"

"I know that she deserves the best and purest love the heart of man can offer," said Mrs. Maylie; "I know that the devotion and affection of her nature require no ordinary return, but one that shall be deep and lasting. If I did not feel this, and know, besides, that a changed behaviour in one she loved would break her heart, I should not feel my task so difficult of performance, or have to encounter so many struggles in my own bosom, when I take what seems to me to be the strict line of duty."

"This is unkind, mother," said Harry. "Do you still suppose that I am a boy, ignorant of my own mind, and mistaking the impulses of my own soul?"

"I think, my dear son," returned Mrs. Maylie, laying her hand upon his shoulder, "that youth has many generous impulses which do not last; and that among them are some, which, being gratified, become only the more fleeting. Above all, I think," said the lady, fixing her eyes on her son's face, "that if an enthusiastic, ardent, and ambitious man marry a wife on whose name there is a stain, which, though it originate in no fault of hers, may be visited by cold and sordid people upon her, and upon his children also, and, in exact proportion to his success in the world, be cast in his teeth, and made the subject of sneers against him, he may, no matter how generous and good his nature, one day repent of the connection he formed in early life. And she may have the pain and torture of knowing that he does so."

"Mother," said the young man impatiently, "he would be a selfish brute, unworthy alike of the name of man and of the woman you describe, who acted thus."

"You think so now, Harry," replied his mother.

"And ever will!" said the young man. "The mental agony I have suffered, during the last two days, wrings from me the undisguised avowal to you of a passion which, as you well know, is not one of yesterday, nor one I have lightly formed. On Rose, sweet, gentle girl! my heart is set, as firmly as ever heart of man was set on woman. I have no thought, no view, no hope in life, beyond her; and if you oppose me in this great stake, you take my peace and happiness in your hands, and cast them to the wind. Mother, think better of this, and of me, and do not disregard the happiness of which you seem to think so little."

"Harry," said Mrs. Maylie, "it is because I think so much of warm and sensitive hearts, that I would spare them from being wounded. But we have said enough, and more than enough, on this matter just now."

"Let it rest with Rose, then," interposed Harry. "You will not press these overstrained opinions of yours, so far as to throw any obstacle in my way?"

"I will not," rejoined Mrs. Maylie; "but I would have you consider—"

"I *have* considered!" was the impatient reply. "Mother, I have considered years and years. I have considered ever since I have been capable of serious reflection. My feelings remain unchanged, as they ever will; and why should I suffer the pain of a delay in giving them vent, which can be productive of no earthly good? No! Before I leave this place Rose shall hear me."

"She shall," said Mrs. Maylie.

"There is something in your manner which would almost imply that she will hear me coldly, mother," said the young man.

"Not coldly," rejoined the old lady; "far from it."

"How then?" urged the young man. "She has formed no other attachment?"

"No, indeed," replied his mother; "you have, or I mistake, too strong a hold on her affections already. What I would say," resumed the old lady, stopping her son as he was about to speak, "is this. Before you stake your all on this chance, before you suffer yourself to be carried to the highest point of hope, reflect for a few moments, my dear child, on Rose's history, and consider what effect the knowledge of her doubtful birth may have on her decision—devoted as she is to us, with all the intensity of her noble mind, and with that perfect sacrifice of self which, in all matters, great or trifling, has always been her characteristic."

"What do you mean?"

"That I leave you to discover," replied Mrs. Maylie. "I must go back to her. God bless you!" And pressing her son's hand affectionately, she hastened from the room.

Mr. Losberne and Oliver had remained at another end of the apartment while this hurried conversation was proceeding. The former now held out his hand to Harry Maylie, and hearty salutations were exchanged between them. The doctor then communicated, in reply to multifarious questions from his young friend, a precise account of his patient's situation, which was quite as consolatory and full of promise as Oliver's statement had encouraged him to hope, and to the whole of which, Mr. Giles, who affected to be busy about the luggage, listened with greedy ears.

The remainder of the evening passed cheerfully away; for the doctor was in high spirits, and however fatigued or thoughtful Harry Maylie might have been at first, he was not proof against the worthy gentleman's good-humour, which displayed itself in a great variety of sallies and professional recollections, and an abundance of small jokes, which struck Oliver as being the drollest things he had ever heard, and caused him to laugh proportionately—to the evident satisfaction of the doctor, who laughed immoderately at himself, and made Harry laugh almost as heartily, by the very force of sympathy.

Oliver rose next morning in better heart, and went about his usual early occupations with more hope and pleasure than he had known for many days. The birds were once more hung out to sing in their old places, and the sweetest wild flowers that could be found were once more gathered to gladden Rose with their beauty and fragrance. The melancholy which had seemed to the sad eyes of the anxious boy to hang, for days past, over every object, beautiful as all were, was dispelled by magic. The dew seemed to sparkle more brightly on the green leaves, the air to rustle among them with a sweeter music, and the sky itself to look more blue and bright.

One beautiful evening, when the first shades of twilight were beginning to settle upon the earth, Oliver sat at the window, intent upon his books. He had been poring over them for some time; and as the day had been uncommonly sultry, and he had exerted himself a great deal, it is no disparagement to the authors, whoever they may have been, to say that gradually, and by slow degrees, he fell asleep.

Oliver knew perfectly well that he was in his own little room; that his books were lying on the table before him; and that the sweet air was stirring among the creeping plants outside. And yet he was asleep. Suddenly, the scene changed; the air became close and confined; and he thought, with a glow of terror, that he was in the Jew's house again. There sat the hideous old man, in his accustomed corner, pointing at him and whispering to another man, with his face averted, who sat beside him.

"Hush, my dear!" he thought he heard the Jew say; "it is he, sure enough. Come away."

"He!" the other man seemed to answer; "could I mistake him, think you? If a crowd of devils were to put themselves into his exact shape, and he stood amongst them, there is something that would tell me how to point him out. If you buried him fifty feet deep, and took me across his grave, I should know, if there wasn't a mark above it, that he lay buried there, I should!"

The man seemed to say this with such dreadful hatred that Oliver awoke with the fear, and started up.

Good Heaven! what was that which sent the blood tingling to his heart, and deprived him of his voice and of power to move? There–there–at the window–close before him–so close that he could have almost touched him before he started back; with his eyes peering into the room, and meeting his–there stood the Jew! and beside him, white with rage or fear, or both, were the scowling features of the very man who had accosted him at the inn-yard!

It was but an instant, a glance, a flash, before his eyes; and they were gone. But they had recognized him, and he them; and their look was as firmly impressed upon his memory as if it had been deeply carved in stone, and set before him from his birth. He stood transfixed for a moment, and then, leaping from the window into the garden, called loudly for help.

Chapter 29

Containing the unsatisfactory result of Oliver's Adventure;
and a conversation of some importance between
Harry Maylie and Rose

WHEN the inmates of the house, attracted by Oliver's cries, hurried to the spot from which they proceeded, they found him pale and agitated, pointing in the direction of the meadows behind the house, and scarcely able to articulate the words, "The Jew! the Jew!"

Mr. Giles was at a loss to comprehend what this outcry meant; but Harry Maylie, whose perceptions were something quicker, and who had heard Oliver's history from his mother, understood it at once.

"What direction did he take?" he asked, catching up a heavy stick which was standing in a corner.

"That," replied Oliver, pointing out the course the men had taken; "I missed them in an instant."

"Then they are in the ditch," said Harry. "Follow, and keep as near me as you can." So saying, he sprang over the hedge, and darted off with a speed which rendered it a matter of exceeding difficulty for the others to keep near him.

Giles followed as well as he could, and Oliver followed too; and in the course of a minute or two Mr. Losberne, who had been out walking, and just then returned, tumbled over the hedge after them, and picking himself up with more agility than he could have been supposed to possess, struck into the same course at no contemptible speed, shouting all the while, most prodigiously, to know what was the matter.

On they all went; nor stopped they once to breathe, until the leader, striking off into an angle of the field indicated by Oliver, began to search narrowly the ditch and hedge adjoining, which afforded time for the remainder of the party to come up, and for Oliver to communicate to Mr. Losberne the circumstances that had led to so vigorous a pursuit.

The search was all in vain; there were not even the traces of recent footsteps to be seen. They stood, now, on the summit of a little hill, commanding the open fields in every direction for three or four miles. There was the village in the hollow on the left; but, in order to gain that, after pursuing the track Oliver had pointed out, the men must have made a circuit of open ground, which it was impossible they could have accomplished in so short a time, A thick wood skirted the meadow land in another direction; but they could not have gained that covert for the same reason.

"It must have been a dream, Oliver," said Harry Maylie.

"Oh, no, indeed, sir," replied Oliver, shuddering at the very recollection of the old wretch's countenance; "I saw him too plainly for that. I saw them both, as plainly as I see you now."

"Who was the other?" inquired Harry and Mr. Losberne together.

"The very same man I told you of who came so suddenly upon me at the inn," said Oliver. "We had our eyes fixed full upon each other, and I could swear to him."

The two gentlemen watched Oliver's earnest face as he spoke, and looking from him to each other, seemed to feel satisfied of the accuracy of what he said.

Notwithstanding the evidently useless nature of their search, they did not desist until the coming on of night rendered its further prosecution hopeless; and, even then, they gave it up with reluctance. Giles was dispatched to the different alehouses in the village, furnished with the best description Oliver could give of the appearance and dress of the strangers. Of these, the Jew was, at all events, sufficiently remarkable to be remembered, supposing he had been seen drinking or loitering about; but Giles returned without any intelligence calculated to dispel or lessen the mystery.

On the next day further search was made, and the inquiries renewed; but with no better success. On the following day, Oliver and Mr. Maylie repaired to the market-town, in the hope of seeing or hearing something of the men there; but this effort was equally fruitless, and after a few days the affair began to be forgotten, as most affairs are, when wonder, having no fresh food to support it, dies away of itself.

Meanwhile Rose was rapidly recovering. She had left her room, was able to go out, and mixing once more with the family, carried joy into the hearts of all.

But, although this happy change had a visible effect on the little circle, and although cheerful voices and merry laughter were once more heard in the cottage, there was at times an unwonted restraint upon some there, even upon Rose herself, which Oliver could not fail to remark. Mrs. Maylie and her son were often closeted together for a long time; and more than once Rose appeared with traces of tears upon her face. After Mr. Losberne had fixed a day for his departure to Chertsey, these symptoms increased; and it became evident that something was in progress which affected the peace of the young lady, and of somebody else besides.

At length, one morning, when Rose was alone in the breakfast-parlour, Harry Maylie entered, and with some hesitation begged permission to speak with her for a few moments.

"A few—a very few—will suffice, Rose," said the young man, drawing his chair towards her. "What I shall have to say has already presented itself to your mind; the most cherished hopes of my heart are not unknown to you, though from my lips you have not yet heard them stated."

Rose had been very pale from the moment of his entrance; but that might have been the effect of her recent illness. She merely bowed, and bending over some plants that stood near, waited in silence for him to proceed.

"I—I—ought to have left here before," said Harry.

"You should, indeed," replied Rose. "Forgive me for saying so, but I wish you had."

"I was brought here by the most dreadful and agonizing of all apprehensions," said the young man—"the fear of losing the one dear being on whom my every wish and hope are fixed. You had been dying—trembling between earth and heaven."

There were tears in the eyes of the gentle girl as these words were spoken; and when one fell upon the flower over which she bent, and glistened brightly in its cup, making it more beautiful, it seemed as though the outpouring of her fresh young heart claimed kindred with the loveliest things in nature.

"An angel," continued the young man passionately, "a creature as fair and innocent of guile as one of God's own angels, fluttered between life and death. Oh! who could hope, when the distant world to which he was akin half opened to her view, that she would return to the sorrow and calamity of this! Rose, Rose, to know that you were passing away like some soft shadow which a light from above cast upon the earth; to have no hope that you would be spared to those who linger here; to know no reason why you should be; to feel that you belonged to that bright sphere whither so many of the fairest and the best have winged their early flight; and yet to pray, amid all these consolations, that you might be restored to those who loved you—these were distractions almost too great to bear. They were mine, by day and night; and with them came such a rushing torrent of fears and apprehensions, and selfish regrets lest you should die and never know how devotedly I loved you, as almost bore down sense and reason in its course. You recovered. Day by day, and almost hour by hour, some drop of health came back, and mingling with the spent and feeble stream of life which circulated languidly within you, swelled it again to a high and rushing tide. I have watched you change almost from death to life, with eyes that moistened with their eagerness and deep affection. Do not tell me that you wish I had lost this, for it has softened my heart to all mankind."

"I did not mean that," said Rose, weeping; "I only wish you had left here, that you might have turned to high and noble pursuits again—to pursuits well worthy of you."

"There is no pursuit more worthy of me, more worthy of the highest nature that exists, than the struggle to win such a heart as yours," said the young man, taking her hand. "Rose, my own dear Rose! for years—for years—I have loved you; hoping to win my way to fame, and then come proudly home and tell you it had been pursued only for you to share; thinking, in my day-dreams, how I would remind you, in that happy moment, of the many silent tokens I had given of a boy's attachment; and claim your hand, as in redemption of some old mute contract that had been sealed between us! That time has not arrived; but here, with no fame won, and no young vision realized, I give to you the heart so long your own, and stake my all upon the words with which you greet the offer."

"Your behaviour has ever been kind and noble," said Rose, mastering the emotions by which she was agitated. "As you believe that I am not insensible or ungrateful, so hear my answer."

"It is, that I may endeavour to deserve you; it is, dear Rose?"

"It is," replied Rose, "that you must endeavour to forget me; not as your old and dearly-attached companion, for that would wound me deeply, but as the object of your love. Look into the world; think how many hearts you would be proud to gain are there. Confide some other passion to me, if you will, and I will be the truest, warmest, and most faithful friend you have."

There was a pause, during which Rose, who had covered her face with one hand, gave free vent to her tears. Harry still retained the other.

"And your reasons, Rose," he said at length, in a low voice–"your reasons for this decision?"

"You have a right to know them," rejoined Rose. "You can say nothing to alter my resolution. It is a duty that I must perform. I owe it, alike to others and to myself."

"To yourself?"

"Yes, Harry. I owe it to myself, that I, a friendless, portionless girl, with a blight upon my name, should not give your friends reason to suspect that I had sordidly yielded to your first passion, and fastened myself, a clog, on all your hopes and projects. I owe it to you and yours, to prevent you from opposing, in the warmth of your generous nature, this great obstacle to your progress in the world."

"If your inclinations chime with your sense of duty—" Harry began.

"They do not," replied Rose, colouring deeply.

"Then you return my love?" said Harry. "Say but that, dear Rose–say but that, and soften the bitterness of this hard disappointment."

"If I could have done so, without doing heavy wrong to him I loved," rejoined Rose, "I could have—"

"Have received this declaration very differently?" said Harry. "Do not conceal that from me, at least, Rose."

"I could," said Rose. "Stay!" she added, disengaging her hand, "why should we prolong this painful interview? Most painful to me, and yet productive of lasting happiness not withstanding; for it *will* be happiness to know that I once held the high place in your regard which I now occupy; and every triumph you achieve in life will animate me with new fortitude and firmness. Farewell, Harry! As we have met to-day, we meet no more; but in other relations than those in which this conversation would have placed us, may we be long and happily entwined; and may every blessing that the prayers of a true and earnest heart can call down from the source of all truth and sincerity cheer and prosper you!

"Another word, Rose," said Harry. "Your reason in your own words. From your own lips let me hear it!"

"The prospect before you," answered Rose, firmly, "is a brilliant one. All the honours to which great talents and powerful connections can help men in public life are in store for you. But those connections are proud; and I will neither mingle with such as hold in scorn the mother who gave me life, nor bring disgrace or failure on the son of her who has so well supplied that mother's place. In a word," said the young lady, turning away, as her temporary firmness forsook her, "there is a stain upon my name which the world visits on innocent heads. I will carry it into no blood but my own, and the reproach shall rest alone on me."

"One world more, Rose. Dearest Rose one more!" cried Harry, throwing himself before her. "If I had been less–less fortunate, the world would call it–if some obscure and peaceful life had been my destiny–if I had been poor, sick, helpless–would you have turned from me then? Or has my probable advancement to riches and honour given this scruple birth?"

"Do not press to reply," answered Rose. "The question does not arise, and never will. It is unfair, unkind, to urge it."

"If your answer be what I almost dare to hope it is," retorted Harry, "it will shed a gleam of happiness upon my lonely way, and light the dreary path before me. It is not an idle thing to do so much, by the utterance of a few brief words, for one who loves you beyond all else. O Rose! in the name of my ardent and enduring attachment, in the name of all I have suffered for you, and all you doom me to undergo, answer me this one question!"

"Then, if your lot had been differently cast," rejoined Rose–"if you had been even a little, but not so far, above me–if I could have been a help and comfort to you in some humble scene of peace and retirement, and not a blot and drawback in ambitious and distinguished crowds, I should have been spared this trial. I have every reason to be happy, very happy, now; but then, Harry, I own I should have been happier."

Busy recollections of old hopes, cherished, as a girl, long ago, crowded into the mind of Rose while making this avowal; but they brought tears with them, as old hopes will when they come back withered, and they relieved her.

"I cannot help this weakness, and it makes my purpose stronger," said Rose, extending her hand. "I must leave you now, indeed."

"I ask one promise," said Harry. "Once, and only once more–say within a year, but it may be much sooner–let me speak to you again on this subject, for the last time."

"Not to press me to alter my right determination," replied Rose, with a melancholy smile; "it will be useless."

"No," said Harry; "to hear you repeat it, if you will–finally repeat it! I will lay at your feet whatever of station or fortune I may possess; and if you still adhere to your present resolution, will not seek, by word or act, to change it."

"Then let it be so," rejoined Rose; "it is but one pang the more, and by that time I may be enabled to bear it better."

She extended her hand again. But the young man caught her to his bosom, and imprinting one kiss on her beautiful forehead, hurried from the room.

CHAPTER 30

In which the reader may perceive a contrast, not uncommon in matrimonial cases

MR. BUMBLE sat in the workhouse parlour, with his eyes moodily fixed on the cheerless grate, whence, as it was stummer time, no brighter gleam proceeded than the reflection of certain sickly rays of the sun which were sent back from its cold and shining surface. A paper fly-cage dangled from the ceiling, to which he occasionally raised his eyes in gloomy thought; and, as the heedless insects hovered round the gaudy network, Mr. Bumble would heave a deep sigh, while a more gloomy shadow overspread his countenance. Mr. Bumble was meditating, and it might be that the insects brought to mind some painful passage in his own past life.

Nor was Mr. Bumble's gloom the only thing calculated to awaken a pleasing melancholy in the bosom of a spectator. There were not wanting other appearances, and those closely connected with his own person, which announced that a great change had taken place in the position of his affairs. The laced coat, and the cocked-hat, where were they? He still wore knee-breeches, and dark cotton stockings on his nether limbs; but they were not *the* breeches. The coat was wideskirted, and in that respect like *the* coat; but, oh, how different! The mighty cocked-hat was replaced by a modest round one. Mr. Bumble was no longer a beadle.

Mr. Bumble had married Mrs. Corney, and was master of the workhouse. Another beadle had come into power, and on him the cocked hat, gold-laced coat, and staff had all three descended.

"And to-morrow two months it was done!" said Mr. Bumble, with a sigh. "It seems a age."

Mr. Bumble might have meant that he had concentrated a whole existence of happiness into the short space of eight weeks; but the sigh—there was a vast deal of meaning in the sigh.

"I sold myself," said Mr. Bumble, pursuing the same train of reflection, "for six teaspoons, a pair of sugar-tongs, and a milk-pot; with a small quantity of second-hand furniture, and twenty pound in money. I went very reasonable, Cheap, dirt cheap!"

After making a tour of the house, and thinking for the first time that the poor-laws really were too hard on people, and that men who ran away from their wives, leaving them chargeable to the parish, ought, in justice, to be visited with no punishment at all, but rather rewarded as meritorious individuals who had suffered much, Mr. Bumble came to a room where some of the female paupers were usually employed in washing the parish linen, and whence the sound of voices in conversation now proceeded.

"Hem!" said Mr. Bumble, summoning up all his native dignity. "These women at least shall continue to respect the prerogative.—Hallo! hallo there! What do you mean by this noise, you hussies?"

Whith these words Mr. Bumble opened the door, and walked in with a very fierce and angry manner; which was at once exchanged for a most humiliated and cowering air, as his eyes unexpectedly rested on the form of his lady wife.

"My dear", said Mr. Bumble. "I didn't know you were here."

"Didn't know I was here!" repeated Mrs. Bumble. "What do *you* do here?"

"I thought they were talking rather too much to be doing their work properly, my dear," replied Mr. Bumble, glancing distractedly at a couple of old women at the wash-tub, who were comparing notes of admiration at the workhouse-master's humility.

"*You* thought they were talking too much?" said Mrs. Bumble. "What business is it of yours?"

"Why, my dear—" urged Mr. Bumble, submissively.

"What business is it of yours?" demanded Mrs. Bumble again.

"It's very true, you're matron here, my dear," submitted Mr. Bumble; "but I thought you mightn't be in the way just then."

"I'll tell you what, Mr. Bumble," returned his lady, "we don't want any of your interference. You're a great deal too fond of poking your nose into things that don't concern you, making everybody in the house laugh the moment your back is turned, and making yourself look like a fool every hour in the day. Be off! come!"

Mr. Bumble, seeing with excruciating feelings the delight of the two old paupers, who were tittering together most rapturously, hesitated for an instant. Mrs. Bumble, whose patience brooked no delay, caught up a bowl of soaps-suds, and motioning him towards the door, ordered him instantly to depart, on pain of receiving the contents upon his portly person.

What could Mr. Bumble do? He looked dejectedly round, and slunk away, and as he reached the door, the titterings of the paupers broke into a shrill chuckle of irrepressible delight. It wanted but this. He was degraded in their eyes; he had lost caste and station before the very paupers; he had fallen from all the height and pomp of beadleship to the lowest depth of the most snubbed henpeckery.

It was too much. Mr. Bumble boxed the ears of the boy who opened the gate for him (for he had reached the portal in his reverie), and walked distractedly into the street.

He walked up one street, and down another, until exercise had abated the first passion of his grief; and then the revulsion of feeling made him thirsty. He passed a great many public-houses, and at length paused before one on a by-way, whose parlour, as he gathered from a hasty peep over the blinds, was deserted, save by one solitary customer. It began to rain heavily at the moment. This determined him. Mr. Bumble stepped in, and ordering something to drink as he passed the bar, entered the apartment into which he had looked from the street.

The man who was seated there was tall and dark, and wore a large cloak. He had the air of a stranger, and seemed, by a certain haggardness in his look, as well as by the dusty soils on his dress, to have travelled some distance. He eyed Bumble askance as he entered, but scarcely deigned to nod his head in acknowledgment of his salutation.

Mr. Bumble had quite dignity enough for two—supposing even that the stranger had been more familiar—so he drank his gin-and-water in silence, and read the paper with great show of pomp and circumstance.

It so happened, however—as it will happen very often, when men fall into company under such circumstances—that Mr. Bumble felt, every now and then, a powerful inducement, which he could not resist, to steal a look at the stranger; and whenever he did so, he withdrew his eyes, in some confusion, to find that the stranger was at that moment stealing a look at him. Mr. Bumble's awkwardness was enhanced by the very remarkable expression of the stranger's eye, which was keen and bright, but shadowed by a scowl of distrust and suspicion, unlike anything he had ever observed before, and most repulsive to behold.

When they had encountered each other's glance several times in this way, the stranger, in a harsh, deep voice, broke silence.

"Were you looking for me," he said, "when you peered in at the window?"

"Not that I am aware of, unless you're Mr.—" Here Mr. Bumble stopped short, for he was curious to know the stranger's name, and thought, in his impatience, he might supply the blank.

"I see you were not," said the stranger, an expression of quiet sarcasm playing about his mouth, "or you would have known my name. You don't know it. I would recommend you not to inquire."

"I meant no harm, young man," observed Mr. Bumble, majestically.

"And have done none," said the stranger.

Another silence succeeded this short dialogue, which was again broken by the stranger.

"I have seen you before, I think," said he. "You were differently dressed at that time, and I only passed you in the street, but I should know you again. You were beadle here once; were you not?"

"I was," said Mr. Bumble, in some surprise; "porochial beadle."

"Just so," rejoined the other, nodding his head. "It was in that character I saw you. What are you now?"

"Master of the workhouse," rejoined Mr. Bumble, slowly and impressively, to check any undue familiarity the stranger might otherwise assume. "Master of the workhouse. young man!"

"You have the same eye to your own interest that you always had, I doubt not!" resumed the stranger, looking keenly into Mr. Bumble's eyes, as he raised them in astonishment at the question. "Don't scruple to answer freely, man. I know you pretty well, you see."

"I suppose a married man," replied Mr. Bumble, shading his eyes with his hand, and surveying the stranger from head to foot, in evident perplexity, "is not more averse to turning an honest penny when he can than a single one. Porochial officers are not so well paid that they can afford to refuse any little extra fee when it comes to them in a civil and proper manner."

The stranger smiled, and nodded his head again, as much as to say he had not mistaken his man; then rang the bell.

"Fill this glass again," he said, handing Mr. Bumble's empty tumbler to the landlord. "Let it be strong and hot. You like it so, I suppose?"

"Not too strong," replied Mr. Bumble, with a delicate cough.

"You understand what that means, landlord!" said the stranger dryly.

The host smiled, disappeared, and shortly afterwards returned with a steaming jorum, of which the first gulp brought the water into Mr. Bumble's eyes.

"Now listen to me," said the stranger, after closing the door and window. "I came down to this place to-day to find you out, and by one of those chances which the devil throws in the way of his friends sometimes, you walked into the very room I was sitting in while you were uppermost in my mind. I want some information from you. I don't ask you to give it for nothing, slight as it is. Put up that to begin with."

As he spoke he pushed a couple of sovereigns across the table to his companion carefully, as though unwilling that the chinking of money should be heard without. When Mr. Bumble had scrupulously examined the coins, to see that they were genuine, and had put them, up, with much satisfaction, in his waistcoat pocket, he went on:–

"Carry your memory back–let me see–twelve years, last winter."

"It's a long time," said Mr. Bumble. "Very good. I've done it."

"The scene, the workhouse."

"Good!"

"And the time, night."

"Yes."

"And the place, the crazy hole, wherever it was, in which miserable drabs brought forth the life and health so often denied to themselves–gave birth to puling children for the parish to rear; and hid their shame, rot 'em in the grave!"

"The lying-in room, I suppose?" said Mr. Bumble, not quite following the stranger's excited description.

"Yes," said the stranger. "A boy was born there."

"A many boys," observed Mr. Bumble, shaking his head, despondingly.

"A murrain on the young devils!" cried the stranger. "I speak of one; a meek-looking, pale-faced hound, who was apprenticed down here to a coffin-maker–I wish he had made his coffin, and screwed his body in it– and who afterwards ran away to London, as it was supposed."

"Why, you mean Oliver!–young Twist!" said Mr. Bumble; "I remember him, of course. There wasn't a obstinater young rascal—"

"It's not of him I want to hear; I've heard enough of him," said the stranger, stopping Mr. Bumble in the very outset of a tirade on the subject of poor Oliver's vices. "It's of a woman; the hag that nursed his mother. Where is she?"

"Where is she?" said Mr. Bumble, whom the gin-and-water had rendered facetious. "It would be hard to tell. There's no midwifery there, whichever place she's gone to; so I suppose she's out of employment, anyway."

"What do you mean?" demanded the stranger, sternly.

"That she died last winter," rejoined Mr. Bumble.

The man looked fixedly at him when he had given this Information, and although he did not withdraw his eyes for some time afterwards, his gaze gradually became vacant and abstracted, and he seemed lost in thought. For some time he appeared doubtful whether he ought to be relieved or disappointed by the intelligence; but at length he breathed more freely, and withdrawing his eyes, observed that it was no great matter. With that he rose as if to depart.

But Mr. Bumble was cunning enough, and he at once saw that an opportunity was open for the lucrative disposal of some secret in the possession of his better-half. He well remembered the night of old Sally's death, which the occurrences of that day had given him good reason to recollect as the occasion on which he had proposed to Mrs. Corney; and although that lady had never confided to him the disclosure of which she had been the solitary witness, he had heard enough to know that it related to something that had occurred in the old woman's attendance, as workhouse nurse, upon the young mother of Oliver Twist. Hastily calling this circumstance to mind, he informed the stranger, with an air of mystery, that one woman had been closeted with the old harridan shortly before she died, and that she could, as he had reason to believe, throw some light on the subject of his inquiry.

"How can I find her?" said the stranger, thrown off his guard, and plainly showing that all his fears (whatever they were) were aroused afresh by the intelligence.

"Only through me," rejoined Mr. Bumble.

"When?" cried the stranger hastily.

"To-morrow," rejoined Bumble.

"At nine in the evening," said the stranger, producing a scrap of paper, and writing down upon it an obscure address by the waterside, in characters that betrayed his agitation; "at nine in the evening bring her to me there. I needn't tell you to be secret. It's your interest."

With these words he led the way to the door, after stopping to pay for the liquor that had been drunk; and shortly remarking that their roads, were different, departed, without more ceremony than an emphatic repetition of the hour of appointment for the following night.

On glancing at the address, the parochial functionary observed that it contained no name. The stranger had not gone far, so he made after him to ask it.

"What do you want?" cried the man, turning quickly round, as Bumble touched him on the arm—"following me!"

"Only to ask a question," said the other, pointing to the scrap of paper. "What name am I to ask for?"

"Monks!" rejoined the man, and strode hastily away.

CHAPTER 31

Containing an account of what passed between
Mr. and Mrs. Bumble, and Monks, at their nocturnal interview

IT was a dull, close, overcast summer evening, and the clouds, which had been threatening all day, spread out in a dense and sluggish mass of vapour, already yielded large drops of rain, and seemed to presage a violent thunderstorm, when Mr. and Mrs. Bumble, turning out of the main street of the town, directed their course towards a scattered little colony of ruinous houses, distant from it some mile-and-a-half, or thereabouts, and erected on a low unwholesome swamp bordering upon the river.

It was before a ruinous building that the worthy couple paused, as the first peal of distant thunder reverberated in the air, and the rain commenced pouring violently down.

"The place should be somewhere here," said Bumble, consulting a scrap of paper he held in his hand.

"Hallo there!" cried a voice from above.

Following the sound, Mr. Bumble raised his head, and descried a man looking out of a door, breast-high, on the second story.

"Stand still a minute," cried the voice; "I'll be with you directly." With which the head disappeared, and the door closed.

"Is that the man?" asked Mr. Bumble's good lady.

Mr. Bumble nodded in the affirmative.

"Then, mind what I told you," said the matron, "and be careful to say as little as you can, or you'll betray us at once."

Mr. Bumble, who had eyed the building with very rueful looks, was apparently about to express some doubts relative to the advisability of proceeding any further with the enterprise just then, when he was prevented by the appearance of Monks, who opened a small door, near which they stood, and beckoned them inwards.

"Come!" he cried impatiently, stamping his foot upon the ground, "don't keep me here!"

The woman, who had hesitated at first, walked boldly in, without any further invitation. Mr. Bumble, who was ashamed or afraid to lag behind, followed, obviously very ill at ease, and with scarcely any of that remarkable dignity which was usually his chief characteristic.

"This is the woman, is it?" demanded Monks.

"Hem! That is the woman," replied Mr. Bumble, mindful of his wife's caution.

Bestowing something half-way between a smile and a scowl upon his two companions, and again beckoning them to follow him, the man hastened across the apartment, which was of considerable extent, but low in the roof. He was preparing to ascend a steep staircase, or rather ladder, leading to another floor of warehouses above, when a bright flash of lightning streamed down the aperture, and a peal of thunder followed, which shook the crazy building to its centre.

He led the way up the ladder and hastily closing the window-shutter of the room into which it led, lowered a lantern which hung at the end of a rope and pulley passed through one of the heavy beams in the ceiling, and which cast a dim light upon an old table and three chairs that were placed beneath it.

"Now," said Monks, when they had all three seated themselves, "the sooner we come to our business the better for all. The woman knows what it is; does she?"

The question was addressed to Bumble; but his wife anticipated the reply, by intimating that she was perfectly acquainted with it.

"He is right in saying that you were with this hag the night she died, and that she told you something—"

"About the mother of the boy you named," replied the matron, interrupting him. "Yes."

"The first question is, of what nature was her communication?" said Monks.

"That's the second," observed the woman, with much deliberation. "The first is, what may the communication be worth?"

"Who the devil can tell that without knowing of what kind it is?" asked Monks.

"Nobody better than you, I am persuaded," answered Mrs. Bumble, who did not want for spirit, as her yokefellow could abundantly testify.

"Humph!" said Monks significantly, and with a look of eager inquiry; "there may be money's worth to get, eh?"

"Perhaps there may," was the composed reply.

"Something that was taken from her," said Monks. "Something that she wore—something that—"

"What's it worth to you?" asked the woman, as collectedly as before.

"It may be nothing; it may be twenty pounds," replied Monks. "Speak out, and let me know which."

"Add five pounds to the sum you have named. Give me five-and-twenty pounds in gold," said the woman, "and I'll tell you all I know. Not before."

"Five-and-twenty pounds!" exclaimed Monks, drawing back.

"I spoke as plainly as I could," replied Mrs. Bumble. "It's not a large sum either."

"Not a large sum for a paltry secret, that may be nothing when it's told!" cried Monks impatiently, "and which has been lying dead for twelve years past or more!"

"Such matters keep well, and, like good wine, often double their value in course of time," answered the matron, still preserving the resolute indifference she had assumed. "As to lying dead, there are those who will lie dead for twelve thousand years to come, or twelve million, for anything you or I know, who will tell strange tales at last!"

"What if I pay it for nothing?" asked Monks, hesitating.

"You can easily take it away again," replied the matron. "I am but a woman–alone here, and unprotected."

"Not alone, my dear, nor unprotected neither," submitted Mr. Bumble, in a voice tremulous with fear; "*I* am here, my dear. And besides," said Mr. Bumble, his teeth chattering as he spoke, "Mr. Monks is too much of a gentleman to attempt any violence on porochial persons. Mr. Monks is aware that I am not a young man, my dear, and also that I am a little run to seed, as I may say; but he has heerd–I say I have no doubt Mr. Monks has heerd, my dear, that I am a very determined officer, with very uncommon, strength, if I'm once roused. I only want a little rousing; that's all."

As Mr. Bumble spoke, he made a melancholy feint of grasping his lantern with fierce determination, and plainly showed, by the alarmed expression of every feature, that he *did* want a little rousing, and not a little, prior to making any very warlike demonstration–unless, indeed, against paupers, or other person or persons trained down for the purpose.

"You are a fool," said Mrs. Bumble in reply, "and had better hold your tongue."

"He had better have cut it out before he came if he can't speak in a lower tone," said Monks grimly. "So! he's your husband, eh?"

"He my husband!" tittered the matron, parrying the question.

"I thought as much when you came in," rejoined Monks, marking the angry glance which the lady darted at her spouse as she spoke. "So much the better; I have less hesitation in dealing with two people, when I find that there's only one will between them. I'm in earnest. See here!"

He thrust his hand into a side-pocket, and producing a canvas bag, told out twenty-five sovereigns on the table, and pushed them over to the woman.

"Now," he said, "gather them up; and let's hear your story."

"When this woman, that we called old Sally, died," the matron began, "she and I were alone."

"Was there no one by?" asked Monks, in the same hollow whisper–"no sick wretch or idiot in some other bed? No one who could hear, and might, by possibility, understand?"

"Not a soul," replied the woman; "we were alone. *I* stood alone beside the body when death came over it."

"Good," said Monks, regarding her attentively. "Go on."

"She spoke of a young creature," resumed the matron, "who had brought a child into the world some years before, not merely in the same room, but in the same bed in which she then lay dying."

"Ay?" said Monks, with quivering lip, and glancing over his shoulder. "Blood! How things come about!"

"The child was the one you named to him last night," said the matron, nodding carelessly towards her husband; "the mother this nurse had robbed."

"In life?" asked Monks.

"In death," replied the woman, with something like a shudder. "She stole from the corpse, when it had hardly turned to one, that which the dead mother had prayed her, with her last breath, to keep for the infant's sake."

"She sold it?" cried Monks, with desperate eagerness; "did she sell it? Where? When? To whom? How long before?"

"As she told me, with great difficulty, that she had done this," said the matron, "she fell back and died."

"Without saying more?" cried Monks, in a voice which, from its very suppression, seemed only the more furious. "It's a lie! I'll not be played with. She said more. I'll tear the life out of you both, but I'll know what it was."

"She didn't utter another word," said the woman, to all appearance unmoved (as Mr. Bumble was very far from being) by the strange man's violence; "but she clutched my gown violently with one hand, which was partly closed; and when I saw that she was dead, and so removed the hand by force, I found it clasped a scrap of dirty paper."

"Which contained—" interposed Monks, stretching forward.

"Nothing," replied the woman; "it was a pawnbroker's duplicate."

"For what?" demanded Monks.

"In good time I'll tell you," said the woman. "I judge that she had kept the trinket for some time, in the hope of turning it to better account; had pawned it, and had saved or scraped together money to pay the pawn-broker's interest year by year, and prevent its running out, so that if anything came of it, it could still be redeemed. Nothing had come of it; and, as I tell you, she died with the scrap of paper, all worn and tattered, in her hand. The time was out in two days. I thought something might one day come of it, too, and so redeemed the pledge."

"Where is it now?" asked Monks, quickly.

"*There!*" replied the woman. And, as if glad to be relieved of it, she hastily threw upon the table a small kid bag, scarcely large enough for a

French watch, which Monks pouncing upon, tore open with trembling hands. It contained a little gold locket, in which were two locks of hair, and a plain gold wedding-ring.

"It has the word 'Agnes' engraved on the inside," said the woman. "There is a blank left for the surname; and then follows the date, which is within a year before the child was born. I found out that."

"And this is all," said Monks, after a close and eager scrutiny of the contents of the little packet.

With these words he suddenly wheeled the table aside, and pulling an iron ring in the boarding, threw back a large trap-door, which opened close at Mr. Bumble's feet, and caused that gentleman to retire several paces backward with great precipitation.

"Look down," said Monks, lowering the lantern into the gulf. "Don't fear me. I could have let you down, quietly enough, when you were seated over it, if that had been my game."

Thus encouraged, the matron drew near to the brink; and even Mr. Bumble himself, impelled by curiosity, ventured to do the same. The turbid water, swollen by the heavy rain, was rushing rapidly on below; and all other sounds were lost in the noise of its plashing and eddying against the green and slimy piles. There had once been a water-mill beneath; and the tide, foaming and chafing round the few rotten stakes and fragments of machinery that yet remained, seemed to dart onward with a new impulse when freed from the obstacles which had unavailingly attempted to stem its headlong course.

"If you flung a man's body down there, where would it be to-morrow morning?" said Monks, swinging the lantern to and fro in the dark well.

"Twelve miles down the river, and cut to pieces besides," replied Bumble, recoiling at the very thought.

Monks drew the little packet from his breast, where he had hurriedly thrust it, and tying it to a leaden weight, which had formed a part of some pulley, and was lying on the floor, dropped it into the stream. It fell straight and true as a die, clove the water with a scarcely audible splash, and was gone.

The three, looking into each other's faces, seemed to breathe more freely.

"There!" said Monks, closing the trap-door, which fell heavily back into its former position. "If the sea ever gives up its dead, as books say it will, it will keep its gold and silver to itself, and that trash among it. We have nothing more to say, and may break up our pleasant party."

They were no sooner gone than Monks, who appeared to entertain invincible repugnance to being left alone, called to a boy who had been hidden somewhere below; and bidding him go first, and bear the light, returned to the chamber he had just quitted.

CHAPTER 32

A strange interview

It was a family hotel in a quiet but handsome street near Hyde Park. As the brilliant light of the lamp which burnt before its door guided Nancy to the spot, the clock struck eleven. She had loitered for a few paces as though irresolute, and making up her mind to advance; but the sound determined her, and she stepped into the hall. The porter's seat was vacant. She looked round with an air of incertitude, and advanced towards the stairs.

"Now, young woman!" said a smartly-dressed female looking out from a door behind her, "who do you want here?"

"A lady who is stopping in this house," answered the girl.

"A lady!" was the reply, accompanied with a scornful look. "What lady?"

"Miss Maylie," said Nancy.

The young woman, who had, by this time, noted her appearance, replied only by a look of virtuous disdain, and summoned a man to answer her. To him Nancy repeated her request.

"What name am I to say?" asked the waiter.

"It's of no use saying any," replied Nancy.

"Nor business?" said the man.

"No, nor that either," rejoined the girl. "I must see the lady."

"Come!" said the man, pushing her towards the door. "None of this! Take yourself off."

"I shall be carried out if I go!" said the girl, violently; "and I can make that a job that two of you won't like to do. Isn't there anybody here?" she said, looking round, "that will see a simple message carried for a poor wretch like me?"

This appeal produced an effect on a good-tempered faced man-cook, who with some other of the servants was looking on, and who stepped forward to interfere.

"Take it up for her, Joe; can't you?" said this person.

"What's the good?" replied the man. "You don't suppose the young lady will see such as her; do you?"

This allusion to Nancy's doubtful character raised a vast quantity of chaste wrath in the bosoms of four housemaids, who remarked, with great fervour, that the creature was a disgrace to her sex, and strongly advocated her being thrown, ruthlessly, into the kennel.

"Do what you like with me," said the girl, turning to the men again; "but do what I ask you first, and I ask you to give this message, for God Almighty's sake."

The soft-hearted cook added his intercession, and the result was that the man who at first appeared undertook its delivery.

"What's it to be?" said the man, with one foot on the stairs.

"That a young woman earnestly asks to speak to Miss Maylie alone," said Nancy; and that if the lady will only hear the first word she has to say, she will know whether to hear her business or to have her turned out of doors as an impostor."

"I say," said the man, "you're coming it strong!"

"You give the message," said the girl, firmly; "and let me hear the answer."

The man ran upstairs. Nancy remained pale and almost breathless, listening with quivering lip to the very audible expression of scorn, of which the chaste housemaids were very prolific, and of which they became still more so when the man returned, and said the young woman was to walk upstairs.

"It's no good being proper in this world," said the first housemaid.

"Brass can do better than the gold what has stood the fire," said the second.

The third contented herself with wondering "what ladies was made of;" and the fourth took the first in a quartette of "Shameful!" with which the Dianas concluded.

Regardless of all this, for she had weightier matters at heart, Nancy followed the man, with trembling limbs, to a small ante-chamber, lighted by a lamp from the ceiling. Here he left her, and retired. The girl's life had been squandered in the streets and among the most noisome of the stews and dens of London, but there was something of the woman's original nature left in her still; and when she heard a light step approaching the door opposite to that by which she had entered, and thought of the wide contrast which the small room would in another moment contain, she felt burdened with the sense of her own deep shame, and shrunk as though she could scarcely bear the presence of her with whom she had sought this interview.

She raised her eyes sufficiently to observe that the figure which presented itself was that of a slight and beautiful girl; and then, bending them on the ground, tossed her head with affected carelessness as she said,—

"It's a hard matter to get to see you, lady. If I had taken offence, and gone away, as many would have done, you'd have been sorry for it one day, and not without reason, either."

"I am very sorry if anyone has behaved harshly to you," replied Rose. "Do not think of that. Tell me why you wished to see me. I am the person you inquired for."

The kind tone of this answer, the sweet voice, the gentle manner, the absence of any accent of haughtiness or displeasure, took the girl completely by surprise, and she burst into tears.

"Oh, lady, lady!" she said, clasping her hands passionately before her face, "if there was more like you, there would be fewer like me—there would, there would!"

"Sit down," said Rose earnestly; "you distress me. If you are in poverty or affliction, I shall be truly glad to relieve you if I can–I shall indeed. Sit down."

"Let me stand, lady," said the girl, still weeping, "and do not speak to me so kindly till you know me better. It is growing late. Is–is–that door shut?"

"Yes," said Rose, recoiling a few steps, as if to be nearer assistance in case she should require it. "Why?"

"Because," said the girl; "I am about to put my life, and the lives of others, in your hands. I am the girl that dragged little Oliver back to old Fagin's, the Jew's, on the night he went out from the house in Pentonville."

"You!" said Rose Maylie.

"I, lady," replied the girl; "I am the infamous creature you have heard of that lives among the thieves, and that never from the first moment I can recollect my eyes and senses opening on London streets have known any better life, or kinder words than they have given me, so help me God! Do not mind shrinking openly from me, lady. I am younger than you would think, to look at me, but I am well used to it. The poorest women fall back as I make my way along the crowded pavement."

"What dreadful things are these!" said Rose, involuntarily falling from her strange companion.

"Thank Heaven upon your knees, dear lady," cried the girl, "that you had friends to care for and keep you in your childhood, and that you were never in the midst of cold and hunger, and riot and drunkenness, and–and something worse than all–as I have been from my cradle. I may use the word, for the alley and the gutter were mine, as they will be my deathbed."

"I pity you!" said Rose in a broken voice. "It wrings my heart to hear you!"

"Heaven bless you for your goodness!" rejoined the girl. "If you knew what I am sometimes, you would pity me indeed. But I have stolen away from those who would surely murder me if they knew I had been here, to tell you what I have overheard. Do you know a man named Monks?"

"No," said Rose.

"He knows you," replied the girl; "and knew you were here, for it was by hearing him tell the place that I found you out."

"I never heard the name," said Rose.

"Then he goes by some other amongst us," rejoined the girl, "which I more than thought before. Some time ago, and soon after Oliver was put into your house on the night of the robbery, I–suspecting this man–listened to a conversation held between him and Fagin in the dark. I found out, from what I heard, that Monks–the man I asked you about, you know—"

"Yes," said Rose, "I understand."

"–That Monks," pursued the girl, "had seen him accidentally with two of our boys on the day we first lost him, and had known him directly to be the same child that he was watching for, though I couldn't make out why. A bargain was struck with Fagin, that if Oliver was got back he should have a certain sum; and he was to have more for making him a thief, which this Monks wanted for some purpose of his own."

"For what purpose?" asked Rose.

"He caught sight of my shadow on the wall as I listened in the hope of finding out," said the girl; "and there are not many people besides me that could have got out of their way in time to escape discovery. But I did; and I saw him no more till last night."

"And what occurred then?"

"I'll tell you, lady. Last night he came again. Again they went upstairs, and I, wrapping myself up so that my shadow should not betray me, again listened at the door. The first words I heard Monks say were these: 'So the only proofs of the boy's identity lie at the bottom of the river, and the old hag that received them from the mother is rotting in her coffin.' They laughed and talked of his success in doing this; and Monks, talking on about the boy, and getting very wild, said, that though he had got the young devil's money safely now, he'd rather have had it the other way; for what a game it would have been to have brought down the boast of the father's will, by driving him through every jail in town, and then hauling him up for some capital felony which Fagin could easily manage, after having made a good profit of him besides."

"What is all this?" said Rose.

"The truth, lady, though it comes from my lips," replied the girl. "Then he said, with oaths common enough in my ears, but strange to yours, that if he could gratify his hatred by taking the boy's life without bringing his own neck in danger, he would; but, as he couldn't, he'd be upon the watch to meet him at every turn in life, and if he took advantage of his birth and history, he might harm him yet. 'In short, Fagin,' he says, 'Jew, as you are, you never laid such snares as I'll contrive for my young brother, Oliver.'"

"His brother!" exclaimed Rose.

"Those were his words," said Nancy, glancing uneasily round, as she had scarcely ceased to do since she began to speak, for a vision of Sikes haunted her perpetually. "And more. When he spoke of you and the other lady, and said it seemed contrived by Heaven, or the devil, against him, that Oliver should come into your hands, he laughed, and said there was some comfort in that too, for how many thousands and hundreds of thousands of pounds would you not give, if you had them, to know who your two-legged spaniel was."

"You do not mean," said Rose, turning very pale, "to tell me that this was said in earnest?"

"He spoke in hard and angry earnest, if a man ever did," replied the girl, shaking her head. "He is an earnest man when his hatred is up. I know many who do worse things, but I'd rather listen to them all a dozen times than to that Monks once. It is growing late, and I have to reach home without suspicion of having been on such an errand as this. I must get back quickly."

"But what can I do?" said Rose. "To what use can I turn this communication without you? Back! Why do you wish to return to companions you paint in such terrible colours? If you repeat: his information to a gentleman whom I can summon in an instant from the next room, you can be consigned to some place of safety without half an hour's delay."

"I wish to go back," said the girl. "I must go back, because–how can I tell such things to an innocent lady like you?–because among the men I have told you of, there is one, the most desperate among them all, that I can't leave; no, not even to be saved from the life I am leading now."

"Your having interfered in this dear boy's behalf before," said Rose; "your coming here, at so great a risk, to tell me what you have heard; your manner, which convinces me of the truth of what you say; your evident contrition and sense of shame, all lead me to believe that you might be yet reclaimed. Oh!" said the earnest girl, folding her hands as the tears coursed down her face, "do not turn a deaf ear to the entreaties of one of your own sex; the first–the first, I do believe, who ever appealed to you in the voice of pity and compassion. Do hear my words, and let me save you yet for better things."

"Lady," cried the girl, sinking on her knees, "dear, sweet, angel lady, you *are* the first that ever blessed me with such words as these; and if I had heard them years ago they might have turned me from a life of sin and sorrow; but it is too late–it is too late!"

"It is never too late," said Rose, "for penitence and atonement."

"It is," cried the girl, writhing in the agony of her mind; "I cannot leave him now! I could not be his death!"

"Why should you be?" asked Rose.

"Nothing could save him," cried the girl. "If I told others what I have told you, and led to their being taken, he would be sure to die. He is the boldest, and has been so cruel!"

"Is it possible," cried Rose, "that for such a man as this you can resign every future hope, and the certainty of immediate rescue? It is madness."

"I don't know what it is," answered the girl; "I only know that it is so, and not with me alone, but with hundreds of others as bad and wretched as myself. I must go back. Whether it is God's wrath for the wrong I have done, I do not know; but I am drawn back to him through every suffering and ill-usage, and should be, I believe, if I knew that I was to die by his hand at last."

"What am I to do?" said Rose. "I should not let you depart from me thus."

"You should, lady, and I know you will," rejoined the girl, rising. "You will not stop my going because I have trusted in your goodness, and forced no promise from you as I might have done."

"Of what use, then, is the communication you have made?" said Rose. "This mystery must be investigated, or how will its disclosure to me benefit Oliver, whom you are anxious to serve?"

"You must have some kind gentleman about you that will hear it as a secret, and advise you what to do," rejoined the girl.

"But where can I find you again when it is necessary?" asked Rose. "I do not seek to know where these dreadful people live, but where will you be walking or passing at any settled period from this time?"

"Will you promise me that you will have my secret strictly kept, and come alone, or with the only other person that knows it; and that I shall not be watched or followed?" asked the girl.

"I promise you solemnly," answered Rose.

"Every Sunday night, from eleven until the clock strikes twelve," said the girl, without hesitation, "I will walk on London Bridge if I am alive."

"You will," said Rose, after a pause, "take some money from me, which may enable you to live without dishonesty—at all events, until we meet again?"

"Not a penny," replied the girl, waving her hand.

"Do not close your heart against all my efforts to help you," said Rose, stepping gently forward. "I wish to serve you indeed."

"You would serve me best, lady," replied the girl, wringing her hands, "if you could take my life at once; for I have felt more grief to think of what I am, to-night, than I ever did before, and it would be something not to die in the same hell in which I have lived. God bless you, sweet lady, and send as much happiness on your head as I have brought shame on mine!"

Thus speaking, and sobbing aloud, the unhappy creature turned away; while Rose Maylie, overpowered by this extraordinary interview, which had more the semblance of a rapid dream than an actual occurrence, sank into a chair, and endeavoured to collect her wandering thoughts.

CHAPTER 33

Containing fresh discoveries, and showing that surprises,
like misfortunes, seldom come alone

HER situation was, indeed, one of no common trial and difficulty. While she felt the most eager and burning desire to penetrate the mystery in which Oliver's history was enveloped, she could not but hold sacred the confidence which the miserable woman with whom she had just conversed had reposed in her, as a young and guileless girl. Her words and manner had touched Rose Maylie's heart; and mingled with her love for her young charge, and scarcely less intense in its truth and fervour, was her fond wish to win the outcast back to repentance and hope.

Disturbed by these different reflections–inclining now to one course and then to another, and again recoiling from all, as each successive consideration presented itself to her mind–Rose passed a sleepless and anxious night. After more communing with herself next day, she arrived at the desperate conclusion of consulting Harry.

"If it be painful to him," she thought, "to come back here, how painful will it be to me! But perhaps he will not come–he may write; or he may come himself, and studiously abstain from meeting me. He did when he went away. I hardly thought he would; but it was better for us both." And here Rose dropped her pen, and turned away, as though the very paper which was to be her messenger should not see her weep.

She had taken up the same pen, and laid it down again fifty times, and had considered and reconsidered the first line of her letter without writing the first word, when Oliver, who had been walking in the streets, with Mr. Giles for a bodyguard, entered the room in such breathless haste and violent agitation as seemed to betoken some new cause of alarm.

"What makes you look so flurried?" asked Rose, advancing to meet him.

"I hardly know how; I feel as if I should be choked," replied the boy. "Oh dear! to think I should see him at last, and you should be able to know that I have told all the truth!"

"I never thought you had told us anything but the truth," said Rose, soothing him. "But what is this?–of whom do you speak?"

"I have seen the gentleman," replied Oliver, scarcely able to articulate, "the gentleman who was so good to me–Mr. Brownlow, that we have so often talked about."

"Where?" asked Rose.

"Getting out of a coach," replied Oliver, shedding tears of delight, "and going into a house. I didn't speak to him–I couldn't speak to him, for he didn't see me, and I trembled so that I was not able to go up to him. But Giles asked for me, whether he lived there, and they said he did. Look here," said Oliver, opening a scrap of paper, "here it is; here's where he lives–I'm going there directly! Oh, dear me, dear me! what shall I do when I come to see him and hear him speak again?"

With her attention not a little distracted by these and a great many other incoherent exclamations of joy, Rose read the address, which was Craven Street, in the Strand, and very soon determined upon turning the discovery to account.

"Quick!" she said, "tell them to fetch a hackney-coach, and be ready to go with me. I will take you there directly, without a minute's loss of time. I will only tell my aunt that we are going out for an hour, and be ready as soon as you are."

Oliver needed no prompting to dispatch, and in little more than five minutes they were on their way to Craven Street. When they arrived there,

Rose left Oliver in the coach, under pretence of preparing the old gentleman to receive him; and sending up her card by the servant requested to see Mr. Brownlow on very pressing business. The servant soon returned, to beg that she would walk upstairs; and following him into an upper room. Miss Maylie was presented to an elderly gentleman of benevolent appearance, in a bottle-green coat. At no great distance from whom was seated another old gentleman, in nankeen breeches and gaiters; who did not look particularly benevolent, and who was sitting with his hands clasped on the top of a thick stick, and his chin propped thereupon.

"Dear me," said the gentleman in the bottle-green coat, hastily rising with great politeness, "I beg your pardon, young lady; I imagined it was some importunate person who—I beg you will excuse me. Be seated, pray."

"Mr. Brownlow, I believe, sir?" said Rose, glancing from the other gentleman to the one who had spoken.

"That is my name," said the old gentleman. "This is my friend, Mr. Grimwig. Grimwig, will you leave us for a few minutes?"

"I believe," interposed Miss Maylie, "that at this period of our interview I need not give that gentleman the trouble of going away. If I am correctly informed, he is cognizant of the business on which I wish to speak to you."

Mr. Brownlow inclined his head. Mr. Grimwig, who had made one very stiff bow, and risen from his chair, made another very stiff bow, and dropped into it again.

"I shall surprise you very much, I have no doubt," said Rose, naturally embarrassed; "but you once showed great benevolence and goodness to a very dear young friend of mine, and I am sure you will take an interest in hearing of him again."

"Indeed!" said Mr. Brownlow.

"Oliver Twist you know him as," replied Rose.

The words no sooner escaped her lips than Mr. Grimwig, who had been affecting to dip into a large book that lay on the table, upset it with a great crash, and, falling back in his chair, discharged from his features every expression but one of the most unmitigated wonder, and indulged in a prolonged and vacant stare; then, as if ashamed of having betrayed so much emotion, he jerked himself, as it were, by a convulsion into his former attitude, and looking out straight before him, emitted a long, deep whistle, which seemed, at last, not to be discharged on empty air, but to die away in the innermost recesses of his stomach.

Mr. Brownlow was no less surprised, although his astonishment was not expressed in the same eccentric manner. He drew his chair nearer to Miss Maylie's, and said,—

"Do me the favour, my dear young lady, to leave entirely out of the question that goodness and benevolence of which you speak, and of which nobody else knows anything, and if you have it in your power to produce any evidence which will alter the unfavourable opinion I was once induced to entertain of that poor child, in Heaven's name put me in possession of it."

"A bad one! I'll eat my head if he is not a bad one," growled Mr. Grimwig, speaking by some ventriloquial power, without moving a muscle of his face.

"He is a child of a noble nature and a warm heart," said Rose, colouring; "and that Power which has thought fit to try him beyond his years, has planted in his breast affections and feelings which would do honour to many who have numbered his days six times over."

"Now, Miss Maylie," said Mr. Brownlow, "to return to the subject in which your humanity is so much interested. Will you let me know what intelligence you have of this poor child? allowing me to premise that I exhausted every means in my power of discovering him; and that since I have been absent from this country, my first impression that he had imposed upon me, and had been persuaded by his former associates to rob me, has been considerably shaken."

Rose, who had had time to collect her thoughts, at once related, in a few natural words, all that had befallen Oliver since he left Mr. Brownlow's house—reserving Nancy's information for that gentleman's private ear—and concluding with the assurance that his only sorrow, for some months past, had been the not being able to meet with his former benefactor and friend.

"Thank God!" said the old gentleman. "This is great happiness to me—great happiness. But you have not told me where he is now, Miss Maylie. You must pardon my finding fault with you—but why not have brought him?"

"He is waiting in a coach at the door," replied Rose.

"At this door!" cried the old gentleman. With which he hurried out of the room, down the stairs, up the coach-steps, and into the coach, without another word.

When the room door closed behind him, Mr. Grimwig lifted up his head, and converting one of the hind legs of his chair into a pivot, described three distinct circles, with the assistance of his stick and the table, sitting in it all the time. After performing this evolution, he rose and limped as fast as he could up and down the room at least a dozen times, and then stopping suddenly before Rose, kissed her without the slightest preface.

"Hush!" he said, as the young lady rose in some alarm at this unusual proceeding. "Don't be afraid. I'm old enough to be your grandfather. You're a sweet girl; I like you. Here they are!"

In fact, as he threw himself at one dexterous dive into his former seat, Mr. Brownlow returned, accompanied by Oliver, whom Mr. Grimwig received very graciously; and if the gratification of that moment had been the only reward for all her anxiety and care in Oliver's behalf, Rose Maylie would have been well repaid.

"There is somebody else who should not be forgotten, by-the-bye," said Mr. Brownlow, ringing the bell. "Send Mrs. Bedwin here, if you please."

The old housekeeper answered the summons with all dispatch, and dropping a curtsy at the door, waited for orders.

"Why, you get blinder every day, Bedwin," said Mr. Brownlow rather testily.

"Well, that I do, sir," replied the old lady. "People's eyes, at my time of life, don't improve with age, sir."

"I could have told you that," rejoined Mr. Brownlow. "But put on your glasses, and see if you can't find out what you were wanted for, will you?"

The old lady began to rummage in her pocket for her spectacles. But Oliver's patience was not proof against this new trial, and yielding to his first impulse, he sprang into her arms.

"God be good to me!" cried the old lady, embracing him, "it is my innocent boy!"

"My dear old nurse!" cried Oliver.

"He would come back—I knew he would," said the old lady, holding him in her arms. "How well he looks, and how like a gentleman's son he is dressed again! Where have you been this long, long while? Ah! the same sweet face, but not so pale; the same soft eye, but not so sad. I never have forgot them or his quiet smile, but have seen them every day, side by side with those of my own dear children, dead and gone since I was a lightsome young creature." Running on thus, and now holding Oliver from her to mark how he had grown, now clasping him to her and passing her fingers fondly through his hair, the good soul laughed and wept upon his neck by turns.

Leaving her and Oliver to compare notes at leisure, Mr. Brownlow led the way into another room, and there heard from Rose a full narration of her interview with Nancy, which occasioned him no little surprise and perplexity. Rose also explained her reasons for not making a confidant of her friend Mr. Losberne in the first instance. The old gentleman considered that she had acted prudently, and readily undertook to hold solemn conference with the worthy doctor himself. To afford him an early opportunity for the execution of this design, it was arranged that he should call at the hotel at eight o'clock that evening, and that in the meantime Mrs. Maylie should be cautiously informed of all that had occurred. These preliminaries adjusted, Rose and Oliver returned home.

Rose had by no means overrated the measure of the good doctor's wrath. Nancy's history was no sooner unfolded to him than he poured forth a shower of mingled threats and execrations—threatened to make her the first victim of the combined ingenuity of Messrs. Blathers and Duff; and actually put on his hat preparatory to sallying forth immediately to obtain the assistance of those worthies. And doubtless he would, in this first outbreak, have carried the intention into effect without a moment's consideration of the consequences, if he had not been restrained, in part, by corresponding violence on the side of Mr. Brownlow, who was himself of an irascible temperament, and partly by such arguments and representations as seemed best calculated to dissuade him from his hot-brained purpose.

"Then what the devil is to be done?" said the impetuous doctor, when they had rejoined the two ladies. "Are we to pass a vote of thanks to all these vagabonds, male and female, and beg them to accept a hundred pounds or so a-piece, as a trifling mark of our esteem, and some slight acknowledgment of their kindness to Oliver?"

"Not exactly that," rejoined Mr. Brownlow, laughing, "but we must proceed gently and with great care."

"Gentleness and care!" exclaimed the doctor. "I'd send them one and all to—"

"Never mind where," interposed Mr. Brownlow. "But reflect whether sending them anywhere is likely to attain the object we have in view."

"What object?" asked the doctor.

"Simply the discovery of Oliver's parentage, and regaining for him the inheritance of which, if this story be true, he has been fraudulently deprived."

"Ah!" said Mr. Losberne, cooling himself with his pocket-handker-chief, "I almost forgot that."

"You see," pursued Mr. Brownlow; "placing this poor girl entirely out of the question and supposing it were possible to bring these scoundrels to justice without compromising her safety, what good should we bring about?"

"Hanging a few of them at least, in all probability," suggested the doctor, "and transporting the rest."

"Very good," replied Mr. Brownlow, smiling; "but no doubt they will bring that about for themselves in the fullness of time; and if we step in to forestall them, it seems to me that we shall be performing a very Quixotic act, in direct opposition to our own interest—or at least to Oliver's, which is the same thing."

"Now?" inquired the doctor.

"Thus. It is quite clear that we shall have extreme difficulty in getting to the bottom of this mystery, unless we can bring this man Monks upon his knees. That can only be done by stratagem, and by catching him when he is not surrounded by these people. For, suppose he were apprehended, we have no proof against him. He is not even (so far as we know, or as the facts appear to us) concerned with the gang in any of their robberies. If he were not discharged, it is very unlikely that he could receive any further punishment than being committed to prison as a rogue and vagabond; and of course ever afterwards his mouth is so obstinately closed that he might as well, for our purposes, be deaf, dumb, blind, and a idiot."

"Then," said the doctor impetuously, "I put it to you again, whether you think it reasonable that this promise to the girl should be considered binding—a promise made with the best and kindest intentions, but really—"

"Do not discuss the point, my dear young lady, pray," said Mr. Brownlow, interrrupting Rose as she was about to speak. "The promise shall be kept. I don't think it will, in the slightest degree, interfere with our proceedings. But before we can resolve upon any precise course of action, it will be necessary to see the girl, to ascertain from her whether she will point out this Monks, on the understanding that he is to be dealt with by us, and not by the law; or, if she will not or cannot do that, to procure from her such an account of his haunts and description of his person as will enable us to identify him. She cannot be seen until next Sunday night; this is Tuesday. I would suggest that in the meantime we remain perfectly quiet, and keep these matters secret even from Oliver himself."

Although Mr. Losberne received with many wry faces a proposal involving a delay of five whole days, he was fain to admit that no better course occurred to him just then; and as both Rose and Mrs. Maylie sided very strongly with Mr. Brownlow, that gentleman's proposition was carried unanimously.

"I should like," he said, "to call in the aid of my friend Grimwig. He is a strange creature, but a shrewd one, and might prove of material assistance to us. I should say that he was bred a lawyer, and quitted the bar in disgust because he had only one brief and a motion of course in twenty years, though whether that is a recommendation or not, you must determine for yourselves."

"I have no objection to your calling in your friend if I may call in mine," said the doctor.

"We must put it to the vote," replied Mr. Brownlow; "who may he be?"

"That lady's son, and this young lady's—very old friend," said the doctor, motioning towards Mrs. Maylie, and concluding with an expressive glance at her niece.

With these words the old gentleman gave his hand to Mrs. Maylie, and escorted her into the supper-room. Mr. Losberne followed, leading Rose; and the council was, for the present, effectually broken up.

Chapter 34

The appointment kept

THE church clock chimed three-quarters past eleven as two figures emerged on London Bridge. One, which advanced with a swift and rapid step, was that of a woman, who looked eagerly about her, as though in quest of some expected object; the other figure was that of a man, who slunk along in the deepest shadow he could find, and, at some distance, accommodated his pace to hers, stopping when she stopped, and as she moved again, creeping stealthily on, but never allowing himself, in the ardour of his pursuit, to gain upon her footsteps. Thus they crossed the bridge, from the Middlesex to the Surrey shore, when the woman, apparently disappointed in her anxious scrutiny of the foot-passengers, turned back. The movement was sudden; but he who watched her was not thrown off his guard by it, for, shrinking into one of the recesses which surmount the piers of the bridge, and leaning over the parapet the better to conceal his figure, he suffered her to pass by on the opposite pavement. When she was about the same distance in advance as she had been before, he slipped quietly down, and followed her again. At nearly the centre of the bridge she stopped. The man stopped too.

The girl had taken a few restless turns to and fro–closely watched meanwhile by her hidden observer–when the heavy bell of St. Paul's tolled for the death of another day. Midnight had come upon the crowded city. The palace, the night-cellar, the jail, the madhouse; the chambers of birth and death, of health and sickness; the rigid face of the corpse and the calm sleep of the child–midnight was upon them all.

The hour had not struck two minutes, when a young lady, accompanied by a grey-haired gentleman, alighted from a hackney-carriage within a short distance of the bridge, and having dismissed the vehicle, walked straight towards it. They had scarcely set foot upon its pavement, when the girl started, and immediately made towards them.

They walked onward, looking about them with the air of persons who entertained some very slight expectation which had little chance of being realized, when they were suddenly joined by this new associate. They halted, with an exclamation of surprise, but suppressed it immediately; for a man in the garments of a countryman came close up–brushed against them, indeed–at that precise moment.

"Not here," said Nancy hurriedly; "I am afraid to speak to you here. Come away–out of the public road–down the steps yonder."

As she uttered these words, and indicated, with her hand, the direction in which she wished them to proceed, the countryman looked round, and roughly asking what they took up the whole pavement for, passed on.

The steps to which the girl had pointed were those which, on the Surrey bank, and on the same side of the bridge as Saint Saviour's church, form a landing-stairs from the river. To this spot the man bearing the appearance of a countryman hastened, unobserved; and after a moment's survey of the place, he began to descend.

These stairs are a part of the bridge; they consist of three flights. Just below the end of the second, going down, the stone wall on the left terminates in an ornamental pilaster facing towards the Thames. At this point the lower steps widen, so that a person turning that angle of the wall is necessarily unseen by any others on the stairs who chance to be above him, if only a step. The countryman looked hastily round when he reached this point; and as there seemed no better place of concealment, and, the tide being out, there was plenty of room, he slipped aside, with his back to the pilaster, and there waited, pretty certain that they would come no lower, and that even if he could not hear what was said, he could follow them again with safety.

So tardily stole the time in this lonely place, and so eager was the spy to penetrate the motives of an interview so different from what he had been led to expect, that he more than once gave the matter up for lost, and persuaded himself either that they had stopped far above, or had resorted to some entirely different spot to hold their mysterious conversation. He was on the very point of emerging from his hiding-place, and regaining the road above, when he heard the sound of footsteps, and directly afterwards of voices almost close at his ear.

He drew himself straight upright against the wall, and, scarcely breathing, listened attentively.

"This is far enough," said a voice, which was evidently that of the gentleman. "I will not suffer the young lady to go any farther. Many people would have distrusted you too much to have come even so far, but you see I am willing to humour you."

"To humour me!" cried the voice of the girl whom he had followed. "You're considerate, indeed, sir. To humour me! Well, well, it's no matter."

"You were not here last Sunday night," he said.

"I couldn't come," replied Nancy; "I was kept by force."

"By whom?"

"Him that I told the young lady of before."

"You were not suspected of holding any communication with anybody on the subject which has brought us here to-night, I hope?" asked the old gentleman.

"No," replied the girl, shaking her head. "It's not very easy for me to leave him unless he knows why; I couldn't have seen the lady when I did, but that I gave him a drink of laudanum before I came away."

"Did he awake before you returned?" inquired the gentleman.

"No; and neither he nor any of them suspect me."

"Good," said the gentleman. "Now listen to me."

"I am ready," replied the girl, as he paused for a moment.

"This young lady," the gentleman began, "has communicated to me, and to some other friends who can be safely trusted, what you told her nearly a fortnight since. I confess to you that I had doubts, at first, whether you were to be implicitly relied upon, but now I firmly believe you are."

"I am," said the girl earnestly.

"I repeat that I firmly believe it. To prove to you that I am disposed to trust you, I tell you without reserve that we propose to extort the secret, whatever it may be, from the fears of this man Monks. But if—if," said the gentleman, "he cannot be secured, or, if secured, cannot be acted upon as we wish, you must deliver up the Jew."

"Fagin!" cried the girl, recoiling.

"That man must be delivered up by you," said the gentleman.

"I will not do it! I will never do it!" replied the girl. "Devil that he is, and worse than devil as he has been to me, I will never do that."

"You will not?" said the gentleman, who seemed fully prepared for this answer.

"Never!" returned the girl.

"Tell me why."

"For one reason," rejoined the girl firmly–"for one reason, that the lady knows and will stand by me in. I know she will, for I have her promise; and for this other reason, besides, that, bad life as he has led, I have led a bad life too. There are many of us who have kept the same courses together, and I'll not turn upon them, who might–any of them–have turned upon me, but didn't, bad as they are."

"Then," said the gentleman quickly, as if this had been the point he had been aiming to attain, "put Monks into my hands, and leave him to me to deal with."

"What if he turns against the others?"

"I promise you that in that case, if the truth is forced from him, there the matter will rest. There must be circumstances in Oliver's little history which it would be painful to drag before the public eye; and if the truth is once elicited, they shall go scot free."

"And if it is not?" suggested the girl.

"Then," pursued the gentleman, "this Jew shall not be brought to justice without your consent. In such a case I could show you reasons, I think, which would induce you to yield it."

"Have I the lady's promise for that?" asked the girl.

"You have," replied Rose–"my true and faithful pledge."

"Monks would never learn how you knew what you do?" said the girl, after a short pause.

"Never," replied the gentleman. "The intelligence should be so brought to bear upon him that he could never even guess."

"I have been a liar, and among liars from a little child," said the girl, after another interval of silence, "but I will take your words."

After receiving an assurance from both that she might safely do so, she proceeded, in a voice so low that it was often difficult for the listener to discover even the purport of what she said, to describe, by name and situation, the public-house whence she had been followed that night. From the manner in which she occasionally paused, it appeared as if the gentleman were making some hasty notes of the information she communicated. When she had thoroughly explained the localities of the place, the best position from which to watch it without exciting observation, and the night and hour on which Monks was most in the habit of frequenting it, she seemed to consider for a few moments, for the purpose of recalling his features and appearance more forcibly to her recollection.

"He is tall," said the girl, "and a strongly made man, but not stout. He has a lurking walk; and as he walks, constantly looks over his shoulder, first on one side and then on the other. Don't forget that, for his eyes are sunk in his head so much deeper than any other man's, that you might almost tell him by that alone. His face is dark, like his hair and eyes; and, although he can't be more than six- or eight-and-twenty, withered and haggard. His lips are often discoloured and disfigured with the marks of teeth; for he has desperate fits, and sometimes even bites his hands and covers them with wounds—why did you start?" said the girl, stopping suddenly.

The gentleman replied, in a hurried manner, that he was not conscious of having done so, and begged her to proceed.

"Part of this," said the girl, "I've drawn out from other people at the house I tell you of, for I have only seen him twice, and both times he was covered up in a large cloak. I think that's all I can give you to know him by. Stay, though," she added. "Upon his throat, so high that you can see a part of it below his neckerchief when he turns his face, there is—"

"A broad red mark, like a burn or scald!" cried the gentleman.

"How's this!" said the girl. "You know him!"

The young lady uttered a cry of surprise, and for a few moments they were so still that the listener could distinctly hear them breathe.

"I think I do," said the gentleman, breaking silence. "I should, by your description. We shall see. Many people are singularly like each other. It may not be the same."

As he expressed himself to this effect, with assumed carelessness, he took a step or two nearer the concealed spy, as the latter could tell from the distinctness with which he heard him mutter, "It must be he!"

"Now," he said, returning—so it seemed by the sound—to the post where he had stood before, "you have given us most valuable assistance, young woman, and I wish you to be the better for it. What can I do to serve you?"

"Nothing," replied Nancy.

"You will not persist in saying that," rejoined the gentleman, with a voice and emphasis of kindness that might have touched a much harder and more obdurate heart. "Think now. Tell me."

"Nothing, sir," rejoined the girl, weeping. "You can do nothing to help me. I am past all hope, indeed."

"You put yourself beyond its pale," said the gentleman. "The past has been a dreary waste with you, of youthful energies misspent, and such priceless treasures lavished, as the Creator bestows but once and never grants again; but, for the future, you may hope. I do not say that it is in our power to offer you peace of heart and mind, for that must come as you seek it; but a quiet asylum, either in England, or, if you fear to remain here, in some foreign country, it is not only within the compass of our ability, but our most anxious wish to secure you. Before the dawn of morning, before this river wakes to the first glimpse of daylight, you shall be placed as entirely beyond the reach of your former associates, and leave as utter an absence of all trace behind you, as if you were to disappear from the earth this moment. Come! I would not have you go back to exchange one word with any old companion, or take one look at any old haunt, or breathe the very air which is pestilence and death to you. Quit them all, while there is time and opportunity!"

"She will be persuaded now!" cried the young lady. "She hesitates, I am sure."

"I fear not, my dear," said the gentleman.

"No, sir, I do not," replied the girl, after a short struggle. "I am chained to my old life. I loathe and hate it now, but I cannot leave it. I must have gone too far to turn back—and yet I didn't know, for if you had spoken to me so, some time ago, I should have laughed it off. But," she said, looking hastily round, "this fear comes over me again. I must go home."

"Home!" repeated the young lady, with great stress upon the word.

"Home, lady," rejoined the girl—"to such a home as I have raised for myself with the work of my whole life. Let us part. I shall be watched or seen. Go! go! If I have done you any service, all I ask is, that you leave me, and let me go my way alone."

"It is useless," said the gentleman with a sigh. "We compromise her safety, perhaps, by staying here. We may have detained her longer than she expected already."

"Yes, yes," urged the girl. "You have."

"What," cried the young lady, "can be the end of this poor creature's life?"

"What?" repeated the girl. "Look before you, lady. Look at that dark water. How many times do you read of such as I who spring into the tide, and leave no living thing to care for or bewail them! It may be years hence, or it may be only months, but I shall come to that at last."

"Do not speak thus, pray," returned the young lady, sobbing.

"It will never reach your ears, dear lady; and God forbid such horrors should!" replied the girl. "Good-night, good-night!"

The gentleman turned away.

"This purse," cried the young lady; "take it for my sake, that you may have some resource in an hour of need and trouble."

"No!" replied the girl. "I have not done this for money. Let me have that to think of. And yet—give me something that you have worn. I should like to have something—no, no, not a ring—your gloves or handkerchief—anything that I can keep, as having belonged to you, sweet lady. There. Bless you! God bless you! Good-night, good-night!"

The violent agitation of the girl, and the apprehension of some discovery which would subject her to ill-usage and violence, seemed to determine the gentleman to leave her, as she requested. The sound of retreating footsteps were audible, and the voices ceased.

The two figures of the young lady and her companion soon afterwards appeared upon the bridge. They stopped at the summit of the stairs.

"Hark!" cried the young lady, listening. "Did she call? I thought I heard her voice."

"No, my love," replied Mr. Brownlow, looking sadly back. "She has not moved, and will not till we are gone."

Rose Maylie lingered, but the old gentleman drew her arm through his, and led her, with gentle force, away. As they disappeared, the girl sunk down nearly at her full length upon one of the stone stairs, and vented the anguish of her heart in bitter tears.

After a time she arose, and with feeble and tottering steps ascended to the street. The astonished listener remained motionless at his post for some minutes afterwards, and having ascertained, with many cautious glances round him, that he was again alone, crept slowly from his hiding-place, and returned stealthily and in the shade of the wall, in the same manner as he had descended.

Peeping out, more than once, when he reached the top, to make sure that he was unobserved, Fagin's spy darted away at his utmost speed, and made for the Jew's house as fast as his legs could carry him.

Chapter 35

Fatal consequences

It was nearly two hours before daybreak—that time which, in the autumn of the year, may be truly called the dead of night, when the streets are silent and deserted, when even sound appears to slumber, and profligacy and riot have staggered home to dream—it was at this still and silent hour that the Jew sat watching in his old lair, with face so distorted and pale, and eyes so red and bloodshot, that he looked less like a man than like some hideous phantom, moist from the grave, and worried by an evil spirit.

He sat crouching over a cold hearth, wrapped in an old torn coverlet, with his face turned towards a wasting candle that stood upon a table by his side. His right hand was raised to his lips; and as, absorbed in thought, he bit his long black nails, he disclosed among his toothless gums, a few such fangs as should have been a dog's or rat's. The candle, which, with long-burnt wick drooping almost double, and hot grease falling down in clots upon the table, plainly showed that his thoughts were busy elsewhere.

Indeed they were. Mortification at the overthrow of his notable scheme; hatred of the girl who had dared to palter with strangers; an utter distrust of the sincerity of her refusal to yield him up; bitter disappointment at the loss of his revenge on Sikes; the fear of detection, and ruin, and death; and a fierce and deadly rage kindled by all—these were the passionate considerations which, following close upon each other with rapid and ceaseless whirl, shot through the brain of Fagin, as every evil thought and blackest purpose lay working at his heart.

He sat without changing his attitude in the least, or appearing to take the smallest heed of time, until his quick ear seemed to be attracted by a footstep in the street.

"At last," muttered the Jew, wiping his dry and fevered mouth. "At last!"

The bell rang gently as he spoke. He crept upstairs to the door, and presently returned accompanied by a man muffled to the chin, who carried a bundle under one arm. Sitting down and throwing back his outer coat, the man displayed the burly frame of Sikes.

"There!" he said, laying the bundle on the table. "Take care of that, and do the most you can with it. It's been trouble enough to get. I thought I should have been here three hours ago."

Fagin laid his hand upon the bundle, and locking it in the cupboard, sat down again without speaking. But he did not take his eyes off the robber for an instant during this action; and now that they sat over against each other, face to face, he looked fixedly at him, with his lips quivering so violently, and his face so altered by the emotions which had mastered him, that the housebreaker involuntarily drew back his chair, and surveyed him with a look of real affright.

"Wot now?" cried Sikes. "Wot do you look at a man so for?"

The Jew raised his right hand, and shook his trembling forefinger in the air; but his passion was so great that the power of speech was for the moment gone.

"D— me!" said Sikes, feeling in his breast with a look of alarm. "He's gone mad. I must look to myself here."

"No, no," rejoined Fagin, finding his voice. "It's not–you're not the person, Bill. I have no–no fault to find with you."

"Oh, you haven't, haven't you?" said Sikes, looking sternly at him, and ostentatiously passing a pistol into a more convenient pocket, "That's lucky –for one of us. Which one that is, don't matter."

"I've got that to tell you, Bill," said the Jew, drawing his chair nearer, "will make you worse than me."

"Ay?" returned the robber, with an incredulous air. "Tell away! Look sharp, or Nance will think I'm lost."

"Lost!" cried Fagin. "She's pretty well settled that, in her own mind, already."

Sikes looked with an aspect of great perplexity into the Jew's face, and reading no satisfactory explanation of the riddle there, clenched his coat collar in his huge hand and shook him soundly.

"Speak, will you!" he said, "or if you don't, it shall be for want of breath. Open your mouth and say what you've got to say in plain words. Out with it, you thundering old cur, out with it!"

"Suppose someone," pursued the Jew, "was to peach–to blow upon us all–first seeking out the right folks for the purpose, and then having a meeting with 'em in the street to paint our likenesses, describe every mark that they might know us by, and the crib where we might be most easily taken. Suppose he was to do all this, and besides to blow upon a plant we've all been in, more or less—of his own fancy; not grabbed, trapped, tried, earwigged by the parson, and brought to it on bread and water—but of his own fancy, to please his own taste; stealing out at nights to find those most interested against us, and peaching to them. Do you hear me?" cried the Jew, his eyes flashing with rage. "Supposing he did all this, what then?"

"What then?" replied Sikes, with a tremendous oath. "If he was left alive till I came, I'd grind his skull under the iron heel of my boot into as many grains as there are hairs upon his head."

"What if *I* did it?" cried the Jew, almost in a yell. "*I,* that know so much, and could hang so many besides myself!"

"I don't know," replied Sikes, clenching his teeth and turning white at the mere suggestion. "I'd do something in the jail that 'ud get me put in irons! and if I was tried along with you, I'd fall upon you with them in the open court, and beat your brains out afore the people. I should have such strength," muttered the robber, poising his brawny arm, "that I could smash your head as if a loaded wagon had gone over it."

"You would!"

"Would I?" said the housebreaker. "Try me."

"If it was Charley, or the Dodger, or Bet, or—"

"I don't care who," replied Sikes impatiently. "Whoever it was, I'd serve them the same."

Fagin again looked hard at the robber; and motioning him to be silent, stooped over the bed upon the floor, and shook the sleeper to rouse him. Sikes leaned forward in his chair, looking on with his hands upon his knees, as if wondering much what all this questioning and preparation was to end in.

"Bolter, Bolter!—Poor lad!" said Fagin, looking up with an expression of devilish anticipation, and speaking slowly and with marked emphasis, "he's tired—tired with watching for *her* so long—watching for *her,* Bill."

"Wo d'ye mean?" asked Sikes, drawing back.

The Jew made no answer. but bending over the sleeper again, hauled him into a sitting posture. When his name had been repeated several times, Noah rubbed his eyes, and, giving a heavy yawn, looked sleepily about him.

"Tell me that again—once again, just for him to hear," said the Jew, pointing to Sikes as he spoke.

"Tell yer what?" asked the sleepy Noah, shaking himself pettishly.

"That about—NANCY," said the Jew, clutching Sikes by the wrist, as if to prevent his leaving the house before he had heard enough. "You followed her?"

"Yes."

"To London Bridge?"

"Yes."

"Where she met two people?"

"So she did."

"A gentleman, and a lady that she had gone to of her own accord before, who asked her to give up all her pals, and Monks first, which she did–and to describe him, which she did–and to tell her what house it was that we meet at, and go to, which she did–and where it could be best watched from, which she did–and what time the people went there, which she did. She did all this. She told it all, every word, without a threat, without a murmur–she did–did she not?" cried the Jew mad with fury.

"All right," replied the other, scratching his head. "That's just what it was!"

"What did they say about last Sunday?" demanded the Jew.

"About last Sunday!" replied the spy, considering. "Why, I told yer that before."

"Again; tell it again!" cried Fagin, tightening his grasp on Sikes, and brandishing his other hand aloft, as the foam flew from his lips.

"They asked her," said the spy, who as he grew more wakeful, seemed to have a dawning perception who Sikes was, "they asked her why she didn't come last Sunday, as she promised. She said she couldn't."

"Why–why?" interrupted the Jew, triumphantly. "Tell him that."

"Because she was forcibly kept at home by Bill, the man she had told them of before," replied the spy.

"What more of him?" cried the Jew. "What more of the man she had told them of before? Tell him that, tell him that."

"Why, that she couldn't very easily get out of doors unless he knew where she was going to," said the spy, "and so the first time she went to see the lady, she–ha! ha! ha! it made me laugh when she said it, that it did–she gave him a drink of laudanum."

"Hell's fire!" cried Sikes, breaking fiercely from the Jew. "Let me go!"

Flinging the old man from him, he rushed from the room, and darted, wildly and furiously, up the stairs.

"Bill! Bill!" cried the Jew, following him hastily. "A word. Only a word."

The word would not have been exchanged, but that the housebreaker was unable to open the door; on which he was expending fruitless oaths and violence, when the Jew came panting up.

"Let me out," said Sikes. "Don't speak to me! it's not safe. Let me out, I say."

"Hear me speak a word," rejoined the Jew, laying his hand upon the lock. "You won't be—"

"Well?" replied the other.

"You won't be–too–violent, Bill?" whined the Jew.

The day was breaking, and there was light enough for the men to see each other's faces. They exchanged one brief glance: there was a fire in the eyes of both which could not be mistaken.

"I mean," said Fagin, showing that he felt all disguise was now useless, "not too violent for safety. Be crafty, Bill, and not too bold."

Sikes made no reply, but, pulling open the door, of which the Jew had turned the lock, dashed into the silent streets.

Without one pause or moment's consideration; without once turning his head to the right or left, or raising his eyes to the sky or lowering them to the ground, but looking straight before him with savage resolution—his teeth so tightly compressed that the strained jaw seemed starting through his skin—the robber held on his headlong course, nor muttered a word, nor relaxed a muscle, until he reached his own door. He opened it softly with a key; strode lightly up the stairs; and entering his own room, double-locked the door, and lifting a heavy table against it, drew back the curtain of the bed.

The girl was lying half-dressed upon it. He had roused her from her sleep, for she raised herself with a hurried and startled look.

"Get up!" said the man.

"It *is* you, Bill!" said the girl, with an expression of pleasure at his return.

"It is," was the reply. "Get up."

There was a candle burning, but the man hastily drew it from the candlestick, and hurled it under the grate. Seeing the faint light of early day without, the girl rose to undraw the curtain.

"Let it be," said Sikes, thrusting his hand before her. "There's light enough for wot I've got to do."

"Bill," said the girl, in a low voice of alarm, "why do you look like that at me?"

The robber sat regarding her, for a few seconds, with dilated nostrils and heaving breast; and then, grasping her by the head and throat, dragged her into the middle of the room, and looking once towards the door, placed his heavy hand upon her mouth.

"Bill, Bill!" gasped the girl, wrestling with the strength of mortal fear—"I–I won't scream or cry—not once—hear me—speak to me—speak to me—tell me what I have done!"

"You know, you she–devil!" returned the robber, suppressing his breath. "You were watched to-night; every word you said was heard."

"Then spare my life for the love of Heaven, as I spared yours," rejoined the girl, clinging to him. "Bill, dear Bill, you cannot have the heart to kill me. Oh! think of all I have given up, only this one night, for you. You *shall* have time to think, and save yourself this crime. I will not loose my hold; you cannot throw me off. Bill, Bill, for dear God's sake, for your own, for mine, stop before you spill my blood! I have been true to you, upon my guilty soul I have!"

The man struggled violently to release his arms; but those of the girl were clasped round his, and tear her as he would, he could not tear them away.

"Bill," cried the girl, striving to lay her head upon his breast, "the gentleman, and that dear lady, told me to-night of a home in some foreign country where I could end my days in solitude and peace. Let me see them again, and beg them, on my knees, to show the same mercy and goodness to you; and let us both leave this dreadful place, and far apart lead better lives, and forget how we have lived, except in prayers, and never see each other more. It is never too late to repent. They told me so—I feel it now—but we must have time—a little, little time!"

The housebreaker freed one arm, and grasped his pistol. The certainty of immediate detection if he fired flashed across his mind even in the midst of his fury; and he beat it twice, with all the force he could summon, upon the upturned face that almost touched his own.

She staggered and fell, nearly blinded with the blood that rained down from a deep gash in her forehead; but raising herself, with difficulty, on her knees, drew from her bosom a white handkerchief—Rose Maylie's own—and holding it up in her folded hands, as high towards heaven as her feeble strength would allow, breathed one prayer for mercy to her Maker.

It was a ghastly figure to look upon. The murderer, staggering backwards to the wall, and shutting out the sight with his hand, seized a heavy club and struck her down.

Chapter 36

The flight of Sikes

Of all bad deeds that, under cover of the darkness, had been committed within wide London's bounds since night hung over it, that was the worst. Of all the horrors that rose with an ill scent upon the morning air, that was the foulest and most cruel.

The sun—the bright sun, that brings back, not light alone, but new life, and hope, and freshness to man—burst upon the crowded city in clear and radiant glory. Through costly coloured glass and paper-mended window, through cathedral dome and rotten crevice, to shed its equal ray. It lighted up the room where the murdered woman lay. It did. He tried to shut it out, but it would stream in. If the sight had been a ghastly one in the dull morning, what was it now, in all that brilliant light!

He struck a light, kindled a fire, and thrust the club into it. There was hair upon the end, which blazed and shrunk into a light cinder, and, caught by the air, whirled up the chimney. Even that frightened him, sturdy as he was; but he held the weapon till it broke, and then piled it on the coals to burn away, and smoulder into ashes. He washed himself, and rubbed his clothes; there were spots that would not be removed, but he cut the pieces out and burnt them. How those stains were dispersed about the room! The very feet of the dog were bloody.

All this time he had, never once, turned his back upon the corpse–no, not for a moment. Such preparations completed, he moved, backward, towards the door: dragging the dog with him, lest he should soil his feet anew and carry out new evidences of the crime into the streets. He shut the door softly, locked it, took the key, and left the house.

He crossed over and glanced up at the window, to be sure that nothing was visible from the outside. There was the curtain still drawn, which she would have opened to admit the light she never saw again. It lay nearly under there. *He* knew that. God, how the sun poured down upon the very spot!

The glance was instantaneous. It was a relief to have got free of the room. He whistled on the dog, and walked rapidly away.

He went through Islington; strode up the hill at Highgate on which stands the stone in honour of Whittington; turned down to Highgate Hill, unsteady of purpose, and uncertain where to go; struck off to the right again, almost as soon as he began to descend it, and taking the footpath across the fields, skirted Caen Wood, and so came out on Hampstead Heath. Traversing the hollow by the Vale of Health, he mounted the opposite bank, and crossing the road which joins the villages of Hampstead and Highgate, made along the remaining portion of the Heath to the fields at North End, in one of which he laid himself down under a hedge and slept.

Soon he was up again and away–not far into the country, but back towards London by the highroad–then back again–then over another part of the same ground as he had already traversed–then wandering up and down in fields, and lying on ditches' brinks to rest, and starting up to make for some other spot, and do the same, and ramble on again.

There was a shed in a field he passed that offered shelter for the night. Before the door were three tall poplar trees, which made it very dark within; and the wind moaned through them with a dismal wail. He *could not* walk on till daylight came again; and here he stretched himself close to the wall–to undergo new torture.

For now, a vision came before him, as constant and more terrible than that from which he had escaped. Those widely staring eyes, so lustreless and so glassy, that he had better borne to see them than think upon them, appeared in the midst of the darkness–light in themselves, but giving light to nothing. There were but two, but they were everywhere. If he shut out the sight, there came the room with every well-known object–some, indeed, that he would have forgotten, if he had gone over its contents from memory–each in its accustomed place. The body was in *its* place, and its eyes were as he saw them when he stole away. He got up and rushed into the field without. The figure was behind him. He re-entered the shed, and shrunk down once more. The eyes were there before he had lain himself along.

In the morning he took the desperate resolution of going back to London.

"There's somebody to speak to there, at all events," he thought. "A good hiding-place, too. They'll never expect to nab me there, after this country scent. Why can't I lay by for a week or so, and, forcing blunt from Fagin, get abroad to France? D— me, I'll risk it."

The dog, though—if any descriptions of him were out, it would not be forgotten that the dog was missing, and had probably gone with him. This might lead to his apprehension as he passed along the streets. He resolved to drown him, and walked on, looking about for a pond, picking up a heavy stone and tying it to his handkerchief as he went.

The animal looked up into his master's face while these preparations were making; and, whether his instinct apprehended something of their purpose, or the robber's sidelong look at him was sterner than ordinary, skulked a little farther in the rear than usual, and cowered as he came more slowly along. When his master halted at the brink of a pool, and looked round to call him, he stopped outright.

"Do you hear me call? Come here!" cried Sikes.

The animal came up from the very force of habit; but as Sikes stooped to attach the handkerchief to his throat, he uttered a low growl and started back.

"Come back!" said the robber, stamping on the ground.

The dog wagged his tail, but moved not. Sikes made a running noose, and called him again.

The dog advanced, retreated, paused an instant, turned, and scoured away at his hardest speed.

The man whistled again and again, and sat down and waited in the expectation that he would return. But no dog appeared, and at length he resumed his journey.

CHAPTER 37

Monks and Mr. Brownlow at length meet

THE twilight was beginning to close in when Mr. Brownlow alighted from a hackney-coach at his own door, and knocked softly. The door being opened, a sturdy man got out of the coach and stationed himself on one side of the steps, while another man, who had been seated on the box, dismounted too, and stood upon the other side. At a sign from Mr. Brownlow they helped out a third man, and taking him between them, hurried him into the house. This man was Monks.

They walked in the same manner up the stairs without speaking, and Mr. Brownlow, preceding them, led the way into a back room. At the door of this apartment Monks, who had ascended with evident reluctance, stopped. The two men looked to the old gentleman as if for instructions.

"He knows the alternative," said Mr. Brownlow. "If he hesitates or moves a finger but as you bid him, drag him into the street, call for the aid of the police, and impeach him as a felon in my name."

"How dare you say this of me?" asked Monks.

"How dare you urge me to it, young man?" replied Mr. Brownlow, confronting him with a steady look. "Are you mad enough to leave this house? Unhand him. There, sir. You are free to go, and we to follow. But I warn you, by all I hold most solemn and most sacred, that the instant you set foot in the street, that instant will I have you apprehended on a charge of fraud and robbery. I am resolute and immovable. If you are determined to be the same, your blood be upon your own head!"

"By what authority am I kidnapped in the street, and brought here by these dogs?" asked Monks, looking from one to the other of the men who stood beside him.

"By mine," replied Mr. Brownlow. "Those persons are indemnified by me. If you complain of being deprived of your liberty–you had power and opportunity to retrieve it as you came along, but you deemed it advisable to remain quiet–I say again, throw yourself for protection on the law. I will appeal to the law too; but when you have gone too far to recede, do not sue to me for leniency, when the power will have passed into other hands, and do not say I plunged you down the gulf into which you rushed yourself."

Monks was plainly disconcerted, and alarmed besides. He hesitated.

"You will decide quickly," said Mr. Brownlow, with perfect firmness and composure. "If you wish me to prefer my charges publicly, and consign you to a punishment the extent of which, although I can with a shudder foresee, I cannot control–once more I say you know the way. If not, and you appeal to my forbearance, and the mercy of those you have deeply injured, seat yourself, without a word, in that chair. It has waited for you two whole days."

Monks muttered some unintelligible words, but wavered still.

"You will be prompt," said Mr. Brownlow. "A word from me, and the alternative has gone for ever."

Still the man hesitated.

"I have not the inclination to parley," said Mr. Brownlow; "and, as I advocate the dearest interests of others, I have not the right."

"Is there," demanded Monks, with a faltering tongue, "is there no middle course?"

"None."

Monks looked at the old gentleman with an anxious eye; but reading in his countenance nothing but severity and determination, walked into the room, and, shrugging his shoulders, sat down.

"Look the door on the outside," said Mr. Brownlow to the attendants, "and come when I ring."

The men obeyed, and the two were left alone together.

"This is pretty treatment, sir," said Monks, throwing down his hat and cloak, "from my father's oldest friend."

"It is because I was your father's oldest friend, young man," returned Mr. Brownlow; "it is because the hopes and wishes of young and happy years were bound up with him and that fair creature of his blood and kindred who rejoined her God in youth, and left me here a solitary, lonely man; it is because he knelt with me beside his only sister's death-bed when he was yet a boy, on the morning that would—but Heaven willed otherwise—have made her my young wife; it is because my seared heart clung to him, from that time forth, through all his trials and errors, till he died; it is because old recollections and associations fill my heart, and even the sight of you brings with it old thoughts of him;—it is because of all these things that I am moved to treat you gently now—yes, Edward Leeford, even now—and blush for your unworthiness who bear the name."

"What has the name to do with it?" asked the other, after contemplating, half in silence and half in dogged wonder, the agitation of his companion. "What is the name to me?"

"Nothing," replied Mr. Brownlow, "nothing to you. But it was *hers*, and even at this distance of time brings back to me, an old man, the glow and thrill which I once felt, only to hear it repeated by a stranger. I am very glad you have changed it—very—very."

"This is all mighty fine," said Monks (to retain his assumed designation) after a long silence, during which he had jerked himself in sullen defiance to and fro, and Mr. Brownlow had sat, shading his face with his hand. "But what do you want with me?"

"You have a brother," said Mr. Brownlow, rousing himself—"a brother, the whisper of whose name in your ear when I came behind you in the street, was, in itself, almost enough to make you accompany me hither in wonder and alarm."

"I have no brother," replied Monks. "You know I was an only child. Why do you talk to me of brothers? You know that as well as I."

"Attend to what I do know, and you may not," said Mr. Brownlow. "I shall interest you by-and-by. I know that of the wretched marriage, into which family pride, and the most sordid and narrowest of all ambition, forced your unhappy father when a mere boy, you were the sole and most unnatural issue."

"I don't care for hard names," interrupted Monks, with a jeering laugh. "You know the fact, and that's enough for me."

"But I also know," pursued the old gentleman, "the misery, the slow torture, the protracted anguish of that ill-assorted union. I know how listlessly and wearily each of that wretched pair dragged on their heavy chain through a world that was poisoned to them both. I know how cold formalities were succeeded by open taunts; how indifference gave place to dislike, dislike to hate, and hate to loathing, until at last they wrenched the clanking bond asunder, and retiring a wide space apart, carried each a galling fragment, of which nothing but death could break the rivets, to hide it in new society beneath the gayest looks they could assume. Your mother succeeded; she forgot it soon. But it rusted and cankered at your father's heart for years."

"Well, they were separated," said Monks, "and what of that?"

"When they had been separated for some time," returned Mr. Brownlow, "and your mother, wholly given up to continental frivolities, had utterly forgotten the young husband ten good years her junior, who, with prospects blighted, lingered on at home, he fell among new friends. *This* circumstance at least you know already."

"Not I," said Monks, turning away his eyes and beating his foot upon the ground, as a man who is determined to deny everything. "Not I."

"Your manner, no less than your actions, assures me that you have never forgotten it, or ceased to think of it with bitterness," returned Mr. Brownlow. "I speak of fifteen years ago, when you were not more than eleven years old, and your father but one-and-thirty, for he was, I repeat, a boy when *his* father ordered him to marry. Must I go back to events which cast a shade upon the memory of your parent, or will you spare it, and disclose to me the truth?"

"I have nothing to disclose," rejoined Monks. "You must talk on if you will."

"These new friends, then," said Mr. Brownlow, "were a naval officer retired from active service, whose wife had died some half a year before, and left him with two children: there had been more, but of all their family, happily but two survived. They were both daughters; one a beautiful creature of nineteen, and the other a mere child of two or three years old."

"What's this to me?" asked Monks.

"They resided," said Mr. Brownlow, without seeming to hear the interruption, "in a part of the country to which your father in his wandering had repaired, and where he had taken up his abode. Acquaintance, intimacy, friendship, fast followed on each other. Your father was gifted as few men are. He had his sister's soul and person. As the old officer knew him more and more, he grew to love him. I would that it had ended there. His daughter did the same."

The old gentleman paused. Monks was biting his lips, with his eyes fixed upon the floor; seeing this, he immediately resumed:—

"The end of a year found him contracted, solemnly contracted, to that daughter; the object of the first, true, ardent, only passion of a guileless untried girl."

"Your tale is of the longest," observed Monks, moving restlessly in his chair.

"It is a true tale of grief, and trial, and sorrow, young man," returned Mr. Brownlow, "and such tales usually are. If it were one of unmixed joy and happiness, it would be very brief. At length one of those rich relations, to strengthen whose interest and importance your father had been sacrificed, as others are often—it is no uncommon case—dies, and to repair the misery he had been instrumental in occasioning, left him *his* panacea for all griefs—Money. It was necessary that he should immediately repair to Rome, whither this man had sped for health, and where he had died, leaving his affairs in great confusion. He went; was seized with mortal illness there; was followed, the moment the intelligence reached Paris, by your mother. who carried you with her; he died the day after her arrival, leaving no will—*no will*—so that the whole property fell to her and you."

At this part of the recital Monks held his breath, and listened with a face of intense eagerness, though his eyes were not directed towards the speaker. As Mr. Brownlow paused, he changed his position with the air of one who has experienced a sudden relief, and wiped his hot face and hands.

"Before he went abroad, and as he passed through London on his way," said Mr. Brownlow, slowly, and fixing his eyes upon the other's face, "he came to me."

"I never heard of that," interrupted Monks, in a tone intended to appear incredulous, but savouring more of disagreeable surprise.

"He came to me, and left with me, among some other things, a picture—a portrait painted by himself—a likeness of this poor girl—which he did not wish to leave behind, and could not carry forward on his hasty journey. He was worn by anxiety and remorse almost to a shadow; talked, in a wild, distracted way, of ruin and dishonour worked by him; confided to me his intention to convert his whole property at any loss into money, and, having settled on his wife and you a portion of his recent acquisition, to fly the country—I guessed too well he would not fly alone—and never see it more. Even from me, his old and early friend, whose strong attachment had taken root in the earth that covered one most dear to both—even from me he withheld any more particular confession, promising to write and tell me all, and after that to see me once again for the last time on earth. Alas! *that* was the last time. I had no letter, and I never saw him more.

"I went," said Mr. Brownlow, after a short pause—"I went, when all was over, to the scene of his—I will use the term the world would freely use, for worldly harshness or favour are now alike to him—of his guilty love, resolved that, if my fears were realized, that erring child should find one heart and home to shelter and compassionate her. The family had left that part a week before; they had called in such trifling debts as were outstanding, discharged them, and left the place by night. Why, or whither, none can tell."

Monks drew his breath yet more freely, and looked round with a smile of triumph.

"When your brother," said Mr. Brownlow, drawing nearer to the other's chair—"when your brother—a feeble, ragged, neglected child—was cast in my way by a stronger hand than chance, and rescued by me from a life of vice and infamy—"

"What?" cried Monks.

"By me," said Mr. Brownlow. "I told you I should interest you before long. I say by me. I see that your cunning associate suppressed my name, although, for aught he knew, it would be quite strange to your ears. When he was rescued by me, then, and lay recovering from sickness in my house, his strong resemblance to this picture I have spoken of struck me with astonishment. Even when I first saw him, in all his dirt and misery, there was a lingering expression in his face that came upon me like a glimpse of some old friend flashing on one in a vivid dream. I need not tell you he was snared away before I knew his history—"

"Why not?" asked Monks hastily.

"Because you know it well."

"I!"

"Denial to me is vain," replied Mr. Brownlow. "I shall show you that I know more than that."

"You—you—can't prove anything against me," stammered Monks. "I defy you to do it!"

"We shall see," returned the old gentleman, with a searching glance. "I lost the boy, and no efforts of mine could recover him. Your mother being dead, I knew that you alone could solve the mystery if anybody could; and as, when I had last heard of you, you were on your own estate in the West Indies—whither, as you well know, you retired upon your mother's death to escape the consequences of vicious courses here—I made the voyage. You had left it, months before, and were supposed to be in London, but no one could tell where. I returned. Your agents had no clue to your residence. You came and went, they said, as strangely as you had ever done—sometimes for days together and sometimes not for months—keeping, to all appearance, the same low haunts and mingling with the same infamous herd who had been your associates when a fierce ungovernable boy. I wearied them with new applications. I paced the streets by night and day, but until two hours ago all my efforts were fruitless, and I never saw you for an instant."

"And now you do see me," said Monks, rising boldly, "what then? Fraud and robbery are high-sounding words—justified, you think, by a fancied resemblance in some young imp to an idle daub of a dead man's. Brother! You don't even know that a child was born of this maudlin pair; you don't even know that."

"I *did not,*" replied Mr. Brownlow, rising too; "but within the last fortnight I have learnt it all. You have a brother; you know it, and him. There was a will, which your mother destroyed, leaving the secret and the gain to you at her own death. It contained a reference to some child likely to be the result of this sad connection, which child was born, and accidentally encountered by you, when your suspicions were first awakened by his resemblance to his father. You repaired to the place of his birth. There existed proofs–proofs long suppressed–of his birth and parentage. Those proofs were destroyed by you, and now, in your own words to your accomplice the Jew, '*the only proofs of the boy's identity lie at the bottom of the river, and the old hag that received them from the mother is rotting in her coffin.*' Unworthy son, coward, liar–you, who hold your councils with thieves and murderers in dark rooms at night–you, whose plots and wiles have brought a violent death upon the head of one worth millions such as you–you, who from your cradle were gall and bitterness to your own father's heart, and in whom all evil passions, vice, and profligacy festered, till they found a vent in a hideous disease which has made your face an index even to your mind–you, Edward Leeford, do you still brave me?"

„No, no, no!" returned the coward, overwhelmed by these accumulated charges.

"Every word," cried the old gentleman, "every word that has passed between you and this detested villain is known to me! Shadows on the wall have caught your whispers, and brought them to my ear; the sight of the persecuted child has turned vice itself, and given it the courage and almost the attributes of virtue. Murder has been done, to which you were morally if not really a party."

"No, no," interposed Monks. "I–I–know nothing of that. I was going to inquire the truth of the story when you overtook me. I didn't know the cause. I thought it was a common quarrel."

"It was the partial disclosure of your secrets," replied Mr. Brownlow. "Will you disclose the whole?"

"Yes, I will."

"Set your hand to a statement of truth and facts, and repeat it before witnesses?"

"That I promise, too."

"Remain quietly here until such a document is drawn up, and proceed with me to such a place as I may deem most advisable, for the purpose of attesting it?"

"If you insist upon that I'll do that also," replied Monks.

"You must do more than that," said Mr. Brownlow. "Make restitution to an innocent and unoffending child, for such he is, although the offspring of a guilty and most miserable love. You have not forgotten the provisions of the will. Carry them into execution so far as your brother is concerned, and then go where you please. In this world you need meet no more."

While Monks was pacing up and down, meditating with dark and evil looks on this proposal, and the possibilities of evading it–torn by his fears on the one hand and his hatred on the other–the door was hurriedly unlocked, and a gentleman (Mr. Losberne) entered the room in violent agitation.

"The man will be taken!" he cried. "He will be taken to-night!"

"The murderer?" asked Mr. Brownlow.

"Yes, yes," replied the other. "His dog has been seen lurking about some old haunt, and there seems little doubt that his master either is or will be there under cover of the darkness. Spies are hovering about in every direction. I have spoken to the men who are charged with his capture, and they tell me he can never escape. A reward of a hundred pounds is proclaimed by Government to-night."

"I will give fifty more," said Mr. Brownlow, "and proclaim it with my own lips upon the spot, if I can reach it. Where is Mr. Maylie?"

"Harry? As soon as he had seen your friend here safe in a coach with you, he hurried off to where he heard this," replied the doctor, "and mounting his horse sallied forth to join the first party at some place in the outskirts agreed upon between them."

"The Jew," said Mr. Brownlow; "what of him?"

"When I last heard he had not been taken, but he will be, or is by this time. They're sure of him."

"Have you made up your mind?" asked Mr. Brownlow, in a low voice, of Monks.

"Yes," he replied. "You—you—will be secret with me?"

"I will. Remain here till I return. It is your only hope of safety."

They left the room, and the door was again locked.

"What have you done?" asked the doctor in a whisper.

"All that I could hope to do, and even more. Coupling the poor girl's intelligence with my previous knowledge, and the result of our good friend's inquiries on the spot, I left him no loop-hole of escape, and laid bare the whole villainy which by these lights became plain as day. Write and appoint the evening after to-morrow, at seven, for the meeting. We shall be down there a few hours before, but shall require rest; especially the young lady, who *may* have greater need of firmness than either you or I can quite foresee just now. But my blood boils to avenge this poor murdered creature. Which way have they taken?"

"Drive straight to the office and you will be in time," replied Mr. Losberne. "I will remain here."

The two gentlemen hastily separated, each in a fever of excitement wholly uncontrollable.

CHAPTER 38

The pursuit and escape

NEAR to that part of the Thames on which the church at Rotherhithe abuts, where the buildings on the banks are dirtiest and the vessels on the river blackest with the dust of colliers and the smoke of closebuilt low-roofed houses, there exists, at the present day, the filthiest, the strangest, the most extraordinary of the many localities that are hidden in London, wholly unknown, even by name, to the great mass of its inhabitants.

In such a neighbourhood, beyond Dockhead, in the Borough of Southwark, stands Jakob's Island, surrounded by a muddy ditch six or eight feet deep and fifteen or twenty wide when the tide is in, once called Mill Pond, but known in these days as Folly Ditch. It is a creek or inlet from the Thames, and can always be filled at high water by opening the sluices at the Lead Mills from which it took its old name.

In Jacob's Island the warehouses are roofless and empty; the walls are crumbling down; the windows are windows no more; the doors are falling into the streets; the chimneys are blackened, but they yield no smoke. Thirty or forty years ago, before losses and chancery suits came upon it, it was a thriving place; but now it is a desolate island indeed. The houses have no owners; they are broken open, and entered upon by those who have the courage; and there they live, and there they die. They must have powerful motives for a secret residence, or be reduced to a destitute condition indeed, who seek a refuge in Jacob's Island.

In an upper room of one of these houses–a detached house of fair size, ruinous in other respects, but strongly defended at door and window, of which house the back commanded the ditch in manner already described– there were assembled three men, who, regarding each other every now and then with looks expressive of perplexity and expectation, sat for some time in profound and gloomy silence. One of these was Toby Crackit, another Mr. Chitling, and the third a robber of fifty years, whose nose had been almost beaten in, in some old scuffle, and whose face bore a frightful scar which might probably be traced to the same occasion. This man was a returned transport, and his name was Kags.

"I wish," said Toby, turning to Mr. Chitling, "that you had picked out some other crib, when the two old ones got too warm, and had not come here, my fine feller."

"Why didn't you, blunder-head?" said Kags.

"Well, I thought you'd have been a little more glad to see me than this," replied Mr. Chitling, with a melancholy air.

"Why, look'e young gentleman," said Toby, "when a man keeps himself so very exclusive as I have done, and by that means has a snug house over his head with nobody praying or smelling about it, it's rather a startling thing to have the honour of a wisit from a young gentleman (however respectable and pleasant a person he may be to play cards with at conweniency) circumstanced as you are."

"Expecially when the exclusive young man has got a friend stopping with him, that's arrived sooner than was expected from foreign parts, and is too modest to want to be presented to the Judges on his return," added Mr. Kags.

There was a short silence, after which Toby Crackit, seeming to abandon as hopeless any further effort to maintain his usual devil-may-care swagger, turned to Chitling and said:

"When was Fagin took, then?"

"Just at dinner-time–two o'clock this afternoon. Charley and I made our lucky up the wash'us chimney, and Bolter got into the empty water-butt, head downwards; but his legs were so precious long that they stuck out at the top, and so they took him too."

"And Bet?"

"Poor Bet! She went to see the body, to speak to who it was," replied Chitling, his countenance falling more and more, "and went off mad, screaming and raving, and beating her head against the boards; so they put a strait-weskut on her and took her to the hospital-and there she is."

"Wot's come of young Bates?" demanded Kags.

"He hung about, not to come over here afore dark, but he'll be here soon," replied Chitling. "There's nowhere else to go to now, for the people at the Cripples are all in custody, and the bar of the ken–I went up there and see it with my own eyes–is filled with traps."

"This is a smash," observed Toby, biting his lips. "There's more than one will go with this."

"The sessions are on," said Kags; "if they get the inquest over, and Bolter turns King's evidence–as of course he will, from what he's said already–they can prove Fagin an accessory before the fact, and get the trial on, on Friday, and he'll swing in six days from this, by G—!"

"You should have heard the people groan," said Chitling; "the officers fought like devils, or they'd have torn him away. He was down once, but they made a ring round him, and fought their way along. You should have seen how he looked about him, all muddy and bleeding, and clung to them as if they were his dearest friends. I can see 'em now, not able to stand upright with the pressing of the mob, and dragging him along amongst 'em; I can see the people jumping up, one behind another, and snarling with their teeth, and making at him like wild beasts; I can see the blood upon his hair and beard, and hear the cries with which the women worked themselves into the centre of the crowd at the street corner, and swore they'd tear his heart out!"

The horror-stricken witness of this scene pressed his hands upon his ears, and with his eyes closed got up and paced violently to and fro, like one distracted.

Whilst he was thus engaged, and the two men sat by in silence with their eyes fixed upon the floor, a pattering noise was heard upon the stairs, and Sikes's dog bounded into the room. They ran to the window, downstairs, and into the street. The dog had jumped in at an open window; he made no attempt to follow them, nor was his master to be seen.

"What's the meaning of this?" said Toby, when they had returned. "He can't be coming here. I–I–hope not."

"If he was coming here he'd have come with the dog," said Kags, stooping down to examine the animal, who lay panting on the floor. "Here! Give us some water for him; he has run himself faint."

"He's drunk it all up, every drop," said Chitling, after watching the dog some time in silence. "Covered with mud—lame—half-blind, he must have come a long way."

"Where can he have come from?" exclaimed Toby. "He's been to the other kens of course, and finding them filled with strangers, come on here, where he's been many a time and often. But where can he have come from first, and how comes he here alone without the other?"

It being now dark the shutter was closed, and a candle lighted and placed upon the table. The terrible events of the last two days had made a deep impression on all three, increased by the danger and uncertainty of their own position. They drew their chairs closer together, starting at every sound. They spoke little, and that in whispers, and were as silent and awestricken as if the remains of the murdered woman lay in the next room.

They had sat thus some time, when suddenly was heard a hurried knocking at the door below.

"Young Bates," said Kags, looking angrily round, to check the fear he felt himself.

The knocking came again. No, it wasn't he. He never knocked like that.

Crackit went to the window, and shaking all over, drew in his head. There was no need to tell them who it was; his pale face was enough. The dog too was on the alert in an instant, and ran whining to the door.

"We must let him in," he said, taking up the candle.

"Isn't there any help for it?" asked the other man in a hoarse voice.

"None. He *must* come in."

"Don't leave us in the dark," said Kags, taking down a candle from the chimney-piece, and lighting it, with such a trembling hand that the knocking was twice repeated before he had finished.

Crackit went down to the door, and returned, followed by a man with the lower part of his face buried in a handkerchief, and another tied over his head under his hat. He drew them slowly off. Blanched face, sunken eyes, hollow cheeks, beard of three day's growth, wasted flesh, short thick breath—it was the very ghost of Sikes.

He laid his hand upon a chair which stood in the middle of the room, but shuddering as he was about to drop into it, and seeming to glance over his shoulder, dragged it back close to the wall—as close as it would go—ground it against it—and sat down.

Not a word had been exchanged. He looked from one to another in silence. If an eye were furtively raised and met his, it was instantly averted. When his hollow voice broke silence, they all three started. They seemed never to have heard its tones before.

"How came that dog here?" he asked.

"Alone. Three hours ago."

"To-night's paper says that Fagin's taken. Is it true, or a lie?"

"True."

They were silent again.

"D— you all," said Sikes, passing his hand across his forehead. "Have you nothing to say to me?"

There was an uneasy movement among them, but nobody spoke.

"You that keep this house," said Sikes, turning his face to Crackit, "do you mean to sell me, or to let me lie here till this hunt is over?"

"You may stop here, if you think it safe," returned the person addressed, after some hesitation.

Sikes carried his eyes slowly up the wall behind him—rather trying to turn his head than actually doing it—and said, "Is–it–the body–is it buried?"

They shook their heads.

"Why isn't it?" he retorted, with the same glance behind him. "Wot do they keep such ugly things above the ground for?–Who's that knocking?"

Crackit intimated, by a motion of his hand as he left the room, that there was nothing to fear; and directly came back with Charley Bates behind him. Sikes sat opposite the door, so that the moment the boy entered the room he encountered his figure.

"Toby," said the boy, falling back, as Sikes turned his eyes towards him, "why didn't you tell me this downstairs?"

There had been something so tremendous in the shrinking off of the three, that the wretched man was willing to propitiate even this lad. Accordingly he nodded, and made as though he would shake hands with him.

"Let me go into some other room," said the boy, retreating still farther.

"Charley!" said Sikes, stepping forward, "don't you–don't you know me?"

"Don't come nearer me," answered the boy, still retreating, and looking with horror in his eyes, upon the murderer's face. "You monster!"

The man stopped half-way, and they looked at each other; but Sikes's eyes sunk gradually to the ground.

"Witness you three," cried the boy, shaking his clenched fist, and becoming more and more excited as he spoke–"witness you three–I'm not afraid of him–if they come here after him, I'll give him up; I will. I tell you out at once. He may kill me for it if he likes, or if he dares, but if I'm here I'll give him up. I'd give him up if he was to be boiled alive. Murder! Help! If there's the pluck of a man among you three, you'll help me. Murder! Help! Down with him!"

Pouring out these cries, and accompanying them with violent gesticulation, the boy actually threw himself, single-handed, upon the strong man, and in the intensity of his energy, and the suddenness of his surprise, brought him heavily to the ground.

The contest, however, was too unequal to last long. Sikes had him down, and his knee was on his throat, when Crackit pulled him back with a look of alarm, and pointed to the window. There were lights gleaming below, voices in loud and earnest conversation, the tramp of hurried footsteps—endless they seemed in number—crossing the nearest wooden bridge. One man on horseback seemed to be among the crowd, for there was the noise of hoofs rattling on the uneven pavement. The gleam of lights increased; the footsteps came more thickly and noisily on. Then came a loud knocking at the door, and then a hoarse murmur from such a multitude of angry voices as would have made the boldest quail.

"Help!" shrieked the boy in a voice that rent the air. "He's here! Break down the door!"

"In the King's name," cried the voices without; and the hoarse cry rose again, but louder.

"Break down the door!" screamed the boy. "I tell you they'll never open it. Run straight to the room where the light is. Break down the door!"

"Open the door of some place where I can lock this screeching Hell-babe," cried Sikes fiercely, running to and fro, and dragging the boy now as easily as if he were an empty sack. "That door. Quick." He flung him in, bolted it, and turned the key. "Is the downstairs door fast?"

"Double-locked and chained," replied Crackit, who with the other two men still remained quite helpless and bewildered.

"The panels—are they strong?"

"Lined with sheet-iron."

"And the windows too?"

"Yes, and the windows."

"D— you!" cried the desperate ruffian, throwing up the sash and menacing the crowd. "Do your worst! I'll cheat you yet!"

Of all the terrific yells that ever fell on mortal ears, none could exceed the cry of the infuriated throng. Some shouted to those who were nearest to set the house on fire; others roared to the officers to shoot him dead. Among them all none showed such fury as the man on horseback, who, throwing himself out of the saddle, and bursting through the crowd as if he were parting water, cried, beneath the window, in a voice that rose above all others. "Twenty guineas to the man who brings a ladder!"

"The tide," cried the murderer, as he staggered back into the room, and shut the faces out, "the tide was in as I came up. Give me a rope, a long rope. They're all in front. I may drop into the Folly Ditch and clear off that way. Give me a rope, or I shall do three more murders and kill myself at last."

The panic-stricken men pointed to where such articles were kept. The murderer, hastily selecting the longest and strongest cord, hurried up to the house-top.

All the windows in the rear of the house had been long ago bricked up, except one small trap in the room where the boy was locked, and that was too small even for the passage of his body. But from this aperture he had never ceased to call on those without to guard the back; and thus when the murderer emerged at last on the house-top by the door in the roof, a loud shout proclaimed the fact to those in front, who immediately began to pour round, pressing upon each other in one unbroken stream.

He planted a board, which he had carried up with him for the purpose, so firmly against the door that it must be a matter of great difficulty to open it from the inside; and creeping over the tiles, looked over the low parapet.

The water was out, and the ditch a bed of mud.

The crowd had been hushed during these few moments, watching his motions, and doubtful of his purpose; but the instant they perceived it, and knew it was defeated, they raised a cry of triumphant execration to which all their previous shouting had been whispers. Again and again it rose. Those who were at too great a distance to know its meaning, took up the sound; it echoed and re-echoed; it seemed as though the whole city had poured its population out to curse him.

On pressed the people from the front—on, on, on, in a strong struggling current of angry faces, with here and there a glaring torch to light them up, and show them out in all their wrath and passion. The houses on the opposite side of the ditch had been entered by the mob; sashes were thrown up, or torn bodily out; there were tiers and tiers of faces in every window, and cluster upon cluster of people clinging to every house-top. Each little bridge (and there were three in sight) bent beneath the weight of the crowd upon it. Still the current poured on to find some nook or hole from which to vent their shouts, and only for an instant to see the wretch.

"They have him now," cried a man on the nearest bridge. "Hurrah!"

"I promise fifty pounds," cried an old gentleman from the same quarter, "fifty pounds to the man who takes him alive. I will remain here till he comes to ask me for it."

There was another roar. At this moment the word was passed among the crowd that the door was forced at last: the immediate attention was distracted from the murderer, although the universal eagerness for his capture was, if possible, increased.

The man had shrunk down, thoroughly quelled by the ferocity of the crowd, and the impossibility of escape; but seeing this sudden change with no less rapidity than it had occurred, he sprung upon his feet, determined to make one last effort for his life by dropping into the ditch, and, at the risk of being stifled, endeavouring to creep away in the darkness and confusion.

Roused into new strength and energy, and stimulated by the noise within the house which announced that an entrance had really been effected, he set his foot against the stack of chimneys, fastened one end of the rope tightly and firmly round it, and with the other made a strong running noose by the aid of his hands and teeth almost in a second. He could let himself down by the cord to within a less distance of the ground than his own height, and had his knife ready in his hand to cut it then and drop.

At the very instant when he brought the loop over his head previous to slipping it beneath his arm-pits, and when the old gentleman before-mentioned (who had clung so tight to the railing of the bridge as to resist the force of the crowd, and retain his position) earnestly warned those about him that the man was about to lower himself down—at that very instant the murderer, looking behind him on the roof, threw his arms above his head, and uttered a yell of terror.

"The eyes again!" he cried, in an unearthly screech.

Staggering as if struck by lightning, he lost his balance and tumbled over the parapet. The noose was at his neck. It ran up with his weight, tight as a bowstring, and swift as the arrow it speeds. He fell for five-and-thirty feet. There was a sudden jerk, a terrific convulsion of the limbs; and there he hung, with the open knife clenched in his stiffening hand.

The old chimney quivered with the shock, but stood it bravely. The murderer swung lifeless against the wall; and the boy, thrusting aside the dangling body which obscured his view, called to the people to come and take him out for God's sake.

A dog which had lain concealed till now, ran backwards and forwards on the parapet with a dismal howl, and collecting himself for a spring, jumped for the dead man's shoulders. Missing his aim, he fell into the ditch, turning completely over as he went, and striking his head against a stone, dashed out his brains.

CHAPTER 39

Affording an explanation of more mysteries than one and comprehending a proposal of marriage, with no word of settlement or pin-money

THE events narrated in the last chapter were yet but two days old, when Oliver found himself, at three o'clock in the afternoon, in a travelling-carriage rolling fast towards his native town. Mrs. Maylie and Rose, and Mrs. Bedwin, and the good doctor, were with him; and Mr. Brownlow followed in a postchaise, accompanied by one other person whose name had not been mentioned.

As they approached the town, and at length drove through its narrow streets, it became matter of no small difficulty to restrain the boy within reasonable bounds. There was Sowerberry's the undertaker's just as it used to be, only smaller and less imposing in appearance than he remembered it; there were all the well-known shops and houses, with almost every one of which he had some slight incident connected; there was Gamfield's cart, the very cart he used to have, standing at the old public-house door; there was the workhouse, the dreary prison of his youthful days, with its dismal windows frowning on the street.

But it was pure, earnest, joyful reality. They drove straight to the door of the chief hotel (which Oliver used to stare up at with awe, and think a mighty palace, but which had somehow fallen off in grandeur and size); and here was Mr. Grimwig all ready to receive them, kissing the young lady, and the old one too, when they got out of the coach, as if he were the grandfather of the whole party, all smiles and kindness, and not offering to eat his head—no, not once; not even when he contradicted a very old postboy about the nearest road to London, and maintained he knew it best, though he had only come that way once, and that time fast asleep. There was dinner prepared, and there were bedrooms ready, and everything was arranged as if by magic.

Notwithstanding all this, when the hurry of the first half-hour was over, the same silence and constraint prevailed that had marked their journey down. Mr. Brownlow did not join them at dinner, but remained in a separate room. The two other gentlemen hurried in and out with anxious faces, and, during the short intervals when they were present, conversed apart. Once, Mrs. Maylie was called away, and after being absent for nearly an hour, returned with eyes swollen with weeping. All these things made Rose and Oliver, who were not in any new secrets, nervous and uncomfortable. They sat wondering in silence; or, if they exchanged a few words, spoke in whispers, as if they were afraid to hear the sound of their own voices.

At length, when nine o'clock had come, and they began to think they were to hear no more that night, Mr. Losberne and Mr. Grimwig entered the room, followed by Mr. Brownlow and a man whom Oliver almost shrieked with surprise to see; for they told him it was his brother, and it was the same man he had met at the market-town, and seen looking in with Fagin at the window of his little room. Monks cast a look of hate, which even then, he could not dissemble, at the astonished boy, and sat down near the door. Mr. Brownlow, who had papers in his hand, walked to a table, near which Rose and Oliver were seated.

"This is a painful task," said he, "but these declarations, which have been signed in London before many gentlemen, must be in substance repeated here. I would have spared you the degradation, but we must hear them from your own lips before we part, and you know why."

"Go on," said the person addressed, turning away his face. "Quick. I have almost done enough, I think. Don't keep me here."

"This child," said Mr. Brownlow, drawing Oliver to him, and laying his hand upon his head, "is your half-brother; the illegitimate son of your father, my dear friend Edwin Leeford, by poor young Agnes Fleming, who died in giving him birth."

"Yes," said Monks, scowling at the trembling boy, the beating of whose heart he might have heard. "That is their bastard child."

"The term you use," said Mr. Brownlow sternly, "is a reproach to those who long since passed beyond the feeble censure of the world. It reflects disgrace on no one living, except you who use it. Let that pass. He was born in this town?"

"In the workhouse of this town," was the sullen reply. "You have the story here." He pointed impatiently to the papers as he spoke.

"I must have it here, too," said Mr. Brownlow, looking round upon the listeners.

"Listen then! You!" returned Monks. "His father being taken ill at Rome, was joined by his wife, my mother, from whom he had been long separated, who went from Paris and took me with her—to look after his property for what I know, for she had no great affection for him, nor he for her. He knew nothing of us, for his senses were gone, and he slumbered on till next day, when he died. Among the papers in his desk were two, dated on the night his illness first came on, directed to yourself"—he addressed himself to Mr. Brownlow—"and enclosed in a few short lines to you, with an intimation on the cover of the package that it was not to be forwarded till after he was dead. One of these papers was a letter to this girl Agnes; the other a will."

"What of the letter?" asked Mr. Brownlow.

"The letter?—a sheet of paper, crossed and crossed again, with a penitent confession, and prayers to God to help her. He had palmed a tale on the girl that some secret mystery—to be explained one day—prevented his marrying her just then; and so she had gone on trusting patiently to him, until she trusted too far, and lost what none could ever give her back. She was, at that time, within a few months of her confinement. He told her all he had meant to do, to hide her shame, if he had lived; and prayed her, if he died, not to curse his memory, or think the consequences of their sin would be visited on her or their young child, for all the guilt was his. He reminded her of the day he had given her the little locket and the ring with her Christian name engraved upon it, and a blank left for that which he hoped one day to have bestowed upon her—prayed her yet to keep it, and wear it next her heart, as she had done before—and then ran on, wildly, in the same words, over and over again, as if he had gone distracted. I believe he had."

"The will," said Mr. Brownlow, as Oliver's tears fell fast.

Monks was silent.

"The will," said Mr. Brownlow, speaking for him, "was in the same spirit as the letter. He talked of miseries which his wife had brought upon him; of the rebellious disposition, vice, malice, and premature bad passions of you, his only son, who had been trained to hate him; and left you and your mother each an annuity of eight hundred pounds. The bulk of his property he divided into two equal portions—one for Agnes Fleming, and the other for their child, if it should be born alive and ever come of age. If it were a girl, it was to inherit the money unconditionally; but if a boy, only on the stipulation that in his minority he should never have stained his name with any public act of dishonour, meanness, cowardice, or wrong. He did this, he said, to mark his confidence in the mother, and his con-viction—only strengthened by approaching death—that the child would share her gentle heart and noble nature. If he were disappointed in this expectation, then the money was to come to you; for then, and not till then, when both children were equal, would he recognize your prior claim upon his purse, who had none upon his heart, but had, from an infant, repulsed him with coldness and aversion."

"My mother," said Monks, in a louder tone, "did what a woman should have done—she burnt this will. The letter never reached its destination; but that, and other proofs, she kept in case they ever tried to lie away the blot. The girl's father had the truth from her with every aggravation that her violent hate—I love her for it now—could add. Goaded by shame and dishonour, he fled with his children into a remote corner of Wales, chang-ing his very name, that his friends might never know of his retreat; and here, no great while afterwards, he was found dead in his bed. The girl had left her home, in secret, some weeks before; he had searched for her, on foot, in every town and village near; and it was on the night when he returned home, assured that she had destroyed herself, to hide her shame and his, that his old heart broke."

There was a short silence here, until Mr. Brownlow took up the thread of the narrative.

"Years after this," he said, "this man's—Edward Leeford's—mother came to me. He had left her, when only eighteen; robbed her of jewels and money; gambled, squandered, forged, and fled to London, where for two years he had associated with the lowest outcasts. She was sinking under a painful and incurable disease, and wished to recover him before she died. Inquiries were set on foot, and strict searches made. They were unavailing for a long time, but ultimately successful; and he went back with her to France."

"There she died," said Monks, "after a lingering illness; and on her death-bed, she bequeathed these secrets to me, together with her un-quenchable and deadly hatred of all whom they involved—though she need not have left me that, for I had inherited it long before. She would not believe that the girl had destroyed herself, and the child too, but was filled with the impression that a male child had been born, and was alive. I swore to her, if ever it crossed my path, to hunt it down; never to let it rest; to pursue it with the bitterest and most unrelenting animosity; to vent upon it the hatred that I deeply felt, and to spit upon the empty vaunt of that insulting will by dragging it; if I could, to the very gallows-foot. She was right. He came in my way at last. I began well, and, but for babbling drabs, I would have finished as I began!"

As the villain folded his arms tight together, and muttered curses on himself in the impotence of baffled malice, Mr. Brownlow turned to the terrified group beside him, and explained that the Jew, who had been his old accomplice and confidant, had a large reward for keeping Oliver ensnared, of which some part was to be given up in the event of his being rescued; and that a dispute on this head had led to their visit to the country house for the purpose of identifying him.

"The locket and ring?" said Mr. Brownlow, turning to Monks.

"I bought them from the man and woman I told you of, who stole them from the nurse, who stole them from the corpse," answered Monks, without raising his eyes. "You know what became of them."

Mr. Brownlow merely nodded to Mr. Grimwig, who, disappearing with great alacrity, shortly returned, pushing in Mrs. Bumble, and dragging her unwilling consort after him.

"Do my hi's deceive me!" cried Mr. Bumble, with ill-feigned enthusiasm, "or is that little Oliver? Oh O-li-ver, if you know'd how I've been a-grieving for you—"

"Hold your tongue, fool," murmured Mrs. Bumble.

"Isn't natur', natur', Mrs. Bumble?" remonstrated the workhouse master. "Can't I be supposed to feel—I as brought him up porochially—when I see him a-setting here among ladies and gentlemen of the very affablest description? I always loved that boy as if he'd been my—my—my own grandfather," said Mr. Bumble, halting for an appropriate comparison. "Master Oliver, my dear, you remember the blessed gentleman in the white waistcoat? Ah! he went to heaven last week, in a oak coffin with plated handles, Oliver."

"Come, sire," said Mr. Grimwig tartly; "suppress your feelings."

"I will do my endeavours, sir," replied Mr. Bumble. "How do you do, sir? I hope you are very well."

This salutation was addressed to Mr. Brownlow, who had stepped up to within a short distance of the respectable couple. He inquired, as he pointed to Monks:

"Do you know that person?"

"No," replied Mrs. Bumble flatly.

"Perhaps *you* don't?" said Mr. Brownlow, addressing her spouse.

"I never saw him in all my life," said Mr. Bumble.

"Nor sold him anything, perhaps?"

"No," replied Mrs. Bumble.

"You never had, perhaps, a certain gold locket and ring?" said Mr. Brownlow.

"Certainly not," replied the matron. "Why are we brought here to answer to such nonsense as this?"

Again Mr. Brownlow nodded to Mr. Grimwig, and again that gentleman limped away with extraordinary readiness. But not again did he return with a stout man and wife; for, this time, he led in two palsied women, who shook and tottered as they walked.

"You shut the door the night old Sally died," said the foremost one, raising her shrivelled hand, "but you couldn't shut out the sound, nor stop the chinks."

"No, no," said the other, looking round her, and wagging her toothless jaw. "No, no, no."

"We heard her try to tell you what she'd done, and saw you take a paper from her hand, and watched you, too, next day to the pawnbroker's shop," said the first.

"Yes," added the second, "and it was a 'locket and gold ring.' We found out that, and saw it given you. We were by. Oh! we were by."

"And we know more than that," resumed the first, "for she told us often, long ago, that the young mother had told her that, feeling she should never get over it, she was on her way, at the time that she was taken ill, to die near the grave of the father of the child."

"Would you like to see the pawnbroker himself?" asked Mr. Grimwig, with a motion towards the door.

"No," replied the woman; "if he"—she pointed to Monks—"has been coward enough to confess, as I see he has, and you have sounded all these hags till you found the right ones, I have nothing more to say. I *did* sell them, and they're where you'll never get them. What then?"

"Nothing," replied Mr. Brownlow, "except that it remains for us to take care that you are neither of you employed in a situation of trust again. You may leave the room."

"I hope," said Mr. Bumble, looking about him with great ruefulness, as Mr. Grimwig disappeared with the two old women—"I hope that this unfortunate little circumstance will not deprive me of my porochial office?"

"Indeed it will," replied Mr. Brownlow. "You may make up your mind to that, and think yourself well off besides."

"It was all Mrs. Bumble. She *would* do it," urged Mr. Bumble, first looking round to ascertain that his partner had left the room.

"That is no excuse," replied Mr. Brownlow. "You were present on the occasion of the destruction of these trinkets, and, indeed, are the more guilty of the two, in the eye of the law; for the law supposes that your wife acts under your direction."

"If the law supposes that," said Mr. Bumble, squeezing his hat emphatically in both hands, "the law is a ass—a idiot. If that's the eye of the law, the law's a bachelor; and the worst I wish the law is, that his eye may be opened by experience—by experience."

Laying great stress on the repetition of these two words, Mr. Bumble fixed his hat on very tight and, putting his hands in his pockets, followed his helpmate downstairs.

"Young lady," said Mr. Brownlow, turning to Rose, "give me your hand. Do not tremble. You need not fear to hear the few remaining words we have to say."

"If they have—I do not know how they can, but if they have—any reference to me," said Rose, "pray let me hear them at some other time. I have not strength or spirits now."

"Nay," returned the old gentleman, drawing her arm through his; "you have more fortitude than this, I am sure. Do you know this young lady, sir?"

"Yes," replied Monks.

"I never saw you before," said Rose faintly.

"I have seen you often," returned Monks.

"The father of the unhappy Agnes had *two* daughters," said Mr. Brownlow. "What was the fate of the other—the child?"

"The child," replied Monks, "when her father died in a strange place, in a strange name, without a letter, book, or scrap of paper that yielded the faintest clue by which his friends or relatives could be traced—the child was taken by some wretched cottagers, who reared it as their own."

"Go on," said Mr. Brownlow, signing to Mrs. Maylie to approach. "Go on!"

"You couldn't find the spot to which these people had repaired," said Monks, "but where friendship fails, hatred will often force a way. My mother found it, after a year of cunning search—ay, and found the child."

"She took it, did she?"

"No. The people were poor, and began to sicken—at least the man did—of their fine humanity; so she left it with them, giving them a small present of money which would not last long, and promising more, which she never meant to send. She didn't quite rely, however, on their discontent and poverty for the child's unhappiness, but told the history of the sister's shame, with such alterations as suited her; bade them take good heed of the child, for she came of bad blood; and told them she was illegitimate, and sure to go wrong at one time or other. The circumstances countenanced all this; the people believed it; and there the child dragged on an existence, miserable enough even to satisfy us, until a widow lady, residing then at Chester, saw the girl by chance, pitied her, and took her home. There was some cursed spell, I think, against us; for in spite of all our efforts she remained there and was happy. I lost sight of her two or three years ago, and saw her no more until a few months back."

"Do you see her now?"

"Yes. Leaning on your arm."

"But not the less my niece," cried Mrs. Maylie, folding the fainting girl in her arms—"not the less my dearest child. I would not lose her now for all the treasures of the world. My sweet companion, my own dear girl!"

"The only friend I ever had," cried Rose, clinging to her. "The kindest, best of friends. My heart will burst. I cannot—cannot bear all this."

"You have borne more, and have been, through all, the best and gentlest creature that ever shed happiness on every one she knew," said Mrs. Maylie, embracing her tenderly. "Come, come, my love, remember who this is who waits to clasp you in his arms, poor child! See here-look, look, my dear!"

"Not aunt," cried Oliver, throwing his arms about her neck; "I'll never call her aunt—sister, my own dear sister, that something taught my heart to love so dearly from the first! Rose, dear, darling Rose!"

Let the tears which fell, and the broken words which were exchanged in the long close embrace between the orphans, be sacred. A father, sister, and mother were gained, and lost, in that one moment. Joy and grief were mingled in the cup. But there were no bitter tears; for even grief itself arose so softened, and clothed in such sweet and tender recollections, that it became a solemn pleasure, and lost all character of pain.

They were a long, long time alone. A soft tap at the door at length announced that some one was without. Oliver opened it, glided away, and gave place to Harry Maylie.

"I know it all," he said, taking a seat beside the lovely girl. "Dear Rose, I know it all."

"I am not here by accident," he added, after a lengthened silence; "nor have I heard all this to-night, for I knew it yesterday—only yesterday. Do you guess that I have come to remind you of a promise?"

"Stay," said Rose. "You *do* know all?"

"All. You gave me leave, at any time within a year, to renew the subject of our last discourse."

"I did."

"Not to press you to alter your determination," pursued the young man, "but to hear you repeat it, if you would. I was to lay whatever of station or fortune I might possess at your feet, and if you still adhered to your former determination, I pledged myself, by no word or act, to seek to change it."

"The same reasons which influenced me then will influence me now," said Rose, firmly. "If I ever owed a strict and rigid duty to her, whose goodness saved me from a life of indigence and suffering, when should I ever feel it as I should to-night? It is a struggle," said Rose, "but one I am proud to make; it is a pang, but one my heart shall bear."

"The disclosure of to-night—" Harry began.

"The disclosure of to-night," replied Rose, softly, "leaves me in the same position, with reference to you, as that in which I stood before."

"You harden your heart against me, Rose," urged her lover.

"Oh, Harry, Harry," said the young lady, bursting into tears. "I wish I could, and spare myself this pain."

"Then why inflict it on yourself?" said Harry, taking her hand. "Think, dear Rose, think what you have heard to-night."

"And what have I heard? What have I heard?" cried Rose. "That a sense of his deep disgrace so worked upon my own father that he shunned all—there, we have said enough, Harry, we have said enough."

"Not yet, not yet," said the young man, detaining her as she rose. "My hopes, my wishes, prospects, feeling, every thought in life except my love for you, have undergone a change. I offer you, now, no distinction among a bustling crowd; no mingling with a world of malice and detraction, where the blood is called into honest cheeks by aught but real disgrace and shame; but a home—a heart and home—yes, dearest Rose, and those, and those alone, are all I have to offer."

"What do you mean?" she faltered.

"I mean but this—that when I left you last, I left you with a firm determination to level all fancied barriers between yourself and me; resolved that if my world could not be yours, I would make yours mine; that no pride of birth should curl the lip at you, for I would turn from it. This I have done. Those who have shrunk from me because of this, have shrunk from you, and proved you so far right. Such power and patronage, such relatives of influence and rank, as smiled upon me then, look coldly now; but there are smiling fields and waving trees in England's richest county, and by one village church—mine, Rose, my own!—there stands a rustic dwelling which you can make me prouder of than all the hopes I have renounced, measured a thousandfold. This is *my* rank and station now, and here I lay it down!"

"It's a trying thing waiting supper for lovers," said Mr. Grimwig, waking up, and pulling his pocket-handkerchief from over his head.

Truth to tell, the supper had been waiting a most unreasonable time. Neither Mrs. Maylie, nor Harry, nor Rose (who all came in together) could offer a word in extenuation.

"I had serious thoughts of eating my head to-night," said Mr. Grimwig, "for I began to think I should get nothing else. I'll take the liberty, if you'll allow me, of saluting the bride that is to be."

Mr. Grimwig lost no time in carrying this notice into effect upon the blushing girl; and the example, being contagious, was followed both by the doctor and Mr. Brownlow. Some people affirm that Harry Maylie had been observed to set it, originally, in a dark room adjoining; but the best authorities consider this downright scandal, he being young and a clergyman.

"Oliver, my child," said Mrs. Maylie, "where have you been, and why do you look so sad? There are tears stealing down your face at this moment. What is the matter?"

It is a world of disappointment—often to the hopes we must cherish, and hopes that do our nature the greatest honour.

Poor Dick was dead!

CHAPTER 40

The Jew's last night alive

THE court was paved, from floor to roof, with human faces. Inquisitive and eager eyes peered from every inch of space. From the rail before the dock, away into the sharpest angle of the smallest corner of the galleries, all looks were fixed upon one man–the Jew. Before him and behind–above, below, on the right and on the left–he seemed to stand surrounded by a firmament all bright with gleaming eyes.

At length there was a cry of silence, and a breathless look from all towards the door. The jury returned, and passed him close. He could glean nothing from their faces; they might as well have been of stone. Perfect stillness ensued–not a rustle–not a breath–Guilty!

The judge assumed the black cap, and the prisoner still stood with the same air and gesture. A woman in the gallery uttered some exclamation, called forth by this dread solemnity; he looked hastily up, as if angry at the interruption, and bent forward yet more attentively. The address was solemn and impressive; the sentence fearful to hear.

They led him through a paved room under the court, where some prisoners were waiting till their turns came, and others were talking to their friends, who crowded round a gate which looked into the open yard. He shook his fist, and would have spat upon them; but his conductors hurried him on through a gloomy passage lighted by a few dim lamps, into the interior of the prison.

Here he was searched, that he might not have about him the means of anticipating the law; this ceremony performed, they led him to one of the condemned cells, and left him there–alone.

It was not until the night of the last awful day, that a withering sense of his helpless, desperate state came in its full intensity upon his blighted soul; not that he had ever held any defined or positive hope of mercy, but that he had never been able to consider more than the dim probability of dying so soon.

He cowered down upon his stone bed, and thought of the past. He had been wounded with some missiles from the crowd on the day of his capture, and his head was bandaged with a linen cloth. His red hair hung down upon his bloodless face; his beard was torn, and twisted into knots; his eyes shone with a terrible light; his unwashed flesh crackled with the fever that burnt him up. Eight–nine–ten. If it was not a trick to frighten him, and those were the real hours treading on each other's heels, where would he be, when they came round again? Eleven! Another struck, before the voice of the previous hour had ceased to vibrate. At eight, he would be the only mourner in his own funeral train; at eleven––

Those dreadful walls of Newgate, which have hidden so much misery and such unspeakable anguish, not only from the eyes, but, too often and too long, from the thoughts of men, never held so dread a spectacle as that. The few who lingered as they passed, and wondered what the man was doing who was to be hung to-morrow, would have slept but ill that night if they could have seen him.

The space before the prison was cleared, and a few strong barriers, painted black, had been already thrown across the road to break the pressure of the expected crowd, when Mr. Brownlow and Oliver appeared at the wicket, and presented an order of admission to the prisoner, signed by one of the sheriffs. They were immediately admitted into the lodge.

"Is the young gentleman to come too, sir?" said the man whose duty it was to conduct them. "It's not a sight for children, sir."

"It is not indeed, my friend," rejoined Mr. Brownlow; "but my business with this man is intimately connected with him; and as this child has seen him in the full career of his success and villainy, I think it well—even at the cost of some pain and fear—that he should see him now."

These few words had been said apart, so as to be inaudible to Oliver. The man touched his hat; and glancing at Oliver with some curiosity, opened another gate, opposite to that by which they had entered, and led them on, through dark and winding ways, towards the cells.

"This," said the man, stopping in a gloomy passage where a couple of workmen were making some preparations in profound silence—"this is the place he passes through. If you step this way, you can see the door he goes out at."

He led them into a stone kitchen, fitted with coppers for dressing the prison food, and pointed to a door. There was an open grating above it, through which came the sound of men's voices, mingled with the noise of hammering and the throwing down of boards. They were putting up the scaffold.

From this place they passed through several strong gates, opened by other turnkeys from the inner side, and, having entered an open yard, ascended a flight of narrow steps, and came into a passage with a row of strong doors on the left hand. Motioning them to remain where they were, the turnkey knocked at one of these with his bunch of keys. The two attendants, after a little whispering, came out into the passage, stretching themselves as if glad of a temporary relief, and motioned the visitors to follow the jailer into the cell. They did so.

The condemned criminal was seated on his bed, rocking himself from side to side, with a countenance more like that of a snared beast than the face of a man. His mind was evidently wandering to his old life, for he continued to mutter, without appearing conscious of their presence otherwise than as a part of his vision.

"Good boy, Charley—well done," he mumbled. "Oliver, too, ha! ha! ha! Oliver, too—quite the gentleman now—quite the— Take the boy away to bed!"

The jailer took the disengaged hand of Oliver, and whispering him not to be alarmed, looked on without speaking.

"Take him away to bed!" cried the Jew. "Do you hear me, some of you? He has been the–the–somehow the cause of all this. It's worth the money to bring him up to it–Bolter's throat, Bill; never mind the girl–Bolter's throat, as deep as you can cut. Saw his head off!"

"Fagin," said the jailer.

"That's me!" cried the Jew, falling instantly into the attitude of listening he had assumed upon his trial. "An old man, my lord; a very old, old man!"

"Here," said the turnkey, laying his hand upon his breast to keep him down–"here's somebody wants to see you–to ask you some questions, I suppose. Fagin, Fagin! Are you a man?"

"I shan't be one long," replied the Jew, looking up with a face retaining no human expression but rage and terror. "Strike them all dead! what right have they to butcher me?"

As he spoke he caught sight of Oliver and Mr. Brownlow. Shrinking to the farthest corner of the seat, he demanded to know what they wanted there.

"Steady," said the turnkey, still holding him down. "Now, sir, tell him what you want–quick, if you please, for he grows worse as the time gets on."

"You have some papers," said Mr. Brownlow, advancing, "which were placed in your hands for better security by a man called Monks."

"It's all a lie together," replied the Jew. "I haven't one–not one."

"For the love of God," said Mr. Brownlow solemnly, "do not say that now, upon the very verge of death, but tell me where they are. You know that Sikes is dead, that Monks has confessed, that there is no hope of further gain. Where are those papers?"

"Oliver," cried the Jew, beckoning to him. "Here, here! Let me whisper to you."

"I am not afraid," said Oliver in a low voice, as he relinquished Mr. Brownlow's hand.

"The papers," said the Jew, drawing him towards him, "are in a canvas bag, in a hole a little way up the chimney in the top front room. I want to talk to you, my dear; I want to talk to you."

"Yes, yes," returned Oliver. "Let us say a prayer. Do! Let me say one prayer–say only one, upon your knees with me, and we will talk till morning."

"Outside, outside," replied the Jew, pushing the boy before him towards the door, and looking vacantly over his head. "Say I've gone to sleep– they'll believe *you*. You can get me out, if you take me so. Now then, now then!"

"Oh! God forgive this wretched man!" cried the boy, with a burst of tears.

"That's right, that's right," said the Jew; "that'll help us on. This door first. If I shake and tremble as we pass the gallows, don't you mind, but hurry on. Now, now, now!"

"Have you nothing else to ask him, sir?" inquired the turnkey.

"No other question," replied Mr. Brownlow. "If I hoped we could recall him to a sense of his position—"

"Nothing will do that, sir," replied the man, shaking his head. "You had better leave him."

The door of the cell opened, and the attendants returned.

"Press on, press on," cried the Jew. "Softly, but not so slow. Faster, faster!"

The men laid hands upon him, and disengaging Oliver from his grasp, held him back. He struggled with the power of desperation for an instant, and then sent up cry upon cry that penetrated even those massive walls, and rang in their ears until they reached the open yard.

It was some time before they left the prison. Oliver nearly swooned after this frightful scene, and was so weak that for an hour or more he had not strength to walk.

CHAPTER 41

'And last

BEFORE three months had passed, Rose Fleming and Harry Maylie were married in the village church which was henceforth to be the scene of the young clergyman's labour; on the same day they entered into possession of their new and happy home.

Mrs. Maylie took up her abode with her son and daughter-in-law, to enjoy, during the tranquil remainder of her days, the greatest felicity that age and worth can know—the contemplation of the happiness of those on whom the warmest affections and tenderest cares of a wellspent life have been unceasingly bestowed.

It appeared, on full and careful investignation, that if the wreck of property remaining in the custody of Monks (which had never prospered either in his hands or in those of his mother) were equally divided between himself and Oliver, it would yield, to each, little more than three thousand pounds. By the provisions of his father's will, Oliver would have been entitled to the whole; but Mr. Brownlow, unwilling to deprive the elder son of the opportunity of retrieving his former vices, and pursuing an honest career, proposed this mode of distribution, to which his young charge joyfully acceded.

Monks, still bearing that assumed name, retired with his portion, to a distant part of the New World, where, having quickly squandered it, he once more fell into his old courses, and, after undergoing a long confinement for some fresh act of fraud and knavery, at length sank under an attack of his old disorder, and died in prison.

Mr. Brownlow adopted Oliver as his own son. Removing with him and the old housekeeper to within a mile of the parsonage-house, where his dear friends resided, he gratified the only remaining wish of Oliver's warm and earnest heart, and thus linked together a little society, whose condition approached as nearly to one of perfect happiness as can ever be known in this changing world.

Soon after the marriage of the young people, the worthy doctor took a bachelor's cottage just outside the village of which his young friend was pastor. Here he took to gardening, planting, fishing, carpentering, and various other pursuits of a similar kind—all undertaken with his characteristic impetuosity; and in each and all he has since become famous throughout the neighbourhood as a most profound authority.

Before his removal he had managed to contract a strong friendship for Mr. Grimwig, which that eccentric gentleman cordially reciprocated. He is accordingly visited by him a great many times in the course of the year. On all such occasions Mr. Grimwig plants, fishes, and carpenters with great ardour; doing everything in a very singular and unprecedented manner, but always maintaining, with his favourite asseveration, that his mode is the right one. On Sundays he never fails to criticise the sermon to the young clergyman's face; always informing Mr. Losberne, in strict confidence afterwards, that he considers it an excellent performance, but deems it as well not to say so.

Mr. and Mrs. Bumble, deprived of their situations, were gradually reduced to great indigence and misery, and finally became paupers in that very workhouse in which they had once lorded it over others. Mr. Bumble has been heard to say, that in this reverse and degradation, he has not even spirits to be thankful for being separated from his wife.

As to Mr. Giles and Brittles, they still remain in their old posts, although the former is bald, and the last-named boy quite grey. They sleep at the parsonage, but divide their attentions so equally among its inmates, and Oliver, and Mr. Brownlow, and Mr. Losberne, that to this day the villagers have never been able to discover to which establishment they properly belong.

Master Charles Bates, appalled by Sikes's crime, fell into a train of reflection whether an honest life was not, after all, the best. Arriving at the conclusion that it certainly was, he turned his back upon the scenes of the past, resolved to amend it in some new sphere of action. He struggled hard, and suffered much for some time; but, having a contented disposition, and a good purpose, succeeded in the end, and, from being a farmer's drudge, and a carrier's lad, is now the merriest young grazier in all Northamptonshire.

And now the hand that traces these words falters as it approaches the conclusion of its task, and would weave, for a little longer space, the thread of these adventures.

I would fain linger yet with a few of those among whom I have so long moved, and share their happiness by endeavouring to depict it. I would show Rose Maylie, in all the bloom and grace of early womanhood, shedding on her secluded path in life such soft and gentle light as fell on all who trod it with her, and shone into their hearts. I would paint her the life and joy of the fireside circle and the lively summer group; I would follow her through the sultry fields at noon, and hear the low tones of her sweet voice in the moonlight evening walk; I would watch her in all her goodness and charity abroad, and the smiling untiring discharge of domestic duties at home; I would paint her and her dead sister's child happy in their mutual love, and passing whole hours together in picturing the friends whom they had so sadly lost; I would summon before me, once again, those joyous little faces that clustered round her knee, and listen to their merry prattle; I would recall the tones of that clear laugh, and conjure up the sympathizing tear that glistened in the soft blue eye. These, and a thousand looks and smiles, and turns of thought and speech–I would fain recall them every one.

How Mr. Brownlow went on, from day to day, filling the mind of his adopted child with stores of knowledge, and becoming attached to him more and more, as his nature developed itself, and showed the thriving seeds of all he wished him to become–how he traced in him new traits of his early friend, that awakened in his own bosom old remembrances, melancholy and yet sweet and soothing–how the two orphans, tired by adversity, remembered its lessons in mercy to others, and mutual love and fervent thanks to Him who had protected and preserved them–these are all matters which need not to be told. I have said that they were truly happy; and without strong affection, and humanity of heart, and gratitude to that Being whose code is Mercy, and whose great attribute is Benevolence to all things that breathe, true happiness can never be attained.

Within the altar of the old village church there stands a white marble table, which bears as yet but one word–"Agnes!" There is no coffin in that tomb; and may it be many, many years, before another name is placed above it! But, if the spirits of the dead ever come back to earth to visit spots hallowed by the love–the love beyond the grave–of those whom they knew in life, I believe that the shade of Agnes sometimes hovers round that solemn nook. I believe it none the less because that nook is in a church, and she was weak and erring.

Printed in Germany